Paul Do⬛⬛⬛⬛⬛⬛⬛⬛⬛⬛⬛⬛⬛⬛⬛⬛⬛⬛⬛ He studied History a⬛⬛⬛⬛ Oxford ⬛⬛⬛⬛⬛⬛⬛⬛⬛⬛ties and obtained a doctorate at Oxford for his thesis on Edward II and Queen Isabella. He is now headmaster of a school in north-east London and lives with his wife and family near Epping Forest.

Paul Doherty is also the author of the Hugh Corbett medieval mysteries, The Sorrowful Mysteries of Brother Athelstan, the Canterbury Tales of mystery and murder, THE SOUL SLAYER, THE ROSE DEMON and THE HAUNTING, all of which have been highly praised.

'Vitality in the cityscape . . . angst in the mystery; it's Peters minus the herbs but plus a few crates of sack' *Oxford Times*

'The book is a pleasure to read and written in an uncompromising prose, the plot developed with intriguing twists and turns. Doherty's deep understanding of the period and the nitty-gritty of historical detail are to the fore without intruding on the rhythm of the plot. Superb entertainment' *Historical Novels Review*

'The maestro of medieval mystery . . . packed with salty dialogue, the smells and superstitions of the fourteenth century, not to mention the political intrigues' *Books Magazine*

'Paul Doherty has a lively sense of history . . . evocative and lyrical descriptions' *New Statesman*

'As always the author invokes the medieval period in all its muck as well as glory, filling the pages with pungent smells and description. The author brings years of research to his writing; his mastery of the period as well as a disciplined writing schedule have led to a rapidly increasing body of work and a growing reputation' *Mystery News*

# Corpse Candle

## Paul Doherty

## headline

First published in 2001
by HEADLINE BOOK PUBLISHING

First published in paperback in 2001
by HEADLINE BOOK PUBLISHING

7

ISBN 978-0-7472-6467-5

Typeset by Avon Dataset Ltd, Bidford-on-Avon, Warks

Printed and bound in Great Britain by
Clays Ltd, St Ives plc

HEADLINE BOOK PUBLISHING
A division of Hodder Headline plc
338 Euston Road
London NW1 3BH

www.headline.co.uk
www.hodderheadline.com

To D. T. Driscoll

*PRAEPARETUR ANIMUS CONTRA OMNIA*

PREPARE YOUR SOUL FOR THE UNEXPECTED

SENECA

# Prologue

Shadows, black as pitch, cloaked the abbey of St Martin's-in-the-Marsh which nestled amongst the fens of Lincolnshire. 'A jewel on a green cushion' was how one visitor described it. Others, who had experienced the marsh's quagmires, treacherous byways and hidden traps, called the fens a place of wickedness. 'The Sacristy of Hell' was how one ancient historian described the deceitful morasses and water-logged fields of this wilderness. Of course, the abbey of St Martin's, founded during the reign of the second Henry, was a hallowed place. Its buildings, and the divine services conducted within, had repelled back to Hell the demons who supposedly wandered such a desolate landscape.

St Martin's had grown into a great abbey: its monks had drained the fens, creating meadow and pasture, plough land, fisheries, stew ponds, as well as building their lavish church, granaries, outhouses, infirmary, scriptorium and library. The abbey estates neighboured those of the Harcourt family. Sir Eustace Harcourt had founded St Martin's after safely returning from a pilgrimage to Outremer where he had survived both the heat and the infidel to worship at the Holy Sepulchre.

Sir Eustace had ignored the legends about how the

3

fens were haunted by the ghost of Sir Geoffrey Mandeville, a robber baron who, with his retinue of ruffians, had harassed the fen men, their towns and villages, and even plundered chapels and churches. Mandeville had died a violent death but, according to the locals, he was condemned for all eternity to haunt this place with his devilish retinue. Many claimed to have heard the rumble of their horses' hooves and seen the black-garbed figures sweep through the night. It was an interesting legend but the good brothers of St Martin's paid little heed to it, dismissing as preposterous the stories of ghastly horsemen who carried blood-red banners with a huge black 'V' in the centre, the personal escutcheon, or livery, of the demon Mandeville. True, some of the more sharp-eared brothers did whisper how, recently, when they met in the refectory at night, they had heard the shrill blast of a hunting horn, and claimed that some retainers of Lady Margaret Harcourt, a virtual recluse since her husband's disappearance, had heard the same haunting blast. Hadn't Sir Reginald, Lady Margaret's former husband, and his cronies once galloped around the fens blowing hunting horns as some sort of madcap joke? Or was it someone else who'd gone out at night and pretended to be a ghostly horseman? Perhaps, they concluded, a peasant had heard this story and decided to play a childish game?

The black-garbed Benedictine monks of St Martin's were not too anxious about such tales. They lived comfortably and confidently behind their high curtain wall, protected by an army of lay brothers and estate workers, not to mention their powerful Abbot Stephen, a personal friend of the King. Under his rule, St Martin's had grown in wealth and power, patronised by both Crown and Church. Didn't the King and his retinue often stay here when they journeyed into the eastern shires on holy pilgrimage or marched north to war against the Scots? The brothers were only interested in their house, their rule, and the calm routine which marked their day; the wild fens, and the hideous stories about them, were best left to children. The grey-haired hermit, however, who lived by the abbey walls thought otherwise. Few knew his real name. He had been there for years and been given the title of the 'Watcher by the Gates'. Abbot Stephen had allowed him to build a small bothy or hut of intertwined branches which he called 'his windswept castle'. The Watcher by the Gates was more convinced than the monks. According to him, demons, howling like wolves, swept back and forth across the wild fens, particularly when the night turned misty and the corpse candles glowed across the marsh. The good brothers tolerated the Watcher. He was not too clean but lived an austere, shameless life; if the Watcher wished to see things they didn't, why should they object? In the main, their life was one of serenity, of holy calmness. However, from the eve of the feast of St Leo the Great, 10 November in the year of Our Lord 1303, the thirty-first year in the reign of King Edward, the brothers would hastily revise their opinion, for on that night the devil and all his hordes appeared to breach the walls of St Martin's.

Prior Cuthbert, Abbot Stephen's powerful lieutenant and leader of the concilium, the council of principal officers of the abbey, was certainly not at peace. Tall and beetle-browed, Prior Cuthbert had not returned to his chamber after the community had risen to chant, sleepy-eyed and slouched in their stalls, the beautiful hymns of the office of Prime. Prior Cuthbert was so distracted, he'd left the abbey by its Judas gate to stand on the edge of Bloody Meadow. The night was brilliantly cold and the stars, in a cloud-free sky, hung like fragments of ice. Prior Cuthbert stared across the great, circular meadow, its frosted grass glinting under the white light of a full moon. The meadow was fringed by great oak trees as it stretched from the abbey walls down to Falcon Brook, from which a mist was rising. By morning it would be thicker, cloaking the trees, and Prior Cuthbert could already see the corpse candles glowing. The local peasants maintained these were candles carried by devils: depending on how close they came, their light meant that someone was soon going to die. Prior Cuthbert's narrow face broke into a smile at the very idea of such stories. Didn't Brother Francis, their learned archivist and librarian, claim such lights were only foul gases emitted by the marshes, and not to be feared? Prior Cuthbert sheltered in the shadow of the gate, hands up the voluminous sleeves of his black woollen gown. This field, for so many reasons, was constantly in his thoughts. Time and again, he and the concilium had argued with Abbot Stephen that the meadow, used for grazing, was the ideal place to build a large guesthouse: a new, spacious mansion with dormitory, refectory, kitchens and butteries, storerooms and cellars to accommodate, in a more luxurious fashion, the many visitors to their abbey.

'We must build it, Father Abbot,' Prior Cuthbert had insisted. 'Our house becomes more popular by the year. The growth of trade in the Eastern ports means that we are now a favourite stopping place for merchants, not to mention His Grace the King and members of the court. The meadow,' Prior Cuthbert had marshalled his arguments carefully, 'is ideally situated, being outside our enclosure but close enough . . .'

Abbot Stephen, as always, shifted in his high-backed, throne-like chair, hands clasped before him. He listened carefully as, when Prior Cuthbert finished, the others joined in: Francis the librarian, Aelfric the infirmarian, Brother Hamo the sub-prior, Richard the almoner and Cuthbert's great allies, Gildas the stonemason and

Dunstan the treasurer. The latter particularly was always eloquent in his support.

'Father Abbot, we have the means. Our coffers are full. In the spring, stone can be quarried and brought here. Within eighteen months . . .'

The response was always the same. Abbot Stephen would sit back and fiddle with the cords on his hood, his severe face racked in concentration.

'I applaud you all, my brothers, for your hard work and industry in this matter.' Abbot Stephen would tick his fingers to emphasise his counter arguments. 'First, we already have a guesthouse within the abbey walls: it may not be luxurious but this is a house of prayer, not some London tavern or hostelry. Secondly, the meadow is used for grazing. Thirdly, as you know, I have great trouble with Lady Margaret Harcourt over who owns Falcon Brook, from which we would have to draw water for a new guesthouse. Brother Cuthbert, you yourself have visited Lady Margaret on a number of occasions: you know she has no time for me or this abbey. She recoils in disgust at my name, God knows why, and claims that I already encroach on her rights. If we try to draw water from Falcon Brook, she would undoubtedly appeal to the King's Council in London.'

Abbot Stephen would pause and the brothers seated round the great, oval-shaped oaken table would quietly groan to themselves. They'd look at each other and raise their eyes heavenwards. On this matter they could agree with their abbot. Lady Margaret Harcourt was a recluse, a widow lost in her own memories and dreams but, she was a fearsome opponent to Abbot Stephen. If the abbey cattle or sheep grazed on her lands, if an abbey servant wandered onto her fields, she would cry trespass. She may live like a grieving widow but Lady Margaret had the ear of skilful lawyers in both Lincoln and Ely. Finally, Abbot

Stephen would come to his most telling argument.

'And then there is the tumulus, the King's grave in the centre of the meadow. Is it right for us to desecrate such a tomb?'

'Abbot Stephen,' Prior Cuthbert would retort. 'How do we know it is a royal burial place?'

'We don't,' Abbot Stephen would respond. 'But, according to the ancient chronicles kept in our library, this was the last resting place of Sigbert, formerly King of these parts, who fought the heathen Northmen. He protected Holy Mother Church and was captured and martyred, clubbed to death. According to tradition, Sigbert's corpse was later rescued by his followers and given honourable burial in our meadow. I consider it unseemly to disturb such a grave.'

'But can't we find out for sure?' Prior Cuthbert had protested. 'How do we know anyone is really buried there? The meadow is owned by us, the tumulus is on abbey property. Surely there is nothing wrong if we dug a tunnel into the tumulus to discover the truth? If Sigbert is truly buried there,' Prior Cuthbert would continue triumphantly, 'then, as a saint and a martyr, shouldn't his holy remains be transferred to a consecrated burial place like our abbey church? Our monastery would then truly become a place of pilgrimage.'

Abbot Stephen would shake his head. 'It is not our task to do that. Whilst I am Abbot of St Martin's, it shall not be done.'

Prior Cuthbert leaned against the Judas gate, stared up at the sky and prayed for patience. The words kept echoing through his mind.

'As long as I am Abbot of St Martin's.'

How long would Abbot Stephen remain? A former soldier, a tall, vigorous man, he could be their Abbot for the next twenty or thirty years. Prior Cuthbert's dream would become a nightmare, years of frustration, failed expectations and dashed hopes. Prior Cuthbert could imagine in his mind's eye the new guesthouse with its stately buildings, small cloister and rose garden. He had pored over the plans of Brother Gildas, their architect and stonemason. He had sought private interviews with Abbot Stephen but the response was always the same.

'As long as I am Abbot of St Martin's, Bloody Meadow will be used only for our cattle and sheep.'

Prior Cuthbert stamped his sandalled foot. It was well named Bloody Meadow! According to local lore, as well as the ancient chronicles, this was where Sigbert had met the heathen Northmen and fought them from dawn till dusk. His army had broken but Sigbert had stood and fought with his house carls until they had died, one by one. Sigbert had been captured and offered his life if he rejected Christ and accepted the heathen gods. Sigbert had rejected this and been cruelly clubbed to death. Prior Cuthbert stared across at the huge tumulus in the centre of the meadow. Was that truly Sigbert's burial mound? He would love to find out. He walked across the frosty grass and stopped before the disputed tumulus. He ignored the call of a screech owl and the yelp of some animal caught in the bracken down near Falcon Brook. Prior Cuthbert felt slightly anxious. He did not believe in goblins and sprites, hideous woodmen or the ghosts of the dead. Yet, this was Sigbert's last resting place. Did his ghost haunt this meadow? Or worse, those of his killers? Prior Cuthbert shook himself free from this sombre reverie. He once again measured out the tumulus: it was about three yards high, a rectangle sloping at the top. He'd already measured the sides, top and base: five yards long, three yards wide. What could it be? The Prior started as he heard an animal screech and felt the sweat break out between his shoulder blades. He gazed round. In the moonlight, the shadows round the oaks seemed deeper, darker, longer. He really should return to his community. But what about the future? He clasped his hands and closed his eyes. In many ways he admired Abbot Stephen but he would not hesitate to use any weapons he was given in his fight for the new guesthouse. The Prior had hinted at what he'd seen here in Bloody Meadow but Abbot Stephen had only stared coldly back.

Prior Cuthbert turned back. He was halfway across the meadow when he heard a sound and whirled round. Surely not? Then he heard it again – the haunting blast of a hunting horn! He paused, holding his breath. Again the sound echoed, braying through the night. Prior Cuthbert's stomach lurched and his sweat ran cold. So the stories were true! Yet who could be blowing a hunting horn at the dead of night? The sound had seemed to echo across Falcon Brook from Lady Margaret's place: perhaps a retainer who had drunk too much? It couldn't be a ghost! Prior Cuthbert did not believe in spectral horsemen or the Mandeville demon. He glared back at the tumulus. Soon the sun would rise and the night would disappear. The abbey of St Martin's would remain, as would this meadow, but the dreams Prior Cuthbert had nourished would fade into nothing. Perhaps it was a time for action? The Prior turned back, went through the Judas gate and down by the side of the church towards his lodgings. He paused in the courtyard and stared up at the great bay windows of the Abbot's lodgings. The shutters were open and he glimpsed the glow of candlelight. He smiled grimly to himself. Abbot Stephen, too, was thinking. Perhaps in time he might bow to the sound arguments and ominous threats of his prior.

* * *

10

Abbot Stephen had also heard the hunting horn. He sighed, got up, walked to the bay window and stared out into the night.

'Go away!' he prayed. 'Please stop that!'

The final blast of the hunting horn seemed to mock him. It invoked memories long hidden, buried beneath years of service as a monk: the hours of prayer, the fasting, the hair shirts, the private pilgrimages on bruised knees up the long nave of the abbey church. Oh yes, Abbot Stephen thought of the past with its nightmares, haunting dreams, soul-wrestling anguish and heartbreak. Wasn't his reparation accepted? Hadn't God forgiven him for his sins? Couldn't he be allowed to continue his great work? Was there a God who listened? Was there a God at all? Abbot Stephen heard a footstep from the courtyard below and peered quickly through the mullioned glass. He couldn't make out the shadowy form but he knew it must be Prior Cuthbert. Abbot Stephen stepped away and crossed to the small wood fire burning in the canopied hearth. The Abbot crouched down and stretched his hands towards the flames.

'Perhaps I should resign?' he whispered.

He stared at the small gargoyles on either side of the hearth, the wizened faces of monkeys each surmounted by a pair of horns.

I could resign, he reflected, but what then? He was not only Father Abbot but also Exorcist in the dioceses of Lincoln and Ely. He had work to do, both as a monk and a priest, so why should he give it up? Especially now, when Prior Cuthbert was so concerned about that meadow and his new guesthouse! His hands now warm, Abbot Stephen returned to his long polished desk and sat down. Before him was a triptych, the central scene showing Christ on the cross and the side panels, Mary and St John. It was the Abbot's favourite picture. He looked at the great book before him which he had taken from the library. Beside it was a sheet of vellum where he made his own notes. This was his world; prayer and study, ink horn and quill, pumice stone and freshly prepared parchment. Abbot Stephen was a great letter writer. In the past two years he had been engaged in academic debate with his old adversary Archdeacon Adrian and the great Dominican Order at Blackfriars in London over the nature of demonic possession and the rite of exorcism. The debate had been sharp but scholarly. The Dominicans supported the Archdeacon of St Paul's, Master Adrian Wallasby maintaining that exorcism was much exaggerated and those described as possessed, were more sick in mind than in the possession of the Lords of the Air, the demons of Hell. Abbot Stephen had been vigorously challenged so, in three days' time, he planned to hold an exorcism in his own abbey church. The candidate had been chosen, a man who'd sought the Abbot's help and was now kept in close quarters in a private chamber adjoining the infirmary. Five days ago Archdeacon Adrian had arrived at St Martin's. He seemed to have relinquished his long-standing grudges against the Abbot, insisting that he only wished to interrogate the possessed man and witness the exorcism. Abbot Stephen had been concentrating on that until the past had intruded in a harsh and brutal way.

Abbot Stephen picked up the book, pulling closer the silver-gilt candelabra so he could read more quickly with the special magnifying glass he had bought in Norwich. He tried to let the words soothe his mind but suddenly he let the book fall back on the table as a wave of depression made him slump deeper in the chair. It was useless! He was hedged in, confined, trapped. Abbot Stephen, despite the warmth of the room, the logs crackling in the fire, the perfumed braziers, grew cold and trembled. He closed his eyes, and faces from

the past appeared. If all this became known? If he was
forced to confess in public? What would happen then?
He couldn't face Prior Cuthbert's threats yet that burial
mound could not be opened. Abbot Stephen closed the
book with a snap. He got up and walked towards the
door. He made sure it was locked, the bolts drawn. He
went round the windows, making sure everything was
closed. He took a wine jug and goblet and brought them
over to the desk. He filled the cup to the brim and
drank quickly. He picked up his ring of keys, rose and
unlocked his private chest, throwing back the lid. Inside
lay a helmet, greaves, gauntlets and a breastplate
bearing his escutcheon. On top of all this lay a brocaded
sword belt. He lifted this out and strapped it around
him, for the first time in over thirty years. He gripped
the pommel of the sword and the handle of the long
stabbing dirk on the other side. He turned and saw his
reflection in the window. Was that him or someone
else?

Abbot Stephen unstrapped the war belt, threw it on
the floor and slumped to his knees. He gazed expectantly at the mullioned glass window and once again
studied his reflection. The glass also caught the light
from the candles and oil lamps. A phrase from St Pauls'
Epistle to the Corinthians echoed in his imagination:
'For now we see through a glass, darkly'. Abbot Stephen
simply had to look into the mirror to know himself
for what he was, what he had done and how he had
tried to hide it. He closed his eyes but he couldn't pray.
He sighed and got to his feet: as he did, his attention
was caught by the reflection of candlelight. Were those
his corpse candles? Were they really reflections? Or
was the legend true? Those strange lights, which
appeared over the marshes and the fens, had they drawn
so close as to flicker outside his chamber, beckoning,
threatening?

Abbot Stephen returned to his desk and sat down. He picked up a quill. He wanted to write, distract himself but he felt alone, frightened. He must concentrate! He scrawled down the quotation from St Paul but mixed it with a reference to corpse candles. A line from the philosopher Seneca pricked his memory. How did it go? Ah yes, that was it: 'Anyone can take away a man's life, but no one his death'. Abbot Stephen threw the quill down. The night breeze gently rattled the windows. Abbot Stephen put his face in his hands. He stared bleakly into the dark as his soul sank deeper and deeper into a morass of despair.

*NIL POSSE CREARI DE NILO*

NOTHING CAN BE CREATED OUT OF NOTHING

LUCRETIUS

# Chapter 1

Prior Cuthbert had turned one of the vesting rooms, which lay off the gallery leading to the sacristy, into a mourning chamber. The white plaster walls were covered in gold and black drapes. On either side of the bier stood three great brass candlesticks with dark-purple candles specially made by the abbey's chandler. A huge cross was nailed to the wall. The drapes covering Abbot Stephen's corpse were embroidered in silver thread depicting Christ harrowing Hell. Despite the late season, some flowers had been found and placed in silver vases at each corner of the bier. Scented braziers, sprinkled with dried thyme, kept the air sweet. Prior Cuthbert felt proud of what he had achieved since the Abbot's death four days earlier. The corpse had been washed, cleaned and prepared for burial. Later that day, just after noon, he would celebrate the solemn requiem Mass in the abbey church. Prior Cuthbert had warned the brothers not to gossip. The abbey had expected some representative from the King. As soon as Abbot Stephen's corpse had been discovered, an abbey messenger, taking two of the swiftest horses from the stables, had ridden to Norwich where the King and court were on royal progress through the Eastern shires.

Prior Cuthbert stood aside and allowed his visitors

to approach the bier. He felt distinctly nervous. He'd expected the King to send an earl, or one of his principal barons. Instead the tall, dark, close-faced Sir Hugh Corbett, Keeper of the King's Secret Seal, had arrived, together with his henchman, Ranulf-atte-Newgate, the red-haired, sharp-featured Clerk of the Green Wax, and Chanson, that strange-looking clerk of the stables with a mop of unruly hair and a cast in one eye. All three were dressed in travel-stained clothes, dark-brown cote-hardies, leggings of the same colour pushed into high-heeled Spanish leather riding boots. Spurs clinked, sword and dagger tapped against thigh. They were men of war, Prior Cuthbert reflected, yet they emanated as well an air of quiet authority and menace: Corbett in particular, handsome, clean-shaven, pleasant-featured but with deep-set, brooding eyes. A man who didn't say much but seemed to listen and watch everything around him. He didn't stand on ceremony. As soon as he was ushered into the Prior's quarters, he showed his warrant bearing the King's Seal, splaying out his fingers to display the Chancery ring emblazoned with the arms of England.

'We expected someone else,' Prior Cuthbert murmured.

Corbett unfastened his cloak and tossed it to Chanson. Ranulf did the same, stretching his arms and legs to ease the cramp after the long ride in the saddle.

'Whom did you expect?' Corbett asked, a half-smile on his face.

'I . . . I . . .' Prior Cuthbert's words died on his lips. 'Do you wish some wine? Some food?'

He gestured Corbett to a chair. Ranulf he ignored. He didn't like the cynical look in the clerk's keen, green eyes.

'No, thank you.' Corbett ignored the chair. 'We have ridden hard, Prior Cuthbert, but the King was most insistent that I view Abbot Stephen's corpse and pay my respects. I would be grateful if you would show it to me now.'

Prior Cuthbert had hastened to obey. He kept silent as Corbett, without any ceremony, pulled back the coverlet. Abbot Stephen was serene and composed in death, dressed in the full pontificals of an abbot, his body was placed in an open casket before being taken into the church. Prior Cuthbert watched the clerk closely: the raven-black hair was streaked with grey, pulled back and tied at the nape of the neck; his face was more olive-skinned than sallow; the hands now free of their heavy gauntlets were soft-looking, the fingers long and strong. An orderly, precise man, Prior Cuthbert concluded: the clerk's cote-hardie and leggings were of pure wool, the shirt beneath crisp and white. The sword belt which Corbett had not taken off, as was customary in an abbey, was of thick brown leather: the sheaths for both dagger and sword were brocaded with red and blue stitching. Prior Cuthbert thought hard and fast as Corbett stood staring down at the dead Abbot's face. Yes, he had heard about this clerk. More powerful than an earl, Corbett was King Edward's spy master, his limner, his greyhound, his searcher for the truth. Abbot Stephen had once spoken of how Corbett had investigated a strange community, the Pastorales out on the Norfolk coast. Oh yes, a clerk who enjoyed the King's favour without stint or hindrance! Prior Cuthbert felt the sweat break out on his brow. Even before Corbett spoke he knew which way this was going. Edward of England was not going to be satisfied with some coroner's report. Abbot Stephen's death was to be investigated. Corbett stood, staring down at the dead Abbot's face as if memorising every detail. Then he went and knelt on the prie-dieu and crossed himself. Ranulf and Chanson knelt on the hard paving floor so

Prior Cuthbert had no choice but to follow.

'*Requiem eternam*,' Corbett intoned. 'Eternal rest grant unto Abbot Stephen, Oh Lord, and let perpetual light shine upon him. May he find a place of light and peace. May he rest in your favour and enjoy your smile for all eternity.'

Corbett crossed himself, got to his feet and replaced the purple cloth over the Abbot's face.

'I will not speak to you now, Prior Cuthbert. I want to see you and the Abbey Concilium, shall we say within a quarter of the hour? You have chambers prepared for us?'

'Yes, yes, in our guesthouse.'

Corbett took his cloak from Chanson.

'One for me and one for my companions?'

'Yes, Sir Hugh.'

Prior Cuthbert felt uneasy, used to exercising authority, Corbett made him nervous, agitated. The clerk seemed to sense this.

'Prior Cuthbert, I am here on the King's business. I understand the grief of your community but Abbot Stephen was a close friend of the King. A priest, one of the leading clerics of the Lords Spiritual. His death, or rather his murder, has saddened and angered the King. The assassin undoubtedly was a member of your community. I and my companions, and I swear this in the presence of Abbot Stephen's corpse, will not leave this abbey until both God and the King's justice is done and seen to be done!'

'Of course.' Prior Cuthbert tried to assert himself. 'We understand the King's grief, indeed, anger. Abbot Stephen was much loved. Yet his assassin may not be a member of our community. Sinister figures prowl the fens outside: outlaws, wolfs-heads under their leader Scaribrick. It is not unknown for such reprobates to trespass on our property.'

'In which case,' Corbett replied drily, tightening his sword belt, 'they have powers denied to you and me, Prior Cuthbert. Wasn't Abbot Stephen's chamber locked and bolted from the inside, its latticed windows firmly closed? There are no secret entrances, I suppose?'

Prior Cuthbert stepped back.

'What are you implying, Sir Hugh?'

'I am implying nothing,' Corbett declared, 'except that Abbot Stephen was found in his chamber with a dagger from his own coffer thrust deep into his chest. No one heard a sound, let alone a cry for help. The room was not disturbed. Nothing was stolen. How could some ragged-arsed outlaw perpetrate such a crime, waft in and out like God's own air?'

'You are implying,' Prior Cuthbert declared, 'that Abbot Stephen was murdered and his assassin must be a member of our community? If that is true then it is a matter for the church courts. This is church property. Until the election and installation of a new abbot, I am the law in this abbey.'

Corbett put on his cloak. He fiddled with the clasp as if ignoring what the Prior had said. He glanced over his shoulder at Ranulf who stood, thumbs tucked into his sword belt. The Prior could see the Clerk of the Green Wax was enjoying himself. Corbett's henchman, Prior Cuthbert thought, his bully-boy, was clearly not impressed by church authority. His cat-like eyes were half-closed and he was biting his lip to hide the mockery bubbling inside. Chanson, their groom, stood open-mouthed like some peasant watching a mummer's play. Prior Cuthbert knew that he was handling this matter badly yet Corbett wasn't going to let him off the hook so lightly.

'What do you think, Ranulf? Shall we collect our saddle-bags and horses, ride back to Norwich and tell the King that his writ does not run in certain parts of Lincolnshire?'

'I have a better idea,' Ranulf retorted. 'Why not call up the local sheriff's posse and have them escort Prior Cuthbert to Norwich so he can explain to the King personally? And, whilst he is gone, we can get on with this business.' He grinned at the Prior. 'As well as God's.'

Prior Cuthbert spread his hands.

'You have me wrong, sirs. However, I am Prior of this abbey. I have certain powers and jurisdiction. We are in the archdiocese of Canterbury, the local bishop will expect me to act in accordance with the Constitutions of Clarendon.'

Corbett walked over and placed a hand on the Prior's shoulder.

'Prior Cuthbert.' Corbett's face was now unsmiling. 'I respect what you say: you are a churchman and must protect the rights of Holy Mother Church. However,' Corbett tightened his grip, 'one of the lords spiritual – a leading abbot of this country, a personal friend of the King, a theologian of some renown, an envoy who has led embassies abroad – has been found murdered in his own chamber. Holy Mother Church is going to demand an explanation. The King wants justice. If you frustrate me, people will begin to wonder whether Prior Cuthbert is the man to lead an abbey. Indeed, some will whisper that he may have things to hide.'

The Prior shook off Corbett's hand.

'You are threatening me.'

'I am not threatening you,' Corbett retorted, eyes blazing with anger. 'I have a task to do, Prior Cuthbert, and I shall do it! I am merely giving you a choice. You can either co-operate or be summoned by the King to explain why you will not. So, before we leave this room, what is it to be?'

Prior Cuthbert swallowed hard.

'You want to meet the Concilium?'

'Yes, I do, in the Abbot's own chamber.'

Corbett stopped and cocked his head to one side as if listening to the faint strains of chanting coming from the abbey church.

'I agree!'

Prior Cuthbert walked to the door.

'I will send Brother Perditus, a lay brother who was the Abbot's manservant. He will take you to your quarters and show you the Abbot's chamber. I will make sure it is unlocked. Since the Abbot's death I have kept it secure, and the doors sealed.'

'Good!' Corbett murmured.

He extended his hand for the Prior to clasp. Cuthbert did so reluctantly and quietly left.

Corbett made sure the door was closed behind him. He stood for a while, listening to the sound of the sandals slapping on the hard paved floor before he turned and looked at his companions.

'He still shows a lack of respect,' Ranulf declared.

He picked at the hem of his cloak, scraping some mud off before remembering where he was and letting it fall.

'He's a churchman,' Corbett replied coming away from the door. 'He's protecting his rights, his jurisdiction. I expected him to do that. I've met his like before. It's a little dance we have to perform, like knights testing each other on the tournament ground before the real battle begins.'

'Did you ever meet Abbot Stephen?' Ranulf asked.

'On a few occasions.' Corbett stared down at the figure lying beneath the purple cloth. 'He was a good man, a scholar, very erudite, skilled in a number of languages. He led embassies to Flanders and the German States. He did good work for the King.'

23

'You said he was a good friend of the King's?'

'Perhaps I should have said "had been". Many years ago, Ranulf, long before you saw the light of day, our Abbot was a knight banneret, a member of the King's own personal bodyguard. He fought with Edward at Evesham against de Montfort. When the King was struck down during the battle, Sir Stephen Daubigny, as he was then known, saved the King's life. They became boon companions, drinking from the same loving cup. There was another, Sir Reginald Harcourt. He and Daubigny were the firmest of friends, close allies. In fact, people thought they were brothers. They went everywhere together.'

'What happened?' Ranulf asked.

'We don't know. Before I left Norwich I asked the King, but even he did not know the details. Apparently Sir Reginald left on some mysterious pilgrimage.'

'To the Holy Land?'

'No, no, to Cologne in Germany. According to rumour, he left by one of the Eastern ports and landed at Dordrecht in Hainault but then disappeared.'

'Disappeared?' Chanson queried, he loved to eavesdrop on his master's conversations.

'That's right, my cross-eyed clerk of the stables,' Ranulf declared. 'Disappeared. That's what Sir Hugh said.'

'Hush now!'

Corbett walked to the door and opened it but the gallery outside was empty. He could still hear the chant of the monks. He closed the door.

'Harcourt's wife, Lady Margaret, was so distraught she begged Sir Stephen to help find her husband. They both travelled abroad. They were away for months. When they came back, according to the King, they were sworn enemies. Lady Margaret became a recluse. The King tried to find her a suitable husband but she always refused to marry again and he respected her wishes.'

'And Sir Stephen?'

'He entered the abbey of St Martin's as a brother and was ordained a priest. He would not explain his decision to the King. He became as good a monk as he had been a knight. He was able, a skilled administrator. He became prior and, after the death of Abbot Benedict, the obvious successor.'

'And Lady Margaret?'

'The King does not know the cause of the enmity between the two. Lady Margaret once confided to the Queen that she believed if Stephen Daubigny had gone with her husband, he would not have disappeared. She also begged Sir Stephen, when they were looking for Sir Reginald, to continue the search but he claimed Sir Reginald had vanished. He refused to travel any further and returned to England. She followed some months afterwards. From the day they separated, they never spoke to each other again.'

'But they were neighbours!' Ranulf exclaimed.

'Aye, but ones who never talked or met. Lady Margaret refused to do business with Abbot Stephen and earnestly challenged any attempt by the abbey to extend its rights. She jealously guarded the privileges of her estates. There was bad blood between them.' Corbett stared down at the corpse. 'I wonder if she has come to pay her last respects? It's something I must ask Prior Cuthbert. Well, what have you learnt, my clerk of the Green Wax?'

Ranulf loosened his sword belt and rubbed where it was chafing his side. He had left Norwich before his master and spent the previous night at a local tavern, The Lantern-in-the-Woods, listening to the tales of chapmen, travellers and tinkers.

'I heard about the enmity between Lady Margaret and Abbot Stephen though people seem to regard it as they do the weather, something to be accepted. Abbot Stephen was respected and loved by his monks. The abbey was well managed, with no hint of laxity or scandal. There's a hermit who calls himself the "Watcher by the Gates". Abbot Stephen allowed him to build a small bothy close to the wall. People regarded him as a madcap, slightly uncanny. He tells travellers chilling tales about demonic horsemen and the ghost of Geoffrey Mandeville.'

'Ah yes, I have heard of that.'

'Nothing but fireside tales,' Ranulf continued, 'except for one thing. A tinker told me how, over the last few weeks, a hunting horn has been heard at night.'

'A horn?' Corbett exclaimed.

'That's what the tinker claimed. One night he was unable to get lodgings, and the abbey gates were closed so he went to seek help from Lady Margaret. She allowed him to sleep in one of the outhouses. He woke in the middle of the night when it was dark, and as clear as a clarion call on a summer's day, he heard three long blasts and then silence. The following day he made enquiries. It seems to be quite common, occurring two or three times a week for the last few months. No one knows why or who is doing it?'

Ranulf was about to continue when there was a knock on the door.

'Come in!' Corbett ordered.

The lay brother who stepped through was dressed in a long, woollen gown, with a white cord around his waist, and stout brown sandals on his feet. He was tall, his fair hair cropped in a tonsure, bold-eyed and firm-jawed. His face was pale, rather ascetic, and the high cheek-bones gave him an imperious air. He seemed unabashed by Corbett.

'I am Brother Perditus,' he declared in a loud, guttural voice.

Corbett noticed his eyes were red-rimmed from weeping. He suspected the man had just washed his face and was putting on a brave front.

'You've been crying, haven't you?'

The lay brother's haughty expression crumpled, his hands fell loosely by his side. He stared down at the floor and nodded. When he lifted his head tears glistened in his eyes. He refused to look at the funeral bier but kept close to the door, glancing at Corbett then at Ranulf.

'I think we'll leave,' Corbett said softly.

Brother Perditus led them out. He walked quickly before them, using the opportunity to dry his eyes on the sleeve of his gown. They went down the gallery and out across the great cloister garth. A weak sun had melted the frost on the grass. The desks and lecterns used by the monks for their study were all deserted, books firmly closed, ink pots sealed. Usually this would be a hive of activity; the abbey illuminators and scribes using the precious daylight to continue their work.

'The brothers are still in church,' Perditus explained over his shoulder. 'But I wager they all know you've arrived.'

He led them down another gallery, out past the church where Corbett could smell the fragrant incense and beeswax, and into a courtyard. In the centre stood a rose garden. On the far side was a half-timbered building with black beams and white plaster. Inside the polished floor gleamed in the weak morning sunlight. The lower storey of the guesthouse consisted of small, white-washed rooms. Brother Perditus explained that meals could be served to them in one of these, which served as a small refectory. He led them up the wooden staircase. The walls were decorated with pictures and coloured hangings. A crucifix hung in the stairwell, and small statues stood in the niches. Rather incongruously the carving of a woodman, with popping eyes and snarling mouth, had also been placed on the wall. Corbett smiled, it was a carving which would frighten his little daughter Eleanor and it certainly jarred with the serenity and calmness of the guesthouse. The top floor was a polished gallery, with large arrow-slit windows on one side and the doors to the chambers on the other. Corbett was shown the first.

'There's a key in the inside lock,' Brother Perditus explained. 'The door can also be bolted.' He blinked in embarrassment. 'Not that we need such protection in an abbey!'

He then took Ranulf and Chanson to their room. Corbett's saddle-bag had already been placed on the small chest at the foot of the bed. He quickly checked the buckles and straps; they had not been tampered with. He stared around at the white-washed walls, and the window which overlooked the courtyard, its glass thick and mullioned with a small latticed door that could be shuttered from the inside. The bed was long and narrow with grey woollen blankets, crisp white linen sheets and bolsters. Corbett felt the mattress, it was thick and soft.

'Probably featherdown,' he murmured.

The rest of the furniture was simple but beautifully carved. A writing table stood under the window, a smaller table by the bed. A chair, stools, coffers, chests and a large aumbry were also available. Corbett placed his war belt on a peg driven into the wall. He removed his spurs from the pocket of his cloak and placed them on the window sill, undid his cloak and loosened his shirt. Corbett sat on the edge of the bed and took off his boots. He closed his eyes as the tension and cramp of his long ride eased. In one corner stood a small wooden lavarium, jug, bowl and coloured cloths. Corbett went across and washed his hands and face, half-listening to

the sounds from the gallery. Brother Perditus knocked
on the door and came in.

'Prior Cuthbert says you are most welcome to join
us in church. He would like you to be his guest in the
refectory. Otherwise you may eat in here or downstairs.'

'You are still mourning, aren't you?' Corbett asked.
'Come in, man.' He gestured to a stool.

Corbett couldn't make up his mind about this abbey.
Everything was clean, serene, orderly and harmonious.
The brothers went about their duties. Prior Cuthbert
had protested but he seemed upright and capable
enough. Brother Perditus was the ideal host and guide.
Yet Corbett felt the hairs on the nape of his neck curl
in danger. Once, while soldiering in Wales, he had
stumbled into a sun-filled glade. Butterflies danced in
the breeze, the air was sweet with the fragrance of wild
flowers. Wood pigeons cooed, birds sang. Corbett had
sensed that, beyond the glade, hideous dangers lurked.
One of his companions had scoffed and abruptly
changed his mind as cruel barbed arrows whipped above
their heads. So it is now, Corbett thought. The lake
may be serene on the surface but he wondered how
deep it was and what treacheries lurked beneath.

Perditus sat, head bowed, hands dutifully up the
sleeves of his gown, patiently waiting to answer anything Corbett asked.

'You are a lay brother?'

'Yes, sir. I have been for four years.'

'And you were the Abbot's personal servant?'

'Yes, sir.'

'And you liked him?'

'I loved him.'

Perditus's head came up. Corbett was surprised at
the fierce expression in his eyes.

'He was truly a father to me, kind and learned. You
are here to trap his murderer, aren't you?'

29

Corbett took a stool and sat opposite.

'He was murdered,' Perditus continued. 'I have heard the whispers amongst the brothers. It was not the work of some outlaw or wolf's-head, wild men from the fens. They had no quarrel with Father Abbot.'

'So, who do you think murdered him?'

Perditus's face broke into a sneer.

'One of our Christ-like community.'

'And why?'

'Because he was a hard taskmaster. He made them obey the rule of St Benedict. He wanted the abbey to remain an abbey, not some glorified guesthouse for the powerful lords of the soil!'

'Tell me.' Corbett undid his leather wrist guard and threw it on the chest at the bottom of the bed. 'How did you serve Father Abbot?'

'I would bring him meals to the refectory, clean his chamber, collect books from the libraries, run errands.'

'And the night he died?'

'I was sleeping in a small chamber nearby.'

'And you heard nothing untoward?'

'No, sir, I did not. The bell rang for matins. Father Abbot did not come down so I thought he was sleeping late or working, he had so much to do. Later in the morning, when he didn't appear and wouldn't answer my calls, I became alarmed. I summoned Prior Cuthbert.'

Corbett held a hand up. 'Enough for now. I wish you to join the Concilium when it meets in the Abbot's quarters.'

'But they will object. I am only a lay brother!'

'And I am only a King's clerk.' Corbett smiled. 'Brother Perditus, I would be grateful if you would bring my companions and myself a jug of ale, some bread and dried meat. We would like to break our fast.'

The lay brother agreed. He almost leapt from the

stool, eager to be out of the way of this hard-eyed clerk. Corbett went to the window and watched Perditus scurry across the courtyard. Ranulf and Chanson entered the room. They, too, had taken off their belts, cloaks and boots. Ranulf had splashed water on his hair, forcing it back from his brow, and this gave him a lean and hungry look. Corbett studied this Clerk of the Green Wax: Ranulf was changing. Tall and muscular, his interests in the ladies hadn't waned but he now had a greater hunger, a burning ambition to rise high in the King's service. Ranulf had hired an Oxford clerk, one of his own subordinates, to teach him Latin and Norman French as well as perfect his handwriting, both the cursive script and the elegant copperplate used on charters and official proclamations. Now he stood on the balls of his feet, eager to press on with the task in hand.

'A serene place, Sir Hugh, though not what it appears . . .?'

'No abbey or monastery is,' Corbett replied, leaning against the window sill and folding his arms. 'Or any community! That even goes for my own family, Ranulf. Look at the tension which can surface at Leighton. The sea of troubles which,' he grinned, 'sends us both scurrying to our private chambers.'

Ranulf coloured slightly with embarrassment. Leighton Manor was ruled by Corbett's wife, the Lady Maeve. A small, beautiful, blonde-haired, Welsh woman, Maeve had the face of an angel and a tongue like a sharpened razor. When she lost her temper, Ranulf particularly would always find something interesting to do at the other side of the manor. Everyone – Uncle Morgan who was their permanent guest, Corbett, Ranulf and even Chanson, who rarely reflected on anything – feared the dimunitive Lady Maeve more than they did the King.

'I thought we were going back home,' Chanson moaned.

The groom had two gifts. He could manage any horse and he loved Corbett's children, Eleanor and Baby Edward. Although not the cleanest or best looking of men, Chanson was always a source of delightful curiosity to them as well as the other children on the manor.

'Aye.' Corbett sighed. 'We were supposed to go home.'

He half closed his eyes. He had joined the King at Norwich after that business in Suffolk. Edward had promised him leave from his service but then the dusty, mud-spattered courier had arrived from St Martin's. The King had begged him to take on this task and what could Corbett do?

'It was murder, wasn't it?' Ranulf asked sitting down on a stool.

'Murder and a cunning one,' Corbett agreed. 'But proving it and discovering the assassin will be difficult. We are going to have to poke with a long, sharp stick. In many ways Abbot Stephen was a strange man. Oh, he was holy enough and learned but self-contained and mysterious; a knight-banneret who decided to become a priest. A soldier who decided to hunt demons.'

'Demons!' Ranulf exclaimed.

Corbett smiled thinly. 'Yes, Ranulf, our late Abbot was an officially appointed exorcist. Abbot Stephen would be called to assist with people who claimed to be possessed, and houses that were reputedly haunted.'

'Sprites and goblins!' Ranulf scoffed. 'A legion of devils wander Whitefriars and Southwark, but they are all flesh and blood. The wickedness they perpetrate would shame any self-respecting demon. You don't believe in that nonsense, do you?'

Corbett pursed his lips. Ranulf stared in disbelief. Chanson, delighted, stood rooted to the spot. He loved

nothing better, as he'd often whispered to Ranulf, than
sombre tales about witches, warlocks and sorcerers.

'Surely, Sir Hugh, it's arrant nonsense!'

'Yes and no,' Corbett replied slowly. 'Ranulf, I am a
true son of Holy Mother Church, as you should be.'

'But you are also an Oxford clerk skilled in logic.
You deal in evidence, in that which can be proved.'

'But I can give you proof,' Corbett teased back.
'Ranulf, think of something.'

The Clerk of the Green Wax closed his eyes.

'Well, of what are you thinking?'

'Sweet Amasia.' Ranulf grinned. 'Her father owns a
tavern on the road outside Leighton.'

'And do you see her?'

'Oh yes, Master.'

'But I can't.'

Ranulf opened his eyes. 'Well, of course not, it's just
an idea in my head.'

'So, it's invisible to me.' Corbett warmed to his
theme. He enjoyed such debate. He recalled the hurly-
burly days in the schools of Oxford, of argument and
disputation, the clash of mind and wit. 'The point I am
making, Ranulf, is that there is evil in our own experience, both visible and invisible. Indeed, following the
great Plato, I would argue that that which is visible
only comes into being from that which is invisible!'

Ranulf glared at Chanson who giggled softly.

'A tree's visible,' he countered.

'But a tree came from that which is hardly visible
and, if you push the argument through, I would say a
tree is the work of the mind of God. Man is the same:
he is conceived in a woman's womb but born of a love,
an idea, which existed before he did.'

'Or lust?' Ranulf added.

'Or lust,' Corbett conceded. 'However, my hypothesis
could apply to anything.' He pointed to a coloured

tapestry on the wall depicting St Antony preaching to the birds. 'Before that picture existed, someone must have conceived it, had an idea. He, or she, worked out what colours would be used, how the scene would be depicted.'

'What's this got to do with demons?' Chanson broke in.

'Everything,' Corbett declared. 'My learned Clerk of the Green Wax challenged my belief in the invisible. In a word, I believe two worlds exist at the same time, the visible and the invisible. In both worlds, beings exist who possess intelligence and will. Whether that intelligence and will are inclined for good or evil is a matter for individual choice. More importantly . . .'

Corbett was about to continue when they heard footsteps on the stairs. Brother Perditus came in carrying a tray with a jug, three cups and a small breadboard. The white manchet loaf had been cut, and each piece smeared with butter and honey.

'Father Prior asks for more time,' he stuttered. 'Nones have just finished. He has to summon the others.' He placed the tray on the table and stepped back. 'I have other duties. Father Prior does not believe that I should attend the meeting in the Abbot's chamber.'

'I thank you for the refreshments,' Corbett replied kindly. 'And never mind what Prior Cuthbert says. Please be there.'

The lay brother fled. Chanson went to serve them but Ranulf pulled at his sleeve and pointed to the groom's dirty hands.

'I know enough about physic,' he said.

Chanson, scowling, stepped back. Ranulf filled three tankards and served them. Each took a piece of bread and ate hungrily.

'There's no meat,' Chanson declared mournfully. 'They've forgotten the meat.'

'We'll dine soon enough,' Corbett declared.

Ranulf drained his tankard and smacked his lips, the ale was tangy sweet. He took the jug and refilled it.

'One thing about monks,' he muttered. 'They make good ale. Master, you were saying?'

'Ah yes, I believe two worlds exist and the beings I described can cross from one to the other.'

'Rubbish!' Ranulf declared, his mouth full of bread.

'I believe it,' Corbett declared. 'Every time you pray you enter the invisible world. Every time you love and, more dangerously, hate or curse. When you call out into the dark, Ranulf, and if you call long and hard enough, someone always answers.'

'Like murder?' Chanson asked.

'Like murder,' Corbett agreed. 'A man or a woman can decide on evil. The idea takes root first. Only afterwards comes their bloody work.'

'You don't need a demon to be an assassin,' Ranulf countered.

'No, but when you kill, you're allying your will with the powers of darkness. Read the gospels, Ranulf, especially St John's. Christ describes Satan as a "killer from the start". Adam's sin was disobeying God but the first real sin was that of Cain slaying his brother, hiding his corpse and refusing to answer God's summons. We all have some of Cain in us,' Corbett murmured.

'Not you, Master, surely?'

Corbett closed his eyes. He recalled the bloody hand-to-hand fighting in Wales when the wild tribesmen broke into the royal camp: the painted faces, glaring eyes, the clash of sword, the sheer desperation to kill and survive.

'Oh yes, I have.' He opened his eyes. 'But I pray God that I never be put into that position.'

Ranulf was about to continue when they heard fresh sounds outside: someone slowly climbing the stairs.

'Our Perditus has returned,' Ranulf observed.

But the man who entered was a stranger. He was small, thickset, and youngish-looking, with closely cropped black hair, a smiling rubicund face, snub nose and the bright eyes of a sparrow. He was dressed in a long, dark-green gown, soft brown leather boots, with a cloak of dark murrey fastened round the neck with a gold clasp. Beneath it was a white collar band, with a small and elegant crucifix on a gold chain round his neck, and rings sparkling on his plump fingers. He stood in the doorway and smiled round.

'Am I interrupting something?'

'It depends on who you are,' Corbett declared.

He could tell from the man's dress that he was a priest and vaguely recalled Edward telling him what had been planned at St Martin's Abbey.

'Archdeacon Adrian Wallasby.'

The man's face broke into a gap-toothed smile. He stretched out his hand and walked towards Corbett.

'Like you, I am a visitor to this holy place. I heard about your arrival and thought I should meet you.'

Corbett shook his hand and introductions were made.

'I am Archdeacon of St Paul's,' Wallasby declared, 'sent here by the Archbishop of Canterbury and the Dominican Order.'

'For what purpose?'

'Oh, to confront the devil and all his demons!' Wallasby threw his head back and gave a deep belly laugh. 'A wasted journey, mind you. I am well entertained in the guesthouse across the courtyard but my journey was fruitless. And you, Sir Hugh, you must be here because of Abbot Stephen's mysterious death?'

'Murder,' Corbett replied. 'I believe the abbot was murdered. Anyway, what has the devil and all his demons to do with the Abbey of St Martin's? I know Abbot Stephen was an exorcist . . . ?'

'And a famous one,' the Archdeacon countered. 'That's why I was here. Abbot Stephen wrote extensively on demonic possession. He performed exorcism both in Lincolnshire and in London, very celebrated cases. He was supposed to carry one out here: a man named Taverner has asked for the abbot's help.'

'And you came to witness this?'

'No, Sir Hugh, I came to disprove it. I agree with the Dominican school of thought. What many people regard as possession is, I believe, some sickness of the mind, a malady of the humours, lunacy, madness and, in many cases, simply suggestion or even downright trickery.'

Ranulf clapped his hands quietly.

'Ah!' The Archdeacon smiled at him. 'I believe I have a kindred spirit here?'

'And when was this exorcism to take place?' Corbett asked.

'Tomorrow.'

'And have you met this Taverner?'

'I have interrogated him.'

'And?'

The Archdeacon shrugged, took a piece of bread from the platter and popped it into his mouth, chewing slowly.

'He's one of the strangest cases I've encountered. I half believed I'd chosen the wrong ground to fight Abbot Stephen.'

'You mean to say the man is truly possessed?'

'Perhaps?'

The Archdeacon paused as footsteps were heard on the stairs. Brother Perditus almost stumbled into the room.

'Prior Cuthbert and the Concilium are ready,' he gasped.

Sir Hugh picked up his boots.

'Then we'd best join them and, as we are going to

deal with the workings of the devil,' he smiled at the Archdeacon, 'perhaps you would be so kind as to join us?'

*NAM FORTUNA SUA*
*TEMPORA LEGE REGIT*

FORTUNE RULES OUR DESTINY
JUST AS SHE PLEASES

TIBULLUS

# Chapter 2

Brother Gildas, architect and stonemason in the Abbey of St Martin's-in-the-Marsh, always prided himself that he would be ready for death. He was an old man but still keen-eyed, a former soldier, a craftsman who had helped build Edward's great castles in South Wales. Brother Gildas had often confronted death, in lonely, mist-filled valleys or forest clearings, where it could strike quickly with arrow, lance, club, axe or dagger. To prepare for death, Brother Gildas had entered the abbey twenty years ago and the brothers had been quick to use his skill. A close friend of Prior Cuthbert, Brother Gildas loved to sketch plans with quill and parchment, to choose stone and feel its texture, to cut and measure, to design and build in his mind before the first sod was cut and the corner stone laid.

Contented, grey-haired and calm-faced, Brother Gildas liked to be on his own. True, he felt a deep sorrow at Abbot Stephen's death and looked forward to singing the psalms at the requiem Mass. Yet life would go on. Gildas was now busy in his own workshop at the far end of the abbey. The table beside him was littered with different types of stone, mallets, chisels and scraps of parchment. Brother Gildas hummed one of his favourite psalms.

'Out of the depths have I cried unto thee, Oh Lord! Lord, hear my voice!'

Brother Gildas loved that song: surely it must have been written by a soldier. Didn't the psalm refer to watchmen, to God the redeemer? Brother Gildas sat at his high desk, beating a slight tattoo on its hard, polished surface whilst he studied, yet again, his plans for the new guesthouse. Now Abbot Stephen was dead Brother Cuthbert would surely be elected Abbot. The burial mound in the Bloody Meadow would be removed. Brother Gildas felt excited at the prospect of fresh building work. Perhaps he should choose the hard grey stone from South Yorkshire? Or maybe he should have selected something new like that beautiful, honey-coloured stone in Oxfordshire now being used in the building of colleges and halls at the university? Gildas felt a pang of regret, closed his eyes and whispered a prayer. He should not be thinking like this! Abbot Stephen's body was not yet buried. Gildas picked up the quill and sharpened it. How could their Father Abbot be murdered in such eerie circumstances? Gildas didn't believe any outlaw had broken in, yet he'd been present when the door had been forced. There were no other entrances or passageways. The windows had been closed and, as a mason, Gildas knew it would be impossible for even the most nimble-footed assassin to climb those walls. They were sheer and smooth, offering no crevice or crack for toe or hand. Gildas wondered if the murder had anything to do with that mysterious, perfumed figure he'd met in his restless wanderings at night. Gildas was a light sleeper so he often went for a walk at night and, twice now, he'd passed that enigmatic figure. He'd thought he'd been dreaming and, to save himself from embarrassment and ridicule, had only confided in Brother Hamo. The sub-prior had agreed that it was impossible for a woman, disguised as a monk, to wander the abbey at night. Perhaps Gildas had been mistaken? Still dreaming? Ah well!

Brother Gildas stared round his workshop. He would have to leave soon. Prior Cuthbert had called a meeting of the Concilium. Gildas had glimpsed the arrival of that tall clerk in his heavy military riding cloak, its cowl making his dark face even more enigmatic. With the King involved, no doubt Corbett would haunt this abbey until the truth was found. Gildas climbed down from his high stool and walked over to a bench. For some strange reason he stared up at a painting on the far wall, a gift from a local merchant. It had been painted on wood and depicted Death outside a house knocking on the door. Death was dressed like a knight, one hand on his sword, the other beating angrily as if determined to collect the soul within. Brother Gildas did not realise it but Death was close by, hunting for his soul.

He was about to return to his desk when he heard sounds from the storeroom, just near the side door.

'Who's that?' he called. Perhaps it was a rat, or it was not unknown for a fox, or even one of the wild cats which haunted the marshy copses, to come inside in search of warmth. Gildas walked to the half-open door and pushed it open. 'Who's there?' he repeated. He walked inside, narrowing his eyes against the gloom. 'Who's there?' he called.

'Gildas!' The words came as a hiss. 'Gildas! Guilty Gildas!'

The stonemason decided to flee. Yet, even as he made to hasten away, he realised his mistake: no soldier should turn his back on an enemy. His foot slithering, Gildas turned. A dark figure hurtled towards him and then a club smacked against his head, sending him crashing to the ground. Brother Gildas lay half unconscious, his head throbbing with pain.

'Please!' he whispered. 'Don't . . .!'

He was aware of his hands being tied behind his back, as the blood trickling from the gash in his head almost blinded him. His mouth was bone dry. He tried to look up at his assailant but all he could see were soft leather riding boots. His hands bound, he tried to struggle onto one side. He glimpsed his assailant who had closed the door to the workshop and was now standing over the brazier. Gildas gazed in horror as his attacker looked round. A red executioner's mask covered his entire face. A cloak swathed his body. He could not be a monk, a brother of the abbey. Gildas recalled the stories of Mandeville's wild huntsmen prowling along the fens. Gildas could smell something burning: his assailant was poking the coals. He turned and came back.

'Gildas! Murderer!' The words came out slowly, more of a hiss than a voice.

The assailant was moving behind him then suddenly he was standing over him. Gildas heard shallow breathing and glanced up. The black-garbed assassin was now carrying a heavy block of stone.

'Oh no, please!'

The assailant lifted the stone higher and let go; it fell smashing Brother Gildas's skull like a mallet would an egg.

Corbett sat behind Abbot Stephen's great oaken desk. The clerk disliked such trappings of power and hid a self-conscious smile. He felt like one of the King's Justices holding a court of Oyer and Terminer or Gaol Delivery. The desk itself had been cleared and Corbett had laid out sheets of vellum, a pumice stone and quill. Ranulf sat at the corner similarly prepared. Chanson stood guard at the door. Around the desk in a semi-circle were chairs and stools for the Abbey Concilium,

Prior Cuthbert sitting in the centre. Corbett looked at these powerful monks, in truth lords of this abbey. Brother Francis, the archivist and librarian, rather elegant, soft-faced and dreamy-eyed. Aelfric the infirmarian who looked as if he suffered from a permanent cold, with white sallow cheeks, protruding red nose and watery eyes which never stopped blinking. Brother Hamo, plump and grey as a pigeon, with staring eyes and lips tightly compressed, he looked like a man ever ready to give others the benefit of his wisdom. Brother Richard the almoner, young, smooth-faced, he kept dabbing his lips and rubbing his protruding stomach. Dunstan the treasurer, being bald he had no tonsure, was heavy-featured, small-eyed and tight-lipped: a monk, Corbett considered, used to accounts, tallies, ledgers, bills and indentures. A man who would seek a profit in everything. Their lord and master, Prior Cuthbert, was more relaxed, studying Corbett, assessing his worth. Corbett realised why there had been a delay. Prior Cuthbert had probably gathered these monks together in his room and told them what he had learnt, how this King's clerk would not stand on ceremony or be cowed by appeals to Canon Law, the Rule of St Benedict or the customs of the abbey. At the far end of the semi-circle sat Brother Perditus. The young man looked decidedly out of place, nervously plucking at his robe and shuffling his feet. Archdeacon Adrian, however, seemed to be enjoying himself, like a spectator at a mummer's play. He clearly did not view Abbot Stephen's death as a matter of concern to himself. Corbett sat up in the chair.

'Are we all here?'

'Brother Gildas is absent,' Prior Cuthbert declared.

'I delivered the summons, Father Prior,' Perditus declared. 'Gildas was the first I told but you know how busy he is: you can't distract him from his work.'

'Then we'll begin.' Corbett picked up his warrant, tapping the black and red seal at the bottom. 'This is the King's own seal,' he declared. 'It gives me the power to act as Commissioner over the death of Abbot Stephen or any other matter of concern. I do not wish to be challenged. The King's writ runs here, as it does in Wales or the Marches of Scotland.'

Prior Cuthbert opened his mouth to protest. Corbett held his gaze. The other members of the Concilium stirred restlessly.

'We have a requiem Mass starting soon,' Brother Aelfric wailed. 'For Abbot Stephen.'

'If the Mass is delayed,' Corbett declared, 'then so be it.'

He got to his feet, turning his back on the Concilium, and walked to the great bay window and stared down into the courtyard.

'Correct me if I am wrong but as I understand it, four days ago, on Tuesday the eve of the feast of St Leo the Great, Abbot Stephen did not go down to the abbey church to sing Matins?'

Prior Cuthbert agreed.

'You, Brother Perditus, were the Abbot's manservant. Was it customary for the Abbot to miss the hours of Divine Office occasionally?'

'He was often busy, sometimes distracted,' Perditus replied. 'As the morning went on and Abbot Stephen hadn't appeared, I became alarmed. I knocked on the door and tried the handle of the latch, but it held fast. I went and informed Prior Cuthbert.'

Corbett came back and rested his hands on the back of the chair.

'Then what happened?'

The Prior gestured over his shoulder at the door.

'We forced the lock. When we broke in, Abbot Stephen was sitting in his chair, slightly slumped, with his head to one side. The dagger had been driven in,' he pointed, 'just above his stomach. The thrust was deep, almost up to the hilt.'

'It was obvious,' Brother Aelfric declared, 'the Abbot was dead, and had been for some time.'

'And the door was definitely locked?' Corbett asked.

He went round and studied the door. He could see it had been re-hung on new leather hinges. The carpenter had also repaired the inside latch as well as the bolt and clasps at top and bottom.

'Of course it was,' Prior Cuthbert snapped, half turning in his chair.

He resented being questioned like a criminal, as this soft-footed clerk walked round the Abbot's chamber, and Corbett's red-haired henchman sat carefully taking down everything said. Now and again Ranulf would lift his head. Prior Cuthbert didn't like the faint smile, or those heavy-lidded eyes which seemed to be mocking him, as if Ranulf didn't believe anything he saw or heard.

'Continue!' Corbett demanded.

'The Abbot's body was removed.'

'And the chamber itself?'

'There were papers on the desk, the fire had burnt low. Abbot Stephen had drunk some wine but, apart from the pool of blood on the floor . . .'

'There was also this.' Corbett held up a scrap of parchment.

'Ah yes.' Prior Cuthbert smiled bleakly.

'Look.' Corbett turned it round. 'What does this wheel mean? I have glimpsed it on a number of the abbot's papers.'

'It was just a favourite sketch of his.'

Corbett turned the paper round. 'And these quotations? Both are rather garbled. One from St Paul's about seeing through a glass darkly and the corpse candles beckoning. The other,' Corbett narrowed his eyes, 'is quite famous, often quoted by the spiritual writers: a saying of the Roman writer Seneca. "Anyone can take away a man's life but no one his death".' He gazed round, they all stared blankly back. 'These were the last words Abbot Stephen wrote. He was apparently fearful of something.' Corbett paused. 'What did he mean about "Seeing through a glass, darkly"? Whilst the quotation from Seneca seems to indicate that he was expecting death?'

'I don't know,' Prior Cuthbert retorted tartly. 'Sir Hugh, I can't say what was in our abbot's mind that night.'

'Can anyone?' Corbett asked expectantly but no one answered. 'Ah well!' Corbett threw the piece of parchment down. 'We were talking of the Abbot's blood. Was it fresh or congealed?'

'It was congealed.' Aelfric spoke up.

The rest of the brothers agreed.

'So, Abbot Stephen had been dead for some time?'

'Naturally,' Hamo snapped. 'As the blood had congealed.'

'What's your name?' Ranulf interrupted.

'Hamo.'

'And you are sub-prior?' Ranulf smiled at his master.

'You know both my name and my office.'

'Yes I do, Brother, just as you know my Lord Corbett's name and office. You will keep your tone respectful.'

Corbett, standing behind the brothers, crossed his arms and stared at the floor. He and Ranulf had held so many investigations. He felt like an actor in a play. They assumed their roles without even thinking. Ranulf, who regarded it as his own private privilege to tease and mock his solemn master, was very keen not to allow anyone else to do likewise. Hamo muttered an apology.

'So, there was nothing wrong?' Corbett came back and sat down, beating his hands on top of the desk. 'This room has no other door, the windows were locked, no secret passageways exist yet someone came here and thrust a dagger deep into your Abbot's chest.' Corbett didn't wait for the chorus of agreement. 'The Abbot was sitting slumped, yes?'

'I've told you that,' Prior Cuthbert declared.

'And his hands?'

'They were down by his side.'

'And there was no disturbance? Nothing else appeared wrong?'

'Nothing.'

'But the dagger was Abbot Stephen's?'

'Ah, that's right,' Hamo said. 'Only one thing I noticed. Abbot Stephen had taken his old war belt out of the coffer. It lay on the floor. His dagger sheath was empty.'

'Fetch me this dagger!' Corbett insisted.

Prior Cuthbert snapped his fingers at Perditus who left and came back holding a folded cloth. Corbett undid the cloth and took the dagger out. It had been cleaned and polished. The hilt was of steel, the handle specially wrought so as not to slip in the hand, its blade was long, ugly and sharp. Corbett wore something similar: close up, a thrust from such a weapon was deadly. He sat for a while balancing the dagger in his hand before putting it down on the table.

'Had the doors really to be forced?' he asked.

'I was there!' the Prior exclaimed. 'So were Hamo, Aelfric and Brother Dunstan. We went straight to the Abbot's corpse.'

'No one wandered off?' Corbett insisted.

'Of course not! We were shocked at what we saw.'

Corbett stared down at the dagger and hid his unease. Before this meeting had begun, he had carefully inspected this chamber as well as the outside. The door was locked and the window closed. How could anyone get in?

'And none of you?' he asked, voicing his concern, 'know how the assassin entered this chamber or how he left?'

The row of monks shook their heads. Corbett caught a gleam of triumph in Prior Cuthbert's eyes. You know I am trapped, Corbett reflected, and can make no sense of this. He stared towards the door. It was heavy oak, its outside was reinforced with metal studs and hung on thick leather hinges. It would take hours for someone to prise it free.

'What if someone had come through a window?' Chanson had queried. 'And, when the door was forced, the assassin used the ensuing chaos to seal this?'

Ranulf, who in a former life had been a night-walker in London, declared it virtually impossible to climb the sheer outside wall. And, of course, there was one further problem . . .

'Abbot Stephen was in good health?' Corbett asked.

'Oh yes, a vigorous man in good health.'

Corbett smiled. 'So, you know what I am going to say? Your Abbot was also a former knight-banneret, a warrior, a soldier. He was used to the cut and thrust of battle. Such a man would not give up his life lightly, would he?'

He paused at the sound of a sob. Perditus sat, head down, hands in his lap, shoulders shaking.

'Abbot Stephen would have resisted. There would have been shouts, noise, tumult. Brother Perditus, I am sorry for your grief but are you a light sleeper?'

'I would have heard such a commotion!'

Corbett shifted in his chair; he glanced at Ranulf who was making notes, using the cipher Corbett had taught him.

'Let's be honest,' he said. 'I do not want to put you on oath but did Abbot Stephen have any enemies in the community?'

'None whatsoever,' Brother Richard answered swiftly. 'He was our Father Abbot. He was severe but he could also be gentle and kind, a true scholar, a holy man.' He glared at his companions.

'Brother Richard speaks the truth,' Prior Cuthbert declared.

'But come, in a community such as this there are always jealousies, rivalries . . .?'

'Father Abbot was above such rivalries, Sir Hugh.'

'Are you accusing one of us?' The sub-prior demanded. 'Sir Hugh, there are other monks in this community?'

'Brother Hamo, I thought you would never ask that. You are here for three reasons. First, you are all members of the Concilium. You had direct dealings with the Abbot, whilst the other brothers did not. Secondly, I understand you all have your own bed-chambers? So, if you went missing during the night, it would not be noticed, as it would in the cells and dormitories of the other monks. Finally,' Corbett continued remorselessly, 'the Abbot's quarters are approached by a staircase. The door to the outside courtyard is always locked at night. Brother Perditus, I believe that was your responsibility?'

The lay brother nodded.

'The only people who have keys to that door are the Abbot's manservant and members of the Concilium.'

'So, you are accusing one of us?' the Prior demanded.

'I am not accusing anyone. I am simply answering your sub-prior's question. So, let's return to your relationship with the Father Abbot. There was no disagreement?'

Brother Richard the almoner now became agitated. He was glaring along the table at Prior Cuthbert.

'There was something, wasn't there, Brother Richard? Please, tell me!'

'There is no need to,' the Prior declared. 'We had one disagreement with Father Abbot. We own a field called Bloody Meadow, which has a tumulus or burial mound in the centre. According to local lore, many centuries

51

ago, one of the first Christian Kings, Sigbert, was martyred and buried there. We, the members of the Concilium, believed the meadow would have been an ideal site for an enlarged guesthouse. Abbot Stephen disagreed. He said the meadow and the burial mound were sacred and should not be disturbed.'

Corbett studied the Prior closely. You speak so quickly, he thought, as if it was a minor matter. Yet I suspect it was very important to you but would it lead to murder? He glanced sideways, to where Archdeacon Adrian Wallasby sat bored, picking at his teeth.

'And you?' Corbett pointed to him. 'You had been in the abbey days before the murder took place? You met with Abbot Stephen? He gave you a key to his lodgings?'

Archdeacon Adrian was no longer bored. He scratched his cheek nervously.

'Abbot Stephen was well known as an exorcist,' Wallasby replied. 'He carried out exorcisms both here and in London witnessed by scholars and theologians.' He paused, choosing his words carefully. 'As you know, Sir Hugh, the Dominican Order are the papal inquisitors. They are used to root out heresy and magic. Many Dominicans now agree with me: the so-called possessed are either sick in their souls, counterfeit or simply madcaps.'

'And Abbot Stephen challenged that?'

'The challenge was scholarly, an exchange of letters. A few weeks ago Abbot Stephen wrote to me about a man called Taverner who had come to St Martin's asking for his help. Taverner claims that he is possessed by the demon spirit of Geoffrey Mandeville.'

Corbett started in surprise.

'The robber baron who plagued this area?'

'The same.'

'And how does Taverner express this?' Ranulf asked curiously.

'I have questioned him,' Prior Cuthbert replied. 'He is a man of no learning but he can lapse into Norman French or Latin. He also seems to know a great deal about Mandeville's life. He is, in fact, two people in one.'

'This man I must meet,' Corbett declared. 'Is he safe?'

'He's kept in a chamber near the infirmary,' Prior Cuthbert declared. 'He is given good lodgings, food and drink. Abbot Stephen was particularly interested in him.'

'And what do you think?' Corbett asked.

The Prior pulled a face. 'Sir Hugh, I am a Benedictine monk, I have my duties and tasks.'

'So, you don't see the devil peeping round corners or hiding in the shadows?'

'Neither did Father Abbot.' Perditus had lost his nervousness. He was hard-faced and defiant. 'Father Abbot didn't see demons and imps lurking in trees or hiding in pools. He truly believed that demons were lords of the air and were given the authority to enter certain people.'

'Abbot Stephen doesn't need your defence,' Cuthbert snapped. 'The gospels talk of demons. Didn't the Gadarene claim to have a legion of devils possessing him?'

Corbett pointed at the Archdeacon.

'And what were your thoughts on Taverner?'

'A remarkable case.' The Archdeacon rubbed his hands together. 'Sir Hugh, in London I have met counterfeit men, cunning deceivers, but I must admit Taverner half convinced me.'

'Half convinced?'

'I don't deny the existence of Satan and his legions,' the Archdeacon simpered. 'It's just that I don't accept they have power to interfere in our lives. After all, human will can perpetrate enough wickedness without those our learned lay brother calls lords of the air. My

discussions with Abbot Stephen were over the writings
of the Fathers such as Ambrose and Augustine. Yet it is
rather strange,' he mused.

'What?' Corbett demanded.

'The sorcerers and necromancers, those who study
the Kabbala, believe in powerful spells and incantations.
Sir Hugh, have you heard about the College of the
Invisibles?'

Corbett shook his head.

'It's a belief that a sorcerer, by certain spells, can
make himself invisible for a matter of hours and pass
through matter such as wood and stone.'

Corbett caught his meaning.

'You are referring to the murder of Abbot Stephen?'

'I have listened to you carefully, Sir Hugh. How else,
except through the black arts, could the Abbot be
stabbed to death in his own chamber? The door at the
foot of the stairs was unlocked, the lay brother Perditus
heard no one come up. The Abbot's windows and doors
were firmly closed. There are no secret passageways.
There appears to have been no struggle yet our Abbot
was found murdered. I wonder—'

Corbett interrupted. 'Before we move to matters
celestial, to quote you, Archdeacon Adrian, the human
will can perpetrate evil enough.'

'But it's still a mystery,' the Archdeacon insisted.

Corbett beat his fingers on the table.

'For the moment it is. Tell me, Prior Cuthbert, did
anything extraordinary happen, in or around the abbey,
in the days preceding Abbot Stephen's death?'

'Our abbey is a place of calm and harmony, Sir Hugh.
Beyond the walls, however, you've seen the country-
side; marshes, swamps, fields, thick copses of woods.
Outlaws such as Scaribrick prowl there.'

'But they are no threat to the abbey?'

'None whatsoever.'

'And Lady Margaret Harcourt?'

'The dislike between her and the Abbot was well known. They never met or corresponded.'

'Falcon Brook,' Dunstan the treasurer intervened. He saw Corbett's look of surprise. 'Falcon Brook,' he explained, 'is a stream which runs at the foot of Bloody Meadow. Lady Margaret and our Father Abbot disputed its true ownership.'

'But I managed the dispute,' Prior Cuthbert intervened. 'That's how Father Abbot wanted it.'

Corbett stared across at a painting on the wall, a piece of canvas stretched across a block of wood. Its colours were brilliantly vivid, the brushwork vigorous. He narrowed his eyes. At first the figures it contained meant nothing: he glimpsed a tower in the background all a-fire. A young man in armour was leading an older one whose eyes were bandaged. Corbett at last recognised the scene: Aeneas leading his father from Troy. He gazed round the room. Other paintings had similar motifs. He recognised the story of Romulus and Remus, Caesar and other themes from the history and legends of ancient Rome. Prior Cuthbert had followed his gaze.

'An idiosyncrasy of Father Abbot,' he explained. 'He liked all things Roman. I understand that, both as a knight-banneret and as a monk, he often served on embassies to the Holy Father in Rome. He was much taken by the ruins there and collected ancient histories.'

'Abbot Stephen was, in all things, a lover of ancient Rome.' Brother Francis the librarian spoke up. 'He collected books and manuscripts about it.'

'Why?' Corbett queried.

'I asked him that once myself,' the librarian replied. 'Abbot Stephen answered that he admired the gravitas of ancient Rome, its honour, its love of order and discipline. We even have a copy of the "Acts of Pilate". He was a great scholar,' the librarian added wistfully.

'He lived a good life and deserved a better death.'

Corbett glanced quickly at Ranulf who was busily writing. He found it difficult to hide his disappointment and frustration. Here was an Abbot foully murdered but, apart from the issue of Bloody Meadow, Corbett could sense no antipathy or hatred towards the dead man, certainly not enough to cause murder. And just how had it been perpetrated? He closed his eyes and suddenly felt the weariness of his rushed journey here. The King had been so insistent that they leave immediately. Corbett wished he could lie on his bed and pull the coverlets over his head to sleep and dream.

'Sir Hugh?'

He opened his eyes quickly.

'Sir Hugh.' Prior Cuthbert smiled placatingly. 'If there are no other questions? The daily business of the abbey demands our attention and we do have the requiem Mass?'

Corbett apologised and agreed. The Concilium left, followed by Archdeacon Adrian and Perditus. Corbett waited until Chanson had closed the door behind them. Ranulf threw his quill down on the desk and buried his face in his hands.

'Nothing, Master, nothing at all! Here we have an abbot, a scholar, a theologian with an interest in antiquities, well loved and respected by his community.'

'But is that only the surface?' Corbett asked. 'Or is there something else?'

He banged the desk in frustration. He was about to continue when there was a knock on the door. Archdeacon Adrian stepped into the chamber.

'There is one thing, Sir Hugh, that the brothers never mentioned.' He took the seat Ranulf offered. 'I have only been here a few days . . .'

'And how do you find the community?' Corbett

asked. 'After all, Master Wallasby, you are an arch-deacon, a sniffer-out of scandal and sin.'

Wallasby took this in good heart.

'I'll be honest, Sir Hugh, the abbey is well managed. If I was making an official visitation . . .' He shook his head. 'The divine office is orderly and well sung. The brothers work assiduously in the library, scriptorium, kitchen and fields. No women are allowed within the enclosures. There are the usual petty rivalries but nothing significant except . . .'

'And that's why you've come back?'

'It's the huntsman,' the Archdeacon explained. 'Two nights before the Abbot died I couldn't sleep. I went for a walk in the grounds. At first I thought I imagined the first blast but two more followed, similar to that heard in a hunt before the hounds are released. I understand, from talking to some of the older brothers, that Lady Margaret Harcourt's husband, the one who disappeared, used to sound a hunting horn at night as a jest, pretending to be the ghost of Sir Geoffrey Mandeville. I have also learnt that the horn has been heard frequently over the last four or five months.' He got to his feet. 'But more than that I cannot say.'

'What will happen to Taverner?' Corbett asked.

The Archdeacon shrugged. 'I suppose the good brothers will give him some money, food, a change of clothing and he'll be sent on his way. However, I understand from Brother Richard that Taverner has asked to stay for a while, and our good Prior is inclined to permit this.'

He left quietly. Corbett turned to his companions.

'Ranulf, Chanson, I want you to wander the abbey.' He grinned. 'Act, if you can, like wide-eyed innocents.'

'You mean snout amongst the rubbish?' Ranulf retorted.

'Yes, to be blunt.'

Ranulf and Chanson left. Corbett stared round the chamber and got to his feet. It was well furnished, with paintings and crucifixes on the wall, statues of the Virgin and saints in small niches. The floor was of polished wood, and the many beeswax candles exuded their own special fragrance. In a small recess stood the bed, a narrow four-poster with curtains, testers and blankets. Woollen carpets, dyed different colours, covered some of the floor. Corbett moved these aside and began to look for any secret entrances or trap door but there was none. The walls were of hard stone, the floor of unbroken, shiny planks of wood. He moved the bed, desk and tables but could detect nothing.

Corbett then moved to the chests and coffers but these only confirmed Abbot Stephen's ascetic nature. There were very few rings or trinkets; the large chest contained pieces of armour, a surcoat, war belt, relics of the Abbot's days as a knight. Nothing remarkable or significant. Corbett gathered up the papers and books and placed these on the desk and slowly began to go through them. He could find nothing untoward: letters, bills, treatises, most of these concerned the government of the abbey, Abbot Stephen's journeys abroad and, of course, his work as an exorcist. Some of the books were histories of ancient Rome or tracts by Fathers of the Church on demonology and possession. There was a Book of Remembrance listing those individuals Abbot Stephen would pray for at Mass but this too was unremarkable. Corbett picked up the sheet of vellum containing the quotation from St Paul about seeing through a glass darkly, the reference to corpse candles and that enigmatic quotation from the Roman philosopher Seneca. What did all these mean? Corbett studied the doodle or diagram at the bottom. He'd seen it on other scraps of parchment: a wheel sketched in ink with a hub, spokes and rim.

Did this hold any special significance?

Corbett pushed the parchment away and stared at the door. Here was a man, he reflected, a churchman, between fifty-three and fifty-five summers old, with very little to show concerning his past. Corbett, exasperated, left the chamber and went down to the spacious abbey kitchens for some bread, meat and ale. The brothers there were kindly but distant and Corbett realised that the abbey was now preparing for the solemn requiem Mass. He met Ranulf and Chanson wandering like lost souls along the corridors and galleries. They, too, reported that the brothers were friendly enough but they had learnt nothing from them. Corbett sent them back to the guesthouse and returned to the abbot's chamber. Going through letters and books, he could find no clue, no reason why this saintly abbot's life ended so brutally.

A servant came to announce that the requiem Mass was about to begin. Corbett joined the community in the great abbey church with its long nave and shadow-filled transepts, cut off from the sanctuary by an ornately carved rood screen. The lay brothers gathered here whilst the monks sat in their stalls. Prior Cuthbert entered, garbed in the magnificent pontificals for the mass of the dead: black and gold vestments. The Abbot's coffin, draped in purple cloth of gold, lay in state on trestles before the high altar.

Corbett was lulled by the rise and fall of the plain chant, the solemn words of invocation as censors swung, sending up billowing clouds of perfumed incense. The sanctuary was ablaze with the light from tall purple candles. The clerk felt as though he was in another world. He was aware of statues, the faces of gargoyles peering down at him; of Father Prior and his concelebrants moving round the high altar, lifting chalice and host, interceding with God for the soul of their departed brother. He was chilled by the final, solemn invocation to the Archangels of heaven that they go out to meet the Abbot's soul and not allow him to 'fall into the hands of the enemy'. Corbett became acutely aware of his own mortality and recalled Maeve's warning about tasks such as this, investigating sudden, mysterious death, hunting down the bloody-handed sons of Cain. He found it difficult to accept, in the midst of so much peace, that members of this community, participating in this sacred, gorgeous ceremony, could have planned, plotted and perpetrated this foul murder. Nevertheless, that was the conclusion Corbett had reached and he would have to stay here until it was resolved.

Corbett gazed up at the stained-glass windows of the sanctuary. Darkness was falling. He glanced over his shoulder back through the rood screen. The shadows in the nave were growing longer like extended, dark fingers stretching towards him. Were Maeve's warnings relevant to this sacred place? Would he and his two companions escape unscathed? He turned back and watched Prior Cuthbert solemnly wave incense over the coffin. Corbett had hunted many an assassin and, although he accepted the serenity and harmony of St Martin's-in-the-Marsh, he had his own premonitions that the Abbot's murder was the flower of a hideous plant with deep, twisted roots.

Corbett had not shared such macabre thoughts with his companions but this abbey, with its shadow-filled corridors and galleries, its lonely fields and gardens was just as dangerous as any battlefield, or the alleys in Whitefriars or Southwark. Indeed, death had already struck and would be all the more surprising and sudden in any fresh assault. Corbett's hand fell to the hilt of his dagger. He studied the brothers in their stalls and the three celebrants, Prior Cuthbert, Hamo and Aelfric.

They seemed to ignore his presence but now and again a cowled head would turn and he would catch a furtive glance or a sharp look.

After the Mass was finished Corbett returned to the nave. He leaned against a pillar as the brothers lowered the coffin into a prepared pit just before the Lady Chapel. Corbett said his own prayers, crossed himself and left. He walked down to the guesthouse and found Ranulf and Chanson fast asleep. Corbett returned to his own chamber. For a while he lay on the bed reflecting on what he had heard and seen but nothing made any sense. He drifted into sleep and was awoken by the abbey bell tolling the Vespers for the Dead. Again he joined the brothers in the sanctuary, sitting on a stool just within the rood screen. This time he joined in the singing. Corbett loved the melodious descants of plain chant and many of the vesper psalms were his favourites. Corbett was a strong, vigorous singer, and his participation provoked smiles and welcoming glances. The sanctuary was starker than it had been earlier in the afternoon. Only one candle glowed on the altar. Prior Cuthbert sat in the Abbot's seat. Corbett had the opportunity to study the other brothers. Most of them were middle-aged men with a sprinkling of novices and newly professed brothers. He noticed a few stalls were empty. He recalled that Gildas the architect and stonemason, had not attended the meeting of the Concilium and wondered what had happened to him. Vespers drew to an end. Prior Cuthbert was about to give the final blessing when the service was interrupted by the sound of hurried footsteps. A sweating lay brother came hurtling through the door of the rood screen and stopped, one hand resting against the polished wood as he caught his breath.

'Father Prior!' he gasped. 'Father Prior, you've got to come!'

'We have not finished vespers,' the Prior replied, leaning down from his stall. 'You know the rule, Brother Norbert, Divine Office is never interrupted.'

'It's Gildas!' the lay brother gasped. 'On the burial mound in Bloody Meadow!'

The Prior looked at Corbett who grasped the lay brother by the arm and led him out. The man was shaking.

'He's dead!' he gasped. 'Oh sir, he's dead! In a hideous way!'

'Show me.'

Corbett almost pushed the lay brother down the nave, aware of others following him. They went out through the main door. Corbett flinched at the blast of cold night air. He glanced up; the sky had remained overcast and it was pitch black. He had to depend on the lay brother as they raced across the cloisters and gardens, down pebble-dashed paths and out through what the lay brother described as the Judas Gate. Corbett waited until the others caught up with him, Prior Cuthbert and members of the community carrying blazing pitch torches.

'The ground is hard underfoot,' the Prior declared.

He led Corbett across the meadow. The clerk's eyes grew accustomed to the darkness. To his left he was aware of a long line of trees. He heard a bird call and saw the great burial mound looming up before him. The lay brother pointed upwards. Corbett grasped a torch and, slipping and cursing, he climbed to the top. The corpse of Gildas sprawled there. Corbett covered his mouth as he saw the hideous wounds to the side of his head. In the flickering flame of the torch he glimpsed a dark bubbling mess. He was aware of staring eyes and the hideous mark, in the shape of a 'V', which had been branded on the dead man's forehead.

*NEC MIHI VERA*
*LOQUI PUDOR EST*

NEVER BE ASHAMED TO
SPEAK THE TRUTH

ANON

# Chapter 3

Corbett, helped by the lay brothers, managed to slide the corpse down the frost-encrusted grass. In the torch light, Gildas's face, with that fearsome brand mark and the great open wound in the side of the head, drew horrified gasps and muttered prayers. Ranulf and Chanson, alarmed by the commotion, also joined them. For a while chaos reigned until Prior Cuthbert, at Corbett's insistence, ordered the corpse to be taken to the death house under the care of Brother Aelfric. A cowled, shadowy figure thrust through the group, ignoring the protests of the brothers. When he reached the corpse, the man pulled his hood back to reveal a mass of wiry grey hair, glittering sharp eyes and a face half hidden by a luxurious beard and moustache. He was short and squat and smelt like a midden.

'You have no right to be here!' Brother Hamo declared.

Corbett realised this was the Watcher by the Gates.

'I don't give a fig what you think,' the fellow grated. 'I have warned you before and I will warn you again. The demon Mandeville is loose and Death rides in his retinue!'

Corbett half smiled as he recognised the mis-quotation from the Book of Revelation.

'And you!' The Watcher turned, pointing at Corbett. 'I saw you arrive. You are the King's emissary? Come to wreak justice. Well, your Abbot is dead.' He stared round the group.

'And by the way you smell, you'd think you were!'

Ranulf grasped the man by the shoulder but the hermit shook him off.

'Ah now!' he exclaimed, peering up at Ranulf. 'There's a pretty boy, a street fighter if I ever saw one. Not like your master, eh? And, as for my smell, that's because my body's ripe.' The Watcher's voice fell to a dramatic whisper. 'As are the bodies of these monks for death!'

'That's enough!' Corbett intervened. He gestured at the lay brothers. 'Take the corpse away!'

The hermit was about to leave.

'No, sir, you'll stay.' Corbett lifted a hand. 'I do not wish to hear your protests.'

The Watcher now preened himself.

'I'll follow where the King's emissary says,' he declared dramatically. 'And I'll thank you for a goblet of wine and some meat, juicy and hot from the spit.'

'You'll get that,' Corbett stared down at him, 'only when I learn why you are here. You didn't see the corpse. So, how did you know he bore the brand of Mandeville on him?'

The Watcher looked crestfallen. He would have backed away but Ranulf now blocked his path.

'Questions first, food later,' Corbett declared. 'Prior Cuthbert, Brother Hamo, let's return.'

Corbett followed the lay brothers who carried the corpse back through the Judas Gate, across the abbey grounds to the white-washed infirmary. A chamber at the far end served as a corpse room. A great wooden table like that of a butcher's stall stood in the centre. Trestle tables ranged round the sides bore bowls, jugs and jars of ointment. A single candle glowed. At Aelfric's instructions, sconce torches were hastily lit, making the hollowed, canopied chamber even more macabre and ghoulish. Gildas's body was placed on the table where Corbett studied it more carefully. Ignoring the rictus of horror carved on the dead man's face, the clerk reckoned the brand mark was about an inch long.

'That was burnt in,' Corbett declared, 'with a branding iron, probably after he was killed.'

He turned the head and looked at the bloody mess of what used to be the side of the monk's head, now a congealed mass of blood, bone and brain. Corbett examined this carefully and, using the point of his dagger, lifted out small grains of stone. Helped by Aelfric, he turned the corpse over on its face. He felt a large bump, a raised bruise, at the back of the head. The hands were dusty but Corbett noticed the little red cuts on each wrist. The rest now clustered around: Prior Cuthbert, Hamo, Aelfric, Ranulf and Chanson, with the Watcher standing between them.

'He was killed by a stone,' Corbett declared, 'dropped from a great force on to the side of his head.'

'But surely, Sir Hugh,' Prior Cuthbert stood, hand over his mouth, gagging at the grievous wound, 'Gildas was a soldier, he would have resisted.'

'No, I think he was struck first at the back of the head, probably with a club, and would drop to the ground stunned. The attacker then tied his hands behind him and brought down a heavy stone and crushed the side of his skull. He also took a branding-iron and put the bloody mark on his forehead. Now, why is that, eh? When was Gildas last seen?'

Prior Cuthbert turned and whispered to Hamo, who hurried off. He returned a short while later with the lay brother Perditus. A brief conversation took place between the monks. When Perditus glimpsed Gildas's head, he retched and, holding his mouth, had to leave for a while. When he returned, he was wiping his lips.

'I saw Brother Gildas this morning, when I delivered the Prior's message about the meeting of the Concilium in the abbot's quarters!'

'Did anyone else see him?'

'I saw him a short while later,' Hamo declared. 'I went across to consult him regarding some building work in one of our granges.'

'Where was this?' Corbett demanded.

'The far side of the abbey,' Hamo declared. 'That's where Gildas had his workshops, rather a lonely spot.'

'And he had stone there?'

'Oh yes, cut and hewn.'

'And a brazier?'

'Yes.'

Prior Cuthbert paused, rocking backwards and forwards on his feet.

'What is it?' Corbett demanded.

'I have just realised,' the Prior replied. 'What with your meeting this morning, Sir Hugh, the requiem Mass and Abbot Stephen's funeral, no one has seen Brother Gildas for the rest of the day.'

'What I suspect . . .' Corbett declared. He paused and felt the corpse's hands, shoulders, legs and ankles, the cadaver was already beginning to stiffen. 'I suspect Brother Gildas has been dead for hours. Notice the hardness of the muscle, the chilling flesh, the stomach beginning to swell. Gildas was probably killed this morning in his workshop. The attacker stunned him, tied his hands and crushed his skull. But then he hid the corpse and, under the cover of darkness, brought it out and laid it on the tumulus: that's where you saw it, wasn't it?' Corbett glanced at the Watcher.

In the light of the torches, the Watcher looked even more grotesque with his broad shoulders and squat body, dark eyes, straggling hair, moustache and beard, his face as brown as a nut. He reminded Corbett of some wood goblin or forest sprite. He was certainly strong enough to kill a man like Gildas and carry his corpse out here.

'I know what you are thinking.' The Watcher by the Gates stamped his foot. 'You think it's me, don't you?'

'And why not?' Corbett declared. 'You may have grey locks but you are strong and thickset, and your arms are muscular. You babble about Mandeville's ghost. You know the corpse had a brand mark and you have no right to be wandering this abbey.'

The Watcher by the Gates blinked, his face crestfallen.

'It's not right,' he moaned. 'All because I wanted some meat!' He waved his stubby fingers.

'To be fair,' Prior Cuthbert spoke up. 'Our Watcher by the Gates is allowed to wander the abbey grounds. As a kindness, we often feed him from our kitchens.'

'See,' the Watcher replied, baring his teeth at Corbett. 'I'll tell you what happened. I came in, and was given some ale and a juicy strip of pork, salty and thick, and a small loaf of rye bread. I went out into Bloody Meadow to eat it.'

'Do you always go there?'

'I like it there, away from prying eyes! The burial mound is sacred and I am sure the fairies gather there. When I came out I noticed something lying on the top. I went up and even in the poor light I could see it was one of the monks. All I could glimpse was Mandeville's mark on his forehead. "Oh, Lord save us!" said I. "Oh, Virgin Queen of Heaven, help me!"' The Watcher clapped his hands. 'I ran back in, got the lay brother, told him what I had seen, the rest you know.'

'Cover Gildas's corpse,' Prior Cuthbert ordered.

Aelfric went to one of the chests. He brought out a

large white cloth which he draped over the corpse.
Corbett waited until he'd finished.

'And what makes you think it's Mandeville?' he
asked turning to the Watcher. 'I don't believe in ghosts.
I don't believe the dead ride. Gildas was killed by flesh
and blood.'

'Gildas was killed by something evil.' The Watcher's
face became sly. 'It's a warning to the good brothers
here.'

'About what?' Prior Cuthbert asked sharply.

The Watcher danced from foot to foot.

'This is what I think! This is what I think! Abbot
Stephen was going to allow you to build your guesthouse in Bloody Meadow, desecrate the sacred burial
ground.'

'How do you know that?' Corbett demanded.

'Oh, I know what I know,' the Watcher replied. He
tapped the side of his head. 'I can hear things on the
breeze.'

'You'll hear me,' Ranulf declared, gripping him by
the shoulder. 'Tell my master, how did you know?'

'The Abbot told me.' The Watcher squirmed in
Ranulf's grip. 'Take your hand off me, Red Hair!'

Corbett nodded at Ranulf who stepped back.

'This is new to me,' Brother Hamo declared. 'Why
should our Father Abbot tell such a thing to a hermit
and not to members of his Concilium?'

'Perhaps it was just a passing fancy?' the Watcher
declared. 'You know how Abbot Stephen liked to walk
outside the walls of the abbey, ave beads in one hand,
crucifix in the other. And you, his shadow,' he pointed
at Perditus, 'always walking behind him. Well, the day
before he died . . .'

'That's right,' Perditus interrupted. 'Father Abbot did
stop and speak to you.'

'I asked him why he looked so troubled,' the Watcher

70

continued. ' "Guesthouses" the Abbot replied quickly. "Perhaps I should allow a new one to be built?" He seemed distracted and walked on. I tell you the truth, I tell you the truth!'

Corbett glanced back at the sheeted corpse and round at the others. Chanson guarded the door. Ranulf lounged, eyes on his master, watchful, tense as a cat. The monks stood like statues as if unable to cope with what had happened.

I could question you further, Corbett thought. Yet, in his mind's eye he recalled the sprawling abbey buildings, the Judas Gate, the postern doors, the lonely fields and orchards outside beyond the wall. With darkness falling early, Gildas's assassin could move with impunity, protected by the commotion caused by Abbot Stephen's death and burial as well as Corbett's arrival.

'I think there's nothing more we can do for the moment,' Corbett declared. 'The hour grows late.'

He was going across to take a sconce torch out of its bracket when the abbey bell began to toll, like a tocsin; not the slow melodious clang which is an invitation to prayer, but sharp and quick.

'God and his Saints!' Prior Cuthbert declared. 'What's the matter now?'

There was a pounding at the door. Chanson pulled it open. Brother Richard the almoner, out of breath, burst in, hand out to the Prior.

'Father, you must come and see this! You, too, Sir Hugh!'

'What about me?' the Watcher by the Gates demanded.

'Go home!' Corbett retorted. 'Though we'll have words later, Watcher by the Gates.'

Corbett went out into the cold night air, striding fast to keep up with Brother Richard.

'It's in the church – desecration, blasphemy!'

They went up the steps and through the main door. To Corbett's left, a monk still pulled at the bell.

'Thank you!' the clerk shouted. 'We realise something's wrong.' He grasped the almoner by the arm. 'But what?'

Brother Richard pointed down the nave. A few candles still glowed in the sanctuary. Corbett studied the entrance to the rood screen. Ranulf saw it first.

'Angels' wings!' he breathed. 'In God's name, what is it?'

Corbett felt his skin prickle with fear. Brother Richard hung back as he walked up the nave, footsteps echoing hollowly. He could hear voices behind him. As he drew closer, Corbett's stomach heaved. The corpse of a cat, throat cut, had been hooked by its tail and left to swing from the beam above the rood screen door. Its bristling fur, swinging body and the pool of blood beneath, turned his stomach and made his gorge rise. Corbett was about to turn away when he saw the piece of parchment pinned to the corpse. He covered his mouth and snatched at it. Plucking it out, his fingers brushed the animal's fur, and Corbett felt as if he was going to be sick.

'Ranulf!' he shouted. 'For God's sake, take care of it!'

His henchman, muttering and cursing, cut the corpse down. Brother Richard hurried up with a wooden box he'd found in the bell tower. Ranulf put the cat in this and took it through a side door. Corbett stood for a while breathing deeply. He felt his stomach calm.

'Are you all right, Sir Hugh?'

Chanson came up. His master's face had gone pale.

'It's not the poor creature,' Corbett replied, 'but it just looked so hideous swinging there.'

He walked down the church. In the light of the torch he read the scrap of parchment. The words were

72

scrawled like those of a child on a piece of slate:
'JUSTICE WILL BE DONE. THE SWORD OF
MANDEVILLE WILL NOT BE FAR FROM THIS
HOUSE'. Corbett studied it carefully. The parchment
could have come from anywhere: it was jagged, rather
dirty, the black ink was common and the words had
been deliberately scrawled to conceal the writer's style.
Corbett handed it to Prior Cuthbert.

'Where was the cat from?' he asked.

'One of the many we have round here, Sir Hugh.
They wage eternal war against the rats in our barns. A
senseless cruelty.'

'Yes,' Corbett agreed.

He took the Prior by the shoulder and led him away.
Cuthbert looked frightened, agitated.

'Believe me, Brother,' Corbett whispered. 'Abbot
Stephen's murder was not the last, neither will Gildas's
be. Someone with a sick mind and a rotten soul has
declared war against your community. More deaths will
occur. So, tell me, is there anything I should know?'

The Prior licked dry lips, and dropped his gaze.

'There's nothing,' he declared. 'Nothing at all. We
have done no wrong, there is no sin here.'

'In which case I would like to see Gildas's workshop.'

Corbett joined Ranulf and Chanson outside the
church.

'I have disposed of the cat,' Ranulf declared. 'Poor
animal! To be caught, have its throat cut and then
trussed up like that.'

'Thank you.' Corbett patted him on the shoulder.
'Long ago I saw a cat crushed by a cart, it's an image
which has never left me.'

'And the message?' Ranulf asked.

Corbett told him. A lay brother came out carrying a
torch and led them across the abbey. Gildas's workshop
lay near the far wall. They went inside, where candles

and oil lamps were lit. Corbett stared round at the table and work benches, the racks of tools, the heap of cut stone. The floor was covered with dust. He scraped it with his foot and eventually found a dark, wine-like stain.

'This is where Gildas lay,' he declared, crouching down. 'He was probably struck on the head and then had his hands tied.' He pointed to the pile of stone and the brazier. 'He was killed here and branded.'

Corbett went outside. On the far side of the work-shops stood an orchard, the stripped branches of its trees stark against the night sky.

'A lonely enough place to hide a corpse,' Corbett observed. 'Then it would be carried out through that gate and taken to Bloody Meadow.'

'Do you think,' Ranulf asked, 'that we are dealing with one assassin or two?'

'I don't know,' Corbett said. 'One fact I have grasped: Abbot Stephen and the leading officials of this abbey clashed over Bloody Meadow and the building of that guesthouse.'

He walked to the small postern gate built into the wall, drew back the bolts and went through: a narrow path divided the wall from a small copse of trees.

'Bloody Meadow,' Corbett whispered. 'Gildas's killer placed that corpse on the burial mound deliberately. But why? And why did Abbot Stephen change his mind so abruptly? If we believe our Watcher, the abbot was deep in thought, considering all possibilities and let slip that he was thinking of changing his mind. So why was he killed? And what is all this nonsense about Mandeville?'

He walked up the path, the curtain wall beside him rose high and sheer. On his left the woods gave way to grass and shrubs. A mist was curling in. Corbett paused and saw the lights flickering.

'Corpse Candles,' he declared. 'I remember these when I was a child, they always terrified me. Some people claimed they were candles held by the angels of death hovering to reap their harvest.' His voice sounded strange in the dark stillness. 'Only when I was at Oxford, did a Magister explain how swamps and marshes give off a substance which can glow in the dark. Yet even knowing this, they are still frightening.'

Ranulf repressed a shiver and tapped the hilt of his dagger. He hated the countryside; he found it more dangerous and threatening than any alleyway in Southwark. Corbett was about to go back when he heard a hunting horn braying. He paused. The sound came from some distance away. Ranulf cursed under his breath as the shrill blast was repeated, two, three times.

'It's easy to scoff at Mandeville's ghost,' Ranulf declared. 'But, out here in the dark, with the mist curling in . . .?'

'I wonder what that could be?' Corbett murmured. 'Why has it started again now? And what connection does it have with these deaths?'

'Shall we try and find out?' Chanson asked.

'Not now, it is too dark for chasing ghostly huntsmen!'

And the clerk went back through the gate into the abbey grounds. Corbett told Ranulf and Chanson to return to the guesthouse.

'Stay together,' he warned.

Ranulf gestured at Chanson to walk away. He tugged at Corbett's sleeve and pulled him into the buttress of one of the buildings.

'And what about you, Master?'

Corbett felt how tense and watchful his companion had become.

'You know the Lady Maeve's instructions!' Ranulf insisted. 'I am not to leave you alone. This may be a house of God, Sir Hugh, but it is also the abode of murder with its lonely chambers, empty galleries and passageways. One monk looks much like another,' Ranulf jibed. 'They are quite capable of thrusting a dagger or loosing an arrow through the dark.'

'And the King?' Corbett asked. He wanted to resolve an issue which had been nagging at him since he'd left Norwich. 'Why do you start, Ranulf? Are you under secret instructions from him?'

Ranulf stepped back and leaned against the wall.

'Come, come, Ranulf-atte-Newgate, principal Clerk in the Chancery of the Green Wax,' Corbett teased. 'How ambitious are you? Why did the King take you by the arm and stroll through the rose garden with you?'

'Why, Master, were you spying on me?'

'Why, Ranulf, I didn't have to. Most of those at the Bishop of Norwich's palace saw you.'

'Are you jealous?'

Corbett laughed merrily.

'I am sorry,' Ranulf apologised.

'Ranulf, Ranulf!' Corbett gripped him by the shoulder. 'Once you ran ragged-arsed through the alleyways of White Friars and Southwark. Ranulf the riffler, the roaring boy, the night-walker, the footpad. Now you are a clerk with good linen shirts, and woollen hose, your shoulders protected by thick warm cloaks, and a broad leather belt strapped round your waist. Spanish boots are on your feet with clinking spurs; sword and dagger are fastened at your side. You carry the King's Seal, you are his man in peace and war. What more do you want, Ranulf-atte-Newgate? You have monies salted away with the goldsmiths in London. You've hired a chantry priest to sing Masses for your soul. How many horses do you own – three or four, including one from Barbary, in our stables at Leighton. You are skilled in every form of writing, drawing up an indenture, sealing a charter, issuing a proclamation. Now the King walks with you arm-in-arm. Why, Ranulf-atte-Newgate? Does he trust you? Do you trust me, Ranulf?'

'With my life, Master. You know that. Your enemies are mine.'

Corbett let his hand fall away. He thought of Edward the King: hair and beard now iron-grey; those cynical, watchful eyes, the right one slightly drooping; his swift changes of mood, either charming or coldly ruthless. Edward was a King who didn't stand on ceremony; and could also play the warrior, clad in his black armour on Bayard his war horse, hanging Scottish rebels by the dozen, not turning a hair as villages were ravaged by fire and sword.

'The devil can come in many forms, Ranulf, and tempt in many ways. Did the King take you up to a high mountain and show you the glory which could be yours?'

'I don't understand,' Ranulf stammered.

'My friend, you do. The King is impatient. I have read the records. Sir Stephen Daubigny, late Abbot of this place, was once one of the King's boon companions, a knight who fought with him during the dark days of Simon de Montfort. The King owes Abbot Stephen his life. Remember the King's motto: "My word is my bond". Now, Ranulf-atte-Newgate, you know and I know, and the King suspects, that Abbot Stephen's killer is a monk, a priest, a member of the Body Spiritual. If I catch him, and God willing I shall, I cannot hand him over to the sheriff or carry out judgement myself and hang him from the nearest gallows. So, what has the King told you? To carry out justice on his behalf? Summary execution? Do you carry in your wallet one of those writs: "What Ranulf-Atte-Newgate has done, he has done for the good of the King and the safety of his realm".' Corbett stepped closer. 'You can't do that, Ranulf. There is the King but above him stands the law. The law is all-important.'

Ranulf stepped aside.

'I am your friend and henchman,' he spoke quickly. 'But, as you said, I am the King's man in peace and war. Have you ever thought, Sir Hugh,' he stepped forward, 'of Ranulf-atte-Newgate as a knight? Ranulf-atte-Newgate as a courtier, or even a churchman?'

Although it was dark Corbett could sense the passion seething in this man whom he secretly regarded as his brother.

'I made a mistake, Ranulf,' Corbett whispered. 'I thought you were my man in peace and war. I am certainly yours.' His hand went out, then fell away. 'I tell you this, Ranulf, here, in this dark, silent place, if I had to choose between Ranulf-atte-Newgate and Edward of England then Edward of England would come a poor second.' Corbett gathered his cloak about him. 'I will be in the Abbot's lodgings and I will be safe.'

And, turning on his heel, Corbett walked away.

'Ranulf! Ranulf!' he whispered once he was out of earshot, tears stinging his eyes. He quietly cursed the King. Edward used Corbett by appealing to his loyalty, his love of the law, his need to create order and harmony. With Ranulf the King had played a different game, appealing to his ambition, playing on the fears of his poverty-stricken past, and the possibilities of a glorious future.

Engrossed in his own thoughts, Corbett, gripping the hilt of his sword beneath his cloak, walked along shadowy porticoes and across dark courtyards. Occasionally a figure flitted by, the silence broken by the slap of sandals. Corbett trusted Ranulf, except where the King's secret orders cut like a knife, dividing them one from the other. Ranulf would have no qualms about executing the King's enemy, as a soldier would a traitor after a battle. He'd force him to his knees and slice off his head as quickly and as coldly as a gardener would snip a rose. Ah well! Corbett paused and stared up at the star-filled sky. He would cross that bridge when he came to it. He revisited the church for a short prayer and then entered the abbey buildings. He lost his way until a lay brother directed him towards the Abbot's lodgings. The door was locked so he carefully examined the outside. The lodgings were really a small mansion or manor house, the top and bottom floors linked by an inside staircase. He looked up at the great bay window and, to satisfy his own curiosity, tried to climb the wall but it was nigh impossible. Unless I was a monkey or a squirrel, Corbett thought. He smiled and thanked God the Lady Maeve couldn't see him clambering like a schoolboy out in the dark. He went back to the door, knocked again and then banged with the pommel of his dagger. He heard an exclamation inside, the sound of footsteps and Brother Perditus, carrying a candle, unlocked the door and swung it open.

'Ah, Sir Hugh, I . . .!'

'What are you doing here?' Corbett asked. 'I know you have a chamber here but the Abbot's now dead and buried?'

'Prior Cuthbert ordered me to stay here to assist you, as well as to look after the Abbot's chamber.'

Corbett followed him up the stone steps. Perditus went to his own chamber further down the gallery and brought back two keys.

'Here, Sir Hugh, you may as well have these.' He thrust both keys into the clerk's hand. 'The larger key is for the outside door.' He smiled through the dark. 'I'll open the Abbot's chamber for you and light a candle. I know my way around.'

Corbett thanked him. Perditus opened the Abbot's

chamber. Corbett smelt the faint fragrance of incense and beeswax, the perfume of wood polish. Apologising loudly, Perditus stumbled around in the dark but, at last, oil lamps and candles were lit and placed on the mantel over the hearth. The fire was already prepared: using a little oil and a pair of bellows, Perditus soon had the dry wood crackling.

'Well.' He got to his feet. He looked more composed than he had earlier in the day. He wiped the dust from his hands. 'There's wine over there and, if you want, I can get you food from the kitchens. You know where my chamber is and . . .' His voice faltered.

'Why did Father Abbot choose you to serve him?' Corbett asked. 'You've been a lay brother here for only a few years, yes?'

'It was because of that.' Perditus grinned. 'Abbot Stephen confided that I was not a lifelong member of his community, so my loyalty would be to him.'

Corbett gestured at the door.

'Close that and sit down. Let's share a goblet of wine.'

Perditus looked surprised but agreed. Corbett studied the lay brother closely. Tall, youthful-faced, with broad shoulders and strong arms, he moved quickly and easily. A suitable candidate, Corbett reflected, to have as a manservant, fetching and carrying things up those stone stairs, protecting the Abbot when he left the abbey. Perditus poured two goblets of wine. He gave one to Corbett and sat opposite on a stool. Corbett leaned against the desk.

'I hoped you'd be here, Brother, without your superiors flapping around like crows ready to pick at any morsel.'

'I have little to say, Sir Hugh, or to add to what you already know. I loved Abbot Stephen as a father.'

'The night he died you really heard nothing?'

'Abbot Stephen was working late: he often did that,

especially since Taverner has been here.'

'Did he ever talk to you about his work?'

Perditus slurped the wine and shook his head.

'He told me a few things but really nothing much. He was looking forward to the dispute with Archdeacon Adrian and there was the business of the Concilium, his relationship with the Prior and the others. Abbot Stephen was a true spiritual lord,' Perditus continued. 'He knew it would be inappropriate to discuss such matters with a lay brother. Oh, he was kind and friendly. We discussed crops, the buildings, news brought by pedlars and tinkers but never once did I hear him criticise another member of this community.'

'And the business of building on Bloody Meadow?'

'Abbot Stephen was worried about that but he decided against it.'

'The Watcher thought differently.'

'Oh!' Perditus gestured with his hands. 'Our Watcher by the Gates wanders in his wits. True, Abbot Stephen did tell me on one occasion that he wondered if he should concede to Prior Cuthbert's demands. But, remember Sir Hugh, I am a lay brother. I was never present at their discussions or any meeting of the Concilium.'

'Isn't there anything that you can tell me?' Corbett demanded. 'Look, I know you are not my spy on the brothers but Abbot Stephen lies dead and buried. Gildas has been murdered in a most hideous way, his corpse tossed onto the tumulus. I believe these killings are somehow connected with Bloody Meadow, possibly even with the disagreements between the Abbot and his Concilium.'

'But they wouldn't lead to murder, surely?' Perditus rolled the wine cup between his hands. 'Abbot Stephen was concerned about the meadow, as was Prior Cuthbert, but it was not a matter of life and death. The

81

debate has been going on for as long as I was here. True, Prior Cuthbert had grown more insistent but . . .'

Corbett sighed and sipped at the wine.

'Do you think both deaths are linked to Bloody Meadow?' Perditus asked.

Corbett nodded absentmindedly. 'Oh, I meant to ask you: Perditus, is that your real name?'

'No, I was baptised Peter in the city of Bristol. I became a merchant's apprentice and worked in the Low Countries, in Flanders and Hainault selling wool and cloth. I was good at my trade, and became accomplished as a traveller. I am fluent in French and Flemish. Abbot Stephen was impressed by that. We had something in common because, as you know, he led embassies there on behalf of the King.'

'And how did you come to St Martin's-in-the-Marsh?'

'I went to a number of abbeys. However, as I was familiar with the Eastern ports, and Abbot Stephen and St Martin's were well thought of, I came here. I didn't want to join some lax house where the routine was disorderly and the monks lazy.' He grinned. 'I also came here because I thought I had a vocation. I have seen the world, Sir Hugh, or the little I lived in. What does it profit a man if he gain the whole world and lose his soul? I wanted to become a priest, a monk. Abbot Stephen said I should wait, remain for a while as a lay brother.'

'And what will you do now?' Corbett asked.

'I don't know.'

'Have you ever met Lady Margaret Harcourt?' Corbett asked.

Perditus shook his head.

'Abbot Stephen was a charitable man but he said he didn't want anything to do with that woman. He told us to stay away from her. Prior Cuthbert dealt with the lady.' Perditus drained the cup and got to his feet. 'Sir

82

Hugh, if there's nothing else? The hour is late and the bell will ring soon enough for Matins and Prime. I'll be in my chamber when you leave.'

Corbett thanked him. Perditus closed the door. Corbett shot the bolts and turned the key in the inside lock. He went across to the fire and, pulling up a stool, warmed his hands, watching the flames turn the dry wood to white-hot ash. Corbett closed his eyes and thought of Lady Maeve and their two babes, Eleanor and Edward. They would be in bed now: the children in their cots and Maeve in her four-poster. Maeve would be lying against the bolsters, her beautiful, serene face composed in sleep, with her long, blonde hair like a halo around her head, and those red lips that Corbett loved to kiss both playfully and passionately, when he lay next to her. Corbett felt a pang of homesickness. He was tired, rather depressed after his conversation with Ranulf. He and his companion had walked the same road for many a year. Were they now approaching the crossroads? Corbett's eyes grew heavy. For a while he dozed, drifting in and out of sleep. A log burst in a flurry of sparks. Corbett shook himself awake. He stared round the chamber. Never once, he reflected, have I met a man like Abbot Stephen. Everything in his room had its own place, the books and papers, household accounts, ledgers but there was nothing which betrayed the inner soul of the man, his likes and dislikes, virtues or faults. What had happened in his past? Corbett sighed and got to his feet. He searched the chests and coffers looking for a secret drawer, a hidden compartment, but there was nothing. He picked up breviaries, psalters and a Book of Hours, all well thumbed: little was written on the inside pages except prayers or notes for a homily. Nothing was out of the ordinary except those quotations from Seneca and St Paul and the reference to Corpse Candles scrawled on a scrap of parchment.

Corbett opened one ledger and studied it. This was an account of the Abbot's different embassies on behalf of the King, to the Scottish march, a few to France, some to Hainault, Flanders or Germany. Corbett smiled. He would have liked to have talked to Abbot Stephen about the King and his plans against Philip of France. Perhaps Stephen had met Corbett's old enemy, Amaury de Craon? He noticed how Abbot Stephen's handwriting was precise and neat. He always described things in the third person as if he was an observer, a spectator. Corbett closed the ledger and pushed it away. He took a piece of parchment, a tray of quills and an ink pot and began to list a series of questions.

Why did Abbot Stephen die?
Because of Bloody Meadow?
How was he killed?
Who killed him?
Was it a member of the Concilium?
Why was Gildas murdered?
Was his corpse thrown on the tumulus in Bloody
    Meadow as a warning?
And why the brand mark?
What did the stories about Mandeville's ghost have
    to do with this place?

Corbett studied the questions. He put his quill down.
'Nothing,' he murmured. 'Nothing at all.'

He had done enough, he would have to leave. He blew out the candles and oil lamps, placing a wire mesh grille up against the fire. He left the chamber and knocked on Perditus's door. The lay brother opened it, sleepy-eyed, dressed in his shift.

'I am going now,' Corbett declared. 'I would be grateful if you would check the Abbot's chamber. Perhaps the fire should be doused?'

Perditus said he would do so. Corbett went down the steps. He opened the door at the bottom and flinched at the blast of cold night air. He realised how tired he was. He tried to close the door but couldn't. He crouched down; a piece of timber, stacked just inside, had slipped. Corbett worked this loose, placed it back and closed the door. He stood for a while to get his bearings and leisurely made his way across the grounds into the abbey buildings. He lost his way once and found himself in the cloister garth but, at last, he reached the portico which would take him down out to the courtyard before the guesthouse. He now walked quickly, his footsteps sounding hollow. The night was cold, and Corbett grew uneasy. He felt as if he was being watched, yet all around him the abbey lay silent. He paused halfway down the passageway and stared through one of the narrow windows. He recalled Ranulf's warnings. He continued on and reached the heavy wooden door at the far end. He pulled at the ring but the latch didn't lift. He tried again, pulling it vigorously but it still wouldn't move. Corbett whirled round, to see nothing but shadows behind him. He didn't want to go back. He tugged again. He started as the Judas squint high in the door suddenly had its flap thrown open. Corbett couldn't see through due to the glow from a candle, which was held up, obscuring his view.

'Who's there?' he demanded.

'Corbett, Sir Hugh Corbett?' The voice sounded muffled, the speaker was disguising his voice.

'Let me through,' Corbett replied.

'Keeper of the King's secrets, eh? Welcome to the Mansions of Cain!'

'What do you mean?' Corbett declared.

'Murderers all!' hissed the reply. 'Steeped in blood!'

'Who are?' Corbett demanded.

'Not men of God but hounds of the devil!'

'What are you talking about?' Corbett demanded. He grasped the iron ring and tugged but the door still held fast.

'A place of sudden death, Sir Hugh, of wickedness. All have to be punished. Sentence has been passed. Stand back, Sir Hugh, for your own safety's sake!'

Corbett had no choice but to obey. He heard footsteps. He tried the latch again, and this time the door gave way to reveal the empty darkness beyond.

86

*NAM CONCORDIA PARVAE RES CRESCUNT,*
*DISCORDIA MAXIMAE DILABUNTUR*

HARMONY MAKES SMALL THINGS GROW,
WHILE DISCORD DESTROYS EVEN WHAT IS
GREAT

SENECA

# *Chapter 4*

Corbett gazed in astonishment round Taverner's chamber. He had never seen so many crosses and statues: these seemed to cover the walls, filling every niche. Triptychs and crucifixes stood on tables. Fronds from Palm Sunday hung above the door. The chamber was spacious and clean. It was the only room in the abbey where Corbett had seen rushes, green and supple, strewn with herbs, scattered on the floor. A shelf high on one wall held some books, a bible and a tattered psalter. Taverner, sitting on the edge of the small four-poster bed, looked like some venerable monk. Dressed in a grey robe, with a balding pate, grey hair on either side of his head fell in tangled curls to his shoulders. He was bright-eyed and chirpy as a magpie with a round, florid face; Corbett noticed the generous bulging paunch above the cord round his waist. The room was warmed by a scented brazier and a small log fire burned in the hearth; it was a warm, comfortable place. Corbett had noticed the smoke coming out of the vent as he approached the far side of the infirmary. As usual, Chanson stood on guard outside. Ranulf looked subdued and sat on a bench just inside the door. Corbett stared curiously at this remarkable man who claimed to be possessed by a demon, the damned soul of Geoffrey

Mandeville. So far Corbett had seen nothing remarkable about this middle-aged man, keen-eyed and sharp-witted, who'd welcomed them and offered some wine.

Corbett picked a scrap of parchment off the desk and noticed the ink-filled 'V' drawn there. He stared down as he collected his thoughts. He had not told Ranulf what had occurred the previous night: about that mysterious visitor who had confronted him behind the grille, drawn the bolts and fled. Corbett had returned to the guesthouse in silence, his relationship with Ranulf still frosty. They had been woken early by a tolling bell, attended Mass in a side chapel and broken their fast in the abbey kitchens. Prior Cuthbert had met them briefly but he had been all a-fluster, claiming he had other business and knew nothing of the death of poor Gildas ... Corbett had nodded and declared he needed to question Taverner. The Prior had shrugged in acceptance.

Corbett still felt tired, heavy-eyed. He held up the piece of parchment. Taverner now had his head down.

'Who drew Mandeville's mark?'

'How dare you!'

Corbett gaped in astonishment. Taverner's head came up, his face had completely changed, with hate-filled eyes, a snarling mouth, his voice totally different.

'How dare you, you whoreson varlet! You base-born clerk! Question me, Mandeville, Custos of the Tower, Earl of Essex!'

Ranulf leaned forward, ready to spring up.

What Corbett found remarkable was the change in voice, which had become harsh and guttural. When they had first entered, Taverner's voice was soft, barely above a whisper.

'That's my escutcheon, my livery,' he continued, jerking his fingers towards the parchment. 'Black chevrons on a red banner. "Scourge of Essex" they called

90

me. "Plunderer of Ely". I showed those mealy-mouthed monks, those fornicating friars and their soft-skinned nuns! I gave them fire and sword! *"Igne Gladioque. Fire and sword! Gero bellum contra Deum.* I wage war against God and strive to breach the very gates of Paradise!" ' Taverner lapsed into old Norman French, ' "*Le Roi Se Avisera.* The King was advised. *Sed Rex territus,* but the King was terrified." '

'Who was King?' Corbett asked.

Taverner glanced slyly at him. 'Why, Stephen, but he was challenged by Mathilda, Henry's arrogant daughter. I lead a legion, do you know that, clerk? Men on horses who still ride the fens at night.'

Corbett closed his eyes and tried to recall the rite of exorcism.

'By what name are you called?' he asked abruptly.

'My name is Geoffrey Mandeville, damned in life and damned in death. I wander the dark places. I seek a place, a house to dwell.'

'And you have chosen Taverner?'

'The door was open,' came the harsh reply. 'The dwelling was prepared.'

'And what do you do when you leave?' Corbett asked curiously. He noticed the white foam gathering at either corner of Taverner's mouth.

'I go back into the darkness, into eternal night. You are Corbett, aren't you? Keeper of the Secret Seal? Your wife is Maeve with the long, blonde hair, and that body, eh Corbett? Soft and white like skimmed milk.'

'Watch your lewdness!' Ranulf declared.

Corbett held a hand up.

'And where do I live?'

'In Leighton Manor, in Essex, my shire, with fat, little Eleanor and Baby Edward. Come from the King, have we?'

Corbett studied the man. He was surprised that

Taverner, or whatever possessed him, knew as much as he did. But, there again, most of it was fairly common knowledge.

'If you are a demon.' Corbett smiled, 'then you should know more. Have you met Abbot Stephen? His soul has left his body.'

Taverner didn't blink or change expression.

'He has gone to judgement,' he declared. 'His crossing was never challenged. He's begun his journey.'

'But why was he killed? How was he murdered?'

'I am not here to help you, Corbett!'

'Come, come,' the clerk teased. 'You claim to be the great Geoffrey Mandeville who roams the fens, yet know less than a scullion in the abbey kitchens?'

'He was killed by a dagger, thrust into his chest,' came the sharp reply. 'Always the Roman was Abbot Stephen. A man who will have to pay for his sin against the Holy Ghost.'

'What do you mean, his sin against the Holy Ghost?' Corbett demanded. Taverner seemed to know a little more than he should about the Abbot's death.

'Oh, he was murdered all right, like Abel, slain by Cain, by his brother . . .'

'By the monks of St Martin's?' Corbett demanded.

'*Tu dixisti clerice*,' Taverner lapsed into Latin. 'You have said it, clerk.'

'Which monk?' Corbett barked.

'All are guilty in some way. Abbot Stephen's blood stains their hands.'

Corbett felt a chill of fear. He'd attended two exorcisms as a royal witness. One in Bermondsey Abbey and the other in St Peter ad Vincula in the Tower. Both had taken place years before, and had been terrifying experiences! Taverner's hand snaked out, his fingers curled like the claw of some hunting bird.

'Plucked he was, taken out of life, sent unprepared

92

into the dark. I feel at home at St Martin's, clerk. It is a house of demons.' The white froth now laced his lips. 'And you can tell Chanson outside the door to stop listening.'

Ranulf, light-footed, opened the door. Chanson almost fell into the room. He stumbled and looked, embarrassed, at Corbett.

'You are supposed to be guarding not eavesdropping.' Corbett glanced quickly at Taverner. 'But go now to the library. Ask Brother Aelfric if he has any books or chronicles about Geoffrey Mandeville.'

'He has one there,' Taverner declared.

'What did Abbot Stephen say to you?'

'He was going to help me.' Taverner's voice turned ugly. 'But he couldn't even help himself!'

Corbett watched him in amazement. Taverner was two people: himself and the spirit who possessed him, alternating in both expression and voice, sometimes lapsing into French or Latin. Corbett glanced across at Ranulf: his henchman seemed fascinated by Taverner. At last the babble of conversation died. The possessed man sat on the edge of the bed, hands hanging by his side, head down.

'Who are you now?' Corbett asked.

Taverner dipped his fingers into a stoup of holy water on the table near the bed: he blessed himself quickly three or four times. He dug into his gown and pulled out a bible which he clutched to his chest.

'I am the man that I was born,' he replied weakly. The white froth had disappeared. 'Matthew Taverner.'

'And why did you come here?' Corbett demanded.

'I lived out in Essex, in a village near Chelmsford. Ever since I was a child I have been plagued by fanciful dreams and hideous nightmares. My father died when I was young. My mother dabbled in the black arts. She sacrificed to Achitopel and Asrael, Beelzebub and the other Lords of the Wasteland. One afternoon I was out near a brook, fishing by myself. The sun went behind a cloud and I looked up. A man stood on the far side of the bank beneath the outstretched branches of an oak tree. He was tall, dressed in black from head to toe and his face was white and haggard.' Taverner blinked. 'He had eyes as cruel as a hawk's. "Who are you, Sir?" I asked. "Why, Matthew, I am your old friend Geoffrey Mandeville." I ran away and told my mother. She just laughed and said we all had demons. Mandeville kept returning. I met him in taverns and on lonely roads. "I'm hunting you, Matthew," he'd taunt, "like a hound does a deer".'

'And he caught you?' Corbett asked.

'I hid in London,' Taverner replied. 'I took up with whores but Mandeville sought me out.'

He undid the collar of his robe and pulled it down. Corbett flinched at the great cruel 'V' etched on the man's left shoulder. He got up and peered at it. The wound had now healed but it looked as if a branding mark had been used. Corbett returned to his chair.

'And so you came to Abbot Stephen?'

'At first I went for help to the Dominicans at Blackfriars. Oh yes, and Archdeacon Adrian.'

'So, you know him?'

'Oh yes.'

'And what did Abbot Stephen promise?'

'That he would exorcise me. He treated me like a son. He was kind and gentle. He said that afterwards I might be able to stay here. I sometimes helped Brother Aelfric in the library.'

'Do you know why Abbot Stephen died?' Corbett asked.

Taverner shook his head. 'We never talked about anything except my possession and my earlier life. Sometimes he looked worried and distracted. I would often find him deep in conversation with his man-servant, the lay brother Perditus.'

Corbett heard a sound outside, probably Chanson returning. Somewhere a bell began to toll. Ranulf started to get up but then sat down again.

'And Abbot Stephen discussed nothing about the abbey?'

Taverner shook his head. 'I feel sick.' He murmured clutching his stomach. 'I need . . .'

He gestured feebly towards the tray containing the cup and platter of food on the table at the far side of the room. Ranulf sprang to his feet. He filled a cup and thrust it into the man's hand. He then walked to the window behind the bed and pulled back the shutters. He seemed engrossed by something outside.

'Did you ever talk to any of the other monks?' Corbett demanded. 'Prior Cuthbert?'

Taverner's head came up: he was once more possessed.

'Narrow heart, narrow soul,' came the harsh reply. 'In love with their abbey more than God. Them and their guesthouse. They want to plunder Bloody Meadow, dig up old Sigbert's rotting bones, build a mansion for the fat ones of the soil. Have more visitors. Increase their revenue.'

'John Carrefour!'

Corbett jumped at Ranulf's harsh voice. Taverner whipped round.

'John Carrefour!' Ranulf repeated. He sauntered over to the bed and sat beside Taverner. 'I'll wager that on your right shoulder here,' he punched Taverner's shoulder, 'is another brand mark in the shape of a diamond. An enpurpled birthmark.'

Ranulf glanced across at his master and smiled in apology.

'What is all this?' Taverner's voice rose to a screech.

95

Ranulf, however, took out his dagger and pricked him under the chin.

'Sir Hugh Corbett,' he declared. 'Keeper of the King's Secret Seal, may I introduce the venerable and venomous John Carrefour, the mummer's man, the cunning man, the faker and the counterfeit. Formerly a clerk in minor orders, taken up by the King's Assizes, he's spent some time abroad in exile. He was forced to serve in the King's armies in both Flanders and Northern France.'

Taverner gazed beseechingly at Corbett.

'I don't know what he's saying.'

Ranulf, however, had now loosed Taverner's gown at the neck, roughly pulling down the grey robe, not caring whether he ripped it. He exposed Taverner's shoulder and made the man turn to reveal the deep purple birthmark. Ranulf pricked the dagger a little deeper until a small trickle of blood appeared under Taverner's chin.

'I am ashamed of you, John,' Ranulf continued conversationally. 'Your memory is beginning to fade, isn't it? I am Ranulf-atte-Newgate.'

'I don't know you,' Taverner stammered.

Corbett remained silent.

'No, you wouldn't. When I met you I was simply Ranulf. I hadn't yet been imprisoned. You knew my mother, Isolda: remember her? Red-haired and green-eyed, generous to a fault she was. She entertained you free, Master Carrefour.' Ranulf winked at Corbett. 'I don't know if that's his true name. He was called John of the Crossroads or, in French, Carrefour. He was nicknamed that because no one knew which direction he would take. A man of many parts is our John. A mummer's man: a member of an actors' troupe. He can mimic and imitate whomever he wishes. He doesn't remember me: the little, red-haired boy sitting in a corner, thumb in mouth, watching Carrefour entertain his mother and other ladies. I bear you no ill will, John.' Ranulf lowered the dagger. 'You made my mother laugh. Do you remember your favourite roles? The begging friar? The portly priest?'

Taverner now looked woebegone and miserable.

'I do admire your Mandeville,' Ranulf continued. 'But you made a mistake. You talked of fornicating friars, yet during the reign of Stephen there were no friars, as the Franciscan order had yet to be founded in this country. The rest was very good indeed: the Norman French, the Latin. He's quite the scholar, our John!'

Ranulf re-sheathed his dagger and walked back to his stool. Corbett quietly admitted that it was rare for Ranulf to astonish him. He felt slightly embarrassed, Taverner had certainly fooled him.

'Is this true?' he demanded.

Taverner opened his mouth to reply but changed his mind. He sat in a crumpled heap on the edge of the bed, hands in his lap.

'I don't know what you are talking about,' he mumbled.

'Oh come!' Ranulf teased. 'He was once famous in the city, Master. He has since spent a considerable part of his life abroad, one step ahead of the sheriff's men, particularly after his success as a relic-seller in Cheapside. He forged letters and licences, stained his skin and claimed to have a box of rocks from the Holy Sepulchre in Jerusalem. He fooled quite a few with his letters from the Patriarch and his marvellous tales about his pilgrimage. And, of course, there was the amazing jar of wine which he claimed to be Falernian, drawn from Pontius Pilate's own cellar. The list of trickery is endless. Our friend has been everything: a pardoner, a summoner, a friar, a priest.' Ranulf laughed and smacked his knee. 'He provided more amusement in the taverns of Southwark than any troupe of jesters. What's the matter, Taverner, are you becoming ill? I'll call you Taverner, as it keeps things simple.'

His hapless victim continued to sit, head down.

'I don't want to hear anything more about Mandeville,' Ranulf added. 'Shall I tell you the truth, Sir Hugh? Our good friend here has become tired and old. He's sick of trudging the lanes, keeping a wary eye out for the sheriff's men. He wants a comfortable place to reside: some little burrow where he can nestle down and spend the rest of his days. Now, he can't knock on a monastery door and declare himself to be a postulant or a novice, as enquiries would be made. I suspect our good friend came back here through the Eastern ports where he wouldn't be noticed or recognised. He heard about Abbot Stephen at St Martin's-in-the-Marsh and he prepared his charade, including the self-inflicted brand mark, and came seeking help.'

'But he claimed to have met Archdeacon Adrian and the Dominicans at Blackfrairs?'

'He may have done, over the years. However, I wager Master Taverner, as he now calls himself, would count on those busy men not recalling him. He arrived at St Martin's-in-the-Marsh, where the other brothers ignored him but Abbot Stephen regarded him as a gift from heaven.' Ranulf gestured round the chamber. 'Our friend was shown every hospitality: good food and drink, a soft bed, a warm room. He had nothing to worry about. He could stay here for three or four years licking his wounds and leave whenever he wished.'

'And Mandeville?' Corbett asked.

'If I remember correctly,' Ranulf replied, 'our friend was born in Essex. He'd know all about the legends. Of course, on his return he'd have refreshed his memory. St-Martin's-in-the-Marsh does have chronicles and accounts. He probably volunteered to help Brother

Aelfric and learnt a little bit more about exorcism and the black arts, not to mention his patron demon, Geoffrey Mandeville. Taverner is a good-enough scholar: he can read, write and, I suspect, is well versed in a number of tongues.'

Corbett got to his feet; he went and stood over Taverner.

'Look at me,' he demanded. 'I am the King's Commissioner.'

Taverner raised his head, his eyes filled with tears. He clasped his hands together as if in prayer.

'Mercy, great lord!' he wailed. 'I was cold and lonely.'

'Still acting!' Ranulf laughed.

Corbett gazed down at the man.

'Matthew Taverner, John Carrefour, Geoffrey Mandeville, whoever you are, I think you are a scoundrel, a rogue born and bred. You probably regard getting caught as simply a hazard of your trade.' Corbett bit back his smile. 'You've proved the old proverb: "It takes one rogue to recognise another". Ranulf-atte-Newgate is correct, isn't he? Don't lie!' Corbett pressed his finger against Taverner's lips. 'If you lie, Taverner, I shall drag you out and hang you!'

'You can't do that,' the fellow whined. 'I have done no wrong.'

'You've stolen. You've defrauded. Come, Master Taverner, no one wants to hang you. I don't even want you to leave the abbey. I am more interested in Abbot Stephen's murder.'

The veteran cunning man sighed and stared down at his feet. He smiled slyly up at Ranulf.

'I remember you now. God bless her, Ranulf, but I liked your mother. She died of a sickness, didn't she? I always remember her red hair, thick and glorious, falling down beyond her waist, the tight dresses, the way she moved.' He raised a hand.

Ranulf's face was like cold stone.

'I mean no offence. In many ways she had more courtesy than any lady at court.'

Ranulf's face softened.

'She did love you,' Taverner continued. 'Called you her pride and joy.'

'Stop it!' Ranulf snapped, making a cutting movement with his hand.

Corbett could see Ranulf was not far from tears.

'She did love you,' Taverner replied defiantly. 'And I had forgotten all about you till now. You always sat watching in the corner when I visited: you reminded me of a little cat. Now, look at you. A fighting man, a clerk! God be blessed! Fortune's fickle wheel is a thing to wonder at! You carry the King's commission, eh? Not like poor me.' He pressed his lips together. 'God forgive me, Sir Hugh, but I have tried every cunning trick I know. I am not going to fool you. One of the great miracles of my life is that I've never been hanged. An old witch once told me: "You'll never climb the ladder. Never feel the noose round your neck though you'll die violently enough". Everything turned to ashes in my mouth. All my plots and schemes came to nothing. I had to flee abroad. I even travelled into the German states for a while. I came back and landed in Hunstanton, cold, miserable and sick. I travelled inland and I knew I had to do something. I was tired of it all. I wanted a warm bed, a hot meal, a refuge from the law, the sheriffs, bailiffs and tipstaffs. I travelled to Ely and begged outside the cathedral, and there I heard about Abbot Stephen and St Martin's-in-the-Marsh. I acted the madcap, the fey, the poor soul possessed by a demon called Mandeville and I travelled here.'

'Did Abbot Stephen believe you?'

'Listen to Ranulf, Sir Hugh. In my time I was

the best. I have been taken for a bishop and, on one occasion, even a Royal Justice!'

Corbett hid his smile.

'I felt guilty but what else could I do? Abbot Stephen was kind and gentle. Sometimes I'd catch him watching me carefully. You could see the smile behind his eyes. I even wondered if we were in a conspiracy together? He was so keen to prove a human soul could be possessed.' He gestured round. 'He gave me this chamber, warm clothes, good food. He said I could stay here if I wanted to when it was all finished. After a while I became aware of how determined he was to prove his theory. He was so generous, I did my best for him.'

'And the night he was killed?'

'I had nothing to do with that,' Taverner retorted. 'I was here, tucked up like a bird in its nest, snoring like a pig. Why should I want Abbot Stephen dead, or Prior Cuthbert and any of the others? They've left me alone till now but Cuthbert's a hard man. He might ask me to move on. I would be grateful, sir, if you could do something for me.'

'They are going to think it's rather strange,' Ranulf interrupted, 'if Geoffrey Mandeville fails to reappear.'

Taverner grinned through chapped lips.

'I've considered that. I was beginning to wonder whether I should go and pray before Abbot Stephen's tomb, give one of the best performances of my life.'

'Oh, I see.' Corbett laughed. 'A miraculous cure?'

'Why not? I'd then go to see Archdeacon Adrian. Perhaps he could help?'

'Do you know of any reason why the Abbot was murdered?'

'No, Sir Hugh. The abbey here is a God-fearing community.'

Corbett recalled the hate-filled words hissed at him the previous evening. Taverner was a cunning man, who'd always lived by his wits, surely he'd sensed something was wrong?

'You are certain of that?' he demanded. 'No bitter rivalry, no blood feuds?'

'Not that I know of. Abbot Stephen walked quietly, talked quietly but carried a big stick. He was gentle but very, very firm. In this abbey his word was law.'

'And his relationship with the Concilium? When you were pretending to be Mandeville, you said Abbot Stephen's blood was on their hands!'

'I was pretending.'

'Were you?' Corbett insisted. 'Or do you think the resentment over Bloody Meadow might have boiled over into something worse?'

Taverner pulled a face.

'From what I understand, they were certainly in fear and awe of him.'

'Except over Bloody Meadow?'

'The Abbot referred to that. I asked him once why he didn't agree to their demands. "It's a sacred place," he replied. "It contains a tomb of a royal martyr who should be left in peace".'

'Was there anything else?' Corbett demanded.

'The Abbot seemed to like that lay brother, Perditus. I often saw them in deep conversation with each other.'

'About what?'

'Oh, the Abbot was a busy man. I think he found it easy to talk to Perditus. No wonder the other monks called him "the Abbot's shadow".'

'Could Perditus have murdered the Abbot?'

'No.'

'How are you so sure?'

'The morning Abbot Stephen was found murdered, I came across here, very early before dawn, as I often did. The Abbot liked to talk to me. I waited outside Perditus's chamber. He woke up and let me stay in his room.' Taverner tapped the side of his nose. 'I know people, clerk, and I'd go on oath: Perditus worshipped his Abbot and, when I met him that morning, he was not upset or disturbed. Of course, all that changed when he failed to rouse Abbot Stephen.'

'Did Perditus become agitated?'

'At first, no. Abbot Stephen often worked late. He sometimes missed attending Divine Office, which he read in his own room.'

'And you never left Perditus that morning?'

'Never. Another monk came to see what was wrong: that's when the alarm was raised. I was present when they forced the door. We all stood shocked, surprised. Perditus went to the Abbot's chair, fell on his knees, put his face in his hands and began to sob. I have never seen a man cry like that before.'

'You are keen eyed,' Corbett murmured. 'Did you see anything untoward in that chamber?'

'Oh, I looked round immediately. I know every trick and sleight of hand. Yet, that door was locked and the windows secure. I noticed the Abbot's war belt was lying on the floor. He must have taken it from his chest near the wall.'

'Did Perditus ever talk to you?'

'Sometimes. He liked me to read to him: his eyesight is not too good.'

'And the other brothers?'

Taverner rocked backwards and forwards on the bed.

'Many of them are former soldiers or clerks in the royal service.' He grinned impishly at Ranulf. 'Perhaps that's how you will end your career?'

'The other brothers?' Corbett insisted.

'Perhaps I am wrong, Sir Hugh. Perhaps there were rancourous feelings? Sometimes I overheard them talking, and it is true they were becoming increasingly angry with the Abbot's refusal to build a guesthouse in

Bloody Meadow. He fended them off, claiming the place was a sacred site. Of course, Lady Margaret Harcourt disputed the ownership of Falcon Brook, not that I could see why.'

'What do you mean?' Corbett asked.

'Well, it's only a rivulet. It's not stocked with fat carp or salmon. For God's sake, Sir Hugh, these are the fens! One thing this place is not short of is water!'

'And who was the prime mover behind the plans for a guesthouse?'

'Oh, certainly Prior Cuthbert. As the weeks passed I often wondered whether he wanted to be Father Abbot. He certainly had support from some of the others. Gildas, the one who was killed, his fingers positively itched to cut the ground and lay the first stone.'

'And did Abbot Stephen ever talk to you? Discuss the past? Come on!' Corbett urged. 'You'll be well rewarded, Master Taverner.'

The cunning man picked up the wine goblet and drank swiftly.

'On occasions, Abbot Stephen talked as if I wasn't there. He once said that everyone had demons, either in the present or from the past and, unless reparation was made, these demons would harass him: his face grew sad and tears pricked his eyes.'

'Did Abbot Stephen elaborate?'

'I teased him. I asked if a holy abbot could also be guilty of sin? "Some sins remain." The Abbot replied. "And I am always fearful of the sin against the Holy Ghost".'

'Did he tell you what that was?'

Taverner shook his head. 'He just said his life was a wheel: that what happened at the hub, or the centre, stretched out its spokes to affect the rim and all within it. Strange thing to say, wasn't it, Sir Hugh?'

'Do you think he had any secrets?'

Taverner looked at Corbett slyly from under his eyebrows.

'He liked all things Roman.'

'Meaning what?'

'He showed me his secret.'

'Secret?'

'Yes, yes, come with me!'

Corbett got to his feet and went to the door. He'd been sure someone was outside but, when he opened it, the small entrance hallway was empty and the door to the abbey grounds was half open, through which a cold draught seeped. Ranulf joined him.

'Our cunning man is searching for his sandals.'

Corbett gripped Ranulf by the arm.

'That was very good, Ranulf. A memory worthy of a royal clerk! If it hadn't been for you, Taverner would have fooled me as he did the Abbot and Archdeacon Adrian.'

Ranulf coloured with embarrassment.

'I am sorry about last night, Master.'

Corbett linked his arm through Ranulf's and they went out of the doorway into the grounds. The heavy mist was now clearing, and a weak sun making its presence felt: a sharp breeze had sprung up, sending the leaves whirling. Corbett stood and revelled in the silence. He was aware of the grey abbey buildings. Now and again a figure moved through the mist. He faintly heard the neigh of a horse and, on the morning breeze, the melodious chant from the church. He caught the words: 'The Lord will rescue me from the huntsmen's nets'. Corbett released Ranulf's arm. But who is the huntsman here, he wondered? How could he find his way through the thick, treacherous mysteries which shrouded these heinous murders? A sound echoed behind him. Taverner came out, clasping a cloak.

'Come with me! Come with me!'

They went down the side of the infirmary and almost bumped into Chanson who, helped by Perditus, was carrying some books.

'Brother Aelfric sent these,' Chanson gasped.

'We don't need them now,' Corbett declared. 'Master Taverner has other things to show us. Chanson, Brother Perditus, I would be grateful if you would take the books to my chamber in the guesthouse.'

He walked by them. Taverner was trotting ahead, beckoning them to follow as if they were playing some childish game. They crossed the empty cloisters, going past the main door of the abbey church and towards the refectory: a long, oblong building of grey ragstone with a red tiled roof. Taverner led them down the outside steps and pushed open the door. They stepped into a hollow, cavernous chamber. Taverner took a tinder and lit a sconce torch. Corbett realised they were in the cellars of the abbey. There was a long, dark gallery with open store chambers on one side which contained tuns of wine, sacks of grain, boxes of fruits and vegetables, some now shrivelled as winter approached. The air was flavoured with different fragrances and smells. Taverner hurried on, pausing now and again to light a sconce torch. Corbett felt as if he was in the underworld. He was aware of the passageway stretching before him, the hard cobbled ground and the yawning chambers to his left. At last they reached the end and went down some steps. Taverner pushed open a door and they stepped into a chamber. Corbett was aware of barrels and pallets of wood, shelves with pots on. One corner was completely empty except for a canvas cloth stretched over the ground. Taverner lit another sconce torch and pulled away the sheeting. At first Corbett couldn't understand what it was until he grasped the torch and knelt down.

He exclaimed, marvelling at the different colours,

the reds, greens, golds and blues. He studied it more carefully.

'Abbot Stephen said it was very old,' Taverner explained.

Corbett stroked its shiny smoothness.

'It's a mosaic,' he explained. 'I've seen similar both in this country and abroad. Beautiful isn't it, Ranulf?'

'The work of the monks?' his manservant asked.

'No, no, this is Roman.' Corbett glanced up at the ceiling. 'Of course it makes sense. This land must have always been cleared. I suspect the abbey was founded on an ancient Roman settlement, perhaps a farmhouse, or a temple, or both?'

'How did Abbot Stephen find this?'

'Years ago when he was Sub-prior,' Taverner explained, 'work was carried out on the foundations. The floor to this chamber was raised. When the paving stones were lifted, Abbot Stephen discovered this and kept it free. He always liked to come here. He'd sit and kneel before it as if it was a shrine.'

Corbett, his eyes now accustomed to the dark and the flickering torchlight, could admire the beauty of the mosaic. It was a square, probably part of a floor, of which only this section had been preserved, and depicted a huge wheel: its hub was of gold with red spokes and blue rim. Between the spokes were different colours, and in each corner were small figures dressed in tunics, carrying grapes and what resembled jugs of wine.

'Why did Abbot Stephen love it so much?'

'I don't know. He said it was beautiful. He used to place his hand on the centre of the wheel as if it was something sacred. Ask the brothers, particularly Cuthbert. Abbot Stephen would often disappear down here and just kneel. Sometimes he'd bring a cushion. Sometimes . . .'

'Sometimes what?' Ranulf demanded harshly.

'One day, two weeks before his death,' Taverner explained, 'I went to see Father Abbot. He was not in his chamber so I came here. I reached the door to the steps. I could hear him praying, weeping, and the lash of a whip.'

'What?' Corbett exclaimed.

'Abbot Stephen was leaning over the mosaic. He'd pulled his robe down to his waist. In one hand he held his ave beads, in the other a whip which he was using to lash his shoulders. "Father Abbot!" I exclaimed. He turned and stared at me, tears rolling down his cheeks. "I'm doing penance, Master Taverner," he declared. "And you must never tell anyone what you have seen today. This is my secret".'

Corbett stared down at the mosaic: the more he studied it the more intrigued he became. He recalled the pieces of parchment he had seen in the Abbot's lodgings. He had dismissed these but now he remembered the doodles and etchings, which were always the same, a wheel with its rim, spokes and hub. What did that mean to the Abbot? And why had he to inflict such terrible penance on himself? Sins he had to atone for? And why here? Many monks would dismiss this mosaic as a pagan symbol. True, the abbot had liked all things Roman but he seemed to have revered this as he would a shrine or reliquary. This mosaic obviously symbolised something for Abbot Stephen. He'd confessed as much to Taverner whilst his obssession with the wheel explained his constant sketches. Wheels? Hidden sins? The dead Abbot did indeed have secrets but they were buried deep and hidden well. Corbett got to his feet and ordered Taverner to cover the mosaic.

'I've told you all I could, Master.' Taverner's voice rose to a wail.

'Don't worry,' Corbett reassured him, tapping him

on the shoulder. 'You are not going to be turned out in
your shift on the highway. We have other people to
visit.' He walked to the steps and then turned. 'Tell
me, Master Taverner, last night, as I was walking back
to the guesthouse, I tried to open a door but it held fast.
I heard a voice hissing at me through the grille. It was
muffled, disguised. It told me that the Abbey of St
Martin's was a house of demons, a place of Cain?'

'You didn't tell me of this!' Ranulf exclaimed.

'Hush!' Corbett gazed round. 'Was that you, Master
Taverner?'

'Oh no!'

'Then which monk do you think wanders the corridors and passageways? I know it wasn't Brother
Perditus. He was in his shift when I left him. So, which
monk is known for his wanderings?'

'They all are, Sir Hugh, especially members of the
Concilium, Prior Cuthbert in particular. The night
Abbot Stephen was killed some of the brothers claimed
he visited Bloody Meadow, staring at that burial
mound.'

Corbett sighed. 'Very well.'

Ranulf and Taverner doused the lights. They went
back along the corridor and out into the abbey grounds.
Perditus, carrying a basket to the kitchens, shouted a
greeting. Corbett raised his hand in reply.

'Where to now, Master?'

'The guesthouse, Ranulf. Perhaps we should have
something to eat? Master Taverner, I thank you. Stay
where you are and tell no one what has happened.'

The cunning man needed no second urging. He
bobbed in gratitude, profuse in his thanks and assurances before he hastened off into the mist. Taverner
was pleased to be free of Corbett. He had told that
harsh-faced clerk a great deal so perhaps he would be
safe for a while. He paused and looked up at the tower

of the abbey church looming above the mist. This was a good place to live. Perhaps even to die? He reached the path leading down past the infirmary. He heard a sound and stopped. A cowled figure had stepped out from behind a bush. He was holding something in his hands. Taverner, eyes popping, mouth gaping, realised it was a longbow. He could see the string pulled right back, the cruel barbed arrow – aimed directly at him. He could glimpse no face.

'What do you want? What is it?'

He was about to sink to his knees but the arrow was already loosed. At such close range it thudded into Taverner's body, thrusting deep into his chest. Taverner staggered forward, the blood already bubbling in his throat. He sank to his knees and, with a gasp, fell on his side.

*JUSTITIA EST CONSTANS ET PERPETUA*
*VOLUNTAS IUS SUUM CUIQUE TRIBUENS*

JUSTICE IS THE CONSTANT AND PERPETUAL
WISH TO GIVE EACH PERSON HIS DUE

[JUSTINIAN]

# Chapter 5

The Concilium of St Martin's-in-the-Marsh was meeting in the Star Chamber, a large room at the centre of the abbey building. It had its name because of the gold stars on the lime-painted walls whilst similar emblems were carved on the stone floor. A spacious, circular chamber with windows looking out over every aspect of the abbey: a place of solemn conferrings and council. However, on that morning, the feast of St Clement the Martyr, confusion and chaos reigned. Taverner's corpse had been found slumped on an abbey path. The arrow which had killed him had passed almost clean through his body. Of course that interfering royal clerk had taken over and the corpse had been taken to the death house.

Prior Cuthbert declared he'd convoked this meeting of the Concilium to discuss the deteriorating situation. For the first time since it had happened, Prior Cuthbert deeply regretted Abbot Stephen's death and wished he could exercise the authority of his late, if not lamented, superior. The principal officers of the abbey clustered round the oak table staring up at him. They were led by Aelfric the infirmarian, Cuthbert's bitter rival. Now Abbot Stephen had departed this life, such intense rivalries were beginning to surface. Aelfric, with his red nose and watery eyes, sat, tight-lipped, next to his henchman, Brother Richard the almoner.

'Father Prior,' Brother Richard led the attack, 'things are not going well. We have royal emissaries prowling our abbey whilst the number of corpses increases daily.'

'Listen! Listen!' Prior Cuthbert held up his hand. 'Abbot Stephen died, we don't know how or why. He was stabbed. Gildas's murder is also a mystery. Now Taverner has been killed too but whose fault is that? Moreover, we cannot oppose the royal clerk. If we did, the King himself may come here, or worse, we might be summoned to appear before him in Norwich, or even in London. Do you want that?'

'We want these hideous deaths stopped!' Brother Richard snapped. 'And the clerks to go about their business. To be frank, Father Prior, matters are going from bad to worse.'

'And there's the question of the guesthouse,' Aelfric spoke up. 'Now Abbot Stephen is dead, why can't the building work begin? The tumulus or burial mound can be levelled. We could even open it up and see what's inside.'

'That would be inappropriate!' Prior Cuthbert retorted. 'An unseemly haste and a lack of reverence for Abbot Stephen's memory: the rest of the community would not like it.'

'That's true,' Brother Francis the librarian spoke up. 'We really should wait for the new abbot.' He smiled dreamily at Cuthbert. 'Whoever that may be?'

The monks sat in silence. Prior Cuthbert smoothed the top of the table with his fingers. Matters were not going to plan. Abbot Stephen had said that Bloody Meadow would never be built upon as long as he was leader of this community. Now, even dead, he still remained Father Abbot. Did his ghost haunt these buildings? It was possible, with his unseemly interest in demonic possessions. On one matter Prior Cuthbert was quietly relieved: Taverner, Abbot Stephen's protégé, was dead. The man had been a nuisance and would have posed problems. What could they have done with him?

'Father Prior?' Aelfric asked softly. 'What do you counsel? What is your advice?'

Prior Cuthbert glared malevolently back.

'Perhaps we should be more honest,' Aelfric declared, pushing back the sleeves of his robe.

'Honest? What do you mean by that?'

'About Abbot Stephen's death! We all know about your plans for Bloody Meadow.'

Prior Cuthbert jabbed a finger at him. 'And you were party to those plans!'

'Are you implying that Abbot Stephen's death was caused by one of us?' Brother Richard demanded. 'We might be holy men but we cannot go through locked doors or walls!'

'I have looked at that door,' Aelfric retorted. 'Perhaps the hinges were loosened?'

His sallow cheeks blushed as the other monks guffawed with laughter.

'And why did Gildas die?' the infirmarian almost screeched. 'Brother Aelfric, spit out what you are saying!'

'Gildas was your confidant, Prior! His fingers positively itched to build that guesthouse. He lived, dreamed and drank what he called his vision. You supported him in that. How often did we sit here as you hectored Father Abbot?'

'I didn't hector him.' Prior Cuthbert tried to control his anger; he could see Aelfric was losing his temper. He was just pleased Corbett wasn't present.

'And there's the other matter!'

Cuthbert's heart sank. Aelfric leaned on the table.

'What other matter, Brother?'

'You know full well! We all do: Sir Eustace's codicil.'

Prior Cuthbert's throat went dry. Aelfric was now pointing at him, a skeletal finger wagging the air. Cuthbert wanted to stretch forward, grasp and snap it.

'We all know about Sir Eustace's codicil,' Cuthbert explained. 'We all agreed to keep it from Abbot Stephen, though of course we would have told him eventually.'

'I found it, you know,' Brother Francis the librarian spoke up, 'in a book of charters high in the library.'

'We haven't had it tested,' Prior Cuthbert declared. 'We all recognise,' he continued, 'that Sir Eustace Harcourt founded this abbey. If the document that Brother Francis discovered is genuine, then we own not only Falcon Brook but the meadows lying on the other side of it, which are still part of Lady Margaret's estate. However, the charter is old; it bears no seal so it cannot be verified.'

'There may be a copy at Westminster?'

'Why didn't you show it to Abbot Stephen?' Aelfric demanded.

'Because we all decided on that. Of course,' Prior Cutbert added slowly, 'I can only speak for myself.' He looked for help from Hamo and Dunstan the treasurer but they sat silent. 'I mean,' Cuthbert continued, 'one of us could have told Abbot Stephen?'

'Did you tell Lady Margaret Harcourt?' Aelfric retorted.

Prior Cuthbert squirmed in his chair.

'You did, didn't you?' Hamo, sitting on his left, leaned forward, hands joined as if in prayer.

'I didn't tell her. I simply hinted that if we built the guesthouse, she could either concede gracefully to our demands or there might be another way.'

'You did that!' Hamo hissed. 'Lady Margaret's dislike for Abbot Stephen was well known. Could she be behind these murders? Did the mention of some secret codicil tip her into killing?'

'Oh, don't be ridiculous!' Prior Cuthbert snapped. 'No woman is allowed in this abbey.'

'Father Prior, I know the rule of St Benedict as well as you do. Just because a woman is not allowed in our abbey, doesn't mean they are not welcome.'

Prior Cuthbert stared in disbelief. The Star Chamber had fallen silent. Hamo was hinting at something.

'We have pilgrims,' the almoner declared. 'Travellers, their wives, the womenfolk of merchants . . .? And we also have mysterious visitors at night.' Hamo was now enjoying himself.

'Impossible!' Prior Cuthbert snapped.

'Is it really?' Hamo stared up at the ceiling. 'We all know about Brother Gildas: a man who found it difficult to sleep at night. Perhaps he wasn't the only one?'

'Oh, come to the point!'

'Our abbey is a large, sprawling place,' Hamo continued. 'We have a gatehouse but there are small postern doors, not to mention the Judas Gate. Gildas could never stay still. Remember, he was always first in the abbey church to sing the divine office. Anyway, at night he often used to go for a walk. Now, the rule is that a monk, if he meets another monk at night, simply whispers "*Pax Vobiscum*" and offers a blessing. Gildas claimed that, on two occasions, he passed a robed, cowled figure who did not respond to his blessing, whilst he also caught a faint trace of perfume.'

His words created uproar.

'A woman in our abbey at night! There's certainly no proof of that!' Brother Francis shouted.

Hamo banged on the table. 'Well, there wouldn't be, would there? It is not something you proclaim to the sound of trumpet and tambour.'

'And Gildas told you this?' The Prior leaned forward.

'Why didn't you inform me? I am responsible for discipline.'

'Brother Gildas was uncertain.'

'Didn't you try and find out yourself?'

Hamo snorted with laughter. 'I like my sleep, Prior Cuthbert. I am not wandering St Martin's at night looking for some mysterious woman. After all, if it was true, such a visitation could be the work of one of the other monks or a lay brother. Some wench brought in from the villages. Or that tavern girl from the Lantern-in-the-Woods.'

Prior Cuthbert leaned back in his chair, fingers to his lips. He would have loved to have screamed at Hamo. If such scandal became known, together with these mysterious deaths whilst the abbey was in his charge, what chance did he have of being elected as Abbot and his appointment confirmed?

'Gildas said she was dressed like a monk?'

'I can only report what he told me. The figure was robed, cowled, with sandals on the feet. It was the fragrance which puzzled him. He would have challenged her but,' Hamo sighed, 'if he'd been wrong, he would have become the laughing stock of the abbey.'

'Perfume?' Prior Cuthbert exclaimed. 'Does that mean someone high-born like Lady Margaret? If so, whom was she visiting?'

'Well, not Father Abbot,' Aelfric jibed. 'Not only did they dislike each other, but the door to the abbot's quarters is most visible. Prior Cuthbert, you are the one who deals with Lady Margaret.'

He saw the anger flush Prior Cuthbert's face.

'I am not implying anything,' Aelfric hurriedly continued. 'Like you, I am trying to find out who is responsible for these deaths. Lady Margaret is a strong-willed woman. If she thought the abbey of St Martin's was going to seize some of her estate, her dislike of Abbot Stephen may have spilled over into murderous hatred.'

'And, of course,' Hamo interrupted, 'Gildas may have been killed because of what he saw.'

'And Taverner?' Prior Cuthbert tried to keep the sneer out of his voice. 'Perhaps he saw something as well?'

'One other matter.' Hamo clapped his hands softly. 'The burial mound in Bloody Meadow. I decided to inspect it this morning. It's got a grassy bank, and I noticed that a sod had been cut away so I pulled it out. Someone had burrowed into the mound and then replaced the sod to hide their handiwork. It was craftily done, I discovered it only by accident.'

'You are not,' Aelfric jokingly accused, 'already destroying the burial mound, Father Prior?'

'I know nothing of it.' Cuthbert gestured at a side table where a jug of ale and small tankards had been placed, together with a platter of bread and cheese. The kitchen always sent refreshments up whenever the Concilium met. 'We need to pause and reflect.'

Prior Cuthbert tried to recall what Abbot Stephen would have done when disagreements had taken place in this chamber. They had to speak, *una voce*, with one voice. Brother Dunstan, the treasurer, who had sat in silence during the entire meeting, was only too eager to push his chair back and serve his colleagues tankards of ale. The platter of bread and cheese was passed round. Prior Cuthbert shook his head. I am in a labyrinth, the Prior reflected. Cuthbert had been born in Kent, the younger son of a manor lord. One summer's day his father had taken him to a friend's house, a powerful merchant who had laid out a maze in his extensive garden, where Cuthbert had become lost, trapped in the narrowing rows of privet hedges. Even in his days as a soldier, Cuthbert had never experienced such terror.

He felt as if he was back in that maze now but, this time, there was no one to lead him out. He closed his eyes and quietly thanked God that there had been no witness to the private conversations between him and Abbot Stephen. No one to eavesdrop on Cuthbert's implied threats and warnings. Cuthbert accepted he had committed a sin and vowed that, next time he travelled to Norwich, he would seek absolution. He had hidden his sin away, buried deep in his soul. One thing truly worried him: had Abbot Stephen confided in anybody else? The Abbot had a confessor somewhere in the abbey. But who was it? One of the old monks, whose eyesight was too dim for the library? Their bodies too weak for any work in the monastery, they spent what was left of their lives in private, little cells, praying and sleeping. Now and again they joined the rest of the community in the abbey church for divine office or in the refectory for meals. Prior Cuthbert had often wondered if one of these – Luke, Simon or Ignatius – had been Father Abbot's confessor? Yet, if that was true, they couldn't say anything. Such confidences were covered by the seal of confession.

Prior Cuthbert picked up his tankard and sipped at the ale. He really shouldn't drink, his stomach was already upset. He glanced down the table. Aelfric was deep in conversation with the librarian. The almoner and sub-prior were exchanging confidences. Dunstan the treasurer, however, just sat staring across the chamber. Prior Cuthbert studied him out of the corner of his eye. A strange one, Dunstan, with his small eyes and balding head. Secretive and rather sly! He now looked very worried.

'Brother Dunstan! Is all well?'

The treasurer forced a smile.

'I am concerned that these present troubles do not affect the abbey's income. If the word spreads, labourers might be unwilling to till our fields or merchants come to buy our produce.'

'Nonsense!' the Prior scoffed, 'these troubles will pass.'

'I don't think so,' Dunstan whispered. He glanced fearfully at the Prior. 'I feel as if we are in the Valley of Death and our sins press heavily against us.'

'What sins?'

Dunstan shook his head and stared into the tankard.

'I feel ill,' he muttered, slamming his tankard down. 'I need some fresh air.'

The treasurer walked out of the chamber. Prior Cuthbert finished his ale. He clapped his hands softly.

'Brothers,' he announced, 'it's time to return to the business in hand. First, I must warn the rest of the community to be vigilant against strangers and perhaps not to walk by themselves.'

'That's going to be difficult,' Aelfric jibed. 'Many of us sleep in separate cells. Moreover, the victims have all been members of this Concilium.'

'Taverner wasn't,' Prior Cuthbert retorted.

He paused as the door opened and the treasurer rejoined them.

'There must be peace . . .'

Prior Cuthbert broke off. Hamo the sub-prior had pushed back his chair and was clutching his stomach, his fat face pallid.

'Oh Lord!' he breathed. 'Oh, my God, the pain!'

Prior Cuthbert thought it must be a seizure. Hamo flailed his hands, head going back. The other brothers jumped to their feet and hastened to help. Hamo pushed them away, trying to rise. The Prior stared in horror. It was as if his colleague was being slowly strangled: his face sweat-soaked, his eyes popping, mouth opening and closing as if desperate for air. A froth appeared at Hamo's lips. He turned as if he could walk away from the pain but collapsed to his knees, hands across his belly. The seizure grew worse. He crumpled to his side, legs kicking. Some of the others were shouting. Aelfric the infirmarian tried to grab Hamo by the shoulder.

'Perhaps he's choking!'

Prior Cuthbert knew what was wrong: a heart-stopping premonition. Hamo was now lost in his world of pain, arms and legs flailing, body jerking. Strange gargling sounds came from his throat. Aelfric tried to help him but it was impossible. Hamo was struggling like a landed fish. He gave a deep choking sound deep in his throat, shuddered once more and lay still, head slightly turned, eyes staring. Aelfric pulled him over on his back and desperately searched for a heart beat in the neck and wrists. He forced his fingers into the sub-prior's mouth.

'What is it?' Brother Dunstan asked fearfully. 'A seizure?'

'I don't think so.' Aelfric pressed the back of his hand against the dead man's cheek. 'Father Prior, Brother Hamo has been poisoned.'

Prior Cuthbert just shook his head. 'He can't have been! He can't have been!'

'He has all the symptoms,' Aelfric insisted. 'The pains were in his belly, not his chest or head. He was hale and hearty till he drank the ale and ate the bread and cheese.'

Prior Cuthbert gestured at the table.

'Take your seats. No one must touch the food or drink. Brother Aelfric, you know something of noxious substances?'

The infirmarian picked up the jug of ale. He sniffed at it and carefully scrutinised what was left on the platter. He examined his own cup.

'No one else is ill,' Brother Francis declared.

Aelfric picked up Hamo's small tankard. He took a

sheet of vellum and poured the dregs out onto it. He then thrust the tankard towards Prior Cuthbert. The Prior could see the grains on the bottom, as if some powder had been distilled.

'I do not think ale was poisoned,' Aelfric declared. 'Or the bread and cheese. The poison was placed in Brother Hamo's tankard. I can detect no odour and, if there was any taste, the ale would hide it.'

'What is it?' Prior Cuthbert asked.

Aelfric, his hands trembling, put the tankard down on the table. He stared down at the dregs forming little pools on the piece of vellum.

'God knows,' he whispered. 'I have many such powders in my infirmary. Whilst our herb garden contains henbane, foxglove, belladonna, potions which . . .'

'Can kill,' Prior Cuthbert finished the sentence for him.

Brother Dunstan, collapsed in his chair, put his face in his hands and began to sob. Prior Cuthbert sighed.

'Sir Hugh Corbett must be informed.'

Corbett was busy in Taverner's chamber, with Ranulf the other side of the room, and Chanson on guard outside.

'Who do you think killed our cunning man?' Ranulf asked.

'I don't know,' Corbett sifted through Taverner's possessions, 'but, looking at the corpse, it wouldn't have taken a master archer. Mind you, an arrow straight through the heart requires some skill.' He paused in his searches. 'One thing is missing. There was no brand mark on Taverner's forehead. I wonder whether it was because the assassin had to act quickly or because he doesn't regard Taverner in the same way as Gildas?'

'Or there are two assassins?'

123

'Very good, my Clerk of the Green Wax. God knows what's happening here? Taverner's might not be connected to the other deaths.'

'But why kill him?' Ranulf demanded. 'He was just a trickster.'

'I think he was more than that,' Corbett breathed. 'Do you know, Ranulf, when I was questioning him, just for a moment, I thought I heard someone outside. I assumed it was Chanson returning with the books but, of course, we met him after with Perditus.'

'So, what are we searching for now?'

'I'm not sure, Ranulf-atte-Newgate. You knew the dead man better than I. I think he did not tell us the full truth.'

'He wouldn't know what that was if it jumped up and bit him on the arse!'

'Precisely,' Corbett replied. 'I find it difficult to believe that Taverner simply turned up at St Martin's with this farrago of nonsense. True, like any wandering sailor, he may have looked for a quiet port to shelter in, but put yourself in his place, Ranulf. If you came to this grand abbey with all its wealth, what would you do?'

Ranulf, at a half-crouch, turned.

'I'd sit, wait and watch.'

'Taverner did the same.' Corbett opened a battered leather saddlebag and fished around inside. 'Taverner would demand some surety, just in case his trickery went wrong. I have never yet known a villain who hasn't got a bolt hole ready, should his villainy turn awry.'

'Does the abbey hold bows and arrows?'

'Probably more than a castle. They have to hunt, don't they? Defend themselves. When we went into the storerooms I glimpsed baskets full of arrows as well as stacks of bow shafts.'

'And the skill to use them?'

'Most men can use a bow,' Corbett declared absent-mindedly. 'Many of these monks were former soldiers. I wager a few were royal clerks. They would have been trained to stand in the battle line. I am truly intrigued by Taverner's death. His assassin wanted him out of the way as quickly as possible. I wonder why?'

Ranulf watched as Corbett grasped one of Taverner's boots and searched carefully inside.

'You don't think . . .?'

'Yes, I do.' Corbett pushed his hand further down. 'Do you remember when Taverner was about to lead us down to the cellars? He said he wanted to change his sandals?'

'He did.'

'I also think that he was busy hiding documents: Taverner knew I would be back. Ah, here we have it.'

Corbett drew out a small ledger bound by a red cord, as well as a thin, battered leather wallet, worn with age and covered in dark patches of mildew.

'I thought as much.'

Corbett finished his search and went and sat on a stool, his back to the window so he could use the light.

'Ha!'

'What is it?'

'Licences, warrants, letters of permission: some old, some new, some genuine, others probably forged.'

'Why didn't you persist with Taverner?' Ranulf murmured. 'Let me take him by the neck and shake him?'

'Taverner had told us enough for one day. Like any cunning man he'd wait to find out the lie of the land, see what arrangements he could reach, what he might garner. A man like Taverner, Ranulf, as you know, doesn't chatter like a squirrel.'

Corbett was about to continue when he heard the

sound of running footsteps; a brief conversation outside and Chanson burst into the room.

'Master, you are needed in what they call the Star Chamber – one of these monks has died!'

Corbett grasped the manuscripts he'd found in Taverner's room and pushed them inside his jerkin. The old lay brother outside was deeply agitated and scurried off, shouting over his shoulder to follow hastily. When they reached the Star Chamber, Hamo's corpse has already been laid out in a more composed fashion on the floor. Someone had brought a blanket and draped it over him. Ignoring Prior Cuthbert and the rest; Corbett went across and pulled the blanket back. One look was enough. Hamo's popping eyes, gaping mouth and discoloured swollen tongue, the strange pallor of his face and the hard tension of his muscles, showed he'd been poisoned.

'God save him!'

Corbett threw the sheet back over the face and got to his feet. He quickly muttered a requiem.

'Poisoned!' he exclaimed. 'No man should die like that, certainly not a priest, a man dedicated to the work of Christ.' He stared round at each member of the Concilium. 'There is no brand mark on his forehead,' Corbett declared. 'But,' he chewed the corner of his lip, 'I suspect it's the work of the same bloody-handed assassin!'

He paused as Brother Perditus brought Archdeacon Adrian, and both stood in the doorway.

'What do you want?' Corbett demanded.

'I heard about the death,' the Archdeacon replied. 'I was talking to Brother Perditus about Abbot Stephen's writings when the message arrived . . .' He swallowed hard. 'I wish to be away from here. Prior Cuthbert, there's no need for me to delay.'

'Oh, there's every reason.'

Corbett came across and tapped him lightly on the shoulder. The Archdeacon's face was no longer jovial. A deeply frightened man, so agitated he couldn't keep still, he tried to avert his gaze from the corpse sprawled beneath the blanket.

'No one will leave here,' Corbett declared, 'until I say. Especially you,' he added in a whisper, 'Archdeacon Adrian.'

The Archdeacon's head came back. He tried to speak but Corbett turned away.

'Brother Perditus, you can stay as well.'

Corbett rested against a chair at the end of the table.

'I suggest we all sit down. Prior Cuthbert,' he gazed round the chamber, 'you all gathered here after Taverner's death?'

'Of course, there were matters to discuss.'

'Good!' Corbett smiled. 'Then you can discuss them with me.'

Brother Dunstan was about to protest but Corbett smacked the table with his fist. Ranulf went across, kicked the door shut and stood with his back to it. Chanson sat on a stool on the far side. Corbett clasped his hands and gestured at the table. The monks and Archdeacon Adrian dutifully took their seats. Corbett could tell, by the way they pushed the tankards away, what had been the source of the poison.

'Brother Hamo lies dead,' Corbett began. 'His corpse lies sprawled over there, his soul has gone to God. The source of the poison?'

'It wasn't in the jug of ale or the bread and cheese,' Aelfric replied, 'but in Hamo's tankard.'

'And who served these?'

'I did,' Dunstan replied meekly, raising his hand. 'But my colleagues saw me. I held the tray in both hands. The brothers could take whatever tankard they wanted.'

'Shouldn't we have the corpse removed?' Prior Cuthbert demanded.

'Read your history,' Corbett replied. 'Years ago, after a man was murdered, the questioning took place in the presence of his corpse. They claimed that his ghost would stay to help find the truth, though I suspect this will take a little longer. I mean no disrespect but Hamo can wait a while. So,' Corbett rubbed his hands, 'Brother Dunstan took the tray and went round the table? You each took a tankard?'

Again nods of agreement.

'I then put the jug on the table. The bread and cheese were passed round.'

'And Brother Hamo's ale was poisoned?' Corbett asked. 'But no one knew which tankard Hamo would take?'

'Of course not,' the almoner replied. 'They are all the same. No one gave it a second thought.'

'And when was this tray brought up?' Corbett demanded. 'Before the Concilium met or during it?'

'Just after we'd begun,' Prior Cuthbert replied. 'We were busy taking our seats when Brother Oswald brought it in.'

Corbett nodded at Chanson who scurried away. They sat in silence. Corbett deliberately wanted that. The pool is being stirred, he reflected, yet its calm surface still hides a lot. One of these men was an assassin but which? Prior Cuthbert, now looking so worried? Aelfric, preening himself as if pleased at the way things were going? Francis the librarian, who kept glancing over his shoulder at Corbett? Richard the almoner, hands clasped together as if reciting his beads? Brother Dunstan, with that faraway look in his eyes as if he couldn't believe what was happening? Archdeacon Adrian sat with his head down, moving backwards and forwards in his chair. Beside him Perditus, his eyes screwed up, stared across at the corpse as if fascinated by it. There was a knock on the door: a grey-haired, ashen-faced lay brother was ushered in. He immediately fell to his knees, hands clasped.

'Father Prior! Father Prior!' he wailed. 'I brought the ale and tankards up.'

'Speak to me,' Corbett said gently.

The man turned, still on his knees.

'You are Oswald the scullion?'

The man blinked through rheumy eyes and nodded, clearly terrified out of his wits.

'You have nothing to worry about,' Corbett reassured him. 'Who told you there was a meeting of the Concilium?'

'Hamo. He came down to the kitchen. I laid out the usual platter of bread and cheese, tankards and a jug of ale. I covered the jug with a napkin and left them there. I sent up one of the kitchen boys, a lad from the village. He came back and reported that the meeting had begun, so I brought up the tray.'

'And no one stopped you?'

A shake of the head.

'Father Prior and the others were just getting ready. The meeting hadn't really begun. I placed the tray on the table and left immediately.'

'Prior Cuthbert,' Corbett demanded, 'did anyone go across to the table whilst the meeting was taking place?'

'Not till I did,' Brother Dunstan answered.

'In which case,' Corbett turned to Oswald, 'when the tray was in the kitchen, who came in?'

The lay brother waved his arms in exasperation.

'Sir, how can I say?'

'Try and think,' Corbett urged. 'Look around this chamber. Study each face carefully.'

Oswald moved restlessly on his knees.

'There were some strangers,' he declared. 'Well,

visitors. Talbot the taverner from the Lantern-in-the-Woods, with that saucy-eyed daughter of his. What's her name?'

'Blanche,' Prior Cuthbert provided the name. 'They often come here to buy provisions. Talbot is a good customer.'

'He is,' Oswald said abruptly. 'But she's bold-eyed and sniggers too much.'

'Did they go near the table?' Corbett asked.

'I can't tell you. Anyway, why would they do something like that?' Oswald's eyes were now shifting about the chamber. 'We had brothers coming in and out, a stack of wood was brought for the ovens but none of the Concilium entered.' Oswald licked his lips. 'Though he did!' He shifted and pointed to Archdeacon Adrian.

'God's teeth!' Wallasby bellowed. 'I was hungry, I wanted some ale, something to eat. I was preparing to leave.'

'But now you're not,' Corbett smiled.

'Yes, he came in,' Oswald clambered to his feet, fingers shaking, 'demanding this and demanding that. He had words with Taverner Talbot, asked if he could stay at the inn for the night on his journey back to London.'

Archdeacon Adrian simply waved his hand. Corbett could tell he was furious.

'I will not deign to answer this. I am a priest, Sir Hugh, a high-ranking official of the Church. I was only here at Abbot Stephen's insistence and that of the Dominican Order.'

'Were you?' Corbett asked. 'Were you really?' He turned. 'Brother Oswald, you may go.'

Ranulf let him out and closed the door. He leaned against it, arms crossed, head back, staring at these assembled notables under heavy-lidded eyes. Ranulf watched Corbett like a cat: sometimes old Master Long

Face infuriated him with his brooding ways and taciturn speech. Ranulf had never met a man so self-contained. Corbett was closer than any brother but, over the years, Ranulf had learnt little about this enigmatic clerk. The only passion he showed was when he was with his beautiful wife Maeve. Ranulf smiled to himself. Lady Maeve, with those piercing blue eyes, always frightened Ranulf. It was as if she could stare directly into his soul, and read his thoughts, his secret desires. Oh yes, Corbett's only passions were Lady Maeve, his children and the law. Always the law! Corbett had once told him that he had seen the work of wolf's-heads in Wales, an entire hamlet destroyed: women gutted from crotch to neck; men hanging from trees; children butchered. He had never forgotten the sight and learnt a bitter lesson.

'If the law is removed,' Corbett declared, 'that's what we become, Ranulf: animals in the dark tearing at each other.'

Corbett loved the King but this was tinged with a deep cynicism and wariness, and that was the difference between them. In Ranulf's eyes whatever the King wanted was the law. Ranulf recalled Taverner and the cunning man's description of his early days. Ranulf-atte-Newgate was determined on one thing: he would never go back to that. Corbett was his friend and companion but he was also his master and mentor. Ranulf studied Corbett like a hunting dog did its quarry. He glanced at Corbett who sat, elbows on the table, hands clasped over the lower part of his face: a favourite trick, to sit in silence and make the guilty nervous.

'Murderers always talk,' Corbett had once remarked. 'They begin by being secretive but, after a while, the power they have grasped goes to their heads. When they talk, they make mistakes.'

Ranulf also liked to see the powerful ones, the great

and the so-called good, squirm before his master's gaze.

'Sir Hugh, are you praying?'

'Yes, Brother Aelfric, I am.'

A bell began to toll.

'It is time for divine office,' Brother Dunstan declared, his hand against the table as if ready to rise.

'Sit down,' Corbett ordered. 'I have read the rule of St Benedict. In times of danger and crisis, the office of the day can be suspended. This is the divine office we must address: the matins of murder, the prime of malice, the vespers of death, the nones of justice, the compline of law. I don't think God wants to hear your prayers. He wants to see justice done. Prior Cuthbert, I suggest you hold a chapter meeting and tell your community that, until these matters are resolved, everyone should walk warily with an eye to his own safety.'

'We are all in the hands of God,' Prior Cuthbert declared.

'Some of us are,' Corbett retorted. 'But others?' He stirred in the chair.

'What of others?' Prior Cuthbert demanded.

'There's an assassin in this abbey,' Corbett replied. 'It will take time for the Hand of God to grasp him and mark him like he did Cain.'

'And Brother Hamo?' Prior Cuthbert demanded.

'Shall I tell you something?' Corbett pushed his chair back. He got to his feet and, hands down, leaned against the table. 'Your brother was poisoned. I am no physician so I cannot tell you the substance. Aelfric, in your infirmary you must have many jars, phials, boxes of powder. In the fields outside grow plants which, if ground and drained, would slay a man within a few heartbeats. What chills me about Hamo's death is that it wasn't planned.'

'What?' Aelfric demanded.

'The assassin is playing a game with us,' Corbett

continued. 'Abbot Stephen's puzzling death; Gildas branded, his corpse left sprawling on the burial mound; the cat, its throat slit, fastened to the rood screen; Taverner killed by an arrow. I think the assassin could have killed all of you this morning. Somehow or other he put that poison in the tankard. He really didn't care who drank from it, as long as one of you did.'

Brother Dunstan gave a low groan. He buried his face in his hands.

'Like a gambler playing Hazard.' Corbett gestured with his hand. 'He rolls the dice and it falls as it will. Our assassin does likewise: poison was put in a tankard when the tray was in the kitchen. It was brought up here,' Corbett shrugged, 'and the die was cast.'

'So, any of us could have taken that tankard?' Prior Cuthbert demanded, his eyes wild with horror.

'Oh yes. The assassin is sending you a warning. He can strike when, and wherever, he wishes. If he wanted he could have killed two, three or all of you.' Corbett re-took his seat. 'He'll play that game until he's satisfied.'

'What can we do?' Brother Richard wailed.

'Say your prayers, be careful where you walk, what you eat and drink.' Corbett tapped the table. 'And tell me the truth. So, Prior Cuthbert, you are going to tell me the truth, aren't you? What did the Concilium discuss this morning? What else do I need to know about the abbey of St Martin's-in-the-Marsh?'

*POTEST NOCENTI CONTINGERE, UT
LATEAT, LATENDI FIDES NON POTEST*

THE GUILTY CAN HIDE, BUT
NEVER WITH PEACE OF MIND

SENECA

# *Chapter 6*

The Griffin was snarling, fierce and repellent, its carved lips opened to display a flickering tongue and jagged teeth. Protuberant eyes glared out, its ears were up and pointed back, like a dog ready to attack. Carved in stone the Griffin lurched out of the corner of the wall, eternally springing on some unseen enemy. Corbett studied it carefully. As a boy he'd always been frightened of such images and, when his mother took him to the parish church, he'd avert his eyes. He had this childish fear that, at night, when the sun sank and the clouds gathered to hide the moon, these gargoyles, snarling griffins, tail-lashing dragons, ogres with the heads of baboons, monkeys with the faces of men, all came to life and crawled down the walls to dance on the tombstones in the graveyard. Corbett smiled to himself. In some ways he still believed this. When darkness fell, whatever that darkness was, loathsome creatures came slithering out.

'In the soul,' Corbett whispered. 'That's where you experience the horrid nights of Hell.'

Standing in front of the abbey church, Corbett gazed up at the tympanum above the doorway. Christ stood in eternal judgement, his left hand slightly raised, his right holding the sword of justice. Seraphs clustered about his haloed head. On the Saviour's right were the virtuous, hands extended to receive his mercy. On his left stood the sinners, a line of condemned felons, with halters round their necks, being driven into the eternal fire by demons in the shape of centaurs, all armed with swords, spears, daggers and lances, to prod and prick their victims. Corbett would have loved to have climbed up and studied the carving more closely. The stonemasons had a dark sense of humour and often used such carvings to portray their enemies as well as their friends. On either side of the arched doorway beneath the tympanum, two great faces, carved in stone, peered out. On the right was a saintly monk, his eyes raised heavenwards. The one on the left was certainly drunk, with skewered eyeballs and gagging mouth. Corbett walked round the side of the abbey church and in through the Galilee porch. Benches stood on either side where, during inclement weather, the monks could sit to meditate, reflect or doze according to their inclination. Inside, the abbey church was deserted. Gusts of incense, like the prayers of angels, wafted about on the cold afternoon breeze. Beeswax candles, fixed in their iron sockets, provided light as well as the soft fragrance of summer.

Corbett walked round the church. Occasionally he paused to study the wall paintings, whose vivid colours depicted different themes from the bible. Christ amongst the dead, standing on the shores of Hell gazing sorrowfully across the Sea of Damnation at the army of the lost. Christ feeding the five thousand with little loaves and a basket of fishes. His passion and death depicted in all its horrors: the beaten, crowned head, the blood gushing from the holes in his hands and feet. The Resurrection and all the glories and horrors of the Second Coming. Some of the paintings were ancient and beginning to fade. Others were freshly done. Corbett realised that the more recent had one common theme, the exorcism of demons: Christ healing the Gadarene, a host of black imps bursting out of the poor man's mouth, their leader shouting: 'My name is Legion for we are many!'

Studying the wall paintings, Corbett became acutely aware of the war between the visible and the invisible. He realised most of this must have been done at the behest of Abbot Stephen. The artist had painted dramatically, giving free rein to his vivid imagination. The demons took many forms: sometimes dark figures with eyes burning like coal and the jagged teeth of a hunting dog; monkeys and baboons; even a rabbit with a gargoyle face. In others the theme starkly changed. Corbett recalled the scriptural verse: 'How Satan could appear as an angel of light.' In such paintings the fallen Seraph was portrayed as a beautiful young man with eyes of sapphire, hair of glowing gold and face lit by the sun. He was dressed in silken gowns with gold tassels edged with silver. The only clues to his real identity were the horned hands constantly close to the hilt of a dagger or sword. Beneath this, Christ's words from the gospel of St John, 'Satan was an assassin from the first'. In all these paintings Lucifer, Satan or Beelzebub appeared as a young courtier, even a handsome knight intent on war. Corbett stood fascinated. Abbot Stephen's interest in demonology certainly made itself felt. One painting dominated the wall just before the Lady Chapel. It was entitled 'The First Sin' and showed Cain beating out the brains of his brother Abel with the bone of an animal. To their right was the altar of sacrifice, and above this the all-seeing eye of God. Corbett studied this painting closely. Beneath the altar were wheels with hub and spokes, very similar to that of the Roman mosaic, as well as the drawings Corbett had seen in the Abbot's chamber. Corbett continued into the Lady

Chapel and lit two candles. He placed both on the spiked candelabra, knelt on the cushions and recited three Aves for Maeve and his family. He then took one of the candles and returned to the painting. Corbett guessed it must be only a few months to a year since it was finished. The more he studied it, the deeper his interest grew.

The painting was very subtle. Many of its features were hidden by the dark shadows of the transept but Corbett, using the candle, was able to study every detail. He smiled quietly to himself. At first glance it appeared that Cain and Abel were in a desert, sacrificing on a rocky outcrop: in the far distance lay Paradise. The artist, probably at the Abbot's behest, had depicted this as a place of lush greenness, with trees, plants and elegant buildings. Corbett, however, recognised the abbey of St Martin's-in-the-Marsh surrounded by its pastures and meadowlands, copses and streams. He could even make out Bloody Meadow with its tumulus surmounted by a cross. Corbett, grasping the candle, sat down at the foot of the pillar and tried to see the painting as a whole. Cain and Abel had been painted as two young men and in the background stood a woman. Was that Eve their mother? She was definitely in mourning, clothed in black from head to toe, hands raised supplicatingly to her face. Next to her stood two young men, dressed in full armour as if guarding her. Were these more sons Corbett thought. Or angels or demons?

Corbett rose, took the candle, placed it on its iron spigot and continued his journey. He paused for a while at Abbot Stephen's tomb and murmured a quick prayer. The other side of the church was also decorated with paintings. These were mostly many years old though one was freshly done. It showed the temptations of Christ by Satan, when he was taken up a high mountain and shown all the glory and pomp of the world. Corbett wasn't sure whether the figure was meant to signify Christ or Man in general. Beneath the mountain the artist had painted cities and castles with soaring towers and powerful walls. Sumpter ponies, laden with wealth, entered their gateways. Away to the right stood a place of peace. Once again Corbett recognised the abbey of St Martin's-in-the-Marsh. Is that why Abbot Stephen had become a monk, Corbett wondered? Fleeing from the glories of the world? Corbett went and sat on a bench and stretched out his legs. Ranulf and Chanson had been despatched to the tavern, the 'Lantern-in-the-Woods'. Such a place was always a source of gossip. Perhaps they could learn something there about the abbey and its community. Corbett felt his mind all a-jumble from his meeting with the Concilium. At first Prior Cuthbert had been reluctant to talk but, urged on by Aelfric and the rest, had confessed to certain irregularities in the life of the community. Who had broken into the tumulus? Was it Abbot Stephen? Prior Cuthbert? Or even Taverner? And what of this codicil? Lady Margaret Harcourt was not going to be pleased by that! Corbett was more bemused by Gildas's story about the woman he had glimpsed at night walking through the abbey grounds. She had been disguised as a monk, hence the robe and cowl, but who was she? Some wench from the nearby villages? Or Lady Margaret Harcourt? Corbett had decided that, whilst his companions were gone, he would traverse this so-called House of God. He'd try to grasp its soul as well as to acquaint himself with all its galleries and passages, postern gates and doorways. Especially now when the abbey was fairly deserted. Prior Cuthbert had called a meeting of the Chapter, a gathering of the entire community, to warn and advise them. Corbett felt his eyes grow heavy. Ranulf always asked him whether he thought such mysteries, such investigations, were just puzzles like the conundrums posed in the Schools of Oxford?

'You mean like a mathematician?' Corbett had replied. 'Or a master of logic trying to resolve some problem?'

Corbett breathed in deeply. No, it was not like that. True, he had never met Abbot Stephen. Prior Cuthbert and his community were strangers. This was the first time he had visited St Martin's-in-the-Marsh. Nevertheless, Corbett felt as if he was now part of the abbey and it part of him. He recalled the answer he had given Ranulf.

'I am not now in the Schools of Oxford,' he'd replied. 'The analogy is not suitable, appropriate or logical. My great fear, Ranulf, and that of the Lady Maeve, is that one of these days, in the middle of some bloody intrigue, I'll receive my death blow. No, Ranulf, we are not scholars or masters of logic. More like knights in a tournament – yet this is not some friendly joust on a May Day field. Oh, we are armed with sword and shield but our eyes are blindfolded. We stand in a chamber full of shadows and, before we can escape, we must trap and kill the sons and daughters of Cain.'

Corbett smiled now at the dramatic way he had spoken but it was true. St Martin's-in-the-Marsh was a darkened chamber. God knows what assassins it housed? Corbett opened his eyes and stared down the transept. Even a place like this, the House of God and Gate of Heaven, was no sanctuary against the flying arrow or the sudden, vicious thrust of knife or sword. Corbett listened carefully; but heard nothing, except the wind battering at a loose door above the squeak and scurry of mice. He sighed, got to his feet and went out into the grounds.

Corbett continued his search through herb gardens and courtyards, down porticoes, across small cloister garths, around the infirmary and refectory. He passed the Chapter House, its doors closed, its windows full of light. Corbett heard the murmur of voices. All the time he kept a hand on his dagger, listening for any untoward sound. The abbey lay silent. The sky was grey and lowering. The wind, sharp and bitter, carried small flurries of snow. Corbett wondered if tomorrow all would be carpeted in white. It would make things difficult for the murderer, he reflected, but also for us. At last Corbett was satisfied. He had, in his own mind, a plan of the abbey. He also realised what a powerful and wealthy place it was. He could understand why Prior Cuthbert was so eager to build a new guesthouse. He walked down towards the curtain wall and paused at the Judas gate just as the bell tolled, the sign that the Chapter meeting was over. Corbett opened the gate and went through. Bloody Meadow stretched out like a great circle, oak trees on either side curving down to Falcon's Brook. A mist was seeping in and, through the trees, Corbett glimpsed the labourers in the fields: he heard the wheels of a cart, the crack of a whip and the harsh braying of oxen as they heaved at the plough. Corbett drew his dagger and knelt down. The frozen grass was hard. He cut deep, picked up the small sod and crumbled the ice-hard soil between his fingers.

'Still the farmer's son,' Corbett murmured to himself. He recognised how rich the earth was. In summer the grass would be green, long and lush. It was good meadow land or, if put to the plough, the crops would sprout thick and high. No wonder Abbot Stephen had been reluctant to build on it. Corbett brushed the soil from his fingers and got to his feet. In the centre of the meadow the tumulus rose like a great finger beckoning him forwards. Corbett walked across and inspected it carefully. Abbot Stephen was correct: the tumulus or funeral barrow was man-made and had been carefully laid out in proper proportions. He patted its surface and tried to climb it but the grass was thick with frost and slippery so he contented himself with walking around. The light was fading. At last he found what the sub-prior had seen: just at eye level, someone had cut into the tumulus. Corbett removed the loose earth. The hole beneath was about six inches across. Corbett looked round for the loosened soil but realised that whoever had dug must have gathered it up and taken it away. He felt inside: the man-made burrow was long. Corbett withdrew his hand.

'Of course!' he whispered. Whoever had done this had come out late in the evening and hacked away a piece which could later be used to conceal his handi-work. The intruder had burrowed down and used a long pole or spear shaft to probe, to discover what lay deep within. A coffin – a sarcophagus? Corbett placed the sod back in its place. Had it been Prior Cuthbert, he wondered? Abbot Stephen? Or even Master Taverner, who must have been attracted by the mystery of this place?

Corbett wiped his hands on the wet grass, dried them on his cloak and walked on. The great oak trees stood in a line from the abbey walls down to Falcon Brook, so symmetrical Corbett wondered if they had been planted deliberately? Squat, round trunks with powerful black branches reaching up to the greying sky. Corbett stared back at the tumulus. With the abbey wall at one end, the oaks on either side resembled the pillars of a church whilst the tumulus in the centre looked like a place of worship. He walked into the shadow of the oaks. Corbett could hear faint sounds from the abbey, as well as the trundling of carts and the shouts of the labourers as they finished their work in the far fields. The abbey bell began to toll again. Corbett recalled how Prior Cuthbert had ordered special prayers to be said for both

Taverner and the sub-prior now stiffening under their corpse sheets in the death house.

The undergrowth between the oaks was thick in places. Corbett had to watch his step. He paused at the great burn mark which scorched the grass and brambles. Corbett crouched down and prodded at it with his dagger: black, flakey ash about six inches broad, the scorch mark stretched for at least two yards. Poachers, Corbett wondered? Mystified, he got to his feet and continued. He left the oaks and walked to the edge of Falcon Brook. It was really nothing more than a rivulet about a yard across. On the far bank was a line of straggling bushes and gorse. The brook was sluggish and against each bank a thick green slime had formed. Corbett carefully scrambled down and measured its depth with his boots: no more than a foot. The brook was probably man-made, its water diverted from the swamp or the fens; certainly not used by the Harcourts or the abbey either as a source of fresh water or fish for the kitchens. Corbett pulled himself out and froze. Further along the bank, on a hummock of grass beneath a willow, sat one of the monks, cowl pulled forward, head down, hands up the sleeves of his robe. He was so deep in thought he hadn't heard Corbett approach. He sat like a statue. Corbett drew his dagger, walked softly forward and coughed. The figure didn't stir. Corbett felt a prickle of fear along his back.

'*Pax vobiscum*, Brother!' he called out and sighed with relief as the figure started and turned, one hand going up to push back the cowl. Corbett recognised Brother Dunstan the treasurer. The monk leapt to his feet, hands flailing. Corbett could see he had been crying.

'Brother Dunstan, this is a cold and lonely place to meditate and pray!'

The monk, feet slipping on the wet grass, made his way forward.

'I thought you were at the chapter meeting! Brother, what is the matter?'

Brother Dunstan's eyes were swollen from crying. The man raised a hand to brush away the tears from his cheek, displaying a row of fingernails bitten to the quick.

'We are going to die, aren't we, clerk?'

Corbett stared round the monk and noticed the small wine-skin lying on the grass.

'Brother Dunstan, we are all going to die: that doesn't mean we must camp out in the cemetery and wait for it to happen.'

'I didn't attend the chapter meeting,' Brother Dunstan slurred. 'What's the use, Sir Hugh? I brought some wine here and decided to think.'

'Is there any left?'

The monk grinned and stepped back. He picked up the wineskin and tossed it over. Corbett lifted the wineskin. He drank and handed it back.

'Remember the good book: a little wine gladdens the heart but too much dulls the soul. Brother Dunstan, you sat there like a man the world has forgotten.'

'I am worried, I truly am.' Brother Dunastan grasped the wineskin as if it was a precious relic. 'The news of these deaths will soon spread. Pilgrims won't come. Merchants will be reluctant to stay. Moreover, when the King hears . . .'

'It will pass,' Corbett reassured him. 'You are frightened about the abbey's revenues?'

Brother Dunstan nodded quickly.

You're lying, Corbett thought: this abbey is rich and powerful enough to withstand a year-long siege.

'What are you truly worried about, Brother?'

The monk looked away. 'Sin!'

'I beg your pardon?'

'Sin!' Brother Dunstan repeated. 'It's true what the

proverb says, isn't it, clerk? Your sins will find you out.'

'What sins?'

'Abbot Stephen was a good father. He was strict yet gentle and kind.' Brother Dunstan glanced back towards the massed buildings of St Martin's. 'He knew our sins but was compassionate.'

'Did you confess to him?' Corbett asked.

Brother Dunstan nodded. 'He shrived me and gave me good counsel.' The monk's watery eyes came up. 'He was a good priest, clerk. I have never met his like before. Now we shall be punished for our sins.'

'First, what do you mean, his like?' Corbett stepped closer.

'It was almost,' Brother Dunstan bit his lip, 'almost as if he believed there was no sin.' He glimpsed Corbett's puzzlement. 'You'd have to listen to him to know what I mean.'

'And yet he was an exorcist?' Corbett demanded. 'He believed in Satan and all his power.'

'I know, I know, it's a conundrum.'

'Did Abbot Stephen have a father confessor?'

'Yes, yes, he did.' Brother Dunstan's fingers went to his lips. 'He told me once that sometimes he confessed to a priest he met on his journeys but there was also someone in the abbey. Ah yes, Brother Luke! He used to be the infirmarian here, and is now almost a hundred years old! Brother Luke says he can remember King John when he progressed through Norfolk. Old Luke! A sharp mind in an ageing body!'

Corbett promised himself that he would seek this old one out.

'It's beginning to snow,' Brother Dunstan declared.

White, soft flakes were lazily floating down. The sky was now low, a dark grey.

'It will be a cold night,' Brother Dunstan whispered.

Corbett looked back towards the soaring towers, spires and gables of St Martin's-in-the-Marsh. Strange, he mused, how a place can change. When he'd first approached the gatehouse, the abbey had seemed welcoming, a pleasant refuge from the wilderness which surrounded it. Now it looked sinister, forbidding, even threatening.

'I am cold,' Brother Dunstan murmured, stamping his feet. 'Sir Hugh, are you walking back?'

Corbett agreed. They crossed the field; the snowfall was now heavy.

'What did you mean,' Corbett asked, 'about Abbot Stephen almost believing there was no sin? You called it a conundrum.'

Brother Dunstan pulled up his cowl. Corbett wondered if it was as much to hide his face as for protection against the biting wind.

'This is only a thought, Sir Hugh.' The treasurer measured his words. 'Philosophers argue about the existence of God. Sometimes I had the impression that Abbot Stephen had gone the other way, that it was almost easier for him to discover the spiritual life through the world of demons, though I wouldn't dare say that to our community.'

'So, Abbot Stephen saw the rite of exorcism as a journey into the darkness?'

'Why not?' Brother Dunstan laughed abruptly. 'We live in a sea of evil, Sir Hugh: murder, rape, theft, lawlessness.' He sighed. 'You very rarely meet an Angel of Light.'

Corbett was about to continue the discussion when the Judas gate was abruptly thrown open and Brother Perditus appeared waving his hands.

'Sir Hugh, you'd best come!'

'Oh no!' Brother Dunstan murmured. 'Not another death!'

'What is it?' Corbett shouted.

Perditus just gestured at him to hurry. Corbett quickened his stride. The lay brother stood agitated.

'I bear a message from Brother Aelfric. You must come, he wishes to show you something.'

He led them back through the Judas gate and across the abbey grounds. Aelfric was at the back of the infirmary where a stout shed had been built against the wall. Corbett entered the Death House. Inside it was warm: braziers glowed in the darkness; the hooded candles gleamed and oil lamps threw shifting pools of light. The Death House contained five or six long tables. Hamo and Taverner's corpses occupied two, and heavy canvas sheeting covered them both.

'I came back from the chapter meeting,' Aelfric explained taking a candle, 'and I noticed the door to the Death House was off the latch. Sir Hugh, look at this!'

He pulled back the sheets covering Hamo and Taverner and lowered the candle to reveal a hideous 'V' mark branded into the forehead of each corpse.

'God and his angels!' Corbett exclaimed. 'The assassin has a malevolence all his own. He has come back to claim the corpses – brand them as his own!'

'How could it be done?' Perditus whispered.

Corbett pointed to the brazier. 'It would only take a few seconds. The branding iron would be heated, and then the forehead marked.' He turned to a bucket of water just near the door. 'The iron was probably cooled in that. The courtyard outside is quiet, so the assassin would hear if anyone was around.'

'True,' Aelfric agreed. 'And very few people come here. It's not till the bodies are formally laid out that the community gathers to pay its respects.'

Corbett pulled the sheets back over the bodies. He turned to find Aelfric, Dunstan and Perditus standing in the doorway. The dancing light made them look sinister, secretive.

'I have had enough of the dead,' Corbett murmured, brushing past them. 'Brother Aelfric, there's little I can do here, at least for the moment.'

Corbett went out. Night was falling and the snow was coating the ground with a white dust. The abbey was busy with monks hurrying about finishing their tasks. Smoke billowed out from the kitchens as well as the fragrant odours of cooking meat and baking pies. Corbett pulled up his hood and walked back to the guesthouse. Once he was back in his own chamber he secured the door, drawing across the bolt. He lit the candles and oil lamps. An extra brazier had been wheeled in. Corbett took a pair of bellows and fired the coals until they glowed hot and red. The chamber had a small mantel hearth but Corbett decided not to light the wood. He went across and checked the wine cups, jug and the platter of dried fruit, bread and cheese. He could detect nothing wrong with them. He eased off his boots and lay down on the bed, staring up at the ceiling. He could make no sense of what was happening. Thoughts and images jumbled in his mind. He idly wondered how Ranulf and Chanson were doing.

'A killer prowls here,' Corbett whispered to himself, 'who enjoys what he does. He's turned this abbey on its head – no longer a place of sanctuary and prayer but of fear and sudden death.'

But was it that in the first place? The more he learnt about Abbot Stephen, the more curious Corbett became. On the one hand a devout, learned monk; on the other, Abbot Stephen was a man full of uncertainty, even regret and remorse. Corbett's eyes grew heavy. He drifted into sleep but was rudely awoken by a loud rapping at the door. He rolled off the bed, and picked up his sword belt which he had thrown onto the floor.

'Who is it?' he called.

'Archdeacon Adrian. Sir Hugh, I need to speak to you.'

Corbett withdrew the bolts and the Archdeacon stamped into the room. Without a by-your-leave, he took off his cloak, wet with melting snow, went across and warmed his hands over the brazier.

'Corbett, it's snowing.'

'I can see that.'

'I need to travel back to London. I want to be away from St Martin's-in-the-Marsh.'

'Why?' Corbett demanded.

'Business, my court in London awaits. I see no point in delay.'

'Oh, I see every point.'

Corbett sat on the bed. The Archdeacon turned. Are you frightened, Corbett wondered? Angry, or playing a game? The Archdeacon's lip curled.

'I need not take orders from you, Corbett!'

'Oh yes you must!' Corbett waved at the panniers stacked in the corner. 'I carry the King's commission!'

'I am an ecclesiastic, a clerk in Holy Orders!'

'I wouldn't care if you were the Angel Gabriel. For all I know, Archdeacon Adrian, you could be the assassin.'

'Don't be ridiculous!' The Archdeacon went across, picked up a chair, turned it round and slumped down on it. 'I'm no more guilty than you, Corbett. Indeed,' he spluttered, 'how do we know you're not the assassin?'

'I wasn't here when the Abbot died.'

Corbett pulled the war belt across his lap and played with the dagger, pushing it in and out of its scabbard.

'But you were here, Master Wallasby!'

'Abbot Stephen was my friend, a colleague. You know the reason for my visit.'

'You're lying!' Corbett pointed the dagger at his

univited guest. 'You weren't Abbot Stephen's friend, you were his rival, his opponent. Perhaps you resented his fame, and that's why you devised this stratagem?'

'What are you talking about?'

'Master Taverner, Carrefour, or whatever he's called, whose corpse lies stiffening in the Death House. You know he's been branded?'

The Archdeacon swallowed hard and glanced at the door as if he regretted coming here.

'If you hadn't come, Master Wallasby, I would have sent for you. Now, let me see. You are an opponent of Abbot Stephen's philosophy. You are a pragmatist, a lawyer. You don't believe in elves and goblins, wood sprites or that the Powers of Hell can possess a man. You engaged Abbot Stephen in open debate. However, he proved to be a resourceful opponent with considerable evidence to justify what he did. Now, Archdeacon, you mentioned your court in London? In your role as a Judge of the Church you must have met the cunning man Carrefour, whom we now know as Taverner.' Corbett paused. 'You did know him, didn't you? Master Wallasby, I don't want to put you on oath. However, I am sure, if I searched the records of your court, I'd find reference to Taverner, that father of lies, being a constant visitor at your court.'

The Archdeacon was now visibly nervous.

'Would you like some wine?' Corbett offered. 'Perhaps a piece of bread and cheese? No? Well, when I went through Master Taverner's possessions I came across a small ledger, a journal he kept. More importantly, I discovered a licence to beg, as well as permission to go beyond the seas, both granted by your court. The licences were issued early in the autumn on the eve of the feast of St Matthew the Apostle. Now, correct me if I am wrong, Archdeacon, but I believe you gave Master Taverner both money and licences. He left on a ship from the Thames carrying supplies up the Eastern coast. Taverner secured his passage, landed and made his way to St Martin's-in-the-Marsh. He really was a master of disguise, a deceitful schemer. He had been furnished with other letters and embellished his story with references to being seen by priests in London. Abbot Stephen accepted him as a *bona fide* appellant, desperate for spiritual help and comfort. Taverner proved equal to the task, and convinced Abbot Stephen that he was possessed. Abbot Stephen rose to the bait. He may have had doubts initially but these slowly crumbled away so he wrote to you and your Dominican friends in London.'

Corbett paused, went across and filled a goblet half full of wine and sipped the blood-red claret. Corbett smacked his lips.

'You are sure, Archdeacon, you won't join me? I could even warm you a posset cup?'

Wallasby stared back owl-eyed.

'I did wonder,' Corbett re-took his seat, 'why such a busy cleric as yourself should come hurrying north at Abbot Stephen's behest? Couldn't it have waited – after all you are so busy? Anyway, you arrived here, and proclaimed yourself impressed by Taverner's performance but then the mummery you planned was overtaken by murder.'

The priest rubbed the side of his face as if he was in pain.

'I . . . I . . .' he stammered.

'Please don't lie,' Corbett urged. 'Archdeacon, you should never trust a man like Taverner! He was supposed to get rid of those letters and licences, wasn't he? But a trickster like him never destroys anything, not knowing whether it might come in useful.'

'It's true,' the Archdeacon sighed. 'Sir Hugh,' he paused, 'Abbot Stephen was a man whom, I believe, the

Church did not need. I am orthodox – I believe in Satan and hellfire – but the world is changing. New knowledge, new sciences are coming out of the east. We no longer believe that every disaster is the work of Satan, that contagion, infection, yes even murder and theft, are part of one vast conspiracy by an unseen horde of demons. It's good for priests to use hellfire to frighten the faithful but Abbot Stephen . . .?' He shook his head. 'What had he to do with the Schools of Oxford or Cambridge, the writings of Plato or Aristotle, the business of the law or Parliament?' The Archdeacon regained confidence as he spoke. 'Yes, I am a judge of the Church. I sit in my court and see men like Taverner fleece the superstitious. Now, Taverner I can take care of. But an abbot, a lord spiritual? I wanted to prove him wrong.'

'No,' Corbett interrupted. 'You wanted to teach him a lesson. What would have happened?' he insisted. 'Would the exorcism have collapsed? Would Taverner have proclaimed who he really was and what he was doing? You would have made Abbot Stephen a laughing stock. A mockery from one end of the realm to the other. Do you think the King would have been pleased?'

The Archdeacon made to protest.

'You would have destroyed him! It proves you had little love for Abbot Stephen.'

Wallasby sprang to his feet.

'Sit down!' Corbett ordered. 'You came here to ask me permission to leave, which I've denied. Now, I am giving you the reason why. You hired Taverner to make a mockery of Abbot Stephen's theories. You travelled north to join him in this mummery. I don't believe, Archdeacon, that this was an academic exercise. It goes deeper than that. What was it? A malicious joke? Did Abbot Stephen block your preferment, hinder your progress?' Corbett clapped his hands so noisily the Archdeacon jumped. 'You can make your confession now, priest, or I can wring it from you in the presence of the King. I want the truth!'

'Two years ago,' the Archdeacon muttered, wiping the sweaty palms of his hands down his robe, 'the King sent a solemn embassy to Paris.'

'Ah yes, about the negotiations for the marriage of the Prince of Wales to Isabella, King Philip's daughter?'

'The same. The Bishop of London chose me to be part of the delegation but Abbot Stephen vetoed my place.'

'Did he give a reason?' Corbett demanded.

'He was part of the same embassy. He claimed that the negotiations would be convoluted and prolonged, and that it was therefore inappropriate for men who had clashed in matters spiritual to be together on such an issue.'

'You disliked him, didn't you?' Corbett murmured. 'And Abbot Stephen knew that?'

'I am giving you my reason, Corbett,' Wallasby paused. 'I didn't like Abbot Stephen and he didn't like me. I vowed to teach him a lesson.'

'And what went wrong?'

'What do you . . .'

'I wonder what went wrong?' Corbett repeated. 'When you arrived at St Martin's you must have had private words with Taverner, well away from prying eyes or any eavesdropper. Had Taverner changed his mind? Abbot Stephen was a good priest, who had welcomed Taverner kindly. Perhaps Taverner thought it more profitable to win the Abbot's favour by continuing to act the possessed man, than to be party to your trickery. You must have been furious to see your subtle ploy drain away like water down a hole. Abbot Stephen had, unwittingly, turned the tables so that you, because of your own stupidity, would be forced to watch his greatest triumph.'

'You have no proof of that!'

Corbett got up, went across and opened the shutters. He pushed open the small latticed door window.

'It's snowing heavily,' he murmured. 'I doubt if you could travel to London anyway.'

Corbett stared down at the courtyard and the pool of light thrown by a cresset torch in its bracket on the corner of the building. He heard a sound, closed the window and turned round. Archdeacon Wallasby was now helping himself to a goblet of wine.

'Don't talk to me of proof. I'm correct, aren't I?'

'Yes, you are,' Wallasby replied. 'I was furious. I questioned Taverner who acted the holy innocent. He said that he had only met me once in his life and that I had driven him away with curses. I reminded him about the silver I had given him. "What money?" he asked. I threatened to expose him.'

'But, of course, you couldn't do that,' Corbett interrupted. 'To expose Taverner would be to betray yourself as no better than him: a liar and a trickster. What else did Taverner threaten? To go and confess all to Father Abbot?'

The Archdeacon slurped from the wine cup.

'Once he did that, the tables would have been truly turned,' Corbett continued. 'Abbot Stephen could declare that he had seen through the trickery and mummery and secured a full confession from Taverner. Our cunning man must have been delighted. He had you in the palm of his hand. You had no choice but to accept. Were you angry?'

Corbett walked across and pushed his face only a few inches from the priest.

'I wonder if you were angry enough to commit murder?'

Wallasby stepped back and drank quickly from the goblet.

'You shouldn't say that.'

'Why not? You disliked Abbot Stephen and he's dead. You must have been furious with Taverner and he's dead.'

'And sub-prior Hamo?'

'Now, there's a coincidence.' Corbett declared. 'You were in the kitchens this morning when the bread and ale were laid out on that tray. Shall I search your possessions, Archdeacon Wallasby? Will I find powders and potions?'

'You can search where you like!' the priest snarled. 'You have no right to make such allegations!'

'I can't say how you broke into the Abbot's chamber,' Corbett went and sat on the edge of the bed. 'But you are a strong man, Archdeacon Wallasby. Do you carry a bow?'

'Of course I do, as did my escort here.'

'Can you bring it here?'

Wallasby put the cup back on the table, mouth quivering.

'You don't have to, do you?' Corbett demanded. 'I would wager, Master Archdeacon, that the arrow which killed poor Taverner came from the quiver you hold, and you know that!'

*ITA VITAST HOMINUM QUASI QUOM*
*LUDAS TESSERIS*

**HUMAN LIFE IS A**
**GAME OF DICE**

TERENCE

# *Chapter 7*

The Lantern-in-the-Woods was a large, spacious tavern which stood off the muddy trackway under a canopy of surrounding trees. Built of black timbers and snow-white plaster, the sight of its red-tiled roof and the garish sign hung above the doorway, was a welcoming beacon for any traveller. The taproom was broad and well lit. The ale casks and wine tuns stood stacked to the right of the great hearth and, to the left, a narrow passageway led into the kitchen. Chanson slipped the reins into a groom's hands and joined Ranulf as he stood on the threshold peering in.

'What are we to do?'

Ranulf threw his cloak over his shoulder and grasped the hilt of his sword.

'This is the parish well, Chanson.'

The groom gazed back in puzzlement.

'It's where everybody gathers,' Ranulf explained. 'Peasants, tinkers, traders, chapmen, merchants. They all come to listen to the gossip, exchange news, spit and clasp hands on bargains.' Ranulf looked into the taproom. 'As well as drink and eat as much as their bellies can take. Now, Chanson, look at me.'

'Are you making fun of my eye?'

161

'No, I am not. What have I taught you about walking into a tavern?'

Chanson closed his eyes. 'Always throw your cloak back over your shoulder.' He did this hastily. 'Grasp the hilt of your dagger. Swagger in. Stop and, when the landlord comes across, don't look at him but rap out your orders.'

'Very good!' Ranulf smiled. 'And why is that?'

'Because you are a stranger and the people inside must get the measure of you.'

'Very good! What else?'

'Always sit with your back to the wall. Find out which door and windows you can escape through, if you have to leave in a hurry.'

'Excellent!' Ranulf grinned. 'Lovely boy! You're going to be a true clerk of the stables.'

'And what about Sir Hugh's rules?' Chanson added mischievously.

'Oh yes,' Ranulf declared wryly. 'Don't engage in games of dice or hazard. Keep your hands off the wenches and be careful what you drink.'

Ranulf stood aside as a pedlar, a tray around his neck, hurried into the welcoming taproom.

'Well, old Master Long Face would say that, wouldn't he?'

'Why are we here?' Chanson asked.

'Oh, to listen to the tittle-tattle and gossip. Now, come on, my belly thinks my throat's been slit.'

Ranulf swaggered in. He stood, feet apart, staring round the taproom. The conversation died. A relic-seller wiped his nose on his sleeve and peered across.

'Who are you?' he bawled.

Someone grasped the relic-seller by the shoulder and whispered quickly into his ear, and he slunk into the shadows.

'You are from the abbey.'

Talbot the taverner, his head bald as a gleaming egg, eyes almost hidden in folds of fat, his protruding belly covered by a blood-stained apron, bustled out from behind the counter.

'How do you know that?' Ranulf asked.

The taverner tapped his fleshy nose.

'Oh come, sirs.'

He led them across as if they were princes, gesturing at a group of farmers who occupied the table near the window to move away. They hastily obeyed, taking their platters of food with them. A wet cloth appeared in the taverner's hand and he cleaned the grease-covered table.

'You'll try the ale, sir? Home brewed with a dish of eels, salted and roasted? A nice vegetable sauce with chopped parsley and cream?'

'That will do nicely.' Ranulf eased himself down. 'And bring a tankard for yourself.'

The smile disappeared from the taverner's oily face.

'But, sir, I run a tavern. I . . .'

'Sir, you run a tavern,' Ranulf agreed, 'and that's why I want to talk to you. You don't object to talking to a King's man, do you?' His voice rose slightly.

'I'll send Blanche across,' Talbot muttered.

He finished cleaning the table and hurried away. Ranulf took off his war belt and slammed it down on the table. The rest of the customers decided not to continue staring. A young, spotty-faced man picked up his pet weasel and clutched it in his lap, turning his back as if fearful that the King's man would come over and arrest it.

'You enjoy this, don't you?' Chanson muttered. 'You like the power?'

'No, I don't,' Ranulf stared round the tavern. 'If we become unpopular here, Chanson, I am afraid it's through that window, round to the stables and away we go.'

'You expect trouble?'

'Well, as we came in,' Ranulf indicated with his thumb to the door at the rear, 'a small, greasy-haired, rat-faced man disappeared through there like a rabbit down a hole. Now, he's either fearful or gone to warn someone. Ah well, we'll see.' Ranulf peered out through the mullioned glass to stare up at the sky. 'I am not a country man, Chanson. Give me a London tavern and a smelly street in Southwark any day. However, even I know it's going to snow: the clouds are low and grey.'

Chanson recalled their freezing journey along those lonely trackways and shivered.

'We'll be back in the abbey before dark, won't we?'

'We'll be back when we've finished,' Ranulf agreed. 'Ah, who is this?'

A tavern wench came trotting across; she had red, curly hair under a white mobcap, slanted eyes with high cheekbones, and her face was slightly flushed. Ranulf admired her fine lips and the green smock, slightly too tight, which emphasized her generous bosom and broad hips. He looked down at her small buckled boots peeping out from beneath the flounced petticoats. She paused and grinned at Ranulf, allowing him a full view of her. She slowly put the tankards down, brushing Ranulf's hand, almost thrusting her breasts into his face.

'King's men are we?' she grinned. 'With fine leather boots and broad war belts?' She raised an eyebrow archly. 'We don't get your sorts often in these parts.'

'What sorts do you get?' Ranulf demanded.

The girl, hands on hips, shrugged. Ranulf noticed the beautiful gold cross on a silver chain round her neck, the fine rings on both hands and the silver chased bracelet clasping her left wrist.

'You are Blanche, Talbot's daughter?'

Her smile faded. 'How do you know that?'

'Oh, just by the way you act. A potboy was going to bring the tankards across but you took them off him.'

'Why sir,' Blanche cooed, 'you are sharper than I am.'

And, turning on her heel, she flounced off.

'The girls always like you, Ranulf.'

'And I like them, Chanson.' Ranulf leaned across and tapped the groom's face with his gauntlets. 'You are a good-looking lad. If you had your hair cut and washed more often, the girls would like you too.'

Chanson coloured and hid his face in the tankard to hide his embarrassment.

'Would you ever marry, Master Ranulf?'

'Better to marry than to burn, as St Paul says. Sometimes I wonder. Do you think, Chanson,' Ranulf took another sip from the tankard, 'that I should enter the church, become a priest?'

Chanson raised his tankard to hide his face. Ranulf often discussed this, and it was the only time Chanson ever felt like laughing out loud at his companion. Ranulf, however, didn't think it was funny. He sat steely faced.

'But you like the ladies, Master Ranulf?'

'So do many priests.'

'And you have never been in love?'

'You know the answer to that.' Ranulf mockingly toasted him with his tankard.

'Ah sirs, how can I help you?'

The taverner came up, scooped up a stool and sat down between them.

'You promised us some eels?'

'They are coming.'

'How old are you, Master Talbot?'

'According to my accounts, I'll be fifty-six summers on the eve of the Beheading of John the Baptist.'

'And you have always lived here?'

165

'Oh yes, and my father before me.'

'So, you know about the Harcourts?'

'Ah now, there's a mystery.' The landlord put his tankard down on the table. 'Lady Margaret comes here once or twice a year. She's always kindly and gracious, very much the high-born lady.'

'And her husband?'

'That's a strange thing. Their marriage was arranged but the service was performed at the door to the abbey church. I was there as a young man. Oh, it was very splendid, with banners and pennants, lords and ladies in their velvets and silks. Lady Margaret rode a milk-white palfrey, Sir Reginald a great war horse. Sir Stephen Daubigny, who later became Abbot, looked a true warrior in his royal surcoat. There was feasting and revelry. Daubigny and Harcourt.' The landlord held up his hand, two fingers locked together. 'Sworn brothers they were, in peace and war, boon companions.'

'And Lady Margaret? Did she like the man who later became the Abbot?'

'I don't know. I remember watching her, both on that day and afterwards. All three of them came here once to feast,' Talbot pointed towards the doorway, 'One bright summer's day. Sir Reginald came in, one arm linked through Lady Margaret's, the other through Sir Stephen's. Some other guests were present. I laid out a special table and we served them with the best dishes. Roast venison . . .'

'Yes, yes, of course,' Ranulf interrupted. 'But what of Lady Margaret and Sir Stephen?'

'They didn't seem to like each other. Sir Reginald arranged the seating, so that Sir Stephen was supposed to sit on Lady Margaret's left, but she objected. I remember Daubigny just shrugged. He went and sat beside his friend. During the meal, Daubigny and Lady Margaret hardly looked at each other or exchanged a word.'

'And then Sir Reginald disappeared?'

'Yes, one day in autumn. Why, it must be some thirty years ago! A potboy, who has now gone, said he saw Sir Reginald ride by with his pack pony. He recognised him by the livery and escutcheon. According to common report, he went to one of the Eastern ports, took ship and that's the last anyone ever heard or saw of him again. And, before you ask, sir clerk, I don't know why, though everyone has a theory.'

'And what's yours?'

'Sir Reginald was a true fighting man, a knight errant. Perhaps he wanted to go on a pilgrimage?'

'But why didn't he tell his wife? People say she was as perplexed as anyone.'

'I don't know.'

Ranulf turned slightly. Rat Face had reappeared and Ranulf didn't like his companions: men in boots and brown leggings armed with swords and daggers through the rings on their belts, faces almost hidden by cavernous cowls, the front part of their jerkins stretching up to their lower lip. Two carried bows with a quiver of arrows slung on their backs. Talbot followed Ranulf's gaze. He became distinctly nervous whilst the rest of the customers didn't look too happy either. The new arrivals went across and sat in a far corner where the shadows gave them some protection, so they could observe the rest of the taproom as closely as they wanted. Ranulf stared out of the window across the garden: the shrubs, herb plots and flowerbeds were still in the grip of a frost which had not thawed during the day. He glimpsed the first snowflakes fall. He knew what had happened. Taverner Talbot may act nervously but the new arrivals were as much a part of this tavern as the tables and chairs. Outlaws, wolf's-heads, men like Ranulf himself in his early days, who lived in the twilight. They prowled taverns such as this, hunting for easy prey or rich pickings. The taverner always welcomed them, either because he shared their loot or, more importantly, because they provided a constant supply of fresh meat poached from the King's forest – wild boar and venison. Ranulf wondered if they'd attack two officers of the Crown? He gently kicked Chanson under the table. The groom was staring across at the strangers. Chanson got the message and looked away.

'I'll get you those eels,' Talbot blustered.

'And some more ale!' Ranulf insisted. 'And do come back!'

'Do you think those strangers will make trouble for us, Ranulf?' Chanson whispered. 'Would they harm us?'

'Yes, they would.' Ranulf's hand went beneath the table and he tapped his purse. 'I wager a shilling to a shilling, they have already inspected our horses and harness.'

Chanson gulped nervously. Of course the horses were some of the finest from the royal stables, whilst the saddles and harness would fetch high prices in any market.

'Then there's our weapons,' Ranulf continued, 'and our clothes, not to mention the purses we carry. And perhaps,' he sighed, 'just as importantly, there's their reputations.'

'What has that got to do with it?'

'They are wolf's-heads,' Ranulf declared, keeping his voice at a whisper. 'They regard these parts as the King does his crown. They decide who comes and goes. Most of these merchants and tinkers probably pay them to travel unscathed.'

Chanson thought of that cold journey back to the abbey, the silent trees, the deserted, frozen trackway.

'Shouldn't we go?'

Ranulf pulled his war belt nearer. 'I've never run from a fight in my life, Chanson. Do you know why?

It's the best way not to get an arrow in your back.'

Talbot, aided by his now surly-faced daughter, served the eels and ale. Chanson took out his horn spoon and small dagger and began to cut, scooping the food into his mouth. Ranulf ate more slowly, now and again glancing across at the men watching him.

'It's good food,' Chanson murmured between mouthfuls. 'Hot and spicy.'

Talbot waited until they had finished and re-took his seat.

'And what do you know about Lady Margaret?' Ranulf demanded. 'After her husband's disappearance?'

'She was distraught, according to common report. It became well known that she wanted to follow her husband. Sir Stephen Daubigny agreed to help. They both stopped here on their way to the coast. A few months later, Sir Stephen returned, travel-stained, face all haggard. As for Lady Margaret,' Talbot lowered his eyes, 'she was gone over a year and when she came back she was a shadow of her former self: thin, pale-faced. She passed by the tavern with an escort, clothed like the figure of death, in black from head to toe. From that day to this, she has lived as a recluse. I go up to the manor to take supplies and to buy from her. As I said, she comes here very rarely. Our conversations over the years wouldn't fill half a page of a psalter.'

'And Sir Stephen?'

The taverner shrugged his shoulders.

'He went straight back to St Martin's, gave up his arms and took the vows of a monk. The rest you know and, before you ask, clerk, he was a good Father Abbot. Honest and fair in his dealings. Blanche and I were always welcome in the abbey.'

'And the others at St Martin's?' Ranulf insisted.

'Oh, they are monks, priests, slightly pompous. We deal with two of them: Cuthbert the Prior, a man of great ambition, and Dunstan the treasurer. We go to them, sometimes they come to us. Now and again we have wine which they would like or,' he gave a lop-sided smile, 'meat, fresh from the forest. Well, sirs,' Talbot drained his tankard and pushed back his stool, 'more than that I cannot say.'

'Oh, Master Talbot,' Ranulf beckoned him closer. 'I'm going to leave now.'

He was sure the taverner was almost going to thank him but Talbot held his tongue. 'And when we do,' Ranulf warned, 'I don't want our new arrivals to follow us out.'

The taverner leaned over. 'I can only warn you and give some advice.'

'Where will they come.' Ranulf replied.

'Out on the trackway,' the taverner replied. 'You are well mounted. They will try to force you down. You know what will happen then?'

Ranulf nodded.

'And you can't prevent them from leaving?'

Talbot shook his head. 'They're Scaribrick's men. If I interfered, by tomorrow morning this tavern would be gutted.'

'How many?' Ranulf murmured.

'There are five,' Talbot whispered, grasping his empty tankard. 'Thank God for the cold and that they didn't know you were coming, otherwise it would have been a good score.'

He hurried away. Ranulf rose and strapped his sword belt on. They left by the rear entrance and walked round to the stables. Chanson checked the horses, their girths and saddles – nothing had been tampered with. They both swung themselves up.

'Get up close!' Ranulf urged. 'Come on, Chanson, you've got two gifts. One is with horses and the other is with knives.'

'But we are leaving first. They'll never catch up.'

'I wager they've already gone,' Ranulf declared. 'Do you remember how that trackway snakes and curves – they'll be waiting there.'

They left the tavern. Chanson looked longingly over his shoulder at its warmth and light. The day was dying. Mist curled out from the trees. The trackway stretched before them like some haunted path.

'Couldn't we gallop?' Chanson whispered.

'And risk an accident? Haven't you heard of tricks such as a rope tied across the path? Say your prayers, Chanson.'

Ranulf loosed the sword in its scabbard and, for the first time that day, Ranulf-atte-Newgate truly prayed.

'Oh Lord, look after Ranulf-atte-Newgate, as Ranulf-atte-Newgate would look after you, if he was God and you were Ranulf-atte-Newgate.'

He urged his horse slightly forward of Chanson's. The groom was now truly frightened. The trees on either side of the trackway stood like ghostly sentinels wrapped in a mist which shifted to show the darkness beyond. Now and again faint rustling echoed from the undergrowth or the lonely call of a bird shattered the silence. Chanson drew a throwing dagger from his belt and pushed it into the leather strap round his right wrist. They turned a bend. Ranulf almost sighed with relief. Five shadows stood across the path, arrows notched to their bows. He'd expected some sudden rush but the attackers were waiting.

'Don't rein in!' Ranulf whispered. 'Keep the same pace.'

Chanson obeyed. They continued, the silence broken by the clopping of the horses' hooves. The line of men across the path wavered. Ranulf smiled grimly, the oldest trick in the book. Their attackers had expected them to stop within bowshot, even to dismount. Ranulf urged his horse on.

'Stop where you are!' a voice rang out.

'Continue!' Ranulf whispered.

Chanson obeyed, only reining in when an arrow whipped over his head.

'What is it you want?'

Ranulf stood up in the stirrups and looked from left to right. Good, he couldn't see anyone in the trees on either side.

'Your horses, your weapons, your money and then you can go back to the abbey in your shifts!'

Ranulf's hand fell to the hilt of his sword, head down as if he was considering the request.

'Now, Chanson!'

Ranulf dug his spurs in. The horse leapt forward and Ranulf's sword came slithering out of its scabbard. Chanson grasped his throwing dagger. Their attackers had relaxed, and lowered their bows. By the time they realised their mistake it was too late. The two horsemen hit them. Chanson threw his dagger. One of the attackers took it full in the mouth. Ranulf, with a scything cut, hit another on the shoulder and turned just in time to deliver a second blow to the attacker on his right. Chanson was eager to continue the gallop but Ranulf turned his horse and went charging back. Only one bowman remained, the other had fled into the forest. Ranulf used his horse and the man went down under its pounding hooves. Ranulf turned, patting his horse, whispering reassuringly to it. Four bodies lay on the trackway. He dismounted and drew his dagger. Two were already dead. He cut the throats of the wounded men, ignoring Chanson's horrified gasps.

'Well, what am I supposed to do?' Ranulf crouched down and wiped the blood off his dagger on the jerkin of one of the attackers. 'Their wounds are grievous, it's freezing cold and, if we took them back to the abbey, what's the use of tending them? They attacked the King's men, that's treason! They died quickly.'

He ordered Chanson to collect the weapons but, when he inspected these, he kept only a dagger, throwing the rest into the darkness.

'Let Master Talbot bury them,' he murmured. 'Now, let's see what these men have?'

Ranulf opened their wallets and emptied the contents into his hand. He put the coins in his purse but gave a cry of surprise and held up what he had found against the poor light.

'What is it?' Chanson demanded.

'It's a seal,' Ranulf declared, peering at it. 'The seal of St Martin's-in-the-Marsh. Now, why should an outlaw, a wolf's-head, have a seal like this? It's not valuable. So, it's either a keepsake or . . .'

'Or what?' Chanson demanded.

'Something like a licence or a warrant. You show it to someone, they recognise it and allow you to pass. Or it could be a sign?'

'Are you saying the outlaws do business with the abbey?'

'Possibly,' Ranulf declared. 'Perhaps for a payment they left the brothers alone? Allowed them to come and go unhindered.'

Ranulf got to his feet. He stared down at the stiffening corpses. Deep in the trees an owl hooted. Chanson tried not to shiver: the owl was a harbinger of death.

'It's time we returned,' he said.

They remounted leaving their bloody handiwork behind them. Ranulf felt exhausted after the attack. He had no compunction about the men he had slain. They would have taken his life as quickly, and without thought, like someone snuffing a candle. Moreover, such outlaws did not kill swiftly: they often tortured their victims. Ranulf pulled his cloak tighter around him as the snowflakes began to fall. He reflected on what he had seen at the Lantern-in-the-Woods: Talbot's daughter Blanche, her gold cross on its silver chain, the costly-looking bracelet, the rings. Who in these parts could afford such expensive items? Blanche certainly smelt sweetly. Ranulf recalled the story about a scented woman, disguised in the robe and cowl of a monk, being glimpsed in the abbey grounds at night.

'Come on, Chanson!' he urged.

Ranulf dug in his spurs, urging his horse into a gallop. Chanson was only too eager to follow. Darkness had fallen and the snow was already beginning to lie.

'I wonder if it will continue all night?' Chanson shouted.

'I wonder what old Master Long Face is doing?' Ranulf retorted.

At last the abbey came into sight. Dark massed buildings, with sconce torches flickering on either side of the entrance. A lantern gleamed in the window of the small chamber above the gatehouse. Ranulf reined in. A small postern door opened and a brother hurried out carrying a lantern.

'Who are you?' he called.

'Ranulf-atte-Newgate and Chanson.'

'Very well! Very well!'

The monk disappeared inside. The bar was removed and the door swung open. Ranulf was about to dig his spurs in when the first fire arrow shot out of the darkness and fell, leaving a trail of fiery light, into the abbey grounds.

Corbett sat on a stool before the brazier warming his fingers. Archdeacon Adrian had left his room abruptly. Corbett, once again, had ordered him not to leave the abbey until his investigations were completed. Corbett heard the cries from the courtyard below, and hastily

174

put on boots and cloak and hurried down as a second fire arrow smacked into the cobbles, its flame spluttering out in the icy slush.

'What is it?' Corbett demanded of a lay brother who came hurtling round the corner.

'Oh, thanks be to God, Sir Hugh!' He peered through the darkness. 'It is you?'

'Is the abbey under attack?' Corbett demanded.

'We don't know.'

Corbett stared up at the sky. Two more fire arrows were falling in a blazing arc.

'Tell Prior Cuthbert to take comfort,' Corbett declared. 'They can do little harm. By the time they fall they are spent.'

Corbett watched another score through the night sky: the mysterious archer must be just beyond the walls, moving quickly to give the impression that more than one bowman was loosing these fiery shafts. The lay brother scurried off. There was little Corbett could do and it was now freezing cold, so he went back into the guesthouse. He had hardly reached his chamber when he heard voices downstairs. Ranulf and Chanson came clattering up, spurs jingling noisily.

'It's cold,' Ranulf groaned. 'I didn't know how cold it was until after the attack.'

He and Chanson ripped off their gauntlets and held their fingers out to the flames.

'Don't warm them too long,' Corbett warned. 'You'll have chilblains. What's this about an attack?'

Corbett poured goblets of wine. As they drank, Ranulf quickly told him what had happened at the Lantern-in-the-Woods.

'You did well,' Corbett declared. 'The outlaws deserved their deaths. Let me see the seal!'

Ranulf handed it over. Corbett scrutinised it carefully in the light of a candle.

'And what happened here, Master?'

Corbett told him what he had seen, his meetings with Brother Dunstan and the Archdeacon. Ranulf whistled under his breath.

'Nothing is what it appears to be, eh, Master?'

'It never is,' Corbett replied, still examining the seal.

'What is so interesting about it?'

'As you said,' Corbett tossed the seal back to him, 'why should an outlaw be carrying that? It was not taken from a letter or a charter. The seal is not broken. It was specially made and given to someone to use as a sign. You have your suspicions?'

Ranulf quickly told him about Blanche the tavern wench, the costly necklace, bracelet and rings. Corbett heard him out. He sat half listening to the bells tolling for vespers.

'Do you ever read the divine office, Ranulf? The verse about Satan like a raging lion, hunting, seeking whom he may devour. Our assassin's like that. He's observed the foibles and weaknesses of others. I half suspect that Brother Dunstan could be his next victim.'

'Why?'

'Because he's immoral,' Corbett declared. 'Chanson, go and fetch him. Tell him to come alone. I wish to have words.'

'Do you really think he could be the next victim?' Ranulf asked as the groom clattered down the stairs.

'Ranulf, I believe the assassin intends to kill every member of that Concilium. I don't know why, but I suspect that one of the roots of these present troubles is that damnable guesthouse and Bloody Meadow: the Concilium hid their feelings well but, I suspect, Prior Cuthbert and the rest championed that cause as fiercely as any lawyer before King's Bench.'

'You talked of one root?'

'Ah!' Corbett got up and stretched. 'I'm getting

hungry.' He patted his stomach. 'Not just for food but the truth. There is another deeper root, I don't yet know what. Abbot Stephen may be the key.'

Chanson returned, with Brother Dunstan following dolefully behind.

'Close the door,' Corbett ordered. He gestured to a stool. 'Sit down.'

'Why do you wish to question me?' Brother Dunstan's hands were trembling so much he hid them up his sleeves.

Corbett took a stool and sat opposite.

'You know why I do. When I met you down at Falcon Brook, Brother, you were like a man lost in your sins. What caused it? Guilt? Remorse?'

'We all sin,' Brother Dunstan tried to assert himself.

'Yes, we do but some more secretly than others. I don't want to torture you, Brother, so I'll come swiftly to the point. You are treasurer of this great abbey. You and the brothers send carts to buy provender and sell your produce in the markets. You travel hither and thither. How many times have you been attacked by outlaws?'

'Such men would never attack Holy Mother Church.' Brother Dunstan coloured at Ranulf's bellow of laughter.

'That's a lie,' Corbett replied. 'Such men couldn't give a fig about the Church. You do what many abbeys and monasteries, even manor lords, do. You meet these outlaws, or their leaders, and you provide them with money and supplies. In return they give assurances that you can go untroubled about your business and they'll make sure that everybody else who lurks in the woods obeys. It's a convenient way of living. The outlaws really don't want to take on a powerful abbot who might ask the local sheriff to hunt them down. Moreover some, but not all, of their coven are superstitious. They don't want to be excommunicated, cursed and exiled from heaven by bell, book and candle. You, of course, and your abbey don't want any trouble. You are the treasurer and, when these men come looking for food and drink, you pay them off and both parties are happy. The law might not like it but, there again, on a lonely forest path the law can do little to protect some unfortunate monk on an errand for his Father Abbot. Am I correct?'

'It is a commonplace practice,' Brother Dunstan replied. 'Everyone does it.'

'Of course they do and, as long as the outlaws don't become troublesome, greedy or break their word, Abbot Stephen would look the other way. He might not like it but . . .' Corbett waved a hand. 'Now you, Brother Dunstan,' he continued, 'travel for the abbey and often visit the Lantern-in-the-Woods.'

The treasurer put his face in his hands.

'Blanche is pretty, isn't she? Long legs, generous lips, a sweet bosom and, if Ranulf is correct, saucy eyes and a pert mouth. You were much taken with her. Of course, she was flattered that a man of the Church should be interested. She was even more impressed when you took coins from your coffers to buy her bracelets and a silver chain with a gold cross, not to mention the rings and the cloth to make her a fine dress. Now, what began as mere dalliance,' Corbett felt sorry for the monk who was now sobbing quietly, 'became an obsession. Ranulf has travelled to the Lantern-in-the-Woods, and the outlaws also go there. Oh, by the way, some of them are dead – killed,' Corbett added warningly. 'I suggest that for the next few months any traveller from St Martin's has an armed escort.'

Brother Dunstan took his hands away. 'Dead?'

'Well, at least four of them.' Corbett turned to Ranulf and clicked his fingers. 'Now, in one of the wallets of the dead outlaws we found this abbey seal. It's unbroken, and is clearly specially made. You gave it to one of the outlaws? Perhaps their leader, Scaribrick? You must have bribed him. Sometimes you found it difficult to leave the abbey – after all, a monk out of his house is like a fish out of water – but you had a hunger for Blanche. You gave her the robe of a monk with a canopied cowl, and you actually brought her into the abbey, didn't you? One of the outlaws was your go-between and when he showed the seal to Blanche, it was the sign to meet you near one of the postern gates. Now, in the warm days of spring and summer, a tumble in the long grass is perhaps safe enough but our Blanche is haughty. She would object to such rough bedding. On one or two occasions she came disguised to that postern door and made her way to your chamber. No doubt you objected, telling her how dangerous it was.'

Corbett leaned forward and prised Brother Dunstan's fingers away from his face. The monk's eyes were red-rimmed with crying.

'For God's sake,' Corbett reassured him, 'I am not going to denounce you before the full chapter. You won't be the first man to break his vows. The world, the flesh and the devil, eh? It's often the flesh which lays the most cunning traps.'

The treasurer rubbed the tears away from his cheeks.

'It was as you say,' Brother Dunstan declared. 'The dalliance began two years ago. I was a clerk before I became a monk. I thought I could live a chaste life but – Blanche, she was so provocative! At night I used to dream about her hair, her lips, her breasts, her legs. At first she allowed some intimacy – a kiss or a cuddle – but she acted very much the lady. She wanted this and she wanted that. So I used money from the Abbey coffers. Sometimes we met in the cellars of her father's tavern but that was too dangerous. Blanche is a hussy, saucy-eyed and sharp-tongued. She wanted to see my chamber and lie in a proper bed, she said. I tried to refuse but ... One night she came disguised, as you say, and told me she had met a monk on her way. From her description I recognised Gildas. I begged her not to do it again but she refused to obey and only stopped when I bought her some Castilian soap. I confessed my sins to one of the old monks. He gave me absolution but said I should also confess to Father Abbot. I did, in a half-hearted way.'

'So, Abbot Stephen knew?'

'Yes, yes he did. He warned me that I would have to make reparation. Replace the money I had taken and end my relationship.'

'That was compassionate,' Ranulf interrupted. 'Many a Father Abbot would have shown you the gate.'

'Abbot Stephen said that if I truly repented, I would have to do so properly. He did not wish to disgrace me.' Brother Dunstan held Corbett's gaze. 'I was surprised by Abbot Stephen's compassion. He just stared at me, tears in his eyes.'

'Did he give a reason for his compassion?' Corbett asked.

'He just said we were all sinners and, if there was a God, Compassion was His name.'

'If there was a God?' Corbett queried.

'That's what he said. I don't think he was denying the existence of God, just stating that God's compassion was most important.' The treasurer took a deep breath. 'And you, Sir Hugh, will you tell Prior Cuthbert?'

'I'll do nothing of the sort.' Corbett clapped him on the shoulder and got to his feet. 'I am not your father confessor, nor am I here to judge the morals of the monks. I want to catch a murderer. Brother Dunstan, I want to ask you one question, broken into different parts. On your oath now: the Concilium, it wanted that guesthouse built?'

'Very much so.'

'Why?'

'To attract pilgrims, to increase the revenue.'

'And what other reason?' Corbett demanded.

'To secure a relic so as to increase our fame.'

'And would they have murdered for that?'

Brother Dunstan did not deny it but gazed bleakly back.

*QUI CUPIET METUET QUOQUE*

WITH DESIRE COMES ALSO FEAR

HORACE

# *Chapter 8*

Brother Francis, the archivist, was pleased to have the library to himself. The small scriptorium at the far end was also empty. The rest of the brothers had gone to celebrate divine office before the evening meal. Brother Francis was so excited, and his stomach so agitated, that he had no time for food or drink. He hadn't told anybody the reason but had sought permission from Prior Cuthbert to absent himself. The librarian now sat at a table and stared round his domain. This was his kingdom with its specially hooded candles and lanterns to diminish the risk of fire. He gazed lovingly at the stacked rows of shelves containing the abbey archives, as well as the manuscripts collected over the years: Augustine's *Confessions* and *City of God*: Beothius's *On Consolation*, the sermons of Ambrose, the writings of Jerome and other fathers: the theological treatises of Bernard, Aquinas and Anselm. Brother Francis got up and walked along the shelves. Here were the jewels of the collection: the works of Aristotle and Plato, the speeches of Cicero, the histories of Tacitus and the thoughts of the philosopher Seneca. These had been Abbot Stephen's favourites, with his love of Roman culture. Brother Francis stopped, closed his eyes and sniffed. He relished the smell of the library, as a

185

gardener did the fragrance of flowers: the perfume of vellum, of leather, ink, beeswax and the sweet-smelling polish which his assistants used on the shelves, tables and floor. Brother Francis liked nothing better than to check everything was in its appointed place. Some of the books were so rare and precious that they were locked away in heavy coffers. He touched the ring of keys on his belt and recalled why he was here. His face flushed. Brother Francis had thought long and hard about these deaths, these heinous murders, which hadn't just started because of a guesthouse or Prior Cuthbert's desire to acquire a precious relic.

Of all the members of the Concilium, Brother Francis had served the longest at St Martin's. He had entered the abbey as a mere stripling. The old abbot had been so impressed by his desire to learn he had sent him to the cathedral schools of Ely and Norwich, as well as the Benedictine house in Oxford. Francis stopped and gnawed at his lip. He must marshal his thoughts carefully, as a true scholar would. Above all, he had to be sure he was alone. Brother Francis went to one of the latticed windows and peered through. The fire arrows had been alarming but surely they had merely been some cruel jape? Brother Francis moved back to the lectern. Didn't one of those chronicles which described the evil depredations of Geoffrey Mandeville mention how the wicked earl always signalled his coming by fire arrows? So, if it wasn't his ghost or demon, who was loosing such fiery shafts on St Martin's-in-the-Marsh?

'I mustn't be distracted! I mustn't be distracted!' Brother Francis murmured.

He also had to be prudent. Both doors to the library were locked and bolted, the latticed windows were also secure, their handles pulled down. Brother Francis checked the arrow slit apertures. In summer the shutters on the outside of these would be removed to allow in the light. Now, of course, they were clasped firmly shut. Brother Francis picked up his ash walking-cane and tapped at each to ensure this was the case. He returned to the piece of vellum laid out on his writing desk, excited by its blank, creamy smoothness. He sat down, picked up a quill and wrote down Abbot Stephen's name and three words: 'the Roman way?' Brother Francis stared down at what he had written. The murders, he reflected, had begun with Abbot Stephen's death. What was the tinder spark which had started this conflagration? What did he know about Abbot Stephen? A former knight, the boon companion of Sir Reginald Harcourt? The man who had assisted Lady Margaret to search for her husband only to return and spend the rest of his life as a member of St Martin's community.

'I know I have seen it,' Brother Francis whispered.

He rose to his feet and went to a shelf. Somewhere here, many years ago, he'd found a Book of Hours – or maybe a psalter – which had contained a carefully written poem. Brother Francis had suddenly remembered this earlier in the day and begun his searches whilst the library was still busy. He had used the index but had been unable to trace the exact volume. The brothers had become curious as their librarian took one book down after another. Brother Francis glimpsed one slender volume, pulled it out and caressed the calf-skin cover with its decorative glass studs. He opened the crackling yellow pages only to grimace with disappointment. This was not the one! He found two more and carried them to his desk. He was about to continue his searches when one of the shutters rattled. The librarian absentmindedly cursed the wind and continued with his studies, as the rattling increased. Brother Francis got to his feet and hastened along the gallery to the arrow slit which stood between two latticed windows. Bang! bang! The clatter unnerved him. He grasped his stick, took up a lantern and peered closer. A cold draught of air hit him. Brother Francis put the lantern down on a table and peered through the arrow slit. The shutter had fallen loose. He was about to turn away in annoyance when the arrow, loosed by the bowman outside, sped through the slit and struck deep in his chest. Brother Francis staggered back, clasping the shaft, coughing blood. He slumped to his knees and collapsed onto the hard, wooden floor.

'So, it wasn't just a guesthouse Prior Cuthbert wanted?'

Ranulf stared across at Corbett sitting on the bed, his back against the bolsters.

'Oh, no.' Corbett shook his head.

Brother Dunstan had left Corbett and Ranulf to summarise what they had learnt.

'I walked round the church,' Corbett explained. 'Every great religious house, be it Canterbury, Walsingham, Glastonbury or even the abbey of St Paul's, has its relics. St Martin's has none. People travel across Europe to pay respects to the lance which pierced the side of Christ, a phial of his precious blood or the cloth which wiped his face. Now, Ranulf, you know and I know that most of these relics are spurious, and many others are also growing more discerning.' He smiled. 'The best relic is a corpse. Look at the revenues Canterbury receives because they hold the remains of Thomas à Becket. Prior Cuthbert certainly wants to build his guesthouse but, more importantly, he wanted that tumulus opened and the corpse removed to the abbey church. With a bit of luck, and God's own help, a few miracles would take place. The news would spread through the great trading centres of Lincolnshire, Norfolk, and Ely. Remember our journey to Suffolk?'

Ranulf grimly recalled their departure from their last investigation and the sight of that grisly corpse swinging from a stark black gibbet.

'Those townspeople we visited were rich. When people have wealth, Ranulf, they like to travel: that's one of the reasons Brother Dunstan paid off those outlaws. I wager a tun of wine to a cask of malmesy that he did so at Prior Cuthbert's insistence. You can't have stories circulating about wolf's-heads attacking travellers to St Martin's.'

'But would eagerness for a relic lead to murder?'

'It could do, Ranulf. You are talking about a tremendous increase in wealth and importance for this abbey. Moreover, Prior Cuthbert is a stubborn man: he may have fiercely resented Abbot Stephen's intransigence over Bloody Meadow, so that the dispute assumed monstrous proportions for him.' Corbett spread his hands. 'To be fair to Prior Cuthbert, I can understand his frustration.' Corbett ran his thumb nail along his lower lip. 'What is important is how Abbot Stephen was murdered. We know he had a dispute with his Concilium, led by Prior Cuthbert, and now members of that Concilium are being murdered.'

'Taverner wasn't a member,' Chanson called out from where he sat on a stool near the brazier, mending a belt buckle.

'No, he wasn't,' Corbett smiled in agreement. 'And that, too, is a mystery. So, Ranulf, arm yourself with quill and ink, parchment and writing tray. Let's see what sense we can make of this puzzle.'

Ranulf agreed. Once he had made himself comfortable, Corbett emphasised the points on his fingers.

'Abbot Stephen, the noble scion of the Daubigny family and once a knight banneret, was loved by the King, and the boon companion of Sir Reginald Harcourt. In his early years, Daubigny showed no indication of becoming a priest or monk. He was fighting man *par excellence*. His good friend Reginald Harcourt married the Lady Margaret; it was an arranged betrothal but one that seemed happy enough. However, the relationship between Lady Margaret and Sir Stephen, as he was then called, was frosty to say the least. Apparently Sir Stephen was a constant visitor at the Harcourt Manor.'

'Why should Lady Margaret dislike him?'

'A good question, Ranulf, though I have seen such a reaction before. Perhaps she resented the closeness of the two friends. But it certainly means that Lady Margaret and I must meet.' Corbett paused, watching Ranulf's quill skim over the manuscript. 'In addition, we have Sir Reginald's mysterious disappearance, followed by Lady Margaret's search and the help given by Sir Stephen. But we can't comment on that until we have seen Lady Harcourt herself.'

'Shouldn't we have visited her before?'

Corbett shook his head. 'No, no. She'll just give the accepted story and I am convinced there's more to it than that. So, let's stay with Abbot Stephen. To all intents and purposes, he became the model monk and rose swiftly in the Benedictine Order. Probably due to royal influence he was appointed Abbot. How would you describe him, Ranulf?'

The clerk pulled a face. 'Reserved, aloof? Certainly a man of sanctity. A fair and just abbot.'

'Yet a strange one,' Corbett mused. 'To some extent he appeared very strict, particularly about Sigbert's burial mound in Bloody Meadow. He didn't like Lady Margaret yet his treatment of Dunstan was very compassionate. For some strange reason he became interested in demonology, studying to be an exorcist. He won widespread repute which explains the visit of Taverner and Archdeacon Adrian. Abbot Stephen dealt with ghouls and devils but he also had a great love of the classics, to quote one phrase: 'all things Roman'. He treated that mosaic in the abbey cellars as if it was sacred. He referred mysteriously to a wheel of life and hinted at his own secret sins. An enigmatic character! He not only showed compassion to Dunstan but also to Perditus and Taverner. I do wonder if he saw through our cunning man? He also had to manage a Concilium which had become increasingly impatient over his views on Bloody Meadow and the new guesthouse. And then he was murdered. But how did the assassin get in and out of that chamber? Why didn't Abbot Stephen raise the alarm? How did the murderer know there was a war belt in that chest? Or did Abbot Stephen take it out himself? That's another mystery.'

'And the other murders?' Ranulf asked.

'Taverner was a cunning man, hired by Archdeacon Adrian to disgrace Abbot Stephen. However, Abbot Stephen's charm impressed Taverner who may have turned the tables on our visitor from London. He was killed by an arrow, certainly taken from a quiver belonging to Archdeacon Adrian, but that doesn't mean our self-important ecclesiastic is a murderer. Hamo's death? Well, that is truly perplexing. The assassin was lashing out indiscriminately. He didn't really care who drank from the poisoned tankard. Finally, there are other strange occurrences. The cat hung up from the rood screen; the fire arrows; the brand marks left on the victims. These bring us to Sir Geoffrey Mandeville.' Corbett pointed to the chronicles taken from the library. 'Our assassin certainly knows all about him. The brand mark is taken from Mandeville's livery, as are the cat and the fire arrows. The rest is now clear: the mysterious woman glimpsed walking through the abbey grounds at night was certainly Blanche from the Lantern-in-the-Woods.'

'Couldn't Brother Dunstan have told us more?' Corbett disagreed.

'And the assassin?' Ranulf asked.

'Is there one or are there two?' Corbett wondered.

'What do you mean?'

'Well, Abbot Stephen's head wasn't branded, was it? And Taverner wasn't a member of the Concilium?'

'You have forgotten about Gildas?'

'No, no, I haven't. Gildas was certainly murdered in his workshop, his forehead branded and the corpse taken out to the burial mound. Somehow or other we are back to Bloody Meadow, and the rivalry between Abbot Stephen and the Concilium. But all we do is keep going round and round like a dog chasing its tail.'

'Why don't we open the burial mound?' Chanson demanded.

'Perhaps we will,' Corbett declared. 'But we have to show we have good reason. I just wish—' He tapped his fingers on his knee. 'Pieces of the puzzle are missing, Ranulf. I wish I could find them.' He sighed. 'So now we come to the assassin.' He pulled a face. 'It could be anybody. Taverner killed by an arrow. Hamo by poison. Gildas by a stone. You have seen this abbey, Ranulf – think of it as a maze of alleyways in London. I know,' Corbett swung his feet off the bed, 'let's go and look at that mosaic again.'

Chanson and Ranulf grumbled but Corbett insisted. 'It's dark,' Ranulf declared. 'It will be pitch black down there.'

'We can carry torches. Come on!'

They put on boots and cloaks and Corbett strapped on his war belt. They went down the stairs into the courtyard. The snow was now falling heavily, carpeting the yard. From around the abbey rose different sounds: a horse whinnying in its stables; the shouts of the brothers in the kitchen as they prepared the evening meal. Corbett led Ranulf along the same route that Taverner had shown him. The snow was transforming the abbey, carpeting ledges and cornices. It made St Martin's look even more menacing and grim. A sheet of freezing whiteness muffled their footsteps.

'I'll be glad to be gone from this place,' Ranulf murmured. 'Master, is this really necessary?'

Corbett ignored him. They reached the refectory, its windows full of light as the brothers prepared for their evening meal. They went down the steps. Ranulf found an empty brazier full of sconce torches and lit two. Corbett went first. At night the passageway seemed like a tunnel from the underworld, and Corbett recalled the stories his mother had told him about a strange mythical kingdom which lay beneath the earth. It was freezing cold. Every so often Ranulf stopped to light the sconces. At last they reached the end chamber. Corbett had more torches lit and, removing the covering sheet, crouched down to look at the mosaic.

'Why is it so important?' Ranulf insisted.

'Because it's the only thing,' Corbett lowered the torch, 'out of the ordinary about Abbot Stephen. He came here often to look at it. He frequently sketched this image – I wonder why? There is something very familiar about this mosaic but I can't place it. Can you, Ranulf?'

His servant, on his knees, stared at the hub, the spokes, the rim, the strange decorative figures in each corner.

'What's that?'

Chanson had returned to the steps and was peering back down the passageway. Ranulf sprang to his feet. The cellar was cold but he could sense danger, as in some alleyway in London, where though pitch black and seemingly empty, Ranulf would be aware of the footpad lurking in a doorway or down some needle-thin passage. He also trusted Chanson's sharp ears.

'I did hear something,' Chanson warned. 'The slither of a boot?'

Corbett, now alarmed, joined him. He went up the steps and glanced down the passageway, a place of flickering light and dancing shadows.

'This is foolish,' Ranulf whispered.

Corbett agreed and quietly cursed himself. He had broken the first rule. Nobody knew they were here, and there was no other escape except back along this eerie tunnel beneath the earth.

'It could be a brother?' Chanson's voice did not sound convincing.

'If it was a monk,' Ranulf replied, 'he would have seen our light and he would have declared himself.' He pulled Corbett back down the steps. 'If it's one man,' he hissed, 'then he must be carrying a bow and arrow. Against the light we'd be ideal targets. A good archer, a master bowman, could hit all of us.'

'We might be wrong.' Corbett drew his sword. 'It's my mistake, Ranulf, I'll find out.'

His henchman pulled him back.

'No, I prefer to face an archer than Lady Maeve's rage.' He grinned over his shoulder. 'Anyway, I am more nimble on my feet than you.'

Ranulf drew his sword and went up the steps. To his right lay the open caverns and storerooms. He narrowed his eyes against the gloom. He tensed, ready to spring. He heard a sound. Ranulf didn't wait. He darted back, almost throwing himself down the steps, as the long bow, somewhere down the passageway, twanged. The arrow hummed through the air, smacking the wall above their heads.

'I was right.' Ranulf picked himself up. 'One archer but a good one. If we try to go down that passageway, he'll kill us one by one.'

'We could wait,' Chanson declared. 'There are stores here, someone is bound to come down.'

'That might not be for hours,' Corbett replied. He stared round the cellar and glimpsed the wooden pallets. 'Come on, Ranulf, quickly!' Corbett pointed at them.

'What are we going to do?'

'Have you ever stormed a castle, Ranulf, and seen men take the battering ram up to the main gate?'

'Ah, the mantlet!' Ranulf grasped Chanson's arm.

They pulled the pallet up and turned it round.

'It's about two yards high, Ranulf, narrow enough to go down the passageway. He could aim at our feet,' Corbett warned. 'So, slither it along the floor, and crouch behind it.'

Turning the pallet so the wooden boards were facing outwards, Ranulf and Chanson carried their makeshift shield up the steps. Corbett followed behind. They pushed the pallet along the ground. It left about a few inches on either side but afforded good protection. The bow twanged and arrows hurtled into their makeshift shield. They reached one doorway and Corbett sighed with relief as they managed to push their mantlet through. Two more arrows hit the pallet with such force Ranulf and Chanson had to brace themselves. This was followed by the sound of retreating footsteps. They heard a door bang. Ranulf and Chanson put the pallet to one side, and Corbett ran forward at a half-crouch, sword out, but the passageway was deserted. In one corner lay a long bow and a half-empty quiver of arrows. He raced up the steps, out beside the refectory. There was nothing to see but snow coating the dirty slush. Corbett realised the futility of continuing the pursuit. He waited for his two companions to join him.

'We'll never do that again,' he breathed out.

'My mistake as much as yours.' Ranulf sheathed his sword. 'Who is this killer, Master?'

'A child could have done what he did,' Corbett replied. 'He just watched and waited. We went down into the cellar, and our killer followed. There is only one way out and, if that Chanson hadn't been so sharp-eared, he could have taken care of at least two of us, seriously wounding or slaying.'

Corbett sat on a stone plinth. He heard voices and saw a line of monks moving across to the refectory doorway. Now the attack was over Corbett was frightened. The sweat on his body began to freeze. Chanson was shaking, teeth chattering. Ranulf was white-faced with fury, gnawing his lip, fingers nervously tapping the hilt of his dagger.

'Why?' Chanson stuttered. 'We are not members of the Concilium.'

'No,' Ranulf snarled, 'but we are King's clerks. Certainly if Sir Hugh was killed or wounded, St Martin's-in-the-Marsh would be disgraced. The King, his court and council would withdraw their favour from the monastery.'

'Very good,' Corbett murmured. 'The attack opens a window into our would-be assassin's dark soul. I've found his motive: destruction for the sake of destruction. No one is safe. Come on,' he urged. 'I'm freezing! We'll eat in the refectory.'

They joined the monks who glowered at them from underneath their cowls. The refectory was a long hall, with great beams high above their heads. From these hung banners depicting the five wounds of Christ, the cross and an image of the Virgin and Child. As in many refectories, for the sake of cleanliness no rushes cluttered the floor. The wooden wall panelling was highly polished and the trestle tables along each side were covered with snow-white drapes. Halfway down the hall a log fire roared in a great hearth. Herb-scented braziers stood along the walls and in corners. Perditus, just inside the doorway, greeted them and came striding across.

'Where have you been, Sir Hugh? I went to the guestroom to seek you. Prior Cuthbert would like you to join him at the high table.' The lay brother studied him curiously. 'Sir Hugh, is everything all right?'

'Yes, yes.' Corbett waved him forward.

They walked selfconsciously up the hall. Prior Cuthbert and the rest of the Concilium greeted them, and the Prior indicated that Corbett should sit on his right. The clerk glanced quickly around. Brother Dunstan looked fearful. Brother Richard the almoner smiled welcomingly enough whilst Aelfric stood looking like a prophet of old, face drawn, constantly rubbing his hands together. Corbett stared down the refectory. This was no longer a place of harmony, of prayer, worship and work. The atmosphere was of palpable fear. The brothers kept looking up at the dais, glowering at these royal clerks who'd brought so much disruption to their abbey. The muttering grew so loud, Prior Cuthbert picked up a handbell and rang it vigorously for silence. He raised his hand.

'*Benedicite Domine* . . .'

Grace was said. They took their seats. Brother Richard went up to the lectern and, opening the book, read from St Augustine's Sermon on the Resurrection. After he had finished, Prior Cuthbert rang the bell and got to his feet.

'Since,' his voice was tinged with sarcasm, 'we have such distinguished guests amongst us, the rule of silence will be suspended. The community may talk.'

The meal began. Brother Perditus served the high table with fish soup, succulent pork roasted in mustard and pepper, small white loaves and dishes of vegetables. Corbett was offered a choice of wine. Ranulf and Chanson ate as if there was no tomorrow, nodding vigorously at Brother Richard's questions. Prior Cuthbert waited until the courses had been served and then turned to Corbett.

'I understand that your henchmen were attacked by outlaws in the forest today. Has anything else occurred during your investigation?'

Corbett winked quickly at Brother Dunstan.

'No, Father Prior, just one mystery after another.'

'Such as?'

'Not now.' Corbett sipped from his wine. 'But you are pleased the outlaws are dead?'

'Four less to feed,' Prior Cuthbert murmured. 'Even as a monk, Sir Hugh, sometimes you have to sit down and sup with the devil. Your henchman Ranulf-atte-Newgate,' the monk gestured with his head, 'is truly a man of war.'

'He'd make a good Hospitaller or Templar,' Corbett agreed. 'The outlaws were stupid. I would not challenge a man like Ranulf-atte-Newgate.' He glanced sideways and grinned. 'Sometimes he even frightens me.'

'Are you frightened now?' Brother Dunstan asked from where he sat on Corbett's left.

'I'm always fearful, Brother.' He paused. 'Did your Father Abbot fear demons? What persuaded him to become an exorcist and take such an interest in demonology. After all, he was a member of this community, and grew old alongside you.'

'Stephen was always a scholar,' Brother Dunstan replied. 'Theology and philosophy were the fields he furrowed.' He gestured with his spoon. 'You know how it is? Some scholars become interested in the cult of the Virgin or the finer points of philosophy. Stephen chose to specialise in demonology, the power of the night.'

'And in all things Roman?' Corbett added.

'Ah!' Brother Dunstan popped a piece of bread into

his mouth and chewed it slowly. 'That's because of our library; it holds many precious manuscripts. Abbot Stephen used to sit here and regale us with stories of the ancients and the doings of the mad emperors. His great ambition was to visit the Scottish march and inspect the great wall the Romans built. He discussed the classics and the ancient empire of Rome with anyone who would listen. I remember, early in the summer, he and his manservant Perditus in heated discussion over a manuscript on the Roman army. Who was the author? Veg . . .?'

'Vegetius,' Corbett declared. 'He wrote a famous tract *De Re Militari*: a treatise well loved by our King. Oh, by the way,' Corbett looked round, 'where is Brother Francis the librarian?'

'He asked to be excused,' Prior Cuthbert explained. 'He's in the library working, quite excited about something.'

Corbett put down his horn spoon.

'Is anything wrong, Sir Hugh?'

'Is he by himself?'

'Of course.'

'He shouldn't be.' Corbett recalled that dark figure in the passageway, those death-bearing arrows thudding into the darkness.

'He'll be safe,' Brother Dunstan declared.

Corbett half rose to his feet.

'Chanson! Find Perditus! Go to the library!'

'It's not necessary,' Brother Dunstan stuttered.

Corbett sat down. All conversation at the high table died.

'He should not be alone,' Corbett urged. He snapped his fingers at Chanson who was staring lovingly at his soup. 'Don't worry, Chanson, Ranulf won't eat it.'

The groom scurried off into the kitchens for Perditus. Corbett continued eating, half listening to Prior

Cuthbert's protestations. A short while passed and Perditus came hurrying back.

'Prior Cuthbert, you'd best come!'

'What is it?' Corbett glanced at the lay brother.

'We can see lights in the library but the doors and windows are locked. Brother Francis does not reply.'

'Oh, sweet Lord!' Prior Cuthbert whispered. He threw his napkin down. 'Francis would never leave candles glowing in the library.'

The meal ended in confusion. Corbett followed Chanson and Perditus, with Ranulf hastening behind. They reached the library door. Ranulf told them to stand aside and banged with the pommel of his sword. Brother Richard, who had been peering through a window, hurried over, white-faced.

'I am not sure,' he said, 'as the glass is rather thick but I think Francis is lying on the floor. I glimpsed his leg and sandalled foot from behind the table.'

Corbett ordered Perditus to find a heavy log.

'No, use that bench!' Prior Cuthbert pointed to one just inside the porchway.

The door was of thick, solid oak. Corbett told them to hammer on the other side of the lock, loosening the leather hinges. At last the door gave way with a crash and they stumbled in. Corbett ordered them to stay back. The library was a rich, splendid chamber, a place of study. Now all this was shattered. Brother Francis lay in a widening pool of his own blood, slightly turned to one side, a long arrow shaft buried deep in his chest. Corbett felt his neck; there was no blood pulse whilst his skin was a clammy cold.

'Stay back!' Corbett shouted.

He went across to the writing table, picked up the pieces of vellum and read Abbot Stephen's name and the phrase 'the Roman way'. He studied the two books lying there, small, thin volumes. He closed them and hastily put them inside his jerkin.

'You can come forward,' he called.

The monks clustered round Brother Francis's body amidst exclamations of grief echoing Prior Cuthbert's low moan of despair. Brother Dunstan the treasurer was the first to recover his wits. He sent Perditus for the holy oils and quickly administered the sacrament of Extreme Unction, whispering the hallowed words into the dead man's ear. Other members of the community arrived but Prior Cuthbert ordered them to stay outside.

'Take the body to the death house!' Corbett declared. 'This time, Brother Aelfric, put a guard on the door. Let's see if the killer tries to claim this corpse.'

'How was it done?' Ranulf demanded. 'Sir Hugh, I've checked the door – it was locked and bolted and the windows were all closed.'

Corbett glanced back to where the corpse had been found. He went and checked but Ranulf was right, the windows were closed and the outside shutter of the nearest arrow slit looked secure.

'Prior Cuthbert, excuse me.'

He gestured at Ranulf and Chanson to follow him outside. Corbett found the shutter covering the arrow slit: it was clasped securely against the ragstone wall. Chanson went back to fetch a lantern. Corbett inspected the shutter carefully. He loosened its clasps, and as he did so, it rattled and he heard exclamations from inside the library.

'I see how it was done,' Ranulf declared, peering through. 'The librarian was studying inside. The assassin distracted him by rattling the shutter: Brother Francis would come to check. He'd be standing in the light, providing even a novice bowman with a good target. The shaft was loosed. Brother Francis collapsed. The shutter was re-clasped and the assassin came to hunt us down in the cellars.'

'But surely Brother Francis had been warned not to be alone?'

'Yes, he was, Chanson, that's what intrigues me.' Corbett patted the books beneath his doublet. 'He was definitely excited, immersed in his studies. So much so that he neglected food and drink and didn't join the rest of the community in the refectory. Now, why should a monk, in the depths of winter, study so late? Was he looking for something? Some evidence regarding these murders?'

'Sir Hugh, what can be done?' Prior Cuthbert came through the darkness towards them.

'I've told you already,' Corbett urged. 'Members of the Concilium must not, where possible, be by themselves for long periods of time.'

'But we have our own chambers, and our duties to perform!'

'Then be prudent,' Corbett urged. 'Warn them about being ambushed. Oh, and by the way, I'd have all bows and arrows in the cellars collected up, put in one place and secured.'

'And where's Archdeacon Adrian?' Ranulf demanded.

'He refused my invitation to the refectory.' Prior Cuthbert shook his head. 'Perditus said he was in a terrible temper, declaring that he would keep to his own chamber and dine by himself.'

'As we shall too,' Corbett declared. 'Prior Cuthbert, tell your monks to finish their meal. My companions and I will return to the guesthouse. We will eat whatever you send across.'

Once they were back, Chanson lit candles and oil lamps and fired the brazier. Ranulf secured the doors and windows.

'Why?' Ranulf demanded. 'Why slay a librarian? An archivist?'

Corbett sat on the bed and took the books out of his jerkin.

'For the same reason he attacked us, Ranulf.' He smiled grimly. 'To give the assassin his due, he warned me not to stay. If royal emissaries were driven out of an abbey, the King would not be pleased but, because we tarried, he struck. The same is true of poor Brother Francis. Think of a fox stalking chickens, Ranulf; that's what our killer has become. I doubt if he knew Brother Francis was searching for something but he did learn that he was by himself.'

Corbett paused at a knock on the door. Perditus came through bearing a tray of steaming food which he placed on the table.

'What is Father Prior planning?' Ranulf asked.

The lay brother made sure the tray was carefully laid and shrugged.

'I have told him he should send to the sheriff for armed retainers. But,' he sighed, 'that will take days. What we need are spearmen and archers to patrol the passageways. Guards on the trackways outside. I've told Father Prior that more braziers should be lit. There are high places in this abbey where sentinels could be positioned but . . . I am only a lay brother—'

Corbett glanced up. 'Have you taken solemn vows, Perditus?'

'No, just simple ones. I could, if I wished, leave this place.'

'And will you?'

Perditus shook his head. 'I love St Martin's and the community here is good to me.'

'And the killer?' Corbett asked.

'Oh, he is undoubtedly a member of this community.'

'Or Archdeacon Adrian?'

'True,' Perditus agreed. 'He does not like St Martin's-in-the-Marsh. But, I must rejoin my brothers.'

Corbett excused him and opened the first book. He quickly thumbed through the yellowing, crackling papers: it was nothing more than a copy of an Anglo-Saxon chronicle, carefully transcribed by some long-dead monk. The loose pages at either end contained nothing remarkable. The second book was more interesting: it contained extracts of the Latin poet Ovid's great work *On the Art of Loving*. Corbett smiled at some of the verses. In his youth he had seen such poetry in the libraries of Oxford and, in his courting of Lady Maeve, had even used some of the famous verses. The pages at the end allowed scholars to write their own thoughts. Corbett recognised Abbot Stephen's hand in some simple verses of regret. He cleared his throat and studied it more carefully.

'What is it, Master?'

' "In youth I served my time" '

Corbett began.

' "In kissing and making love.
　　Now that I must retreat,
　　I feel my heart breaking.
　　Ah God, it is your food today
　　That feeds me, not kisses." '

'Who wrote that?' Ranulf demanded.

'Abbot Stephen did as a young monk.'

'You can recognise his hand so well?'

Corbett smiled, turned the book and tapped the foot of the page. Ranulf peered at the drawing.

'It's the wheel!' Ranulf exclaimed. 'Look, the hubs, spokes, and rim! It's like the mosaic down in the cellar. Why should Abbot Stephen have written that?'

'A monk besotted by love, Ranulf. As Brother

Dunstan is now, Abbot Stephen in his time was no better. I wonder—?' Corbett weighed the book in his hands.

'Do you want some food?' Chanson called out.

'Of course he does!' Ranulf snapped.

Chanson placed a strip of pork on a trauncher, cut up the bread and served it. Corbett balanced it on his lap.

'Before I left the King,' Corbett paused as if distracted, 'ah, yes, His Grace informed me that there were many theories as to why Stephen Daubigny entered a religious order. One of the most popular was that he fell in love with a young woman who became a nun and died rather young. Now the King said he had little proof of this except for an incident one day when he visited Abbot Stephen here in St Martin's. Now you know our noble King likes nothing better than teasing a churchman, especially when he's in his cups. The Queen was present with her beautiful ladies-in-waiting,' Corbett winked at Ranulf, 'who are always smiling at you. "Stephen", the King declared. "Are you not distracted by beauty such as this?" The abbot replied that he was but he had his calling and they had theirs. His Grace laughed. "Have you ever loved, Stephen?". The abbot grew sad. "Once, my lord, I did but the rose withered in a cold hard frost." "Dead?" the King asked. "Oh yes," Abbot Stephen replied. "And gone to God".'

Ranulf listened with interest. He wished he had met Abbot Stephen, who seemed to have been a man after his own heart. Deep down Ranulf nursed great ambition. He wanted to be like Abbot Stephen: a warrior, a poet, a lover of fine things and beautiful women.

'Ranulf, what's the matter?'

'Sorry, Master, just distracted.'

'Aye.' Corbett put the books down and picked up a piece of pork with his fingers. 'Do you know, Ranulf, I suspect Abbot Stephen was distracted all his life. At first I thought it was by demons or all things Roman. Now, I'm beginning to believe it may have been by love.'

*SEMPER IN ABSENTES*
*FELICIOR AESTUS AMANTES*

PASSION IS ALWAYS STRONGER
FOR ABSENT LOVERS

PROPERTIUS

# *Chapter 9*

Corbett led Ranulf and Chanson out of the line of trees which fringed the trackway to Harcourt Manor. Snow had fallen heavily during the night, blanketing everything in its white stillness. It lay heavy on ledges and cornices, swept up deep against the wall of this great timber and stone mansion. Harcourt Manor was well situated on the brow of a gently sloping hill, surrounded by its own demesne. Corbett had passed barns and granges, seen labourers out in the fields doing what they could in such inclement weather. A line of hunters had greeted them, the corpses of rabbits and other game slung from a pole. Corbett now studied Harcourt Manor: the old house had probably been destroyed and replaced with this three-storeyed building of grey ragstone, red-tiled roof and large windows, some of them filled with coloured glass. The stonemasons had added gargoyles and statues, and it was a place of obvious wealth and power. The manor was approached by sweeping stone steps which led up to double oaken doors. One of these was now pulled apart, as grooms and ostlers hurried round to take their horses. Corbett glimpsed a lady with a white wimple on her head, dressed in a dark-blue dress with a silver belt round her waist.
'My name is Pendler.'

A small, red-faced man bustled up, cowl pulled tightly over his head to protect his ears from the cold. He looked Corbett over from head to toe. He could tell this visitor was important.

'I know who they are.' The woman's voice cut clean through the air. 'The King's emissaries are always welcome. Sir Hugh . . .'

Lady Margaret came and stood at the top of the steps. Corbett smiled, his breath hanging heavy in the air. He went up and kissed Lady Margaret's proffered hand. It was soft and warm. She wore mittens against the cold but on one finger he glimpsed a sparkling amethyst ring.

'Very much the courtier.' Lady Margaret grasped his hand and led him forward. 'And your companions, they are welcome too.'

At first glance Corbett considered Lady Margaret beautiful, despite the greying hair peeping from beneath the wimple, the furrows and lines in her creamy-skinned face. Her lips were full and red, her nose slightly pointed, her eyes large, grey and lustrous, amused but watchful.

'You knew I was coming, Lady Margaret?'

'Sir Hugh, everybody in the shire knows you are here with your henchmen Ranulf-atte-Newgate and Chanson the groom. You are at St Martin's-in-the-Marsh? We have heard of the terrible murders there.' Her eyes were no longer amused. She picked up the hem of her skirt. 'You'd best come in.'

She stepped over the lintel and led Corbett into a dark oak-panelled hallway, warm and fragrant-smelling, its light was mirrored in the polished oak walls, the balustrade and newel post on the wide sweeping staircase. Servants hurried up to take Corbett's cloak and war belt, after which Lady Margaret led her visitors into a small parlour. There was a window seat at one end, with the the shutters pulled back. The chamber was dominated by a huge carved hearth where a fire roared gustily. Lady Margaret gestured at a chair in front of this whilst she took the other. A servant led Chanson and Ranulf over to the window seat. A small table was set between Corbett and Lady Margaret. Plates of sweetmeats and sugared almonds were served whilst a scullion brought deep bowled cups of posset. Corbett took a cup and drank. The wine was hot, laced with nutmeg and other herbs: a welcome relief from the chill of his journey from St Martin's. Lady Margaret sipped at hers, sitting back in the chair with her face slightly turned away. You have a great deal to hide, Corbett thought, you are welcoming but secretive. He stared round the chamber: its walls were half-panelled and above hung paintings, a crucifix and richly coloured cloths. Behind him a large Turkey carpet covered most of the floor. On each side of the fireplace were cupboards and, above these, rows of shelves bearing ornaments, statues, a gold crucifix and a triptych. He glanced back at the fire; its warmth made him relax and he stretched out his legs. Corbett was amused by the gargoyles on either side of the fireplace, which had women's faces framed in chainmail and war-like helmets.

'A fanciful notion of Sir Reginald's father,' Lady Margaret observed, following Corbett's gaze. 'The manor house is full of them. He had more than a fair sense of humour.'

She put the goblet on the table and laid the white napkin across her lap, smoothing it out, folding it and unfolding it.

'Well, Sir Hugh, I am sure you aren't here just out of courtesy.' She turned to face him fully. 'There is other business?'

'Your friend Stephen Daubigny is dead.'

'I had no friend called Stephen Daubigny,' she replied quietly.

Lady Margaret stared across at Ranulf and Chanson in the window seat, both pretending to be distracted by something in the garden outside.

'I do regret Abbot Stephen's death.'

'Murder, Madam! Sir Stephen Daubigny was murdered.'

'Are you sure of that?' Lady Margaret refolded her napkin.

'He was found in his chamber with his own dagger thrust through his chest.'

'I am sorry, Sir Hugh – no man should die like that.' Lady Margaret looked away. 'Abbot Stephen was a good man but, to me . . .' She shrugged one shoulder.

'Did you like him?'

'Abbot Stephen was my rival. He laid claim to Falcon Brook, and that tiresome Prior Cuthbert has also hinted that a codicil existed whereby St Martin's could claim more of our land. I informed him that my lawyers would fight such claims tooth and nail in the Court of Chancery.'

'Did you ever meet Abbot Stephen?'

'On occasions, from afar. But no, Sir Hugh, I did not like him and he did not like me.'

'Because he was an abbot who claimed some of your lands? Or because he was Sir Stephen Daubigny?'

'Both.'

Corbett sipped from his wine and deliberately moved his chair to the side to get a better view. Lady Margaret reminded him of some of the noble widows at Edward's court: graceful, comely, charming but with a tart tongue and a will of steel.

'You manage these estates yourself?'

'I have stewards, bailiffs.' She smiled impishly. 'And, above all, lawyers.'

'And you never married again?'

Lady Margaret blinked. 'Oh, Sir Hugh,' she murmured, 'don't play games with me.' She leaned over and patted his hand. 'I met you at court once. We were not introduced so don't be embarrassed that you can't recall my name or face. It was three years ago, on the Feast of the Epiphany, at a Crown-Wearing ceremony. You know how Edward loves such occasions?'

Corbett laughed softly.

'He was there charging about as he always did. Golden-haired Edward,' she added wistfully, 'with a young man's mind and an old man's body. Lord, how he's changed, eh, with his iron-grey hair? I remember him in his youth: he reminded me of a golden leopard.' She smiled. 'A magnificent animal, coiled and ready to spring. Anyway, His Grace did as he always did: he hugged and kissed me. I looked over his shoulder and saw a tall, dark-faced, sad-eyed man dressed like a priest near the door. "Who's that?" I asked the King. "Oh, that's Corbett my hawk." Edward replied. "He'd prefer to fly than bow and peck at court".'

Corbett smiled.

'You don't like the court, Sir Hugh?'

'Sometimes I find it difficult, Madam.' Corbett ignored Ranulf's sharp bark of laughter. 'Everything is shadows with very little substance.'

'You are married?' Lady Margaret asked.

Corbett's smile answered the question.

'As for my remarriage,' she continued, 'I am sure the King told you. Oh, he wanted me to marry this or that person, but I begged him, for the sake of Reginald, to excuse me and he agreed.' She chewed the corner of her lip. 'I also quoted canon law, and you know how our King loves the law. There is no evidence, I pointed out, that Sir Reginald is dead so I may not be a widow.'

'Do you think he is dead, Madam? Do you consider him so?'

'Yes and no. In the harsh light of reason I know he must be, otherwise he would have returned. But, in my heart, never!'

The words came out almost as a shout.

'Madam,' Corbett chose his words carefully, 'I am here to question you on that, as well as to learn all you know about Sir Stephen Daubigny.'

Lady Margaret put her hands on the arms of the chair and rocked herself backwards and forwards.

'It is painful,' Corbett added, 'but hideous murders are occurring at St Martin's. Abbot Stephen's was the first. Now members of the Abbey Concilium are being slain, each hideously branded.' He paused. 'They have died by poison, and by arrow, whilst Brother Gildas, the mason, had his brain crushed with a rock.'

Lady Margaret gasped and closed her eyes. She tried to stop it but she began to tremble. She took a deep breath, opened her eyes and picked up the posset cup, cradling it in her hands.

'Please, Madam, tell me of Sir Stephen?'

'He and Reginald were like brothers. Remember the Book of Proverbs: "Brothers united are as a fortress"? Well, that's how it was. Stephen came from a noble but poor family. His parents died young and Reginald's father took him in, as an act of kindness. So,' she sighed, 'they were raised as brothers. When civil war broke out between Edward and his barons, led by De Montfort, Reginald and Stephen flocked to the royal banner. Edward called them his young lions. They were his men in peace and war, enduring all the hardships and privations of campaign. As you know, on one occasion, Stephen saved the King's life. The war ended and, to the victors, came the spoils. Reginald's estates were extended: he gained meadows and pastures, granges and barns. I own properties in Cornwall, Somerset, South Yorkshire and Kent. Stephen also prospered. He was given rebels' estates in Lincolnshire and Norfolk. They both became knight bannerets, members of the King's Council. They shared Edward's chamber, and were of that select band of knights who were allowed to carry arms in his presence. They loved each other and Edward loved them both: anything they wanted, they could have. My family come from Lincolnshire. The King arranged our marriage. I was only seventeen but when I met Sir Reginald I fell in love. He was kind and gentle, albeit a born warrior. Oh, he could bore you to death with details about the hunt or the virtues of this war horse compared to another, yet he was a good man.'

'And Sir Stephen?'

'Ah yes! The briar in the garden patch, the thorn on the rose.' Lady Margaret took a deep breath. 'I disliked him from the start: hot-eyed, impetuous, slightly mocking. Sir Hugh, I don't think he believed in anything except the King, Sir Reginald and his own sword arm.'

'Anything?' Corbett queried.

'Oh, he'd go to Mass and chat through it, if he didn't fall asleep. Daubigny had little time for priests or religion. He wasn't blasphemous or offensive, just cynical and mocking. Nobody was more surprised than I when he entered St Martin's.'

'And you continued to dislike him?'

'Sir Hugh, sometimes I hated him.' Lady Margaret turned, her face now harsh, eyes narrowed, lips set in a determined line. 'Reginald talked about him continuously and they couldn't bear to be apart for any length of time. Not a Christmas, Easter, Midsummer or Michaelmas passed without Sir Stephen in attendance. Sometimes I felt as if I was married to two not one man.'

'Was he mocking towards you?'

'He wasn't lecherous, just hot-eyed and slightly insolent. I think he resented Reginald's marriage. The years passed. Sir Stephen was still employed on various tasks by the King. When he went away, I fell to my knees and thanked Le Bon Seigneur but he always came back.' Lady Margaret spat the words out.

'And Sir Reginald?'

'We were happy.'

'How many years were you married?'

'Five.'

'And what of Sir Reginald's disappearance?'

'In my heart I have always blamed Daubigny. You have heard, Sir Hugh, about the legend of Arthur and his knights. Well, Reginald loved such tales. He collected the stories, and never turned away a troubadour or a minstrel. Stephen fed him these fancies like a man would his dog. I grew alarmed. Sir Reginald nourished a great dream to go on crusade, and then, with the Turks so successful in Outremer, Sir Reginald considered travelling east to join the Teutonic knights in their war against the heathen along the Eastern March. I was aghast. I begged him not to go. It was the only matter over which we quarrelled, sometimes bitterly.' Lady Margaret sipped the posset cup. 'One midsummer Stephen arrived here. He and Reginald were like two mischievous schoolboys. They put their heads together and began to plan their crusade. First they would hold a tournament, a tourney here at Harcourt Manor in one of our great meadows. Knights from all over the shire were invited. The feasting and celebrations lasted for days. Reginald was a redoubtable jouster, a master of the tournament. He became full of excitement, talking more and more about his crusade. The wine drank in Sir Stephen's company did not help matters. On the last day of the tournament Reginald told me he would definitely be leaving. We quarrelled late that evening. He slept in a different chamber. The next morning he was gone.'

Lady Margaret cradled the wine goblet and stared into the fire, rocking herself backwards and forwards.

'Madam, how did he leave?'

'He took one war horse, a sumpter pony, money, provisions and clothing. He was seen by some of the tenants but Reginald often travelled—'

'They actually saw him?' Corbett interrupted.

'Well, my husband seemed to be in a hurry, and did not even pause to raise his hand but they recognised his horse and his livery. No one could mistake those.'

'He took no groom or manservant?'

'Nobody. At first I thought he was sulking, indulging in some madcap scheme and that he would soon return. A week passed and I grew alarmed. Sir Stephen was still here. He made careful enquiries. The taverner at the Lantern-in-the-Woods had glimpsed my husband, and he'd also been seen at Hunstanton where he had taken ship for Dodrecht. He paid good silver for he took his horse and sumpter pony with him.'

'And Daubigny?'

'I turned on him. I screamed abuse and threats. I told him it was all his fault and that the least he could do was help me. I left stewards in charge of Harcourt and then Sir Stephen and I followed the same route as my husband did. We journeyed to Hunstanton and endured the most vile sea voyage to Dordrecht. At first we met with good news. Sir Stephen went out and spoke to the burgesses and mayor. He brought back a chapman who definitely swore he had seen Sir Reginald and that my husband had declared he was determined to travel to the Eastern March. We followed but could find no trace. Sir Stephen said he could make little sense of it. After three months he left me on the border outside Cologne.'

'Why there?' Corbett asked.

'So far our journey had been relatively easy. However, Daubigny argued that once we entered the wastelands and the deep forests of Eastern Germany, our task would be impossible. He claimed we should stay in Cologne and wait. I refused. We quarrelled and he left. I cursed him as a coward, a varlet, a caitiff but . . .'

'But what?' Corbett asked.

'He had done what he could. He had been an honourable companion and, on reflection, years later, I realised he was correct. I hired a small household and continued my search. I was away a full year and then came home. By then Stephen Daubigny had changed. No longer the knight errant, the fearsome warrior, he had given up sword and shield, taken the vows of a monk and entered St Martin's-in-the-Marsh.'

'And you never met again?'

'I wrote him one letter. I reminded him that he was responsible for my husband's disappearance and that I did not wish to see or hear from him again. He never replied.'

'And Sir Reginald?'

'From the moment he left Harcourt to this very hour, I have neither seen nor heard from him again. Sometimes rumours come in, that he has been glimpsed in one place or another; nothing more than fanciful tales, not worth a farthing of sense. I became a widow. I consider myself such.'

'And Daubigny?'

'Oh, I watched from afar. The King was bemused but Stephen was able. I watched his ascendancy with the help of royal patronage to sub-prior and eventually Father Abbot. Of course we had business dealings, especially after Cuthbert became Prior. Now, Sir Hugh, there's a jackdaw in human flesh. He wanted this and he wanted that. Wasn't Falcon Brook really the property of the abbey? Cuthbert also informed me he was searching for the codicil and I told him he could go hang. Nevertheless, he was insistent. Insults seemed to have as much effect on him as arrows against a shield.' She smiled. 'I listened to his chatter. How the Abbey of St Martin's did not have a relic, about the burial mound, and how Bloody Meadow could be used for the site of a guesthouse.'

'Were you concerned?'

Lady Margaret laughed and turned to face Corbett squarely.

'Concerned, Sir Hugh? There's not a monk under heaven I fear. What do I care if some mouldy bones are placed in a silver casket? As far as I am concerned, they can build a cathedral in Bloody Meadow, provided they do not interfere with my demesne or infringe my seigneurial rights.'

Corbett drained the posset and put the cup back on the table. He paused as he heard shouting outside but Lady Margaret ignored this.

'And you know nothing about these heinous murders?'

'Sir Hugh, I know nothing about St Martin's-in-the-Marsh that you don't, probably less.'

Corbett felt heavy-eyed, sleepy after the wine. He rubbed his eyes. Just for a moment he felt as if he was back in Leighton Manor and wished to God he was. Lady Margaret Harcourt was of implacable will, yet there was something puzzling about what she had said, as if she was describing a dream rather than what actually happened in the past. He studied her face and, although he could not remember meeting her, now, up close, she looked familiar: the shift in her eyes, the way she spoke. Corbett heard Ranulf cough, and he pulled himself up in his chair.

'So, you had nothing to do with Abbot Stephen?'

'Why should I? He was a priest. I am a widow.'

'But the marshes?' Corbett insisted. 'They contain a close community?'

'There are outlaws in the forest.' Lady Margaret smiled. 'That doesn't mean I have to meet them. Oh, by the way, Sir Hugh,' she glanced across at Ranulf, 'I understand your henchmen killed four such men, leaving their bodies like a farmer would rats at the side of a trackway. The news is all over the area. People are pleased, though they hide their smiles behind their fingers. Nevertheless, you should be careful. Oh yes,' she paused, 'the outlaw leader, Scaribrick, claims to be a small tenant farmer. My steward Pendler believes he organises and leads these wolf's-heads. You have been to the Lantern-in-the-Woods?'

'No, but my henchmen have.'

'Well, according to common report,' Lady Margaret seemed more relaxed now they had moved away from the bloody doings at the abbey, 'Scaribrick was at the Lantern-in-the-Woods last night, breathing threats and curses. You killed four of his men, and made the rest look fools; they are bullyboys used to swaggering around, receiving admiring glances from that hot-eyed wench Blanche.'

Corbett hid his unease.

'You seem very well informed, Madam.'

'I am a seigneur in my own right, Sir Hugh. I look after my tenants and they tell me what's going on.'

'You don't have tenants at the Abbey of St Martin's?'

'No, but I do have the Watcher by the Gates, our self-proclaimed hermit. He worked here once, you know. What was his name? Ah yes, Salyiem! He claims to be the descendant of a French lord. He was a minor official, a bailiff or reeve, I forget which. Sir Reginald liked him. Salyiem's wife died of some contagion so he went on his travels. When he returned, I offered him a cottage

and some work, but the sun had turned his wits. He
built that bothy against the abbey wall, with Abbot
Stephen's permission. I don't know what Salyiem really
is. A man of God? A warlock? Or a madcap? He often
comes to our kitchens when, as he says, he tires of the
monks. He gives us all the news. For the last few days
he has been chattering like a magpie.'

'And does he tell you about the mysterious horn-
blower?'

'Ah yes.'

'Have you searched for him?' Corbett demanded.

Lady Margaret shrugged. 'I don't believe, Sir Hugh,
in legends about wood-goblins and sprites. Or that the
demon ghost of Sir Geoffrey Mandeville prowls the
marshes.'

'So, the horn-blower is flesh and blood?'

'Of course! Apparently,' she continued, 'Mandeville
used to have a standard-bearer, a herald, a trumpeter
who always proclaimed his evil lord's arrival in the
area. As you know, Mandeville was killed and his soul
gone to hell. However, Daubigny, when he was a young
knight, rather liked the story. Whenever he approached
Harcourt Manor, he'd stop and bray his hunting horn.'
Her lips compressed in annoyance. 'He used to come at
all hours. Sir Reginald thought it was a great joke. He'd
go to the window and answer, blowing likewise on a
hunting horn.'

'But Sir Stephen's dead and the horn can still be
heard late at night.'

'I know, I have sent out bailiffs but they cannot
discover who it is. One of these days I'll send them
down to the Watcher by the Gates.'

'Do you think it's him?'

'It must be. I know he has a hunting horn. He is
always chattering about what he hears at night. He
loves to agitate the maids with his gossip.'

Corbett silently promised himself a visit to this eccentric hermit.

'The marshes are full of such incidents,' Lady Margaret continued absentmindedly. 'Ghastly stories about demon riders, the howling of beasts from hell. You know about the Corpse Candles?'

Corbett nodded.

'Be wary of them! Scaribrick has been known to use lanterns and lights at night to trick unwary travellers from their paths.'

Corbett sat and watched a log snap and break in the hearth. His conversation with Lady Margaret had provided no light, nothing new, yet he was certain she could tell him more. He felt as if he had entered a dark chamber, with the lights doused, the windows firmly shuttered. He was just stumbling around, feeling his way, tripping and slipping.

Corbett reflected, staring into the fire: Lady Margaret had everything prepared, the story came tripping off her tongue like the lines of some mummery but for what reason? To hide her own grief? To conceal, perhaps, her deep hatred for Abbot Stephen? She showed little grief at his going and no interest in the details of that hideous death: how a man, who once loved her husband, had a dagger thrust deep into his chest.

'Will you stay the day?' Lady Margaret murmured.

'No, my lady. However, I would like to return to the question of Sir Stephen Daubigny. Madam,' Corbett chose his words carefully, 'what of the relationship between Sir Stephen and your husband?'

'What are you implying, clerk?' Lady Margaret lifted her hand deprecatingly. 'I shouldn't really be angry. So many years have passed. But, yes, there were whispers, malicious gossip that the love between them was like that of David and Jonathan in the bible.'

'And was it true?'

'No.' She shook her head. 'Sir Stephen was a lady's man, heart, body and soul. He loved nothing more than a teasing dalliance. It was all part of being a knight errant, a troubadour. Daubigny knew all about the courts of love, the songs and poems from Provence. Moreover, he did fall in love.'

'Yes, I thought he did,' Corbett interrupted. 'I found a book in the abbey library, which had in the back a love poem in Abbot Stephen's hand.'

'A poem, Sir Hugh? Do you recall it?'

Corbett closed his eyes. 'I only read it quickly. Something about: "In my youth I served my time, in kissing and love-making. Now I must retreat, I feel my heart is breaking" . . .'

Lady Margaret leaned forward: try as she might she could not stop her lower lip quivering, tears pricking her eyes.

'So long ago,' she whispered, 'Reginald use to write love poetry to me.' She paused, composing herself. 'Couplets, quatrains, verses and odes.'

'And Daubigny's great love?'

'I know little about her, Sir Hugh. Reginald told me a few of the details, just before he disappeared. She was a young woman from noble family – I think her name was Heloise Argenteuil. Stephen fell deeply in love with her but she did not respond, and would have nothing to do with him.' Lady Margaret stared blankly at the wall above the hearth. 'She forsook the world and entered a convent, I forget which one, but it was an enclosed community which turned Sir Stephen away. I suppose that was another reason for our enmity: whilst Sir Stephen was with me across the seas, Heloise died and was buried in the convent grounds. Perhaps that turned his mind, tipped his wits. He was never the same again.'

'And all things Roman?' Corbett demanded.

'Ah yes.' Lady Margaret touched the white wimple

on her head, re-arranging its drapes and folds. 'Now, that did fascinate Sir Stephen. During the war against de Montfort, Sir Stephen and my husband had to go into hiding. According to one story, they sheltered in a forest, somewhere in the south-west, and stumbled upon the ruins of a Roman house or villa. Stephen never forgot the beautiful mosaics and pictures. After the war, he spent time visiting the Halls of Oxford and Cambridge, the cathedral schools, begging librarians and archivists for the loan of manuscripts on anything Roman.'

'Sir Stephen was a scholar?'

'Yes, both he and Sir Reginald attended Merton Hall in Oxford. When he talked about the ancient times,' she continued, 'I'll be honest, Sir Hugh, he became a different man, no longer the arrogant knight or the witty courtier. Apart from his love for Heloise and his regard for my husband, the only time he showed true feelings were for "all things Roman", which was his favourite expression.'

'And he continued that interest as a monk, the only link with his former life?'

'Sir Hugh,' Lady Margaret put the cup she had been cradling back on the table, 'I welcome you but I find your visit upsetting. Perhaps, if there is nothing more?'

She got to her feet and extended a hand. Corbett grasped it and kissed her fingers. Despite the fire they felt ice cold.

'I am sorry to have troubled you, Madam, but . . .'

'I know, I know,' she retorted, 'if I recall anything, Sir Hugh, I will let you know.'

Ranulf and Chanson got to their feet. Lady Margaret grasped Corbett by the elbow.

'There is one thing. The abbey has another visitor, Archdeacon Adrian Wallasby? I heard of his arrival. He had no love for Abbot Stephen.'

'I know that.' Corbett laughed. 'They were rivals on the field of Academe.'

'They were more than that.'

Corbett stopped, his hand on the latch of the door. 'Madam?'

'Hasn't Archdeacon Adrian told you?' she teased. 'He comes from these parts. He and Daubigny went to the same cathedral school. More than just theological disputation separated them. There was some incident in their youth, hot words which led to blows. Abbot Stephen may have forgotten but I don't think Wallasby did.'

She led Corbett out into the hallway. A steward brought their cloaks and war belts. Lady Margaret asked about what else was happening in the abbey and Corbett replied absentmindedly. They went out onto the steps. A groom brought their horses round. They whinnied and stamped in the ice-cold air, steam and breath rising like small clouds. Corbett stared up at the sky, which was grey and lowering, threatening more snow. A cold wind whipped their faces.

'A safe journey, Sir Hugh.'

Lady Margaret extended her hand. Corbett kissed it again. He was about to go down the steps when a line of ragged men and women came out of the copse of trees which fringed the path down to the main gate. Corbett stared in amazement. There were thirty or forty people in all, leading short, shaggy ponies, their belongings piled high and lashed with ropes. They walked purposefully towards the manor. Pendler the steward came hurrying from the stables behind the house.

'My lady, we have visitors.'

'No, Pendler,' she called merrily back, 'we have guests!'

Corbett stared in astonishment as the motley collection of beggars drew nearer. They were followed by a cart, its wheels shaking and creaking, pulled by a thin-ribbed horse which looked as if it hadn't eaten for days. The beggars were cloaked in a collection of rags, their heads and faces almost muffled. The leader came forward, hands raised, and greeted Lady Margaret. Corbett couldn't decide whether they were travellers or Moon people, gypsies or an intinerant band of travelling mummers.

'My lady, I did not know you were entertaining?'

Lady Margaret smiled and shook her head.

'They look cold,' she murmured. 'They are travellers, Corbett. They have free passage across my demesne. They will be welcome here until the thaw comes. We give them food and drink, tend their horses, and provide them with fresh clothes.'

'An act of great charity, my lady.'

'Not really, Sir Hugh, more of compassion. I know what it is to travel on a hopeless quest and I have more than enough to share with them. Now I must tend to them.'

Corbett took the hint. He went down the steps, grasped the reins of his horse and pulled himself up into the saddle. His companions did likewise. Corbett lifted his hand in salutation, pulled up his cowl and turned his horse. Lady Margaret, however, was already tripping down the steps, eager to greet the travellers. Corbett was almost at the bend leading down to the gateway when he heard his name being called. Pendler the steward came hurrying up, slipping in the snow. He grasped Corbett's stirrup and stared up, eyes watering.

'A message from the Lady Margaret,' he gasped. 'A warning! In their approach to the manor, the travellers saw men in the forest. They are not of this estate. She tells you to be careful!'

Corbett leaned down and patted his hand.

'Thank Lady Margaret, we will take care.' He held

the man's hand. 'Your mistress is kind and charitable. How long has this been going on?'

'Oh, for a number of years. Longer than I can think. My mistress is a saint, Sir Hugh.' He pulled his hand away. 'And there are few of those.'

Corbett stared back towards the manor. Lady Margaret was now in the centre of the travellers. He gathered his reins, lost in thought, and led his companions towards the main gates.

Brother Richard the almoner came out from his Chamber of Accounts and stood in the small bricked courtyard. He stared up at the sky and quietly cursed the prospect of more snow. After the service of divine office, all lay quiet. Despite the chaos and bloody murder, the brothers were trying to adhere to their routine, working in the scriptorium of the cloister, the library or the infirmary. In a way Brother Richard was pleased at the harsh, cold weather. During the winter months visitors to the abbey were rare. He quietly echoed Prior Cuthbert's belief that the sooner the royal clerks went the better. Perhaps the murders would end then? An idle thought.

Brother Richard sighed and closed the door of his chamber. He pulled up his cowl and reluctantly prepared to carry out the task Prior Cuthbert had assigned him. Since poor Gildas's death, no one had entered the stonemason's workshop. Yet a tally had to be made, and accounts drawn up. The almoner slipped through the snow, stopped and cursed. He had forgotten his writing wallet. He returned to his chamber, picked this up from a bench and placed his cowl over his head. He was about to leave when he saw the thick ash cane in the corner. Brother Richard grasped this. It would keep him steady in the snow as well as act as protection against any would-be attacker. Yet who had a quarrel with him? Brother Richard left and made his way carefully across to Gildas's workshop. The almoner was confused. Why were these hideous murders taking place? Who had a grudge against poor Francis the librarian? Or hard-working Gildas? Even Hamo the sub-prior, an officious little man but kindly enough in his own way? And who would have a grudge against him? Richard had been a man-at-arms, an archer who had served in both Wales and Gascony. He really believed he had a call from God and he tried to live the life of a holy monk. True, he thought, as he swung the ash cane, he had his weaknesses. Women, the allure of soft flesh. Well, temptation came and went like a dream in the night. He did like his food, particularly those golden, tasty crusty pies, a delicacy of the abbey kitchens; he also had a weakness for the sweet white flesh of capon and the crackle of highly flavoured pork.

By the time he'd reached the workshop, Brother Richard's mouth was watering. He took a bundle of keys, opened the door and went in. He looked round and felt a lump in his throat. This had been Gildas's kingdom. A cheery, hard-working monk, Gildas had loved to talk about stone and building. Now he was gone, his head brutally smashed in. Brother Richard went slowly round the chamber, touching mallets, hammers, chisels, caressing the piece of stone Gildas had been working on. He went into the office at the far end of the workshop. Gildas's manuscripts lay open on the table, all covered in intricate drawings, and calculations. There was even a tankard on the table, half full of stale ale. Brother Richard sighed and sat down. He put his writing bag on the floor and began to pull the manuscripts towards him. He tried to make sense of them but he felt uneasy. He went back into the workshop. He felt a draught of cold air and realised he had left the door unlocked.

'No, no, I'll leave it,' he whispered. If anything happened he might wish to get out quickly. He didn't want to die trapped like Brother Francis. The almoner walked round. He still felt uncomfortable as if he was intruding. He glimpsed a shiny brass vase high on the shelf. He smiled. In summer Gildas always took this out and filled it with flowers. The almoner went across and took it down, holding it up, turning it to catch the light. As he did so, he glimpsed a shadow in the reflection. He turned quickly and gaped in terror. Murder had slunk in like a poacher; the awesome figure before him was dressed in the grey robe of a Benedictine but his face was covered by a red leather mask. Black gauntleted hands held a dagger in one and a club in the other. The assassin lurched forward, knife snaking out. Brother Richard, grasping the brass vase, struck out wildly and parried the blow. The assailant stepped back. Brother Richard realised he was wearing soft leather boots. The almoner tried to control his panic, recalling his days as a soldier. He couldn't really see the man's eyes but the vase he grasped had saved his life. If he hadn't turned in that second of time ... Again the assailant came at him but Brother Richard composed himself. He used the vase as a war club: steel and brass clanged together shattering the silence. The red-masked attacker tried once more – a parry, a feint. Brother Richard, torn between fear and courage, lashed back. The attacker drew off. He came dancing forward. Brother Richard gave a loud shout, stepped away and stumbled. He expected his assailant to take full advantage. He twisted round, only to see his red-masked attacker flee towards the door.

*PRIMA EST HAEC ULTIO, QUOD SE*
*IUDICE NEMO NOCENS ABSOLVITUR*

THE GREATEST PUNISHMENT FOR THE GUILTY
IS THAT THEY ARE NEVER ACQUITTED IN
THEIR OWN EYES

JUVENAL

# Chapter 10

'Guard us as thou wouldst the apple of thine eye.
Under the shadow of thy wings keep us safe.'

Corbett mouthed the verse from the psalms as they
made their way along the trackway. It was now almost
noon. The ground underfoot was slushy and wet, and
the horses kept slipping. On either side stretched snow-
filled fields, white empty expanses, their eerie silence,
which so unnerved Ranulf, broken only by the sharp
cawing of circling crows and rooks. Chanson rode
slightly behind Corbett, with Ranulf a little distance
ahead. Corbett tried to hide his unease. They were in
open countryside, with hedges on either side broken
now and again by wide gaps, cut through for drovers
and shepherds. The warning about Scaribrick and his
outlaws had slightly unnerved Corbett. He'd thought of
returning and asking Lady Margaret for an escort but
that would be unfair. Manor tenants and officials were
not soldiers. They would be reluctant to take up arms
against men with whom they were compelled to live.
He could tell by the way Ranulf sat rigid in his saddle
that his henchman was also highly wary. Ahead of them
rose a dark mass of trees on either side of the path.
Corbett made sure his sword slipped easily in and out

of its scabbard. Without warning Ranulf broke into a trot, only to rein in and jump down; he raised his horse's left hind leg to check on the hoof.

'Don't be startled,' he hissed, not looking up. 'Get down and join me.'

Corbett and Chanson obeyed. Ranulf's green eyes gleamed at the prospect of a fight.

'They are waiting up ahead,' he said, 'within the trees.'

'How do you know?' Corbett demanded. 'There was no flurry of birds?'

'It's not the birds,' Ranulf retorted. 'There's a tree, covered in snow, across the trackway. No, Chanson, don't look. Pretend something's wrong with my horse.'

The groom obeyed.

'You saw it?' Corbett asked.

'I glimpsed it. The trackway dips then rises. It's on top of the rise.'

'It could be the work of the assassin from St Martin's.' Chanson murmured.

'Don't be stupid!' Ranulf let his horse's leg fall and patted its neck. 'It wasn't there when we came by and it takes more than one man to fell a tree and drag it out. There's been no fresh snowfall, so where did the snow on top come from? I didn't actually see the trunk, just the branches to one side. Well, Master, what do you recommend?'

'We could go back and seek help but I am not sure what assistance could be given. We could try and find another route but we might become lost and the outlaws would certainly pursue us.' Corbett steadied his voice. 'What I recommend, Ranulf, is that we mount and pretend there is something wrong with your horse. We will ride either side of you as if in deep conversation and then, at my word, charge. However, we must break up. Ranulf, you go first, Chanson second, I'll go last. If the obstacle is too high or too dangerous we'll try and go round it: that's up to you to decide.'

Ranulf kept his back turned to the trees.

'We'll probably have to go round it,' he declared. 'Watch your horses' footing. Either way, we are going to have to fight our way through.'

Ranulf eased his own sword and dagger out.

'Chanson, don't show any weapon until you are round the obstacle. If necessary, lash out with your boot. They will be armed with bows and arrows.' Ranulf grasped Chanson's wrist. 'It doesn't make them skilled bowmen, my master of the horse. They are probably used to loosing at a standing target. They will also be cold, their fingers numb. There's no other way – prayer might help.'

They mounted their horses, Ranulf in the centre. Corbett acted as if he was concerned, paying attention to his henchman's horse whilst, at the same time, trying to control the fear and panic which curled his stomach and set his heart beating faster. He glanced up. The shadowy avenue of trees was drawing closer. He could make out the tree trunk which had been cut down, dragged across the path and covered with a powdering of snow. Images, memories of the war in Wales, rose up to haunt him. Dark valleys, hillsides covered in snow, wild tribesmen breaking out of the brooding line of trees. This would be similar. He closed his eyes and said a quick prayer. They were drawing closer. The silence was ominous, broken not even by a bird call. He glanced up again, his heart sank. The tree had been pulled across at an angle: on the right it was too high to jump.

'Ranulf, go for the left,' he murmured, 'but take care of any ditch.'

Ranulf abruptly spurred forward, his horse breaking into a canter, then into a gallop. Chanson followed.

Corbett came next. His world narrowed to an awareness only of the trees on either side and the pounding hooves of their horses. They drew closer. Ranulf abruptly moved to the left. In one leap he cleared the obstacle. Chanson did likewise. Even as he did so, arrows whipped through the air. Corbett followed suit. His horse cleared the fallen tree but landed clumsily: it skittered, iron hooves scrambling on the forest path. Corbett's right foot broke loose from its stirrup. He was thrown sideways and had to fight to regain his balance. His horse reared up, and Corbett was aware of shouts, and cries. He managed to control his mount but it turned abruptly as if it wanted to go back. Men came rushing out of the trees. An arrow flew by Corbett's face. He was aware of a whirl of faces. Someone came from behind but his war horse, now angry, lashed out with its back legs. The man's scream rent the air even as Corbett drew his sword. A hooded face came round his horse's head. Corbett swiped with his sword, slicing the man from eye to chin. Ranulf and Chanson joined the fray. It was a bloody, bitter struggle, with the three horsemen fighting off assailants desperate to claw them out of the saddle. Corbett felt a slight pain in his right thigh and drove the pommel of his sword into a masked outlaw's face. They were moving forward. The horses settled down. Men garbed in brown and green, their faces covered by hideous masks, clustered about. Chanson was hacking clumsily with his sword but, in the thick of the press, he wreaked as much damage as the skilful, silent swordplay of Ranulf, his bloodlust fully roused.

'Ride!' Corbett shouted.

He dug his spurs in. He was aware of Chanson following; Ranulf left last. He followed a man staggering away and, bringing his sword down, cleft him clear through the skull. Then he, like Corbett, galloped low

in the saddle up the forest path, arrows whipping above
them. They rode until they were safe. Corbett reined
in. He was sweat-soaked, his stomach lurching so badly
he felt he was going to be sick. Chanson, head bowed,
was coughing and retching. If it hadn't been for Ranulf
he would have fallen from the saddle. Corbett began to
tremble. It took three attempts before he could sheath
his sword, which seemed to have become part of his
hand. He checked his horse and looked at his leg. He
could see no blood or cut and realised he must have
been struck by a club or the pommel of a sword. The
Clerk of the Green Wax was composed and impassive.
He betrayed no sign of the conflict except the occasional
gasp. However, his face was white, his lips a thin
bloodless line, his green, cat-like eyes full of fury. Once
he made sure Chanson was well, Ranulf dismounted.
He cleaned his sword in the snow, picking up handfuls
to wash spots of blood and gore from his saddle and
harness.

'You did well, Chanson!' he called out.

'Shouldn't we move on?' the groom mumbled. 'They
may pursue us.'

Corbett turned his horse and looked down the forest
path.

'I doubt it,' Ranulf jibed. 'How many do you think
there were, Sir Hugh? About a baker's dozen, eh? Five
at least dropped. They'll be dead by nightfall. Two or
three others suffered wounds. They have had enough
for one day. We took them by surprise.' He laughed
sharply. 'Thought we'd dismount, eh? They'll be scut-
tling like rabbits into the trees. They'll tend their
wounds and slink back to the Lantern-in-the-Woods to
describe what brave warriors they are.'

Corbett half listened. He felt cold and tired, a sleepy
exhaustion which he recognised as the aftermath of
battle.

'Although it's a place of terror,' Chanson spoke up, 'I think we should go back to the abbey. I want some wine, and hot broth, then to lie on my bed and wrap the coverlet round me.'

Ranulf sheathed his sword and leapt into the saddle.

'You seem as fresh as a spring flower,' Corbett teased.

His henchman stared coolly back.

'You enjoyed that, didn't you?' Corbett murmured. He leaned down and patted his horse's sweat-soaked neck.

'I enjoyed dispensing well-deserved justice to those wolf's-heads,' Ranulf declared. 'I glimpsed Scaribrick the leader. He didn't take part in the fight. He was under the trees watching it all.' He gathered up his reins. 'Well, Master, where to now?'

'We'll go back to the abbey but, first, we'll visit the Watcher by the Gates.' Corbett ignored Chanson's groan. 'We have to see him; he could be our assassin, as much as any monk!'

Ranulf turned his horse. 'Then, as the priests say, *Procedamus in Pace* – let us go forward in peace.'

Corbett followed Ranulf. He pulled his cowl back up, tugging his cloak tighter about him. He tried to think of Maeve, his children, the manor of Leighton on a warm summer's day, of feasts and banquets as he tried to control the terrors which still shook him. He had been in many fights. It was always the same, especially with these sinister ambushes: the sudden lunge of knife and sword; the assassin's arrow whipping through the air. He let his body relax. All he was conscious of was the thinning trees giving way to snow-filled fields, the occasional bird call or sudden flurry in the ditches on either side.

'And there it is!' Ranulf shouted.

They had now entered the abbey demesne: the spire of its church soared up against the grey clouds. Corbett could make out the tiled roofs, the broad gables and fretted stonework of the abbey buildings above the grey curtain wall. They passed Bloody Meadow. Corbett reined in and peered through the oak trees at the burial mound in the centre.

'If the living can't help me,' he whispered, 'perhaps the dead will?'

They went on, past the main gateway, following the wall. Ranulf abruptly reined in and pointed to the small wooden straw-thatched bothy, more like a cow byre, built against the wall near one of the postern gates. A black column of smoke rose from the hole in the roof. The ground outside was littered with broken pots, bits of bones and rags.

'Not the cleanest or tidiest of men,' Ranulf laughed. 'But there's our hermit. Sir Hugh, I wish you well.' He turned his horse.

'Where are you going?' Corbett asked sharply.

'I have business of my own,' Ranulf replied.

And, before Corbett could object, he'd spurred his horse along the trackway.

'Where is he going?' Chanson wailed.

Corbett had his suspicions but he kept them to himself. He dismounted and led his horse along the wall. The Watcher came shambling out of his bothy. He stood, legs apart, hands on his hips.

'You are just in time for some food!' he bawled. 'I wondered when you'd come. Bread and meat?'

He darted back in. Corbett glanced at Chanson: some colour had returned to the groom's face.

'Look after the horses!' the clerk ordered.

He followed the Watcher inside. The bothy was cleaner and tidier than he had expected. It was very similar to a poor peasant's cottage: earth-beaten floor, two makeshift windows on either wall, no door but instead a thick leather covering. The vent in the straw roof allowed smoke to escape from the fire built in a circle of stones. Above it was a bubbling iron pot on a makeshift tripod. The place smelt sweet, rather fragrant. In the far corner stood a trestle bed; in the other a large, battered chest, which bore pewter bowls, cups and jugs, all cracked and weathered.

'Aren't you afraid of fire?' Corbett murmured.

'Well, if there was one,' the Watcher was now crouching by the pot stirring it with a wooden ladle, 'I'd flee like a greyhound and come back and build another. The monks are very kind and so is Lady Margaret, as you probably discovered.'

He brought across a rather unsteady three-legged stool, pressing it down against the floor as if he wanted to make it more secure.

'Sit there!'

He took a bowl and filled it, thrusting it into Corbett's hands. There was a similar one for Chanson waiting outside with the horses. Corbett took his hornspoon out and dipped it in. The broth was very good: thick and dark with pieces of succulent meat, vegetables and bread. He even tasted a little salt. He sipped it carefully. The Watcher by the Gates came back, pulling down the leather awning, turning the hut gloomy.

'I have an oil lamp,' he offered.

'Sit down,' Corbett replied. 'You were expecting me, weren't you?'

The Watcher filled a bowl for himself and crouched cross-legged before Corbett, his face almost masked by the tangle of hair, as he slurped noisily on the broth.

'Of course I expected you. You're a clerk, aren't you? You have questions to ask?'

'You were baptised,' Corbett began, 'Salyiem. I understand from the Lady Margaret that you were born in this area and spent your youth on the Harcourt estates.'

The Watcher smacked his lips.

'If Lady Margaret says that, then she's right.'

'Were you there when Sir Stephen and Sir Reginald were friends?'

'Of course, they were comrades-in-arms.'

'And Lady Margaret's marriage was a happy one?'

The Watcher lowered his face and licked the broth from the battered spoon.

'Of course.'

'Were you there the day Sir Reginald disappeared?'

'Of course.' The Watcher lifted his head, his moustache and beard stained with the broth.

'Of course! Of course! Of course!' Corbett mimicked. 'What were your duties at the manor house?'

'I was what you call a reeve, more concerned with the household than the estates.'

'And you remember the day Sir Reginald left?'

'Yes, early in the morning, I helped him saddle his horse. Don't look surprised,' he continued, 'that was my task.'

'And it was definitely Sir Reginald?'

'Who else could it be?'

'And how was his manner? Was he shaved and changed?'

'He loaded the sumpter pony himself, then he left with hardly a word. I did ask him where he was going. "A great adventure, Salyiem," he replied and he was gone. I believe it was a Friday, the feast of St Iraeneus. The rest of the household were asleep because of the tournament. Sir Stephen was agitated, when Sir Reginald didn't return after a few days, and that's when the search began.'

'Were you involved in it?'

'Of course I was. I liked Sir Reginald. He was always very kind to me. He'd promised to make me his squire.'

Quick and easy, Corbett thought. He recalled the

first time he had met the Watcher by the Gates: he had been tense and excited. Corbett almost had to pinch himself. Was this the same man? The Watcher spoke fluently, without pausing to recall or test his memory.

'I even offered,' he chattered on, 'to accompany Sir Stephen and Lady Margaret but they refused.'

'They took no servants?'

'None whatsoever. A few months later Sir Stephen returned.' The Watcher put down his bowl and gesticulated with his hands. 'All changed he was, thinner, harsh-faced, no longer teasing or laughing. He came back to the hall. I couldn't believe it when he announced that he was entering the Abbey of St Martin's. A few months later Lady Margaret returned. She, too, had changed. She put on widow's weeds, and hung black cloths round the hall. I realised life had altered forever: the summer and autumn had gone, a harsh winter had arrived. It wasn't the same after that. Harcourt Manor became the haunt of ghosts. No more jousting or revelry, troubadours or minstrels, jesters or mummers men.'

'So you went wandering?'

'Aye, I went wandering. Across to France, down into Italy. I even visited Rome and took ship to Outremer. I came back a sick man and spent some time at St Bartholomew's Hospital in Smithfield. Then I travelled north. When I arrived here Stephen Daubigny was Prior.' He heard the horses whinny outside and glanced towards the door.

'Chanson will look after them. Continue with your story.'

'He greeted me like a long-lost brother. He allowed me to build this bothy.' The Watcher pointed to the chest. 'He even gave me a letter of permission and so I settled down. I have bread and meat, and the skies to watch. I love this place.'

'Everybody likes you, don't they?' Corbett remarked. 'Abbot Stephen was kind; Lady Margaret the same, though she's compassionate to everyone, isn't she?'

'Always has been.'

'Even before Sir Reginald disappeared?'

The Watcher opened his mouth, a guarded look in his eyes.

'Well, no,' he stumbled over his reply, 'only since her return.'

'And she and Sir Stephen never met again?'

'Never once.'

'But that's strange? They had so much in common yet they never met?' Corbett insisted. 'Never exchanged letters?'

The hermit picked up his bowl.

'I asked Abbot Stephen about that. He said the past was closed, blocked by a steel door. There was no handle, no lock, only death would open it.'

'And Bloody Meadow?' Corbett decided to change the conversation backwards and forwards as quickly as possible.

The Watcher leaned over to fill his bowl but it was only to gain more time.

'What about Bloody Meadow?' he declared. 'It contains a burial mound, oaks on either side, the abbey wall at the top and Falcon Brook at the bottom.'

'You said Abbot Stephen was going to change his mind?'

'Well, yes he was. I told you he passed me one day and I . . .'

'Why should he tell you?'

'I don't know. Sometimes he did talk to me. He was worried about Bloody Meadow.'

'Have you ever tried to dig into the tumulus, the funeral mound?' Corbett asked.

The Watcher shook his head and slurped more broth into his mouth.

'Oh no, that would have been blasphemous. Why?' He became all agitated. 'Has someone tried?'

'Yes, they did.'

The Watcher put the bowl down and shot to his feet, almost doing a dance. 'But that's sacrilege!' he spluttered. 'It's blasphemy!'

'I suspect the person responsible is now dead, murdered.'

'What? What's that? One of the monks?'

'No, Taverner.'

'Ah!' The Watcher sat down on the floor and grabbed his bowl. 'Now, there's a cunning man if there ever was one.'

'What makes you say that?'

'Oh,' the Watcher tapped the side of his nose, 'I can tell a rogue when I see one.'

'Did Abbot Stephen know Taverner was a villain?'

'He may have done but he was very trusting.'

'Was Abbot Stephen worried or agitated in the days before he died?'

'Murdered, Sir Hugh. He was murdered. And, yes, you could see he was very worried but he kept his own counsel. Only that morning, when he talked to me about giving in to the Concilium, he mentioned something about the Romans. I asked him what he meant but I couldn't understand him. He replied it was a quotation from a philosopher called Sen—'

'Seneca.'

'Ah, that's right.' The Watcher cleaned his bowl with his fingers and licked them hungrily. 'I can't remember the quotation.'

Corbett stared at the bubbling pot. This hermit was a strange one. For an outsider he knew a great deal about Abbot Stephen; the clerk could sense a deep respect, even affection for the dead abbot. Why was this? Because of his kindness? Or what had happened years previously?

'Did Abbot Stephen ever talk about Lady Margaret?'

'Never.'

'Or the great love of his life, a young woman called Heloise Argenteuil?'

'Ah, Heloise!' The hermit bit his lower lip.

'Did you ever meet her?'

'No, no, but we knew about Sir Stephen's passion. She entered a convent and died and that was the end of the matter.'

'Do you think Heloise's death turned Abbot Stephen's mind? Led him to become a monk and a priest?'

'Possibly. He never told me.'

Corbett stared at a point beyond the Watcher's head. He recalled the Book of Remembrance he had seen in Abbot Stephen's chamber, really a psalter for the dead: it also included lists of names the Abbot would remember at Mass. This Watcher was one of them – that's right, the name Salyiem had been inscribed! Now Lady Margaret had mentioned the name, Corbett also recalled seeing an entry for Heloise Argenteuil.

'Who was she?'

The Watcher shook his head.

'Sir Hugh, I really don't know. A young noblewoman at one of the manors Stephen visited. She was frail of health, and would have nothing to do with him. She entered a convent and died there whilst Sir Stephen was abroad, searching for Sir Reginald.'

'And the hunting horn?'

'Ah.' The Watcher's face broke into a smile. 'Sir Stephen used to love doing that. Whenever he approached the hall, he'd always blow three long blasts and Reginald would reply. It was based on one of those legends about knights fighting in valleys and calling on each other for help. They loved that sort of thing,' the Watcher added wistfully. 'Pretending to be members of Arthur's Round Table or the Paladins of Charlemagne.'

'Paladins of Charlemagne?' Corbett echoed his words. 'For a reeve you are very well read.'

'When I was a stripling Sir Stephen taught me. In my travels I learnt even more.'

'So you don't believe in ghosts and demon riders? Or that Sir Geoffrey Mandeville rides the marshes with his legion of the damned? That he's the source of our mysterious hunting horn?'

'Strange things happen here, master clerk.'

'No, they don't,' Corbett replied drily. He leaned closer. 'Master Salyiem, humble hermit, Watcher by the Gates, for a man who wants to leave the world you seem very much part of it. You visit the abbey. You talk to Abbot Stephen. You also visit Lady Margaret. Who do you think is blowing that horn at night? It's not some ghost, some courier from the household of hell. Is it you? You do have a hunting horn?'

'Don't be ridiculous!' The Watcher drew away, a stubborn look on his face.

'Or could it be Scaribrick the outlaw? I am the King's officer,' Corbett added quietly. 'I am sure you know Master Scaribrick.' Corbett rubbed his thigh. 'I had the pleasure of meeting him and his merry men on my journey here.'

'I thought you looked dishevelled, mud-flecked.' The Watcher picked up his bowl and cradled it as if it was a toy.

'Yet you never asked me why. Did you know Scaribrick was out on the marshes hunting me? Don't Scaribrick and his merry coven patrol here at night? Do they pay a certain hermit money to stir the muddy waters and spread stories about ghosts and ghouls on the marshes? Is that where Scaribrick meets with his smugglers, those who bring in illicit goods by sea and river? Of course, you have to live with these people. Does Master Scaribrick slip you a few coins to look the other way? To embroider stories to frighten others?'

'I have never done anything wrong. Yes, Sir Hugh, I am a hermit and I travel hither and thither. I try to live at peace with everyone, it's the only way.'

'Did you go searching for Sir Reginald?' Corbett abruptly changed. 'I mean, in your travels abroad, surely you questioned people? After all, an English knight travelling by himself would attract some attention?'

'Oh yes! Oh yes!' the Watcher gabbled. 'In northern France and Germany I heard rumours, whispers, but they came to nothing.'

Corbett glanced down. Outside he could hear Chanson stamping his feet against the cold and the snorting of the horses eager for their warm stables. The clerk was convinced some great mystery lurked here. He was in a maze but, so far, he kept wandering around and around with no path out. The assassin could be this Watcher! He was strong and resourceful enough. He could have weapons hidden away. He could climb the wall into the abbey and wreak terrible damage. One moment he could be the rather wild-eyed hermit, the next a man bent on vengeance for whatever reason. Corbett wondered what Ranulf was doing? He half suspected but, in such matters, Ranulf was his own man with his own keen sense of justice. Ranulf-atte-Newgate never took kindly to being attacked.

'Are you sleeping, master clerk?'

Corbett opened his eyes and raised his head.

'No, master hermit, I am thinking.' He stretched out his arms. 'On the one hand we have the Harcourt estates and the mystery of Sir Reginald. On the other the Abbey of St Martin's and, in between, these eerie, wild marshlands with their copses and woods. I suspect

Mine Host at the 'Lantern-in-the-Woods' doesn't pay full import duties on his wine or other commodities, whilst Scaribrick the outlaw probably resents my interference here.' Corbett lowered his hands. 'But Ranulf will deal with him. What I am trying to unearth are these mysteries of the marsh. The fire arrows. The hunting horn. Are these part of Scaribrick's world? Or are they part of some other mystery?' Corbett got to his feet. 'Master hermit, I will have other questions for you.' He stared down at him. 'They call you the Watcher by the Gates and I suspect you have seen more than you have told me.'

The Watcher held his gaze.

'You will not be travelling far.'

Corbett opened his purse and threw a silver coin into the man's bowl and, lifting the leather awning, went out to join Chanson.

They mounted their horses. Corbett gathered the reins and they followed the wall back along to the main gate. He called out and the gate was opened and they entered the cobbled yard. They had hardly dismounted, Chanson offering to see to the horses, when Brother Richard came hurrying out of a doorway.

'Sir Hugh, you are back! Thank God!'

And in brief, gasping sentences Brother Richard described what had happened earlier in the morning. Corbett took him by the elbow and led him out of the cold. He asked the monk to go through it once again, told him to be careful, then dismissed him. Corbett walked across to the stables and helped Chanson unsaddle the horses and dry them down. Brother Richard, he reflected, was most fortunate. He had been attacked but had escaped death. So, the killer must be in the abbey, and was definitely not an outsider like Scaribrick who, at the time, must have been planning his ambush. Nor was it Lady Margaret, who had been entertaining him at Harcourt Manor. Brother Richard had described the attack vividly.

'A soldier!' Corbett exclaimed.

'What's that, Master?' Chanson asked.

'Brother Richard the almoner was attacked this morning and was able to defend himself, probably because he was a former soldier. But, listening to his account carefully, I would say the same holds time for the attacker.'

'But there are a number of monks here,' Chanson wiped his nose on the cuff of his jerkin, 'according to Ranulf, who once served in the royal levies.'

'Oh, I know that,' Corbett retorted. 'And there's something else. Lady Margaret talked of a young woman called Heloise Argenteuil with whom our Abbot, in a former life, was supposed to be infatuated. The Watcher repeated the same story.'

'And?'

Corbett shook his head. 'I've heard that name before. I know of no Argenteuil, certainly not at court, but the name strikes a chord. Chanson,' he patted his horse's neck, 'see to the horses. I am going down to the library.'

Corbett left the stables.

'Sir Hugh?'

Prior Cuthbert came bustling up, red-eyed and grey-faced with exhaustion.

'You've heard of the attack on Brother Richard?'

'Aye.' Corbett glanced at the gaggle of monks who stood in the doorway behind the Prior. 'Tell your brothers to be careful. I wish to ask you a question.'

He led the Prior out of earshot.

'Does the name Heloise Argenteuil mean anything to you?'

'Ah yes, Abbot Stephen once mentioned her. As a young knight, he supposedly fell deeply in love with her.'

'And you know nothing else?'

'Oh no.'

Now he was out of the shadows the Prior looked even more stricken. Corbett noticed his face was unshaven, and he had dark circles beneath his eyes.

'Father Prior, I believe you have more to tell me.'

'I assure you, Sir Hugh, I have nothing to say.' The Prior flailed his hands.

Corbett realised that Prior Cuthbert was not prepared to talk.

'Is the library locked?'

The Prior tapped the ring of keys on his belt.

'I'll take you there.'

He seemed only too willing to be away from Corbett's watchful gaze, walking in front, gesturing with his hands for the clerk to follow. Corbett did so and was about to walk up beside him when he noticed the dark blotches high on the back of the Prior's robe. The cowl hid the Prior's neck but Corbett was sure that the stains were caused by blood. Had the Prior been whipping himself? What secret sins would compel this proud priest to inflict such a terrible punishment? They reached the library and Prior Cuthbert unlocked the door. He hastened around to light the candles and oil lamps under their steel caps.

'I'll send a lay brother,' he declared. 'When you are finished he'll lock the door behind you.' He rubbed his hands. 'I have yet to appoint a replacement librarian.'

Prior Cuthbert hurried out, slamming the door behind him. Corbett walked round. The sombre bloodstain still marked the floor where the librarian had been killed – a grim reminder of what horrors haunted this abbey. Corbett sat down at the writing desk. What had the hermit said? He had mentioned the Roman philosopher Seneca and the woman, Heloise Argenteuil. Where had Corbett heard her name before? He stared up at the light pouring through one of the coloured stained-glass windows and idly wondered how long it would be before Ranulf-atte-Newgate returned.

Ranulf-atte-Newgate was furious. The senior Clerk in the Chancery of the Green Wax had made a careful study of the law. He and Corbett were royal messengers, and carried the King's writ: they were his Commissioners in these parts. They had not travelled through bleak freezing marshes to become the playthings of outlaws.

'An attack upon a royal clerk,' Corbett often remarked, 'is an attack upon the King himself, a malicious insult to the Crown, which must be answered.'

Corbett, however, could be lax in his interpretation, accepting insults and obstacles that Ranulf never would. Scaribrick had organised that ambush so why should he be allowed to squat in the Lantern-in-the-Woods and boast about his boldness? Ranulf approached the tavern by a circuitous route. He kept away from the well-worn paths but found it difficult to thread his way through the snow-capped trees, the gorse and briar hidden by an icy-white softness. The journey had not improved his temper. On one occasion he had become lost and had been forced to break cover but, at last, he found the route, led by the smoke which he knew came from the tavern hearth.

Ranulf had hobbled his horse deep in the trees opposite the tavern entrance. He now stood watching the main door, cloak about him, cowl pulled over against the icy splashes from the branches above. He'd watched travellers, tinkers and chapmen enter and leave. So far Ranulf had recognised no one. He calculated the time. Scaribrick and his men would probably have come straight here and were probably within. Blanche came out to empty a pot of dirty water and, eventually, Taverner Talbot emerged with a broken stool which he placed by the entrance. Ranulf called his name, stepped out of the trees, pulled back his cowl and gestured. The taverner looked fearfully back at the inn.

'You'd best come,' Ranulf called out softly. 'Master Talbot, I mean you no mischief, at least not for now.'

The taverner closed the tavern door and hastened across. Ranulf gripped him by the shoulder and dragged him into the trees; his drawn dagger pricked Talbot's fleshy neck, forcing his head back.

'What's the matter?' the man wailed. 'I've done no wrong. I heard about the attack on you but I can say nothing to such men. They will have their way.'

'Aye, Master Talbot, and I will have mine. Scaribrick is in there, isn't he?' Ranulf pressed the tip of his dagger more firmly. 'He's there, isn't he?'

Talbot blinked and nodded, swallowing hard, fearful of this hard-eyed clerk and the long, Welsh, stabbing dagger, its cruel tip like a razor under his chin.

'I want to speak to him. Out here now!'

'He won't come out.' The taverner shook his head. 'And, if he does, sir, he'll bring two or three of his companions with him.'

Ranulf withdrew the dagger. The taverner would have backed away but the clerk grasped him by the shoulder, this time the tip of the dagger rested against his protruding belly.

'Very well,' Ranulf ordered. 'Tell Scaribrick that someone wants to meet him.'

'I can't,' the taverner gasped. 'It's all very well for you, sir. You'll leave this area but I live here and do my trade here.'

'In which case—'

Ranulf re-sheathed his dagger, pushed by the taverner and, walking across the trackway, entered the tavern.

Talbot came hurrying behind him, bleating and protesting. As soon as Ranulf entered he threw back his cloak, his hand on the hilt of his sword. He stared around the taproom at the tinkers and chapmen, traders and farmers, but then he found his quarry: a group of men in the far corner. They sat huddled round the table, hoods back, war belts on the floor beside them. They were sharing a jug of ale and a large platter of bread and meat. Ranulf walked slowly across, his gaze held by a cold-faced, thickset man who sat in the corner. Ranulf had only glimpsed him during the ambush but he recognised the face. Scaribrick muttered something to his companions and they turned, hands going for sword and dagger. Ranulf walked closer. Scaribrick's fleshy face was well fed. A bully-boy, Ranulf thought, used to filling his belly and not so quick on his feet.

'Don't touch your weapons!' Ranulf ordered. He opened the wallet on his belt and drew out a document bearing the King's seal. 'I am Ranulf-atte-Newgate, senior clerk in the Chancery of the Green Wax. You,' he pointed to the outlaw leader, 'are Scaribrick. You must consider yourself under arrest. Your list of crimes reads like a litany but, at the top, stands treason!'

'Treason?' Scaribrick half rose. 'Who are you? A madcap?'

Ranulf was pleased that the other outlaws kept their hands well away from their war belts.

'Where are the rest of your weasels?' Ranulf jibed. 'Nice and warm in some cave in the forest? They are all under arrest too and they can hang.'

Ranulf watched Scaribrick's eyes, but the outlaw's gaze had shifted. He looked at the outlaws and saw that Rat-Face wasn't there. Ranulf heard a sound and, whipping out his dagger, turned round. Rat-Face stood behind him, knife in hand, ready to spring. Ranulf struck first. Moving slightly to one side, he thrust his dagger straight into the man's belly, pulling it out and kicking him away. Stools shifted behind him. Ranulf whirled back, drew his sword and stood, feet apart. The outlaws were clumsy, tired and much the worse for drink. The first almost stumbled on to Ranulf's sword. The clerk thrust deep and stepped away, up the tavern until he felt the barrels against his back. The outlaws, ignoring the cries of their wounded companions, now scrabbling on the floor, fanned out with Scaribrick in the centre. The rest of the customers hurriedly moved away, almost clinging to the walls on either side.

'Two down,' Ranulf jibed. 'Like skittles, eh?'

The outlaws were frightened. They were used to secret attack, the sudden ambush, but a fighting man, sword and dagger ready, his back protected, was a different prospect. The screams of the wounded outlaws only unnerved them further. One of the outlaws on the far right stepped away and, ignoring Scaribrick's curses, headed straight for the window. He jumped on a table, pulled back the shutters and was through.

'I'm not here for all of you!' Ranulf smiled. 'Just your leader!'

That was enough. The outlaws broke and fled in many directions. Scaribrick tried to follow but Ranulf blocked his path.

'I killed four of your companions,' Ranulf taunted, 'and we beat you off this morning.' His voice rose. 'By the time I'm finished, you'll be a laughing stock—' He broke off.

Scaribrick, snarling with rage, his sword and dagger out, came rushing forward. Ranulf stepped swiftly to the left. He parried Scaribrick's weapon, forced his arm up and thrust his sword deep into the outlaw's belly.

*QUASI NIX TABESCIT DIES*

THE DAY MELTS AWAY LIKE SNOW

PLAUTUS

# Chapter 11

Corbett sat in the Abbot's chamber, where Perditus had lit a fire and pulled the shutters close. The room was cold as if it had lost its very soul. The clerk gnawed his lip in frustration. His visit to the library had been fruitless. His mind was puzzled, his wits slightly dulled by the journey to Harcourt and that ferocious ambush on the lonely forest trackway. Corbett stared up at a gargoyle carved in the corner of the room: the face of a jester, staring, popping-eyed, mouth gaping to display a swollen tongue.

'If only the stones could talk,' Corbett murmured.

What had happened in this chamber? he wondered. This is where it had all begun. Corbett still nursed deep suspicions that the solution to all these mysteries lay in the very fabric of the abbey: its manuscripts, Bloody Meadow, that haunting, lonely burial mound. Corbett shuffled together the Abbot's papers. He'd ordered them to be kept here and was searching through them again. He sifted them with his fingers and picked up a piece of paper, a draft of a letter to a merchant in Ipswich. At the end was the usual scribbled sketch of a wheel with its hub, spokes and rim. Corbett pulled across the piece of vellum on which he'd copied the Abbot's quotations. The first came from the letter of St Paul, or rather the

Abbot's own interpretation of it: 'For now I see through a glass, darkly: the corpse candle beckons.' The other was a quotation from Seneca: 'Anyone can take away a man's life but no one his death'. Undoubtedly the Abbot had scrawled these words shortly before his death but what did they mean? What was their significance? Why had Abbot Stephen been so fascinated by the symbol of a wheel? Corbett pulled across the psalter and looked down the list of names at the back. He recognised Salyiem, the Watcher by the Gates' real name, and Reginald Harcourt. Others were probably knights the Abbot had served with in his days as a soldier. Finally, that enigmatic name which pricked Corbett's memory and teased his wits, Heloise Argenteuil! Corbett took his quill and wrote down the other interesting scraps: the Abbot's fascination with Rome and 'the Roman way'. What did that mean? Why had he considered changing his mind about Bloody Meadow? What about Brother Dunstan's enigmatic remarks about his abbot's compassion and his attitude towards sin.

A knock on the door roused him from his studies.

'Come in!' Corbett shouted.

Ranulf slipped like a cat into the room. Just from the way he stood, war belt in one hand, cloak in the other, Corbett knew his henchman had been bloodily busy.

'You went searching for Scaribrick, didn't you?' Corbett accused. 'You didn't have my permission. When I returned to Norwich I would have issued warrants for his arrest.'

Ranulf dropped his cloak and sword belt to the floor.

'Aye and he would have hidden like a rabbit in the forest. He'd have waited until the sheriff's men became tired of the hunt and returned to his villainy. You know the law, Sir Hugh! Scaribrick feloniously and traitorously, with malice in his heart, assaulted and tried to murder three royal emissaries, clerks bearing the royal commission. The King would have had him hanged, drawn and quartered.'

'Did the King order this?' Corbett asked wryly.

'No, Master, Lady Maeve did.'

Corbett glanced up in surprise.

'I swore an oath, Sir Hugh, as I do every time we leave, that I will bring you back safely Master, they deserved to die. One day we will have to leave this benighted place, and travel down lonely, snow-frosted lanes. I don't want Scaribrick and the others waiting amongst the trees with bows bent and arrows aimed.'

Corbett glanced down at a scrap of parchment in front of him. According to the law, particularly the statute of Winchester, Ranulf had acted legally and correctly. Malefactors had assaulted them on the King's highway. As they were royal clerks, the law stringently instructed 'all loyal servants of the Crown to hunt such malefactors down and mete out summary execution'. Corbett just wished that justice could have been carried out by the King's Justices of Assize.

'You met him fairly?' he asked.

Ranulf grinned. 'I even asked him to surrender. He refused and compounded his offence by drawing a sword and attacking me.'

'How many?' Corbett murmured.

'Scaribrick and two others, the rest fled. They have learnt a lesson which will last for many a day. I met them in the Lantern-in-the-Woods tavern.' Ranulf shrugged. 'You can imagine the rest.'

Corbett could: Ranulf dancing like a cat, nimble as a monkey, sword and dagger snaking out.

'Ah well!' Corbett pushed away the manuscript.

'I also found something else when I went through Scaribrick's wallet. The coins I will give to the poor but I also discovered this.'

Ranulf came across and threw a greasy scrap of

parchment onto the desk. Corbett picked it up and smoothed it straight. One name was scrawled on it: Archdeacon Adrian Wallasby.

'What is this?' Corbett handed it back. 'Why would an Archdeacon from St Paul's in London be dealing with a marsh outlaw?'

'He is going to flee,' Ranulf declared. 'Brother Dunstan explained how it could be done.'

'Yes, I believe you are correct,' Corbett agreed. 'Our Archdeacon intends to leave sooner than we think. He's persuaded a member of the Concilium to write out his name and, through Brother Dunstan, passed it to Scaribrick for safe passage along the roads. Yet,' Corbett mused, 'would Brother Dunstan really have much to do with him?'

'I have been thinking about that.' Ranulf pulled up a stool. 'Whenever I kill, Master, by sword or dagger, be it on a trackway, in a tavern, or some filthy London alley, memories come back. The way I used to fight when I was a boy, or the time when I was taken and was for the hangman's cart, ready for that hideous jogging down to The Elms at Smithfield. Do you remember?' Ranulf's eyes grew softer. 'You came into Newgate Yard and pulled me out.'

'I remember.'

'Well, it was the same after I met Scaribrick. Truly, Master, I didn't want to kill him, not really.'

Corbett held his gaze.

'Well, perhaps I did,' Ranulf laughed abruptly. 'I couldn't forget how close we were to death this morning. Anyway, Scaribrick's dead. As I rode back, I was thinking about what Taverner had said about my mother and about his disguise as a possessed man.' Ranulf ran his finger round his lips. 'It appeared as if he was frothing at the mouth. Now,' Ranulf scratched his chin, 'in my lawless youth I saw similar tricks in

London. You have to be very careful what you chew, lest you choke or rot your guts.'

'You mean, someone here supplied him with a powder?'

'He wouldn't have arrived with it,' Ranulf declared. 'Abbot Stephen was sharp and keen-witted: he would have had Taverner searched from head to toe.'

'He didn't find those licences bearing Wallasby's name?'

'Ah no,' Ranulf gestured with his hand, 'but they could be explained away. Abbot Stephen was really looking for the usual tricks; paints and dyes, powders, to change the colour of the face.'

'Or to make a man froth at the mouth?' Corbett added.

'Taverner wasn't skilled in physic,' Ranulf continued, 'so he must have obtained the powder from someone in St Martin's which, logically, brings us to the infirmarian Aelfric.'

Corbett sat back in the chair.

'Ranulf, if you're correct, some of these monks were plotting against Abbot Stephen. Wallasby was at the root of it. He disliked Abbot Stephen and concocted a plot. But, to be successful, he'd need help here in St Martin's.'

'Prior Cuthbert?'

'Perhaps. Certainly Aelfric. If Wallasby and Aelfric would go to such lengths as this, one must speculate as to whether murder was also in their minds? Ranulf, fetch them. Bring them now!'

Whilst his henchman went searching, Corbett paced up and down the room until Ranulf ushered a sombre-faced Wallasby and an agitated Aelfric into the Abbot's chamber.

'I'll come swiftly to the point.' Corbett sat down and rubbed his hands together. 'Abbot Stephen, in many ways, was a compassionate father to his community. On one matter he would not be moved: that of the burial mound in Bloody Meadow! He was an exorcist.' He pointed at Wallasby. 'You not only opposed his views, you didn't like him as a man. You didn't tell us you were born in these parts, Archdeacon, and that your enmity with the Abbot ran so deep?'

Wallasby cleared his throat and shuffled his feet.

'Where's the crime in that, Sir Hugh? There's many a man I don't like, be they clerk or priest.'

Corbett smiled thinly.

'You were trying to disgrace him, I know, under the guise of scholarship and academic friendship. You, Aelfric – infirmarian and a member of the Abbot's Concilium at St Martin's – you were Wallasby's spy. You corresponded secretly and told him when Taverner had arrived and about Abbot Stephen's reaction. You also supplied our cunning man with the necessary powders and potions to assist in his mummery. Is that why Abbot Stephen died? Because he turned the tables on you? Does this account for the arrow in Taverner's heart? Because your well-laid plots and schemes went awry?' Corbett banged his fist on the table. 'The truth, Brother!'

Aelfric looked as if he was going to faint: without a by your leave he went and sat on a chair against the wall and put his face in his hands.

'*Peccavi! Peccavi!*' he intoned, striking his breast. 'I have sinned and sinned again!'

'Oh, don't be so weak!' Wallasby snarled.

'Be quiet!' Aelfric hissed. 'It was your plan! Sir Hugh, you are correct. Abbot Stephen would not be moved on the matter of the guesthouse. Above all, he would not allow us to search for a holy relic. Like others on the Concilium, I dreamt of St Martin's being a second Glastonbury, a shrine to rival Walsingham or even

Canterbury. It wasn't just the guesthouse . . . it was the shrine, the pilgrims . . .'

'Of course,' Corbett interrupted. 'And, where there's a shrine, miracles occur. And where miracles flourish there has to be a physician to attest to their worthiness, not to mention a hospital well furnished with beds and the best medicines. You were all dreaming of greatness, weren't you?'

'Archdeacon Wallasby was born in these parts,' the infirmarian continued, staring at the floor. 'Seven months ago he came here, supposedly visiting his family, and the plot was laid. I corresponded with him. The rest you've surmised. Taverner arrived at St Martin's and I supplied him with the necessary potions and powders. I also wrote to Wallasby, using our own code, informing him that Abbot Stephen was much impressed. I didn't mean any harm.' The infirmarian wiped tears from his eyes. 'I know I have sinned. Trickery was perpetrated. It would have broken Abbot Stephen's heart and he didn't deserve that. I was almost relieved when Taverner turned the tables. He said he would act the part through and not disgrace our Abbot's name.' The infirmarian spread his hands. 'What could I do? The hunter had become the hunted. Taverner said if I told the truth, I'd be disgraced. How could I continue as infirmarian without the trust of Father Abbot? But I had nothing to do with Taverner's murder, I swear. I have confessed my sin. I was going to let matters take their course until the . . .'

'Until these murders began,' Ranulf interrupted.

'Yes,' the infirmarian muttered. 'Wallasby here wanted to get away. He needed a secure passage along the lanes so I went to Brother Dunstan, and Scaribrick was advised to let him pass.'

'Sir,' Corbett pointed at Wallasby, 'I have told you once and I will tell you for the last time: you will remain here until my investigations are finished!'

'I am a clerk in Holy Orders!' Wallasby bellowed.

Ranulf made to rise.

'Lay a hand on me,' Wallasby threatened, 'and I'll have you excommunicated from St Paul's Cross!' He walked to the door and paused, his hand on the latch. 'I am no assassin, Corbett,' he jibed over his shoulder.

'Yes, you are, Archdeacon. You are a man of deep malice. You intended to kill the Abbot's spirit, turn him into a laughing stock. Tell me,' Corbett got to his feet, 'why was it you hated Abbot Stephen so much?'

He knew Wallasby couldn't resist the opportunity. The Archdeacon leaned against the door, face contorted with anger and hate.

'I met Daubigny at the cathedral schools,' he replied. 'Even as a boy he was cynical and mocking, quick of wit, nimble of foot.' Wallasby walked forward. 'He didn't believe in anything, Corbett: in God or his Church. He often mocked the priests and yet,' he paused, 'everywhere he went he won friends. He and Harcourt were like peas in a pod. A man like Daubigny should have been brought to book, but instead he became a knight banneret, friend, counsellor and confidant of the King, a soldier and self-proclaimed scholar. And, when he wanted to . . .' Wallasby snapped his fingers, 'he abruptly converted, became a man of God, a monk. But not your lowly lay brother – oh, not Daubigny! – he not only rose to become Abbot of a great monastery but a scholar, a theologian, an exorcist. In truth, he was a hypocrite!'

'Can't a man change?' Corbett asked. 'Doesn't Christ preach conversion, repentance?'

'Cacullus non facit monachum: the cowl doesn't make the monk,' Wallasby retorted. 'The rat does not change its coat. Yes, I admit I plotted against Daubigny, and I would have proved the truth about him, if Taverner hadn't turned.'

'Tell me,' Corbett went back and sat in his chair, 'have you ever heard of Heloise Argenteuil?'

'The name means something,' Wallasby replied, 'but I cannot say more.'

The Archdeacon bowed mockingly at Ranulf.

'And I must congratulate you. The news of your meeting with Scaribrick is all over the abbey. Sir, you have done more to impose the King's writ than a dozen sheriff's posses. At least, when I do depart this place, I'll be safe.'

And, spinning on his heel, Wallasby left the room, slamming the door behind him.

'No, you stay,' Corbett gestured as Aelfric started to rise. 'I have the further question. What if Abbot Stephen had agreed that the guesthouse could be built?'

'We would have all rejoiced.'

'Then let me take another path. If he continued to refuse,' Corbett measured his words carefully, 'could it have led to murder?'

Aelfric shook his head. 'Not murder, Sir Hugh, but perhaps something just as heinous: hate, resentment, curses. You see, we met with Abbot Stephen as a group and, when we did, followed the Rule of St Benedict: our discussions had to be amicable, in the true spirit of Christ.'

'But individually?' Corbett interrupted.

'God forgive us,' Brother Aelfric breathed. 'We all went our separate paths. You've discovered mine.'

'And the rest?'

Aelfric shook his head. 'As a group we were bound by holy obedience but I cannot speak for what happened in the souls of my brothers. Now, Sir Hugh, I must go.'

Once the infirmarian was gone, Corbett sighed and stood looking out of the window.

'No one is fully truthful,' he murmured. 'You do realise that, Ranulf? Wallasby, Aelfric, Cuthbert – they are still not telling us what we really want to know!'

'Can't we use force?'

'Against a monk, or an archdeacon? Secretly the King would agree. Publicly, we'd spend weeks cooling our heels in the Tower. I think we've exhausted everything.'

'Are we to leave?'

'No. The library won't yield any secrets, Archdeacon Wallasby hides behind his hate and his holy orders, whilst the monks use their vows as a knight would a shield. Lady Margaret Harcourt is polite and courteous whilst the Watcher by the Gates spins his own tale.'

'So, we come back to Abbot Stephen?' Ranulf asked.

'His manuscripts yield nothing,' Corbett replied. 'He did not say or do anything to provide a key to all these mysteries. All that remains is the burial mound in Bloody Meadow. Snow or not, come frost or hail, tomorrow, Ranulf, I intend to open and search that burial mound.'

'For what?'

'To be perfectly honest, I don't know. If it yields nothing, we'll stay two more days.'

Corbett stared at the crucifix and recalled Aelfric's words: 'I have sinned! I have sinned!' The clerk picked up his cloak.

'Where's Chanson?'

'Where he always is, down at the stables admiring the horses.'

'As long as he doesn't sing.'

Corbett smiled as they left the chamber. He had strictly ordered Chanson that, if he attended the Divine Office of the abbey, he was not to sing. Corbett had also warned Ranulf not to bribe or encourage him. Chanson was an excellent groom and a deft hand with the knife, but his singing! Corbett had never heard such an atrocious sound! The only person who appeared to admire it was his daughter Eleanor. She often begged Chanson for a song and, whilst Baby Edward screamed his head off, his daughter would laugh until the tears streamed down her cheeks.

They clattered down the stairs and out into the abbey grounds.

'Where to, Sir Hugh?'

'Why, Ranulf, to be shriven.'

'Confession? Absolution?' Ranulf teased. 'Should the Lady Maeve know of this?'

Corbett threw his cloak over his shoulders and fastened the clasp. He stamped his feet on the icy ground and stared up at the overcast sky.

'Abbot Stephen spoke openly with no one or appeared not to. He had no real confidant but, like any man, he had to be shriven. I am looking for Brother Luke.'

Corbett went up into the cloisters and stopped by a desk. A young monk, his face and hands almost blue with the cold, was poring over a manuscript. Corbett made his enquiries and the young monk's face lit up with a smile.

'My fingers are freezing, even the ink is sluggish. I'll take you to Brother Luke.'

They crossed the abbey grounds to a long, one-storeyed, grey-ragstone building with a red tiled roof and a shaded colonnaded walk on one side. Their guide explained that this was where the 'ancient ones' lived: too old or infirm for other duties except prayer, reflection and, as the young monk laughingly put it, 'chomping on their gums'. He paused at a door and knocked.

'Go away!' a voice bellowed. 'I don't want to be disturbed!'

The monk sighed, pressed down the latch and opened the door. The chamber inside was sweltering: it contained at least four braziers as well as a large chafing dish filled with charcoal on a table beside the high-backed chair where the occupant sat. The chamber also boasted a table, a stool, a small trunk and cupboard, a cot bed in the far corner and a lectern with a psalter on it facing a stark crucifix. Brother Luke certainly looked ancient with his scraggy neck, almost skeletal face stained with dark liverish spots, and a head as bald as an egg, but his eyes were bright with life. He pushed away the footstool and leaned forward.

'You are the clerk,' his voice was surprisingly strong. 'A royal clerk and his bully-boys come to see poor old Brother Luke. I wondered if you would. You, Brother!' he thundered at Corbett's guide, 'stop grinning like a monkey and go back to your studies!'

The young monk fled.

'Prior Waldo once had a monkey,' the Ancient One remarked. 'God knows why the Abbot at the time allowed him to bring it in, for it climbed everywhere whilst its habits were none too clean!' Brother Luke gave Corbett a red-gummed smile. 'But that can be said for many of the sons of God. Come on! Come on!' He gestured at a bench along the far wall. 'Bring that over and sit down. I have some wine.'

Corbett shook his head. He and Ranulf sat down like schoolboys before a master.

'I thought you'd come! I thought you'd come!' A bony finger wagged in Corbett's face.

'Why, Brother?'

'Because of the deaths – the murders! I always said this was an unhallowed place.'

'St Martin's?'

'No, clerk, the marshes!'

'Poor Abbot Stephen. You were his confessor?' Corbett asked.

'Aye, I listened to his sins and shrived him. And, before you ask, clerk, you know I can't tell you anything of that. I have not many days left: for a priest to reveal what's heard in confession is a sin to answer for in hellfire.'

'But what sort of man was he?' Ranulf demanded.

'Why, of mankind.' Brother Luke threw his head back and cackled with laughter. 'He was like you or I, Red Hair.' He peered at Ranulf. 'A fighting man born and bred, eh? I wager the ladies like you.' He patted his stomach. 'They used to like me too. Sprightly, they called me, a nimble dancer. Aye, I've danced on moon-washed greens and listened to the tambour beat and the jingle of the bells.'

Corbett glanced at Ranulf and winked.

'But, to answer your question,' Brother Luke pushed out his chin, 'Abbot Stephen was a good man but very troubled by something in the past. In many ways he was a sinner, perhaps even a great sinner: that's why I felt comfortable with him for so am I.'

'Did he ever talk of Heloise Argenteuil?'

Brother Luke stared impassively back.

'Did he ever talk about Reginald Harcourt?'

Again the hard-eyed stare.

'Did he ever talk about a wheel?' Corbett insisted.

'Yes, but in confession.' The vein-streaked, brown-spotted hand clasped Corbett's. The old monk's eyes grew gentle. 'The Good Lord and his Holy Mother know you have a dreadful task here, yet I can only speak on those matters not heard in the confessional pew.'

'Why was he an exorcist?' Ranulf asked.

'Now, Sharp Eyes, I can answer that! I asked the same. Stephen had doubts, grave doubts, about every-thing! Sometimes he thought there was nothing after death but extinction: no heaven, no hell, no purgatory, no God, no demons. So, he took the view that, if he could prove the existence of demons, then it might mean something.'

Corbett nodded. He had heard this before, not only about Abbot Stephen but about others who struggled with their faith. As one priest had confided in Corbett, 'If there's a hell, there must be a heaven.'

'He was trying to prove to himself,' Brother Luke continued. 'As the Creed puts it, "I believe in things visible and invisible". He wanted to shift the mist which blinded his soul. I suppose he was searching for the truth.'

'And Bloody Meadow?' Corbett asked.

Again the old priest's head went down.

'I can tell you something of that. Abbot Stephen swore that, as long as he lived, that burial mound would not be opened. On that point he was obdurate. I don't . . .' His voice trailed off. 'I have spoken enough.' He sighed.

'What of the days before he died?' Corbett demanded.

The old priest licked his lips. 'Yes, he came to me agitated, troubled. A great darkness clouded his mind, heart and soul. I can tell you this, clerk, and I've told no one else – if you had not come to me, I suppose I would have asked to see you.'

Corbett held his breath. He could see the old monk was torn by the fear of betraying a confidence.

'So, in his last days Abbot Stephen did not come for confession?'

'No, clerk.'

The old priest turned away, his lower jaw trembling. Corbett grasped his hand and squeezed it gently.

'You must help me. Blood has been shed. The souls of your brothers sent brutally, unshriven, before God's tribunal might not cry for vengeance but they do call out for justice. God's justice must be done and the King's law upheld.'

'Very well.' The old priest grasped his Ave beads and threaded them through his fingers. 'Abbot Stephen knelt before me. He did not confess his sin but he claimed how one of his brothers, a man close to him, had accused him of a hideous offence, not against the Rule but against God.'

'A hideous offence!' Ranulf exclaimed. 'What wrong could a holy abbot do in such a hallowed place!'

'Was he talking about the past?' Corbett added.

'No, no, of a recent event.'

'And what was this sin?'

'I will not tell you.'

'But I can ask?'

The old priest nodded.

'Was it murder?'

A shake of the head.

'Was it fornication? Lying with a woman?'

Again the shake of the head.

'Theft? Blasphemy?'

Brother Luke's gaze held Corbett's.

'What sin?' Corbett exclaimed.

'Have you read the Book of Samuel? The story of David?' Luke demanded.

Corbett closed his eyes. David of Israel had been accused of many crimes.

'And Jonathan,' Brother Luke added quietly.

Corbett opened his eyes.

'Abbot Stephen was accused of unnatural practices with a fellow monk!'

'*Tu dixisti*. You have said it, clerk.'

The Ancient One must have seen the consternation in Corbett's face.

'And this was recent?' Ranulf asked.

'Very much so.' Brother Luke shook his head. 'I would say about a month before his death.'

'Did he say why? How?'

'Abbot Stephen simply said that he had been accused of this.'

271

'Did he deny it?' Ranulf asked.

'No. I told you, he just knelt here and sobbed like a child. He said the accusation had been made in a whispered conversation in his own chamber. I tried to reason with him, to soothe his soul but he got up abruptly and left. I sent a messenger after him but he never returned. My Abbot never came back.' The old man's eyes filled with tears. 'Now he has gone. God forbid that he despaired, that he committed the sin against the Holy Ghost before that dreadful act was committed. May the angels take him to a place of peace and light. He was so different.' Luke's old face had a faraway look. 'Do you know, clerk, when I was younger, I was the infirmarian here. Stephen Daubigny was a regular visitor, not so much to the Church, but to our library. He did love the world of books.'

'But why come here?' Corbett asked.

'He came with his friend, Sir Reginald.'

'And why would *he* visit St Martin's?'

'Do you know, clerk,' the old man mused, 'I never understood Sir Reginald, but if I had to choose between Harcourt and Daubigny becoming a monk, I would have chosen Sir Reginald.'

'Why?'

'He was very shy of women, embarrassed. I can tell you this because it is not a matter for the confessional.' Brother Luke poked Ranulf in the shoulder. 'You are a vigorous man, aren't you?'

'Thanks be to God!' Ranulf teased back.

'And you love the pleasures of the bed?'

Ranulf couldn't stop himself blushing. Corbett laughed softly.

'Well, come on!' the old monk teased. 'Are you sprightly or not? Once, I was a clerk, and served in the royal levies. I could resist anything but the temptations of the flesh and a deep bowl of claret. Sir Reginald was

272

different: he came here for my help.'

'He was impotent?' Corbett asked.

'He had problems. Sometimes such failings are a matter of the body: an injury, perhaps a growth. I have treated enough monks in my life to recognise the cause and recommend a possible cure. Other times the cause is not so clear.'

'And Sir Reginald?'

'Both, Sir Hugh.' The old monk tapped his head. 'Though more phantasms of the mind.'

'But he married?'

'I know, I know,' Brother Luke sighed. 'Sir Hugh, we have monks in this abbey who have problems – how can I put it – in relation to the ladies. Being repelled by women, they seek sanctuary and safety behind the walls of a monastery. Other men believe such problems can be resolved in holy wedlock. Sir Reginald was one of the latter. But,' he held up a bony finger, 'I could be wrong. Many men face such difficulties, and they are often of a temporary nature. The only people who can really know the truth in this case are Sir Reginald and Lady Margaret. You have met that redoubtable woman?'

Corbett nodded.

'I doubt if she would say anything on a matter so intimate.'

'And who was the monk that accused the Abbot of unnatural practices?' Ranulf interrupted.

'Not a hint, not a whisper, Red Hair. Do you play hazard?' Brother Luke asked abruptly, not waiting for an answer. 'If I was laying a wager, I would say such a heinous accusation was closely tied up with that damnable funeral barrow and, God forbid, the ambitions of some of my brothers.'

'What did Harcourt ask for when he came to you?'

'Powders, potions, some miraculous elixir. In reality, I was of little help.'

'Did Sir Stephen Daubigny know of this?'

Brother Luke shook his head. 'That's why Harcourt came here. He said he would sooner trust a monk than some local physician.'

'Did he return to you after his marriage to Lady Margaret?'

The old monk shrugged and played with the Ave beads.

'You must have been here when Sir Stephen first entered St Martin's?'

'Oh yes.'

'Were you his confessor then?'

Brother Luke shook his head. 'For many years he avoided me. I admit I was surprised by both the change in him and his rapid promotion, yet he soon proved to be an ideal Benedictine.' He paused. 'More than that, Sir Hugh, I cannot tell you.'

The old man closed his eyes and started threading the beads through his fingers. He sat slumped as if tired by this conversation. Corbett and Ranulf thanked him, rose and moved the bench back.

'I cannot break my vows.'

Corbett turned round. Brother Luke still sat with his eyes closed.

'These bloody murders, Sir Hugh. Why should they start now?'

'I don't know, that's what I am trying to find out.'

'Search the past,' the old priest murmured. 'We sow our sins like seed. They take root and lie dormant but, in time, they sprout like black corn, their leaves full and fat with wickedness.' He opened his eyes. 'I wish you well, clerk. God be with you!'

Brother Luke sketched a blessing in the air as Corbett opened the door to leave.

Prior Cuthbert knelt on the cold flagstones of his own cell. He had locked and barred the door. The fire in the hearth was now dull ash, the braziers unlit. The Prior had removed his gown and undershirt. The hard paving stones bit into his bony knees. He found it difficult to keep his toes against the freezing floor. Above him a huge crucifix, showing Christ writhing in agony, stared down at him. Prior Cuthbert grasped the small whip, closed his eyes, gritted his teeth and began to flail his left and right shoulders. Even here, in the darkness of his cell, the demons seemed to be waiting. He whipped and whipped again as, in his mind, roaring griffins leapt from fires and a dark tunnel opened to spew forth blood-soaked demons, hair writhing like serpents. Prior Cuthbert opened his eyes. He forced himself to look at the crucifix. He had sinned most grievously.

'*Mea culpa*! *Mea culpa*!' He struck his breast. 'Through my fault! Through my fault!'

He would have to make atonement, repent his ambition and greed. If only he could turn back time. He let the whip fall to the floor. He felt as if he was choked and cloaked by sin. All around him clustered its hideous consequences: the scrawny corpse of that cat hanging from the rood screen; the macabre deaths of his brothers; the fire arrows searing the night air; the whispering and the chatter. The Concilium had ceased to act. They were more like frightened rabbits cowering in their cells, terrified of shadows, loneliness and the long stretch of the night. Prior Cuthbert couldn't stop trembling. He clambered to his feet, his knee brushing against the whip. He slipped on his sandals and put on his robe. A loud knocking on his chamber door made him start.

'I am busy!' he called out.

'And so am I, Father Prior!'

Prior Cuthbert moaned in despair: that sharp-eyed clerk with his spate of questions!

'I am busy.' Even Prior Cuthbert realised how his voice was faltering.

'Father, I need to speak to you urgently.'

Prior Cuthbert kicked the whip under a bench and, going across, unbarred and unlocked the door. Corbett and Ranulf stood on the threshold like avenging angels. One look at Sir Hugh's face and Cuthbert knew that he would finally have to tell the truth.

'I think it's best if we came in.'

Prior Cuthbert stood aside. He closed the door behind them.

'Satan's Teeth!' Ranulf clapped his hands together. 'This chamber's cold.'

Corbett had already walked across and stood staring down at where Prior Cuthbert had been kneeling.

'Blood on the flagstones,' he murmured.

Corbett crouched down, his gauntleted hands skimming the floor. He caught sight of the whip under the bench, pulled it out and held it up.

'I am not a monk, Prior Cuthbert,' he said quietly, 'but I am a King's clerk searching for the truth.'

The Prior sat down in a chair, head bowed, hands clasped as if in prayer.

'Why should the Prior of St Martin's whip himself so hard,' Corbett demanded, 'that the blood seeps through his robe?'

He stared round at the well-furnished chamber with its carved chairs and coffers, desk, benches, and shelves bearing books.

'And why should he kneel almost naked,' he pointed to the unstrapped sandal, 'and punish himself in a freezing chamber?'

Prior Cuthbert closed his eyes and muttered.

*'Miserere mei Domine et exaudi vocem meam.'*

'Christ will have mercy on you and hear your voice,' Corbett translated. 'If you tell the truth.' He got to his feet. 'You were the Abbot's loyal prior, weren't you? You had dreams of building a great guesthouse and having Sigbert's remains as a precious relic. What started off as a dream became a burning ambition. Under Abbot Stephen's rule, St Martin's had grown in fame and royal patronage. Yet Abbot Stephen was insistent: Bloody Meadow was not to be touched. So you and the rest of the Concilium plotted, turning a blind eye to each other's activities. Did Aelfric take you into his confidence? Did he tell you the truth about Taverner and Archdeacon Wallasby?'

Prior Cuthbert sat, head bowed.

'Perhaps he hinted at it? You turned a blind eye, didn't you? As you did to Brother Dunstan's infatuation with the tavern wench, Blanche. You are sharp-eyed, Cuthbert, and as Prior you are responsible for the discipline of this abbey, but of course you needed your treasurer's allegiance. Like the priest in the parable of the Good Samaritan, you passed by on the other side and turned a blind eye.'

Corbett came and crouched before him. The Prior's eyes were tightly shut.

'Look at me!' Corbett urged.

Ranulf stood fascinated. When they had first met Cuthbert, he had been very much the haughty prelate, the ruler of this abbey. Now he sat a broken man, on the verge of tears.

'You saw something else, didn't you?' Corbett declared. 'You weren't really concerned with the plottings of Aelfric. You were hunting bigger quarry. You saw what you thought was a secret and hideous sin. You reproached your Father Abbot with it, hinting that if you had your way and were allowed to build a guest-house, that sin would remain a secret between you. So, Father Prior, what did you see?'

Prior Cuthbert sat, shoulders shaking. When he opened his eyes tears coursed down his cheeks.

'It was Gildas,' he sobbed. 'It was really his fault.

The man couldn't sleep and often returned to his workshop. I'd go down there at night and we'd sit and discuss the new guesthouse. One night, late in autumn, as I was coming back, I found the Judas gate off the latch so I went out into the open meadow. The sky was cloud free, the stars seemed to hang low, the meadow was moon-washed; an eerie place. By the burial mound, not hiding behind it but almost, stood two figures. At first I was going to call out but then one moved – his cowl and hood were pushed back and I recognised Father Abbot. The other was also dressed as a monk. I glimpsed cowl and robe but it was impossible to distinguish his features or see who it was. I hid in the shadows of the gate. I saw Father Abbot embrace the other person.'

'How?' Corbett asked.

Prior Cuthbert demonstrated with his hands.

'He put one hand up behind the person's head, and the other round his waist. They embraced and kissed.'

'Full on the lips?' Corbett asked.

'I am not sure.'

'Was the other person male or female?'

'I cannot say.'

'So, it could have been a woman disguised in the robe of a monk? Come, Father Prior,' Corbett urged. 'Up and down the the kingdom, scenes such as this take place in monasteries and abbeys. It is not unknown for a monk to bring his leman into the monastery disguised as one of the brothers. For all you can tell, that is what happened here.'

The Prior refused to hold his gaze.

'Brother Dunstan had his paramour Blanche from the Lantern-in-the-Woods,' Ranulf jibed. 'Could it have been her?'

'I don't know.'

'Why didn't you wait and see?' Corbett asked.

'I intended to but Father Abbot and this mysterious

figure disappeared behind the tumulus. I didn't dare walk across the meadow, as they would have heard me coming and the other person would have fled. I didn't want to be accused of spying. I decided to wait for them to emerge again but Gildas came looking for me. I didn't want him to see what I had so I went back through the Judas gate. I closed the gate more abruptly than I should, and it must have startled Father Abbot. I didn't mention it to anyone else.' The Prior beat his fists against his side. 'I couldn't get that image out of my mind. I was growing more and more frustrated with Abbot Stephen, so one morning I visited him in his chamber, and once again raised the question of the guesthouse, and the possibility of the abbey acquiring Sigbert's holy remains. Abbot Stephen lost his temper and banged his fist on the desk. I was roused to fury and I told him what I had seen.' Prior Cuthbert paused. 'God forgive me, Sir Hugh, I wish I hadn't. I really do. I expected him to deny it. He just sat, stricken, staring at me as I accused him of a hideous sin. I said that unless he agreed to my demands, I would accuse him of such before the full Chapter.'

'And Abbot Stephen didn't deny it?'

'No, he sat like a man pole-axed.'

'Did you repeat the blackmail?'

Prior Cuthbert nodded. 'I was overwhelmed by my anger. I forgot my vows and charity. All I could see was this stubborn old man refusing a reasonable request whilst hiding his own secret sin.'

'And you shared this information with no one?'

'No.'

'What made you think the sin was unnatural?'

'I assumed it since the figure was dressed as a monk. Father Abbot didn't deny it.'

'And on the second occasion?' Corbett asked.

'He was more composed, serene. He quoted from the scriptures, "Your sin will find you out". He said he would consider my request.'

'But the other person could have been a woman? It might have been Blanche. After all, in his youth Abbot Stephen was known as a virile, young knight.'

'True, true.'

'Could it have been Perditus?'

'No, why do you say that?'

'Well, he was the Abbot's manservant. He shared the same quarters.'

'No, I am sure it wasn't he. I went back to talk to Gildas but I was in a hurry to get away, as I thought I might find out who it was by watching the door to the Abbot's lodgings. When I went across, I saw the lights shining from Perditus's chamber. I went up, making some excuse. He was in his chamber reading a psalter by candlelight. I asked where the Abbot was and he replied that he had gone for a walk so I went back and hid again in the shadows. I must have been there some time before Abbot Stephen returned alone.' Prior Cuthbert put his face in his hands. 'I don't know who it was but someone was there whom Abbot Stephen embraced and kissed. It must have been unnatural.'

'It might have been the *osculum pacis*?' Corbett queried. 'The kiss of peace?'

'In the dead of night, out in a lonely meadow?' Prior Cuthbert gestured with his hands. 'If you had seen Abbot Stephen's face the day I accused him, you'd know I spoke the truth.'

The Prior put his face in his hands and began to sob uncontrollably.

*PARVA SAEPE SCINTILLA CONTEMPTA*
*MAGNUM EXCITAVIT INCENDIUM*

OFTEN THE TINIEST OF NEGLECTED
SPARKS HAS WHIPPED UP AN INFERNAL BLAZE

QUINTUS CURTIUS

# *Chapter 12*

Corbett sat in the Abbot's chamber. Ranulf had returned to the guesthouse. Outside the day was drawing on and darkness was falling. They had left Prior Cuthbert to his grief. The man had become so distraught it would have been cruel to question him further. Corbett could make little sense of the Prior's confession. Who had been with the Abbot on that moonlit night out in Bloody Meadow? The clerk sat and meditated, his eyes growing heavy as he turned over and over in his mind the different possibilities. Brother Luke's enigmatic account of Sir Reginald; Prior Cuthbert grieving over his own malice; Abbot Stephen, a priest with a reputation for holiness yet so secretive. Corbett closed his eyes and slept. He started awake as the bells of the abbey marked the time for Divine Office.

Corbett got up and opened the shutters. Would the assassin strike again, he wondered? Or would he be more cautious since his attack on Brother Richard had been repelled?

'If only,' Corbett murmured to himself, 'if only I could resolve Abbot Stephen's death: that's the loose thread.'

He was about to return to his chair when he heard a pounding on the stairs and muffled groans and cries.

Corbett hastened to the door and flung it open. Perditus stood gasping. If Corbett hadn't caught him, he would have collapsed into his arms. The lay brother's face was bruised, and cuts bloodied his hands and face.

'In God's name!' Corbett exclaimed.

He half dragged the man over to a chair and sat him down. Perditus was trembling. Corbett quickly felt his head and patted his arms, looking for serious wounds.

'What happened?' he asked.

Perditus just sat, mouth open, now and again wincing, hands going up to the bruises on his face.

'Are you wounded?' Corbett asked.

The lay brother refused to answer. He was ashen-faced, and a trickle of blood bubbled at the corner of his mouth. Corbett hastily filled a goblet of wine, walked across and held it to Perditus's lips. He heard footsteps outside and Ranulf entered. Corbett held up a hand to fend off his henchman's questions.

'What's the matter, Perditus?'

Corbett crouched by the lay brother, studying him carefully. The bruise just under the eye was now coming out, and there was a similar one on his left jaw. He had cuts on his cheeks, hands and wrists. Corbett felt his chest and back.

'I'm all right.' Perditus gulped at the wine. 'I had been out to Bloody Meadow, and I was just nearing the Judas gate on my way back when I heard a sound as I went past some bushes. I whirled round to find myself under attack. I couldn't see who it was: he was masked, cowled and hooded. He was about to strike me on the back of the head with a club. I moved to the left and he caught me on the chin then smacked me again here, on the cheek. I grappled with him, but he had a dagger in his right hand, and one side of the blade was very sharp. I tried to get a good grip but it was difficult as the blade turned.' He stretched out his hand. 'At one time he caught me here on the cheek with it. It cut like a razor. I pushed him away. I thought he'd attack again but he turned and fled.'

'Shall I go after him?' Ranulf moved to the door.

'No,' Corbett declared. 'The attacker will be gone.' He urged Perditus to drink more wine. 'And you had no sight of him?'

'His cowl was securely tied and never fell back in the struggle. A leather mask covered his face. I only glimpsed his eyes and heard his grunts.'

'Was he strong?' Ranulf asked.

Perditus drained his cup. 'Well, he was fairly muscular and wiry but I would say he was an older man. He wasn't like you.' Perditus pointed at Ranulf. 'I could hold my own against him. I was aware of his strength slipping. His belly was soft, with a slight paunch. He must have realised that if the struggle continued, he would have the worst of it, so he fled.'

'Do you think he was waiting for you?'

'I remember that as I was walking past the gate, the bushes were swaying in the wind. The ground underfoot was slippery, icy, that's how I heard him. I heard the ice crack and turned just in time.'

'Did he speak?'

'No, apart from gasps and groans, he said nothing.' Perditus looked woebegone and scratched his close-cropped hair. 'I had the impression he was waiting there for anyone.'

Corbett moved away and closed the door.

'That would make sense,' he declared, coming back. 'The night is dark and cold. You had your cowl up?'

Perditus agreed.

'And, of course, you would be walking slightly hunched against the cold. He might have mistaken you for one of the older brothers, realised his mistake and fled?'

Corbett was about to continue when a bell began to clang noisily. Perditus sprang to his feet, so quickly he became unsteady. Ranulf caught him and urged him to sit down again. Corbett walked to the door and threw it open.

'That's the tocsin!' Perditus gasped. 'The alarm! Something has happened in the abbey! I must . . .' He tried to rise.

'No, you go to your chamber.' Corbett grasped him by the arm. 'I mean that, Brother, lie down on your bed. I'll tell Aelfric to come and see to you. You have no other wound or bruise?'

Perditus winced and held his left side.

'The attacker hit me here but . . .'

He was distracted by the tocsin, its tolling echoed across the abbey. Corbett escorted Perditus along the passageway to his own chamber, which was smaller and starker than the Abbot's. Corbett made him sit on the side of his bed and told him to stay there. Ranulf lit candles from an oil lamp. Corbett picked up some of the books lying on the floor and placed them on the table. The tocsin continued to toll.

'Stay there!' Corbett ordered.

Followed by Ranulf, the clerk hastened from the chamber and down the stairs. Once they were outside, the source of the crisis was obvious. The cold night air brought the smell of burning and, glancing up, Corbett saw the glow against the night sky from the far end of the abbey.

'A fire,' he declared. 'I wager a shilling to a pound, Ranulf, it's not an accident.'

The whole abbey was now roused. Monks, breaking off from their different duties, hastened across the abbey grounds. Corbett and Ranulf followed. The smell of burning grew stronger and thick tendrils of smoke curled around them. They came round the abbey church, across the cemetery and through a line of trees. Corbett and Ranulf paused. One of the abbey's main storehouses, a timber and plaster building on a red-bricked base, was ablaze from end to end. Flames leapt out of the windows, the plaster was cracking and buckling. Even as they looked, a part of the roof caved in with a crash and the flames roared up to the sky. Prior Cuthbert hadn't arrived but Richard the almoner was busy organising the community to fetch slopping buckets of water from a nearby well. Some of the monks who'd been working there already had blackened faces and hands, their robes stained with dust and ash.

'It's impossible.' The almoner came over, mopping his face with a wet rag. 'Wouldn't you agree, Sir Hugh?'

Corbett stared at the building. Although ablaze from end to end, at least it stood alone with little danger of the fire spreading.

'I would advise, Brother, to let it burn: the real danger is when it collapses.'

The almoner agreed. He hurried off, calling out to the monks to stop their fruitless efforts with the water. Burning plaster and wood were now falling away from the building and the heat, wafted by the night breeze, became searing. Corbett stood with the monks, watching the fire totally destroy the building.

'What was in there?' Corbett asked.

'Wine, corn, flour, some vellum, charcoal and oil.' Brother Richard listed the stores.

'But none of the brothers?'

'No, no, it's a very dark building inside. In autumn and winter the doors are secured late in the afternoon.'

'It could have been an accident.' Aelfric had now joined them.

Corbett shook his head. 'I doubt it,' he replied. 'The fire took hold quickly, yes? There was no reason for candlelight or a fire within?'

Brother Richard agreed. 'Like any house we are most vigilant. I agree, Sir Hugh, our assassin has struck again.'

'But how?' Ranulf demanded.

'Perhaps a fire arrow through the window.'

Corbett watched the flames as they began to die and coughed as a swirl of smoke gusted towards them.

'Yes, a fire arrow or a lighted torch thrown through a window would have started such a blaze, particularly if it landed near the oil.'

Prior Cuthbert came hastening up. In the glow from the fire he still looked pallid-faced and red-eyed. The almoner told him what had happened as Prior Cuthbert stood, eyes half closed.

'I am sorry,' he apologised. 'I was in a deep sleep.'

He walked away to organise the brothers. Some were just sitting on the frozen ground staring helplessly at this fire which had consumed an entire building. The walls and roof had now collapsed, and only the red brick base remained, but flames still leapt up, licking hungrily at blackened timbers. The breeze brought grey and black ash towards them and, occasionally, the sweet smell of the spices stored inside. Prior Cuthbert set up a system of watches and the community began to drift away. Corbett could tell the monks also believed the fire was deliberate: an act of terror by the assassin lurking within their community. Corbett watched the fire as if fascinated.

How could it have happened, he wondered? Who was responsible?

Perditus had been with him for some time before the tocsin began, but what about the rest? Richard and Dunstan had been present. Aelfric had joined them later but the Prior had claimed he had slept through all the commotion.

'Why?' Ranulf asked, standing behind Corbett.

Chanson had already left to make sure his precious horses were safe.

'All men are terrified of fire.' Corbett whispered. 'Sudden and fierce, it wreaks havoc and instils terror: that's what our assassin wanted to do. He's aping the wicked Lord Mandeville who liked nothing better than to see a monastery burn beneath God's own sky. He was probably frustrated that the attacks on Perditus and Dunstan had failed so he lashed out. He doesn't want these monks to forget his presence. Corpses, sacrilege in church, fire arrows and now the destruction of one of their main storehouses.'

'Sir Hugh?' Aelfric hurried through the darkness. 'Sir Hugh, you'd best come!'

'I know why, Aelfric. The corpses in the death house – Hamo and Brother Francis. Both have been branded, haven't they?'

Aelfric pushed his hands up the sleeves of his gown and stifled a sob.

'The tocsin rang and the guard left his post, as did we all,' he explained. 'When I returned the sheets were ripped back.' Aelfric pulled out his hand and tapped his forehead. 'Both bear the brand marks. The killer has claimed his own.'

Aelfric gazed bleakly at the dying fire, then round at the snow-capped buildings as if he was seeing this abbey for the first time.

'This is my home, Sir Hugh, yet it's becoming a place of hideous terrors. We are being punished for our sins.'

He walked off into the darkness. Corbett told Ranulf to bring some food from the abbey kitchens and returned to the guesthouse. He met Wallasby on the stairs.

'You've heard of the fire, Archdeacon?'

'Yes, Sir Hugh, I have, but I will not leave my chamber except for food.'

And, brushing by the clerk, he clattered down the stairs. Corbett went into his own chamber, checked all was well and sat at his writing desk. Ranulf brought across food. Chanson joined them for a meal of pike with galentyne sauce, buttered vegetables, dates and spiced wine. Corbett chewed his food absentmindedly. Once finished, he crossed to his desk and wrote down all that had happened. Ranulf asked questions but he ignored him. Corbett went and lay down on his bed, plucking the coverlet over him. He tried to think of Maeve: how much he loved her, the poetry he would recite to her. He recalled that enigmatic name, Heloise Argenteuil. Corbett sat up so quickly he startled Ranulf.

'Heloise Argenteuil!' Corbett shouted. 'Oh Ranulf, I am dim! Who hasn't heard of Heloise and Abelard!'

'Master?'

Corbett threw back the coverlet.

'Tonight I work. Tomorrow, Ranulf . . .'

Corbett was almost dancing from foot to foot, rubbing his hands.

'Tomorrow, for the first time since we came here, the truth will emerge!'

When he started to unlock a mystery, Corbett hovered like a hawk so that Ranulf was always unsure who was the marked quarry. This time was no different. Corbett began to hum a hymn under his breath. No longer tired, he busied himself about his desk, taking out sheets of vellum, scrubbing them with the pumice stone, sharpening quills, stirring ink pots, talking and singing under his breath as if the rest of the world had disappeared. He looked over his shoulder.

'Go back to your chamber, Ranulf,' Corbett murmured. 'I cannot yet tell you what I do not know for sure myself. However, we will be up early. Make sure you bring your boots and gauntlets. We are going to start digging in Bloody Meadow.'

'What for?'

'The truth. Now leave me.'

Corbett worked late into the night. Now and again Ranulf would check on Chanson, who, fully dressed, lay snoring on his bed oblivious to the cares of the world. Every time he went into his master's chamber, the clerk was still bowed over his desk. Corbett was doing what he loved best. Like an Oxford scholar, he'd form a hypothesis, develop that as far as he could and, for each supposition, look for proof. If the hypothesis didn't work he would simply start again. At last Ranulf himself grew tired, and threw himself on his cot bed. It seemed only a matter of minutes before Corbett, washed and changed, was shaking him by the shoulder urging him to get up. Ranulf hastened to obey. Chanson was already jumping from foot to foot eager to break his fast in the refectory.

'Don't you ever wash or change?' Ranulf asked crossly when they met in the corridor. 'Your horses are cleaner than you.'

'Sir Hugh needs me,' Chanson retorted. 'Ablutions will have to wait.'

'Ablutions? Who taught you that word?'

'Lady Maeve. She told me to attend to my ablutions more often.'

'A wise woman,' Ranulf muttered as they clattered down the stairs.

Corbett was already striding across to the refectory where the monks were filing in after Prime. Corbett didn't go to the High Table but sat down at the table just within the doorway specially reserved for guests. They broke their fast on oatmeal, fresh loaves and butter, with a small pot of honey and stoups of watered ale. Once he had finished, Corbett cleaned his hornspoon with a napkin and put it back in his wallet.

Perditus, still looking bruised and rather tired, came in. Corbett grasped him by the arm.

'I would be grateful if you could ask Father Prior to meet me outside, he and all members of the Concilium.'

Corbett told Ranulf and Chanson to follow him. They went out of the refectory and down the steps. The morning was turning grey and hard. The smell of burning still hung heavy on the breeze but the snow was turning into an icy slush, treacherous underfoot.

Corbett stood clapping his gauntleted hands. Despite his lack of sleep he looked fresh: eyes glittering in the cold, hair tied back. Prior Cuthbert and the rest came bustling up.

'I've held a meeting,' Prior Cuthbert explained. 'After checking the fire damage, we had to discuss all that has happened. Sir Hugh, we can discover no solution.'

'I can,' the clerk declared merrily. He pointed to a carved, gargoyle face on the lintel of the refectory doorway. 'The truth may be as ugly as that but just as real. Right, Cuthbert.' He clapped the Prior on the shoulder as if the monk was a close friend. 'By the powers invested in me and— Well, we don't want to go through that again, do we? I want every able-bodied man with hoe, mattock and spade out in Bloody Meadow.'

Prior Cuthbert's face was a joy to see. He just gaped.

'Well, isn't it the fulfilment of your dreams,' Corbett teased.

'But it's a burial place!'

'That's not what you said to Abbot Stephen. Now look, Father Prior,' Corbett laid a hand on each shoulder, 'the solution to all these bloody mysteries lies in that burial mound. You can either help me or I shall have to send for the sheriff and his posse. The sooner that grave is opened, the sooner these matters can be brought to an end and I will be gone.'

'Open it!' Brother Aelfric snapped. 'Let's put an end to this, Father Prior!'

Prior Cuthbert agreed.

'Have the tocsin rung,' he said. 'I want all the brothers to assemble in the Chapter House. The spiritual hours of this abbey will be set aside. Sir Hugh, you have your way.'

Corbett thanked him and went back to the refectory where he ordered another bowl of oatmeal and a stoup of ale. He ate and drank lustily, tapping his feet, humming between mouthfuls.

'Sir Hugh,' Ranulf leaned across the table, 'won't you share your wisdom with us?'

'It's not wisdom, Ranulf, it's just intuition. So, please, bear with me. I'll explain as this murderous tale unfolds.'

He finished the oatmeal and went back out towards the Judas gate. Father Prior had acted quickly. Labourers and tenant farmers were all assembling in the meadow, their breath rising like steam as they stamped their feet on the icy ground. Bloody Meadow had lost its macabre loneliness and the crows, roused from their nests in the oak trees, cawed raucously, whirling aloft as if they sensed what was about to happen. The sky was full of iron-grey clouds, though these were not threatening or lowering. The only discomfort was the biting breeze and the cold which seemed to creep through boots and gloves to freeze toes and fingers.

'We'll soon be warm,' Corbett murmured. 'And I don't think it will snow.'

'The ground will be hard.' Prior Cuthbert came up.

'Only the top layer will be,' Corbett explained. 'I am a farmer's son so I can tell that winter has yet to set in. Thank God it's not February or March. Now, let's proceed.'

Corbett went and picked up a spade from a barrow.

Using this he climbed to the top of the funeral barrow and called the others around. He felt slightly ridiculous with the breeze whipping his hair and cloak. The ground underfoot was slippery, and he quietly prayed he wouldn't fall. He glanced around the meadow, and the view so startled him he had to steady himself with the spade.

'I didn't think,' he murmured. 'Oh, Corbett, sometimes you can be a great fool!'

'Master, what's the matter?'

Ranulf stared anxiously up, grasping a hoe as if it was a spear. Corbett ignored him. Digging the spade into the ground he slowly turned, making sure he didn't lose his foothold. The top of the funeral barrow was flat, about a yard across. Corbett kept turning as Ranulf, cursing under his breath, used the hoe to climb the mound and join him.

'Oh, you stupid man!' Corbett whispered. 'Why did I never think of . . .?'

'What is it, Sir Hugh? Have you lost your wits?'

'No, I have just regained them. Ranulf, look around this field. What does it remind you of?'

The Clerk of the Green Wax turned so quickly he nearly slipped. Corbett steadied him. At the foot of the mound, Prior Cuthbert and his community were becoming restless. Corbett ignored them.

'Think, Ranulf. This meadow is almost like a circle, with the burial mound in the centre. Look at the furrows leading off. You can only see them from up here.'

'The wheel!' Ranulf exclaimed. 'Abbot Stephen's wheel! The mosaic, the drawings he etched. The burial mound is the hub. These furrows, probably pathways to it, are the spokes, the edge of the field is the rim.'

'Precisely,' Corbett whispered. 'And now we are going to find out why it is so important.'

'Sir Hugh,' Prior Cuthbert called. 'We are beginning to freeze!'

Corbett, grasping the handle of the spade, stared down at them.

'I want you to dig!' he shouted. 'Take away the top soil and begin to burrow in: from the side rather than the top.'

'But it will collapse!' someone shouted.

'No, begin that way,' Corbett declared. 'I am looking for something. It will not be deep within the barrow.'

The monks acquiesced. Prior Cuthbert and members of the Concilium stood aside, wrapped in their cloaks. Brother Dunstan had a portable brazier brought out as well as jugs of mulled wine and trays of pewter cups. The labourers began their task, cursing and muttering, carefully removing the surface of frozen grass. They dug eagerly, now and again breaking off to warm their hands over the brazier, or scooping up handfuls of snow to cool their fingers as they grasped the hot mulled wine. Corbett and Ranulf chose their spot and began to dig whilst Chanson spent more time warming his fingers.

'Not work for royal clerks,' Ranulf muttered.

'It takes me back to being a boy,' Corbett grinned. 'And it's something to do.'

They must have worked for about an hour. Corbett and Ranulf were at the far side of the meadow near the Judas Gate when the alarm was raised. They hastened round: a group of labourers were now leaning on their mattocks and hoes, peering into the hole they had dug. Ranulf grasped a hoe and, pushing the wooden handle in, prodded gently.

'It's not mud,' one of the labourers declared. He plucked a piece of rotting cloth from the soil and handed it to Corbett.

The clerk carefully rubbed it through his fingers.

'I can't tell what fabric it is but, although stained with mud, it was probably once quite costly.'

'Wool?' Ranulf queried. 'It hasn't rotted away very well.'

The labourers now dug more carefully. The rest ceased their labours to stand and watch. The hole widened and, under Corbett's instructions, they gently pulled the bundle they had found out into the open. At last it was free. The top of the skull and the skeletal feet peeping out from beneath the rotting coverlet were quite clear. Everyone drew back. Corbett laid the macabre bundle gently on the ground and undid the makeshift winding-sheet. The skeleton beneath was white; it hadn't yet turned a corrupting yellow, whilst the bones were still hard and firm.

'The coverlet was his cloak,' Corbett declared.

Ranulf could clearly see rotting chainmail which had once covered the chest, and the tabard above bearing a livery. The hose on the legs had rotted away.

'The boots must have been removed,' Corbett declared.

The hauberk was cut and mangled on one side. Corbett lifted this up to expose a smashed rib beneath. He carefully checked for signs of other wounds. Corbett got to his feet and looked down at the pathetic remains. The skull hung sideways, the jaw slightly open.

'That's not the body of King Sigbert!' Brother Aelfric declared. 'The skeleton is too well preserved.' He stared down at the tattered, rotting remains of the livery. 'Those are the Harcourt arms. Who is it?' He glanced at Corbett.

'Sir Reginald,' Corbett replied. He crouched down and tapped the mud-caked coverlet. 'This was probably his cloak, the boots have been removed and, apart from the chainmail and this surcoat, the rest has rotted away. I can detect no other wound except these smashed ribs.'

Once again he pushed back the chainmail.

'It was probably a sword wound. A powerful thrust which penetrated his ribs and went up into his heart. He must have died instantly. Whoever killed him, quickly removed all insignia: the clasp of the cloak, rings – perhaps the boots had recognisable studs or buttons which might have identified the corpse?'

'Then why not remove the surcoat?' Ranulf asked.

'Because it was stained with blood and caught in the mesh of the chainmail. As I said, whoever killed Sir Reginald had to act swiftly.'

Corbett got to his feet, peered into the makeshift grave and used the hoe to make sure there was nothing else.

'But the stories?' Prior Cuthbert protested. 'Sir Reginald was seen leaving his house. Lady Margaret and Sir Stephen spent months searching for him!'

'All a lie,' Corbett replied, 'though I am not too sure who was responsible. What really happened was that one summer's evening, many years ago, Sir Reginald came down to Bloody Meadow to meet his assassin. He was killed and his corpse swiftly buried in the tumulus. His murderer moved quickly and expertly. He probably removed the top soil, dug out this make-shift grave, stripped the corpse as quickly as he could and slipped it in.'

'Who?' Prior Cuthbert asked.

'I have yet to discover that. But look, Prior Cuthbert.' Corbett wiped the mud from his gauntlets. 'The remains of Sir Reginald Harcourt deserve decent burial.'

'Oh, yes, yes.'

'Other pressing matters await me,' Corbett explained. 'Have the remains put in your death house.'

'And the mound?'

Prior Cuthbert's face was white with cold, his eyes watered and his nose had turned a bright red.

'You've been very helpful. The mound has now been disturbed. You and your brothers might as well finish the task and search for Sigbert's corpse.'

Corbett strode away, with Ranulf and Chanson following. Once they were through the Judas Gate, Corbett ordered Chanson to prepare the horses.

'Did you expect that?' Ranulf asked.

'Yes, I did and soon I'll explain why.'

'And the murderer?'

Ranulf peered at his master.

'Sir Reginald was murdered by more than one person. It would have taken two or three people, to dig a hole like that and cover it quickly.'

Corbett didn't wait for further questions but strode on. Chanson had their horses saddled by the main gate. A lay brother swung this open. They went through but, instead of going onto the main trackway, Corbett rode quickly round the walls. He was relieved to find the Watcher squatting outside his bothy.

'He must have drunk deep and late,' Corbett explained. 'Otherwise he might have heard all the excitement and fled.'

The Watcher by the Gates got to his feet as Corbett approached.

'Good morrow, Sir Hugh.' He stared at the mud stains on the clerk's cloak. 'You've been travelling far?'

'No, Master Salyiem. I've been digging! The burial mound in Bloody Meadow contained Sir Reginald Harcourt's corpse, his murdered remains.'

The Watcher stared fearfully and stepped back. If Ranulf hadn't urged his horse up alongside him, he would have fled.

'But Sir Reginald . . .' The hermit's words died on his lips as he gazed up at this severe-faced clerk.

'Come, man,' Corbett stretched out his hand. 'I could arrest you and drag you at the tail of my horse . . .!'

The hermit closed his eyes and quickly crossed himself.

'Get up behind me!'

The Watcher had no choice but to agree. Forcing himself up behind Corbett, he put his arms round the clerk's waist. Corbett could sense his fear from the quick, short gasps, and his trembling arms.

'Where are we going?' he whispered throatily.

'You know where we are going.'

Corbett urged his horse into a canter back along the walls and onto the trackway. They reached Harcourt Manor a short while later. Only once did they pause, at the place in the forest where they had been ambushed. Apart from the scuffed earth and a few broken arrows, all signs of that bloody conflict had disappeared. The manor itself was quiet. Grooms came out to take their horses. Pendler the steward hurried up, huffing and puffing.

'I wish to see the Lady Margaret now,' Corbett demanded, helping the hermit to lower himself out of the saddle.

Pendler looked quickly at the Watcher by the Gates who nodded, his face as white as the snow which still covered the bushes on either side of the main entrance.

Corbett himself dismounted and went quickly up the steps. Ranulf and Chanson, with the Watcher between them, followed. Corbett was about to knock when the door abruptly swung open. Lady Margaret, dressed in a dark-blue robe, her white wimple covered by a furred cowl, greeted them.

'Why, Sir Hugh, I was about to go for a walk.' She grasped a cane in her hand, tapping it on the floor. 'What do you want?'

'I have news about your husband Sir Reginald. I can say it no other way, my lady. He did not leave for an Eastern port. His remains have been discovered in the burial mound at Bloody Meadow.'

Lady Margaret swayed. Corbett hastened to steady her. She lowered her head, gasping as if she found it difficult to breathe and, when she glanced up, Corbett was shocked at the sudden change. Her face seemed to have narrowed, the skin tight on the high cheekbones, her eyes haunted and fearful. Pendler came hurrying up the steps.

'Madam, what is the matter?'

Lady Margaret, grasping Corbett's arm, just lifted the cane, gesturing at him to go away.

'You'd best come in.'

She took a deep breath, pushed away Corbett's arm and led them into the parlour. Corbett sat where he had on his last visit. Lady Margaret, still grasping the cane, sat opposite. The three others came in behind and Corbett waved them to the window seat.

'Do you wish some wine, my lady?

'No. Tell me of Sir Reginald. You say you've discovered his remains? How did he die?'

'Why, Madam, he was murdered.'

'By whom?'

'Madam, we both know that.'

*OMNIBUS IGNOTAE MORTIS TIMOR*

IN ALL CREATURES THERE IS THE FEAR OF
UNKNOWN DEATH

OVID

# Chapter 13

Lady Margaret didn't move. She sat gripping her stick, staring at the weak fire, where the flames spluttered around the slightly damp logs.

'You heard what I said, Madam?'

'I heard what you said, clerk. You'd best say your piece.'

'You loved Sir Stephen Daubigny, didn't you?'

Lady Margaret started, as beads of sweat laced her forehead under the wimple.

'Loved!' she murmured harshly.

'You know you did,' Corbett continued matter of factly. 'You were betrothed to Sir Reginald but your heart was Daubigny's, as his was yours.'

'He had a lover, Heloise Argenteuil.'

'No, Madam, that was a jest or, perhaps it was more a tale to cover up what you had done. Decades ago in Paris the famous theologian Abelard fell in love with Heloise, a woman he was tutoring. Abelard was a brilliant scholar, a subtle theologian, a Master in the Schools. Heloise's relatives, however, were furious. They seized Abelard and castrated him. He later withdrew from society but, in spite of all the protests and violence, Abelard and Heloise continued to love each other. Heloise entered a convent at Argenteuil. You took her name to create this fictitious woman whom Stephen Daubigny was supposed to have loved and lost. In reality, it was just to divert suspicion.'

Lady Margaret didn't disagree. A smile appeared on her bloodless lips as if she was relishing a tale she'd once delighted in.

'Reginald Harcourt was your husband,' Corbett continued, 'but Stephen Daubigny was the knight of your heart. You concealed it well under what others considered to be mutual dislike, even contempt. In truth you were lovers. Sir Reginald may have been a personable man but what of his virility?' Corbett glimpsed the surprise on Lady Margaret's face. 'The old infirmarian from St Martin's remembers him well. Stephen Daubigny became a constant visitor at Harcourt Manor and everyone thought it was for love of Sir Reginald, whereas in fact, it was for love of Harcourt's wife. Daubigny played out a game.' Corbett glanced across at the Watcher. 'Whenever he approached the house, he blew three long blasts on his hunting horn. Sir Reginald considered it a jest and, like Charlemagne's knights at Roncesvalles, he would answer back. If Sir Reginald was absent, the lack of any reply was enough for Daubigny to know he was safe. When he and you were closeted alone together, you could continue your deep love for each other.'

Lady Margaret sat upright, clutching the table. She wasn't staring at the fire but gazing straight across at the Watcher. Corbett followed her gaze.

'No, no, Lady Margaret. He has not betrayed you. What I tell you is merely surmise but based on a logic.'

'Then continue with your logic, clerk!'

'I suspect Sir Reginald never knew of your affair until it was too late. Something occurred during the great tournament held here the summer he disappeared. To cut a long story short, he and Daubigny met late one

304

evening in Bloody Meadow. By then Sir Reginald was highly suspicious and accusations were hurled. God forgive them, perhaps these former friends were even drunk. Swords were drawn and, known for his prowess, Daubigny killed Harcourt instantly. His body was stripped of as much as possible so, if discovered, there would be little indication of who he really was. Daubigny removed the top soil from the burial mound, and dug a makeshift grave. He wrapped Sir Reginald's body in its cloak, eased it in and covered it up. Before Bloody Meadow became a matter of contention between the Abbot and his monks, it was a lonely place, where few people would ever go. Any trace of a furtively dug grave was soon well hidden. Daubigny had chosen well. Local lore regarded the grave as something sacred: protected by its own sanctity as well as the religious fervour, or superstition, of others. Sir Stephen, however, was consumed by guilt. Sir Reginald's death had not been planned or wished for: more a matter of hasty words, red wine and hot blood. The next morning Daubigny left Harcourt manor pretending to be Sir Reginald. Dressed in his clothes, cloaked and hooded, he travelled to the Eastern ports, before slipping quietly back.'

Lady Margaret closed her eyes, breathing in deeply. 'Sir Stephen accompanied you abroad to search for Sir Reginald,' Corbett continued. 'He might as well have been chasing moonbeams. He left you in the Low Countries and returned to England. By now he was a changed man. Consumed by remorse, Daubigny entered the Abbey of St Martin's and became to all appearances a model monk. However, his life was haunted by the hideous murder of his friend. He had only to walk a short distance through the Judas Gate to see that threatening funeral mound, reminding him of his great sin. Abbot Stephen viewed Bloody Meadow as a symbol of his life, in fact a wheel, its hub being the burial mound containing the corpse of his murdered friend. He often drew it, probably sub-consciously, for that meadow in the shape of a wheel was never far from Abbot Stephen's thoughts.'

'And the mosaic?' Ranulf called across.

'Yes, when Abbot Stephen found that he must have regarded it as a sign from God. He must have been fascinated by the similarity between an ancient picture and an image which dominated his very being, his soul, his heart, his mind, his every waking moment. He'd betrayed you not only by taking the life of your husband but also, of course, there was the well-proclaimed story of his abandoning you abroad and returning to England. No wonder there was enmity, a barrier of silence between you – it had its roots in the past.' Corbett paused. 'Of course, Madam, my story is incomplete, isn't it? You were also there when your husband was killed. You, and I suspect Salyiem the reeve, the faithful squire, were both party to it. You must have been. You yourself told me that Sir Reginald had left that morning. You made no mention of not seeing him the night before, whilst Salyiem actually claimed he helped Sir Reginald leave the manor house and watched him go.'

Lady Margaret opened her eyes.

In the window seat the Watcher by the Gates had jumped up as if to protest. Lady Margaret gestured for him to re-take his seat. She sat chewing the corner of her mouth.

'God forgive you, clerk, you are sharp. I'll not deny it. You have the truth. I loved Stephen Daubigny from the day I met him. I committed two great sins. I should have followed my heart and married him but, I didn't, I married Sir Reginald. Harcourt was, as you say, likeable but he was not a lady's man. He was impotent.' She sighed. 'Our lovemaking wasn't how the

troubadours describe the act of love. I tried my best.'
Tears brimmed in her eyes. 'I desperately wanted to
remain faithful to Sir Reginald and, to be fair, so did
Stephen. Yet, we might as well have tried to stop the
sun from rising. We concocted a story that we disliked
each other, couldn't abide to be in one another's
company. And Stephen, to make it even safer, fabri-
cated the tale about being in love with some young
noblewoman called Heloise Argenteuil. At the time
we considered it a piece of trickery to distract others.
Sir Reginald never suspected, not till late that hot,
sun-filled summer's day.'

'You told him?'

'No, Sir Hugh, he found out that I was pregnant.
Stephen asked to meet both of us under the shade of
the oak trees in Bloody Meadow. Sir Reginald had
enjoyed a good day at the tournament but he'd drunk
more than he should have done. We met by Falcon
Brook. Salyiem, here, was Stephen's squire and held
the horses. Daubigny went down on his knees, like a
penitent before his confessor. He told Reginald the
truth. I shall never forget my husband's face. He stood
like a man stricken, all colour drained away from his
face, his tongue searched for words. Then it happened,
like a fire bursting up. He suddenly drew his sword and
raised it in one sweeping arc. Daubigny moved, nimble
as a dancer. He rolled aside and drew his own sword, as
Reginald rushed in. Daubigny tried to disarm him. It
happened in the twinkling of an eye – more of an
accident than an intended blow. Sir Stephen's sword
entered here,' she tapped her left side, 'where the
chainmail shirt was tied, deep up into his chest. I
watched in horror, as did Daubigny. My husband took
one step forward, blood bubbling at his lips. He was
dead before he hit the ground. What could we do on
that beautiful summer's evening, with the brook

gurgling by! Salyiem had heard the clash of swords and came running over.'

'It was my plan,' the Watcher called out. 'My scheme. Sir Stephen would have surrendered his sword to the King but I warned him not to. What use would it be?'

Salyiem approached and, pulling up a stool, sat by Corbett's chair.

'We waited till darkness. We stripped the body but the chainmail and the surcoat proved too difficult to remove so we left them. I went to the burial mound. It was summer but there had been rain and the soil was soft. As a reeve, I knew about cutting and planting, so I removed the top soil, folding back the grass verge and, helped by Sir Stephen using sword and dagger, we hollowed out Sir Reginald's grave. We slipped the corpse inside, wrapped in its cloak, and covered our makeshift grave as best we could. The peasants, even some of the monks, regarded Bloody Meadow as a haunted place. Any sign of our digging was soon covered over. We went back to Falcon Brook and washed ourselves, cleaned away bloodstains. Sir Reginald's clothes, boots and hose were put in a sack, tied with a cord, and burnt. Now the corpse was hidden we were all committed to one plan.' Salyiem glanced at Corbett; he smiled coldly, combing his straggling beard with his fingers. 'Once Sir Reginald was buried, we knew that any discovery could lead to the execution of Sir Stephen, if not all three of us. We then devised our plan and returned to the manor. Early the next morning, Daubigny, cloaked and cowled, and pretending to be Sir Reginald, left Harcourt on his warhorse with his sumpter pony.'

'But wasn't Sir Stephen missed?' Corbett interrupted.

'I gave out he had to leave,' Lady Margaret declared. 'Who would object? At that time the mystery had not begun. Daubigny rode disguised as my husband, to the

Eastern ports. He created quite a fuss so that people would remember him. In looks and colouring, Daubigny and my husband were like brothers. He then got rid of his disguise, sold the horse, pony and harness and, buying the fastest mount, rode swiftly and secretly back to Harcourt.'

'So,' Corbett took up the story, 'Sir Reginald was dead and you were pregnant. You could have claimed the child was posthumous.'

'It would have been too dangerous,' she replied with a shake of her head. 'The pregnancy had hardly begun. People would later think it was a remarkable coincidence. And, as you have discovered, Sir Hugh, Sir Reginald's impotence, his lack of virility, had not remained a chamber secret.'

'So, you pretended to go searching for Sir Reginald?'

'The child was growing within me. Daubigny felt responsible. We crossed the Narrow Seas, through Hainault and Zeeland and into the German states. We deliberately took no servants. We stopped near Cologne, where I stayed in one of the pilgrim taverns. Daubigny went searching and at last discovered a merchant and his wife, who were English and had moved to Germany because of trade. She had always wanted a child but was barren. They accepted Daubigny's suggestion as a parched man would water. I went and lived with them. They never knew who I was: I had changed my name, as had Stephen, and was well furnished with money. We both decided it would be too suspicious if Sir Stephen stayed until I was birthed. Before he left, we discussed the future. Daubigny was distraught. A man who had believed in neither God nor man, a young warrior with his head full of glory, he was now solemn and silent, broken in spirit. He was overcome by guilt at Sir Reginald's death. We both vowed to make reparation.' She tapped the walking cane on the floor. 'The rest you know. Daubigny travelled back to England and entered St Martin's. I gave birth to a beautiful boy. To surrender him broke my heart but that was the price of my sin. When I was ready I left Germany. The merchant furnished me with retainers who took me to the border. There I hired fresh servants and came back to England. Daubigny was already in the monastery.' She pointed across at the Watcher. 'He, too, was consumed with guilt.' She paused. 'I couldn't forget my child. I begged Salyiem to travel back to Cologne to see what had happened to him.'

'I did as my lady asked,' the Watcher interrupted, 'but, when I arrived, the family had gone and a wall of silence greeted me.'

'They suspected that I might return,' Lady Margaret declared, 'so they'd moved elsewhere. Salyiem searched far and wide before coming back. He thought of entering the abbey but,' she gazed sadly at the hermit, 'our Watcher by the Gates had a soft spot for the ladies; the celibate life wasn't for him.'

'He was your go-between, wasn't he?' Corbett asked. 'Between Abbot Stephen and yourself?'

She nodded. 'We had taken a vow never to meet again. Salyiem was our messenger: nothing in writing, just words. We pretended to be enemies, arguing over Falcon Brook. I am sure you guessed, clerk, that I couldn't give a fig for Falcon Brook. I took a vow to entertain no other man. You saw those travellers, the beggars who visited the manor the last time you visited us? They too are part of my reparation. Poor Stephen!' She sighed. 'He became a priest even though he believed in nothing. He was an avid scholar and proved to be a skilled theologian. He thought that by hunting demons he could exorcise his own and find something substantial on which to build his faith.'

Lady Margaret began to cry, not loudly but

dramatically; an old woman, tears streaming down her cheeks.

'God forgive me,' she whispered. 'I loved Daubigny more than life itself, I still do. One night of passion, Corbett.' She held up her hand. 'Just one night and our entire world was shattered. I thought I had made reparation but always, deep in my heart, I knew the demons would return. Sir Reginald's body lay in unhallowed ground. Blood demands blood. Vengeance seeks retribution. Murder shrieks for justice.'

'And Abbot Stephen's death?'

'It came as a bolt out of the blue, like a thunderstorm on a summer's afternoon. I assure you, clerk, I know nothing of it.' She gripped Corbett's hand. 'You do though, don't you?'

Corbett smiled sadly.

'You won't tell me?'

'Not now, not till it's over. Tell me, my lady, did you ever meet Abbot Stephen, by day or night, here or elsewhere?'

'Never! We kept our vow!'

'Did he ever ask about his son?'

'Not at first. But, about three or four years ago, through Salyiem, he began to question me closely. I realised that the loss of his son hurt as much as the death of Sir Reginald.'

'I brought messages,' the Watcher spoke up. 'Abbot Stephen wanted the names of the foster parents, everything Lady Margaret knew about them.'

'He went searching, didn't he?' Lady Margaret asked.

'Of course,' Corbett agreed. 'Abbot Stephen was used by the King to lead embassies to many of the courts of Europe. He had a wide circle of friends, people who could help him.'

Lady Margaret closed her eyes.

'I . . . I think . . .'

311

'You suspect what happened,' Corbett finished the sentence for her.

She glanced at him sharply, opened her mouth to reply but paused at a sound from outside.

'How did you get to know, Corbett? When I heard of your arrival I thought it would take you years even to suspect the truth.'

'Heloise Argenteuil . . .'

'That silly, little secret!' she interrupted. 'A fairy tale, a jest.'

'It was obvious that Sir Stephen loved someone.' Corbett remarked. 'Once I knew Heloise Argenteuil was a fiction I began to wonder why. I suspected that your enmity was not as real as it appeared. And, as for you, Salyiem . . .'

'I didn't betray my master.'

'Not deliberately,' Corbett agreed. 'I always wondered why the Abbot should open his heart to you, but, of course, he was accustomed to do so. And then there was his Remembrance Book – why should Abbot Stephen pray for a woman who never existed? I finally realised that Heloise Argenteuil was what he called you, wasn't it?' Corbett placed his hand over Lady Margaret's.

'Will I be arrested?' Lady Margaret asked.

Corbett shook his head. 'It may be a sin to love unwisely but it's not a crime.'

'I was present at my husband's death.'

'But you did not will it. If the truth be known, I doubt Daubigny wanted him killed either. It just happened and the poisoned flower took root. Now, decades later, it comes to full flower.'

Corbett got to his feet, he felt slightly stiff, tense.

'But you will arrest someone?'

'Oh yes, my lady. I must ask you and your servant Salyiem to remain here at Harcourt. He is not to return to St Martin's until tomorrow.'

Corbett bowed and, followed by Chanson and Ranulf, left the hall. Their horses were brought round. Corbett swiftly mounted, bracing himself against the cold breeze which seemed to have strengthened.

'Heloise Argenteuil!' Ranulf exclaimed. 'So much from so little?'

Corbett gathered the reins. 'So much *for* so little, Ranulf, but that's the way of the human heart, isn't it? We'll travel swiftly back to St Martin's. I will go direct to the Abbot's chamber. Once there I will tell you whom to gather.'

'Will it be dangerous?' Chanson asked.

'Oh yes.' Corbett dug his spurs in. 'We are dealing with a heart full of hate!'

Corbett sat in the Abbot's lodgings. He'd arrived back and walked around St Martin's, measuring out distances. He felt as if the abbey had closed in around him. Gargoyle faces contrasted with the holy demeanour of saints depicted in the stained glass windows. The statues in their carved niches staring stonily down at him. The hollow creak of his boots echoed along pavement and passageways. He opened his eyes and mind to impressions of the abbey: the dark, musty cellars and cavernous chambers; the different smells of the abbey, beeswax and ink, vellum and manuscripts; the coldness of the death house; the sweet warmth of the kitchens. Now he was ready for the final confrontation. There was a knock on the door and Prior Cuthbert came in. He still looked frozen, whilst mud heavily caked his robe and sandals.

'Sir Hugh, I would like to speak to you alone.'

'What is it?'

Prior Cuthbert shuffled his feet in embarrassment. 'We opened the funeral barrow.'

'And?' Corbett asked.

'We found a coffin, many centuries old. The wood was rotting but of good quality. Inside lay a skeleton, a person of rank.'

'So, you found your saintly Sigbert?'

'No, from the fabric and the ornaments we could tell the coffin must have contained the corpse of a woman.'

The Prior looked sheepishly at Corbett, who threw his head back and bellowed with laughter.

'You are sure?' he asked.

'As sure as I am of standing here. The skeleton was whole and undecayed. It is miraculous! It even had tufts of blonde hair still on the skull. It bore a sword mark here.' The Prior touched his left shoulder, just below his neck.

'And who do you think it was?' Corbett asked, drying his eyes on the back of his hand.

'We consulted the manuscripts. It may have been Sigbert's eldest daughter Bertholda, a Frankish princess. She, too, ruled the small kingdom which once existed here. The heathens may have martyred her because of her faith.'

Corbett leaned back in the chair and studied this shrewd Prior.

'So, you have your relic?'

'Yes, Sir Hugh, we have our relic. It's being preserved in the death house.'

Corbett clapped his hands. 'You mean until this matter is over. Ranulf!' he shouted at his henchman who had been guarding the door. 'Bring the rest up! Father Prior, we have business!'

One by one they entered the chamber: the members of the Concilium, Dunstan, Aelfric and Richard; Archdeacon Wallasby and finally Perditus. They sat on the stools Ranulf had prepared. Chanson guarded the door whilst Ranulf came and sat beside Corbett. Sir

Hugh took out his commission, displaying the royal seal, and laid it on the desk. To show he was one of the King's Justices, his sword was placed beside it.

'I am the King's Commissioner in these parts,' Corbett began. 'For all intents and purposes this is a court, busy on the matters of the Crown. First, I wish to comment on the death of Abbot Stephen and the hideous murders perpetrated in this abbey. So, Abbot Stephen's death,' Corbett pulled himself up and stared round. 'To all intents and purposes you are all guilty.' He made a cutting movement with his hand to quell their protests. 'In many ways,' he continued, 'Abbot Stephen was an eccentric man. A priest searching for a reason for both his faith and his vocation. I shall not explain, not yet, why Sir Stephen Daubigny became a monk but he had his secrets, including the violent death of his old friend Sir Reginald Harcourt whose pathetic remains were found in that funeral barrow.' Corbett paused. 'Daubigny was responsible for his death.'

'No!' Aelfric protested. 'It cannot be!'

'Yes, it is true and I can prove it. He killed Harcourt, not maliciously but in a violent quarrel over a woman they both loved. Daubigny hid his sin behind pretence but atoned for it by a life of reparation. Daubigny, however, didn't believe in God, His angels or the power of the Church. He constantly searched for proof. He became an avid scholar, a peritus, a theologian skilled in the study of demonology. By pursuing Satan,' Corbett added, 'Abbot Stephen thought he might find God. I suppose his life as an Abbot provided some peace until his ambitious Concilium started to make demands about the funeral barrow.'

'So, he wasn't protecting sacred remains?' Prior Cuthbert interrupted. 'But his own secret sin?'

'Of course. Now,' Corbett continued, trying to hide his gaze from the man he knew to be the assassin, 'the

Concilium waged their own private secret war against their Abbot.'

'We did not!' Brother Dunstan exclaimed.

'You did!' Corbett banged his fist on the table. 'Not openly! The Rule of St Benedict is quite clear about the obedience of a community to its Abbot. You all went your different ways until Archdeacon Wallasby entered these hallowed precincts to wreak his own mischief. He wanted to humiliate Abbot Stephen, to prove that he wasn't an exorcist. He was helped, was he not, by some of you? But as he plotted, treachery curled back like a viper and struck its handlers. Taverner, the cunning man, was much impressed by your Father Abbot; at first involved in Wallasby's malicious scheming, Taverner later refused any part in the mummery and mischief you'd planned.'

'What is this?' Prior Cuthbert exclaimed.

He stared round at his companions but the expressions on Aelfric's and Wallasby's faces showed him Corbett was telling the truth.

'Oh, Father Prior, don't be so sanctimonious,' Corbett declared, 'you must have heard whispers about what was plotted?'

'Yes, yes, he did,' Aelfric interrupted. 'Oh come, come, Brother,' the infirmarian jibed. 'You knew Wallasby and I met. Surely you suspected Taverner wasn't what he claimed to be?'

'You did worse than that, didn't you, Father Prior?' Corbett tapped his fingers on the pommel of his sword. 'You went hunting by yourself. One night you saw your Father Abbot embrace and kiss a shadowy figure, dressed like a monk, out in Bloody Meadow. You accused him of unnatural vice, hinted that exposure might bring disgrace, threatened that if you did not have your way regarding the building of the guest-house . . .'

Corbett paused at the protests and exclamations which broke out. Prior Cuthbert sat, head down, like a convicted prisoner ready to be led off to Newgate and the executioner's cart. Aelfric sneered whilst Richard and Dunstan looked horrified.

'How could you!' the Almoner shouted. 'How could you!'

'It's a lie,' the treasurer declared leaning forward, red-faced. 'Sir Hugh, that's a lie!'

'No, Prior Cuthbert had half the truth. He saw Father Abbot kiss and embrace a member of his community but he didn't know the reason why. I'll come to that in a while. Anyway, Father Abbot felt trapped. He knew a gulf had opened up between himself and his brothers. The issue of Bloody Meadow was a dagger pointed at his heart, an invitation to all the demons from his past to return. He could never give way, so the tension between him and you only intensified. If he did surrender, his secret sin would be exposed. A man of shaky faith, Abbot Stephen retreated into himself, believing his past had returned to haunt him. On the day that Abbot Stephen died, something in his soul snapped, shattered.' Corbett paused. 'On that same evening Abbot Stephen came up to this chamber. He locked and barred the windows and doors and he began to brood. He could see no way out of his predicament. The night wore on. He drank some wine and glanced through the window.' Corbett half turned and pointed. 'He saw the reflection of the candles in the glass. In the Abbot's fevered, distraught imagination he believed he was seeing his own Corpse Candles beckoning him to death: that's why he wrote down the quotation from St Paul, about seeing things through a glass, darkly and about the Corpse Candles, those mysterious lights seen on the marshes beyond the abbey, beckoning him to death. The Scriptures provided little comfort for him. Instead

Abbot Stephen reflected on the ancient Romans, their culture, the civilisation he so deeply loved. He recalled Seneca, the famous Roman philosopher, who wrote: "Anyone can take away a man's life, but no one his death". Abbot Stephen brooded on those words, sinking deeper and deeper into a morass of despair and depression, what the theologians called the sin against the Holy Ghost.'

Corbett stared at the Prior. The awful realisation had dawned on Cuthbert. He sat like a man facing death, mouth opening and closing as if he wished to speak but couldn't find the words to express himself.

'Oh *Domine Jesu, Miserere Nobis*!' the Prior whispered. 'Sir Hugh, are you saying Abbot Stephen committed suicide?'

The chamber fell deathly silent. Corbett stared at each of them.

'Abbot Stephen,' Corbett chose his words carefully, 'was a man driven to the brink and finally tipped over. He could see no way out except the Roman way, the fate of Seneca.' Corbett pointed at the coffer. 'He took out his dagger, sat in his chair, positioned it carefully and thrust it deep into his chest. It would have taken only a matter of seconds, a terrible searing pain, before he lost consciousness, which is why no clamour was heard, no cry, no disturbance. Abbot Stephen's soul slipped silently into endless night.'

Prior Cuthbert sat with his face in his hands, shoulders shaking.

'You can weep,' Brother Aelfric shouted, 'but his blood is on your hands!'

'His blood is on all your hands!'

Everyone turned to Perditus. He had moved his stool as if he wished to study each of their faces.

'You are all murdering bastards! This is not a monastery, it's the place of the Red Slayer!' He lapsed into German, '*Der Rode Schlächter*. You call yourselves the sons of Benedict? No, you are the sons of Cain!'

They all stared at this lay brother who sat erect, his face contorted with hatred and rage.

'How dare you!' Brother Aelfric shouted.

'Oh be quiet!' Perditus showed his teeth, like the snarl of an attacking dog. 'You with your drooling eyes and ever-wet nose! You are worse than animal shit!'

Corbett watched intently. Perditus wasn't angry with him. All the while Corbett had been speaking, Perditus had sat with a slight smile on his face, head imperceptibly nodding in agreement at his words. Now the truth was out and he couldn't contain himself. Corbett glanced at Ranulf, to see that his henchman had quietly withdrawn his dagger and had it balanced in his lap.

Corbett banged the pommel of his sword on the desk. Perditus paused in his diatribe, not so much because of Corbett but more because he could no longer vent his rage but sat like a man who had run a long, demanding race, gasping and gulping for air.

'Abbot Stephen's death,' Corbett remarked quietly, 'was a hideous sin and the consequence of a heinous threat. It marked the beginning of the real horrors. Isn't that right, Perditus? How much did Abbot Stephen tell you?'

The lay brother's face was ashen except for the red spots of anger high in his cheeks. He shook his head.

'You can speak both English and German,' Corbett continued matter of factly. 'I noticed that when I took you back to your chamber after the alleged attack upon you. One of the manuscripts you were reading was in German. I don't know the tongue but I recognised the cursive script. Where did you get it from, the library?'

Perditus smiled coldly.

'You were raised to speak German and English fluently. You no more come from Bristol than I do. If I made careful search there, I am sure no one would recall you.'

'What is this?' Wallasby demanded, stamping with his boot.

'You!' Perditus turned on him. 'Will ... shut ... up! Because ... you!' Perditus jabbed his finger at the frightened Archdeacon, 'were also on my list. You should thank God, Wallasby, that this clerk kept you from leaving St Martin's. You were special to me, and if you had left, I would have followed.'

Ranulf was about to interrupt but Corbett gestured him to stay silent.

'Scaribrick and his wolf's-heads may not have captured you,' Perditus taunted, 'but I would have done.'

The Archdeacon gulped and looked at Corbett for protection. The clerk stared back.

'I planned to take you on your horse. I was going to put a rope around your neck, half hang you from a branch and use you as an archer's butt, to improve my aim and my skill.'

'Were you an archer?' Corbett interrupted. 'A bowman?'

'I was more than that,' Perditus, now distracted, turned back.

'Yes, I am sure you were,' Corbett agreed. 'Let me see, a professional mercenary, hired by the nobility and powerful merchants of Germany? You and Abbot Stephen discussed Vegetius treatise, *The Art of War*, so you must have been a professional soldier once?'

'I was a Ritter, a knight,' Perditus declared. 'My real name is Franz Chaudenvelt. I led my own company,' he added proudly. He sat, head back as if reminiscing with friends in a tavern, eyes bright with pride. 'I commanded mounted men, hobelars and bowmen.' Perditus faced him squarely.

Corbett wondered whether his look was admiration

at Corbett's discovery or pride in his own bloody deeds.

'I made mistakes, didn't I?' Perditus confessed. 'I knew I shouldn't have left that book on the floor. And, of course . . .'

'Yes,' Corbett interrupted, eager to take over the conversation. 'You talked of phalanxes, describing how the abbey could be defended. Of course, the irony was, you were talking about defending it against yourself!'

'He is the assassin? He killed them all?' Prior Cuthbert exclaimed, shaking his head as if he couldn't believe what he was hearing.

'Of course he is,' Corbett agreed. 'Perditus saw himself as God's justice, his vengeance on the men who had driven Abbot Stephen to his death.'

'He told me, you know,' Perditus almost shouted, 'he told me how the dogs were snapping at his ankles, always demanding . . . Abbot Stephen didn't fear any of you.' His voice turned to a snarl.

'Did he tell you what the funeral barrow contained?' Corbett asked. 'No, he wouldn't, would he?'

Perditus shook his head. 'He simply said it must not be disturbed. He made mysterious references to that funeral barrow being the hub of his life: he never explained what he meant.' He smiled at Corbett. 'You are a clever clerk. Abbot Stephen was always drawing that diagram of the wheel. When I climbed up the funeral barrow I realised what it had meant. No wonder he admired that mosaic in the cellars. But they,' his voice rose as he pointed at the monks, 'are the true assasins. Abbot Stephen was driven distracted by their pleas, their hints, their threats. Oh yes, Prior,' Perditus jibed. 'He told me how you had seen us out in Bloody Meadow; about your blackmail and your nasty threats. If I'd had my way I'd have cut your scrawny throat, but Abbot Stephen would have no violence.'

'You were Abbot Stephen's lover?' Brother Dunstan spoke up.

'Shut up, you fat, lecherous slob! What do you know about love except between the thighs of some tavern wench! Tell them, Corbett. You seem to know everything!'

'Abbot Stephen loved Perditus,' Corbett replied quietly. 'But it was not an unnatural vice but the most natural love: Perditus was his son.'

In any other circumstances the looks on the monks' faces would have provoked Corbett to laughter.

'Son?' Brother Aelfric exclaimed. 'How could a priest have a son?'

'Don't be stupid! Priests' bastards litter one end of Christendom to another,' Perditus snarled.

'Abbot Stephen,' Corbett explained, 'did not father his child when he was a monk but when he was a member of Edward's court, a knight banneret. Perditus?'

The lay brother lifted his head, tears in his eyes.

'Did Abbot Stephen ever tell you about your mother?'

'No.' The reply was a half whisper. 'No, he never did, he never would. He simply said she had died and that her name was Heloise. But, since his death and the events of this morning . . .'

'You mean, what we found in the burial mound?' Corbett asked.

'And when you left for Harcourt Manor,' Perditus replied, 'I began to suspect.'

'Lady Margaret!' Wallasby exclaimed.

'Lady Margaret,' Corbett agreed.

'I didn't know.' Perditus seemed lost in his own thoughts. 'I didn't even suspect. Abbot Stephen hardly mentioned Lady Margaret, and when he did, he described her only as a vexatious neighbour, an old woman he deeply disliked and resented. That was all pretence, wasn't it, Corbett? I should go to her.' He half rose. 'I should see her, shouldn't I?'

In the doorway Chanson quietly withdrew his dagger.

'Sit down!' Corbett ordered. 'Perditus, sit down! Let me finish this matter. Let me explain how you wreaked justice and exacted vengeance?

Perditus, eyes narrowed, sat down.

'There is a likeness, you know,' Corbett said gently. 'When I met Lady Margaret I thought I had seen those features before. You are very like her: the same glance; the way you move your eyes; your iron will; your inflexibility of purpose.'

Corbett deliberately flattered, hoping to soothe this man, whose soul was given up to hate and vengeance.

'Go into the abbey church,' Corbett declared, 'and look carefully at the wall paintings: they describe, in their own secret code, the life of Daubigny and of Daubigny's son. They show how this place became his refuge, his exile, though the painting of Cain slaying Abel was a constant reminder of the evil he had done.'

'I wish Father had told me,' Perditus was speaking to himself.

'Perhaps he would have done,' Corbett reassured. 'In time.'

'How did this all come about?' Prior Cuthbert demanded.

'I will tell you,' Corbett retorted. 'And, when I am finished,' he pointed to the bible resting on the lectern at the far corner of the room, 'you shall all take a solemn oath never to reveal or discuss what you hear today. Sir Stephen Daubigny and Margaret Harcourt have paid for their sins. Hate and rage have had their way. Enough blood has been spilt.' He glanced at Perditus. 'There will be truth and then there will be silence!'

*FRANGIT FORTIA CORDA DOLOR*

REJECTION CAN SMASH EVEN THE
STRONG AT HEART

TIBULLUS

# Chapter 14

'Did Abbot Stephen tell you what he planned?'

'No,' Perditus seemed not to be concentrating. 'No, not really. On one occasion he claimed the best solution was the Roman way. I didn't truly understand what he meant. Afterwards I realised he had taken his own life: that was the only logical explanation.'

'How did you discover you were Abbot Stephen's son?

'I was born and raised in Germany,' Perditus declared. 'For many years I believed the man and woman who raised me were my natural parents. They treated me kindly enough but there was always a distance between me and them. I didn't want to be a merchant but a soldier. My foster father died when I was still young, and his wife later fell ill. On her deathbed she told me some of the truth: that my parents were English born, and my real mother was of noble birth.' He shrugged. 'But that was all. Abbot Stephen later confessed that, as he grew older, the thought of me haunted him. He often led embassies to the courts of Northern Europe and, as you know, he built up a wide circle of friends, who could advise and help him. Four years ago the Archbishop of Mainz asked to see me. He had Abbot Stephen waiting in the chamber. The Archbishop left

327

us alone, and Abbot Stephen went down on his knees.'
Perditus's voice grew thick with emotion. 'He knelt
like a penitent, hands joined before him. He confessed
that he was my natural father, that he and my mother
had travelled from England and given me away as a
foster child.'

'Did you believe him?'

'At first I was dumbfounded yet I knew he spoke the
truth. On one matter he was resolved. He would tell
me very little about my true mother. He simply gave
her name as Heloise and claimed she died shortly after
my birth.'

'Did you follow Abbot Stephen back to England?'

The chamber was now hushed. Archdeacon Wallasby
and the monks sat like scholars in a schoolroom
listening to one of their colleagues make a full confession of every offence he'd committed.

'No, not at first. I cursed him. I nearly lashed out
with my boot as he just knelt there, tears streaming
down his cheeks. He said he loved me, that he'd paid
for his sins, that he'd do anything in atonement. He
was so calm, so full of remorse: it wasn't easy for him.
That same evening we dined alone in one of the city
taverns. Despite my anger,' Perditus half smiled, 'I was
much taken by Abbot Stephen. I considered him a
genuinely holy man, a scholar. When I heard about his
exploits as a warrior my heart glowed with pride. Abbot
Stephen told me he would accept whatever I did; he
said I could even travel to London and denounce him
from St Paul's Cross. He left for England. I waited a
year before I followed, not for revenge or for justice – I
just wanted to be with him. He welcomed me with
open arms. I became a lay brother, and I took the name
Perditus.'

'Ah yes,' Corbett interrupted. 'I thought so. Perditus
is Latin for "that which is lost".'

'Abbot Stephen laughed when I made my choice. I tell you this, clerk, despite the shaven heads around us, those years with my true father were the happiest of my life. Publicly I acted as his manservant, but in private we were truly father and son. He told me all about the marshes, the legends of Mandeville and how, as an impetuous young man he used to go out and blow his hunting horn.'

'And so you did likewise?'

'Yes.' Perditus half laughed as if enjoying himself. 'I never told Abbot Stephen but I think he suspected. I was so happy. I would have remained happy.' Perditus's face turned ugly. 'Perhaps one day I would have been told the truth about my mother if it hadn't been for that damnable Bloody Meadow and the greed of these monks! On spring and summer evenings, Abbot Stephen and I would often go out there to walk and talk. We thought we were safe. One night we heard the Judas Gate clatter and I knew we were being spied on.'

'You hastened back,' Corbett demanded. 'You may be monkish in your studies and your singing but you are still an athletic young man.'

'I climbed the wall, reached the Abbot's lodgings and was there when our prying Prior came slithering along. The threats began soon afterwards. When Abbot Stephen took his own life, I hid my sorrow and turned to vengeance.'

'To murder!'

'No, clerk, I meted out justice. If I had my way I'd have burnt this abbey to the ground, not left one stone upon another. Gildas was first: a monk more at home in his workshop than his choir stall. I brained him, hid his body and, after dark, dragged it out and placed it on the burial mound as a warning to the rest. I went out onto the marshes. My father had hunted demons, but I called upon these same demons to help me.'

'Why did you kill Taverner?' Ranulf interrupted.

'You heard him confess his subterfuge, didn't you?' Corbett said.

'But I thought Perditus was helping Chanson in the library?' Ranulf declared.

'No, no, he was eavesdropping.' Corbett winked at his henchman. 'After Taverner confessed his trickery, Perditus, frightened of being caught, hastened back. He met Chanson coming from the library.' Corbett glanced at his groom. 'He offered to help you, didn't he?'

'Yes.' The groom, in a reverie of astonishment at Corbett's blatant lie, nodded quickly.

'That's the truth,' Perditus remarked. 'Why should that trickster escape? He planned to make a mockery of my father. Abbot Stephen had been so excited about his case. I took the fat Archdeacon's bow and arrows from his quiver. This abbey is like a rabbit warren. Taverner came slipping through the morning mist and took an arrow straight through his heart.'

'And then you branded him?' Corbett demanded.

'I wanted to put the fear of God into those mean-minded monks. I fashioned a branding iron. Gildas was the first and, when I was ready, I placed the same brand, the devil's mark, on Taverner and Hamo. I was so excited about the sub-Prior's death. I went into the kitchen with some powder from the infirmarian's chest. I chose a tankard and slipped it in. It was like playing Hazard. I didn't mind which one of these cowards drank the poison. All I knew was that one of them would die.' Perditus shook his fist in Cuthbert's direction. 'I just hoped it wasn't you. I wanted to save you to the last. I wanted you to experience the same fears and terrors my father did.'

'And the librarian, Brother Francis?' Corbett reminded him.

'Ah, he was different. In a way I felt sorry for him. He was a member of the Concilium and had always been kind to me but he was dangerous. The day he died I went down into the library. I wondered if, perhaps, amongst the books Abbot Stephen borrowed, I might find further clues to my past. Brother Francis took me aside. He told me that he had been reflecting upon Abbot Stephen's death. He wondered if it was suicide and claimed that Abbot Stephen must have had some great secret which perhaps could explain both his death and the bloody murders which followed. He questioned me closely. "Come on, Brother." he urged. "You were not only Abbot Stephen's manservant but also his friend." I could see he was suspicious. I told him that I knew nothing, that I couldn't help him. He still claimed the truth lay somewhere in that library.'

'It was,' Corbett interrupted. 'I discovered a love poem that your father wrote as a farewell when he first entered the abbey.'

'Did you?' Perditus was now like a little boy. 'Can I see it?'

'Brother Francis?' Corbett demanded.

'Oh yes. He was kindly and studious but very much a busybody. I decided he should die quickly. He thought he was safe in the library but, during the day, I had loosened the shutter covering one of the arrow slit windows. That night, while the other monks were stuffing their faces, I took my bow and arrows and went towards the library. I rattled the shutter, removed it and strung my arrow. For a bowman, it was an easy target as Brother Francis had the light behind him. The rest you know.' He grinned. 'My eyesight's better than I pretend.'

'Didn't you care?' Brother Dunstan snarled.

'Of course I cared, about my father. I would have taken you as well, you fat, lecherous monk! My father suspected your visits to the Lantern-in-the-Woods were not just on abbey business. Every day you should slump on your fat knees and thank God you are safe.'

Corbett glanced warningly at Ranulf. Perditus was enjoying himself. He hated these monks so much, he loved the taunting and the jibes describing how clever he was and the vengeance he had planned. But what would happen when it was all finished?

'And the cat?' Ranulf called out.

'Oh, that was to emphasise the parallels with the Mandeville story,' Perditus had now forgotten Dunstan. 'I was sorry for the poor creature, but I had to test the powders I had taken from Aelfric. The cat died very quickly, and then I cut its throat, put it into a sack, with a hook tied to one of its legs by a piece of twine. The abbey church is full of shadows. I bided my time, slipped through the sacristy door and hung the cat up in the twinkling of an eye.' He clapped his hands suddenly, making the monks jump. 'You were all frightened, weren't you?'

'And the fire arrows?'

'Again they came from the Mandeville story. I had to keep these monks on their toes. It was easy: a dish of burning charcoal and arrows dipped in tarred pitch. I slipped through the postern gate, knowing I would not be seen in the dead of night. I didn't want anyone to forget. I didn't want anyone to relax and think it was finished.'

'That's why you trapped us in the cellar, wasn't it?' Ranulf asked.

'Yes,' Perditus glanced sadly back. 'I did warn you.'

'Yes, you did,' Corbett agreed. 'You jammed the door to the Abbot's lodgings that night. By the time I'd freed the wood and, as a new arrival at St Martin's, found my way, you had left by a window. You were waiting for me behind that grille?'

'I could tell, even then, you'd find the truth,' Perditus sighed. 'I didn't really want to kill you but you moved fast, like a greyhound searching out its quarry, backwards and forwards, backwards and forwards.'

'You could have killed us in the cellar?'

'True and the King's anger would have blazed out against the Abbey of St Martin's,' Perditus smiled at Prior Cuthbert. 'It will never be the same now. Corbett is going to report to the King. Oh, our prince will keep it secret, to protect my father's name and that of Lady Margaret!' He smirked. 'However, I don't think he'll forget you, Prior Cuthbert! Your ambition to succeed as Abbot will never be realised.'

'At least I'll be alive!'

'Stop it!' Corbett interrupted. 'You were frightened that we would discover the truth, Perditus.'

'It was only a matter of time.'

'But the fire?' Richard the almoner spoke up. 'I understand that when the fire broke out in the store room, Perditus was here, suffering from injuries.'

'That was another defence.' Corbett leaned forward. 'Perditus had been a soldier and was used to knocks and bruises, so it wasn't difficult to inflict them on himself. He's also skilled in starting slow fires. I've seen the King's men do the same: they take a long piece of heavy cloth and twist it into a rope. They smear it with tar and pitch, place one end in the building about to be destroyed, in a bucket of oil or something dry and combustible.' Corbett paused. 'You did inflict those cuts and bruises on yourself?'

'A small price,' Perditus retorted. 'It gave me more time.'

'Cuts and minor bruises,' Corbett observed. 'You then lit your oil-soaked rope and came hastening to me. I saw where you had practised,' Corbett continued, 'amongst the oak trees which ring Bloody Meadow.'

'I had to make sure it would work,' Perditus observed. 'Do you know what I really planned? The death of every monk in this room.' He pointed at the almoner. 'You would not have escaped if it hadn't been for that damnable vase! Oh, how I would have danced to view your corpse and this entire place in flames.'

'You are mad,' Cuthbert declared. 'Wicked, steeped in sin.'

'We truly are brothers in arms,' Perditus jibed. 'Given enough time I would have taken all your lives.' He snapped his fingers. 'Snuffed them out like candle wicks!'

'You really do believe you are lord of life and death?' Corbett remarked. He noticed how Wallasby was sitting quiet and composed, a look of smug satisfaction on his face.

'What do you mean?' Perditus stamped his foot: that gesture alone warned Corbett. He was no longer dealing with a sane man. Perditus really saw himself as the Vengeance of God.

'Do you consider yourself the reincarnation of Mandeville's ghost?' Corbett tried to keep the taunt out of his voice. 'That you have become the lord of life and death in the Abbey of St Martin's?'

Perditus looked puzzled.

'You brand your victims,' Corbett explained, 'like a farmer would his cattle, marking his possessions – even dead they had to bear your imprint.'

'Of course!'

'Let us return to Taverner's death,' Corbett mused. 'Why should you kill a man whom your father cherished and protected? A man who was going to help him in his study of demonology and provide the proof Abbot Stephen needed that an exorcism, a true exorcism, could take place?'

'Taverner was a trickster. As you said, I eavesdropped

on your conversation and overheard what he said. Taverner was a liar.'

'But that's not quite true, is it?' Corbett declared. 'This morning, after my return from Harcourt Manor, I visited Taverner's chamber. I went inside, closed the door and stood where I had when I questioned the cunning man. Ranulf stayed outside. The doors and walls of this abbey are very thick. Ranulf could hear nothing, not even a murmur. If you *had* overheard Taverner, you would've rejoiced at what he said: the Cunning Man was not going to betray Abbot Stephen, he was going to help him.'

'What are you saying?' Prior Cuthbert demanded.

Corbett turned to Wallasby.

'You really did hate Abbot Stephen, didn't you?'

The Archdeacon swallowed hard, his smug smile had disappeared.

'You were going to destroy him,' Corbett continued, 'and Taverner was your weapon. Perditus tried to eavesdrop on Taverner's confession but couldn't hear anything, whereas you, of course, knew the truth. Your treacherous plot had collapsed and Abbot Stephen was dead. You knew that, as a royal clerk, I would be reporting my findings to the King who would not be best pleased to learn that the Archdeacon of St Paul's was involved in such trickery. But the only proof I had was Taverner.'

The Archdeacon scraped back his stool. Perditus, as if he was an accomplice, stretched out his hand, forcing him to stay still.

'You'd sown the tempest,' Corbett declared, 'and now you had to reap the whirlwind. Instead of Abbot Stephen facing disgrace and humiliation, it was the turn of Adrian Wallasby, Archdeacon of St Paul's.'

'I didn't . . .'

'Oh, yes, you did,' Corbett interrupted. 'Taverner was

a very dangerous man to you. He had been looking forward to a life of leisure at the Abbey of St Martin's until his protector, Abbot Stephen, died. He could blackmail you. In fact, I suspect he already had. Amongst his possessions I found some silver and gold coins. The Abbot's personal accounts showed no disbursements to Taverner, so that gold and silver came from you. You seized your chance when Abbot Stephen and Gildas had been murdered. It was clear that an assassin was loose amongst the monks so you thought one more death wouldn't matter?'

'You can't prove anything!' Wallasby regained his composure. 'True, an arrow from my quiver was used but Perditus could have stolen it: he has already confessed to the crime.'

'But he didn't do it,' Corbett replied. 'You did. On the morning Taverner died, he took us down to the cellar to see the Abbot's Roman mosaic. When we came back I met Perditus busy with some task. We walked a little further and then Taverner left us and was killed shortly afterwards. I have walked this abbey time and again, and this morning I measured the distances. No matter how athletic or nimble-footed Perditus might be, he could not possibly have gone to fetch a bow and arrows and return to lurk on that misty path. It was you, Archdeacon Wallasby. One well-aimed arrow and all the proof of your trickery, all the menaces Taverner could muster were silenced. Another death at St Martin's, for which someone else could take the blame. No wonder you wanted to leave so urgently. Of course,' Corbett concluded, 'Perditus was glad Taverner was dead. In his own frenetic mind perhaps he believed he was responsible. You must have been relieved when Taverner's forehead, as well as Hamo's, was branded with the Mandeville mark.'

Perditus had now turned on his stool and was looking

full at the Archdeacon, head slightly to one side. He glanced at Corbett, a puzzled look in his eye. The monks just sat shocked at the devastating revelations. The assassin was correct: these were broken men, monks who must bear some responsibility for the bloody events in this abbey.

'Are you saying, Sir Hugh, that I did not kill Taverner? That this one was the culprit?' Perditus tapped the Archdeacon's hand. Wallasby removed it abruptly.

'You can't prove anything,' Wallasby declared. 'This man is the true assassin.' His face turned ugly. 'His hands should be bound like a common malefactor. He can be taken back to London and tried before the King's Bench for murder, blasphemy and sacrilege. He'll die at the Elms with the noose around his neck, face turning purple, feet kicking. A fitting end,' he taunted, 'for the son of our holy Abbot Stephen!'

'Will I hang?' Perditus asked, eyes rounded in consternation. 'I am a cleric in holy orders.'

'No, you are not!' Wallasby jibed. 'You are a—'

Corbett sensed the coming danger but it was too late. Perditus, taunted by Wallasby's jibes, abruptly sprang to his feet. He picked up the stool and threw it at Corbett. The clerk moved sideways so that the stool crashed behind him. Wallasby was not so quick. Perditus drew a dagger from the sleeve of his gown and sliced the Archdeacon deeply across the neck, from underneath his right ear up under his chin. The Archdeacon sat slightly forward, hands to his wound, the blood pouring out between his fingers. Ranulf leapt to his feet but Perditus was already across the chamber. He knocked Brother Dunstan aside and, before the almoner could intervene, had seized the surprised Prior Cuthbert round the neck, pushing the dagger up under his chin.

'Stand back!'

Ranulf looked at Corbett who shook his head. The clerk knew he had made a mistake. Perhaps he should have restrained Perditus from the beginning but then he would not have confessed. The assassin was now dragging Prior Cuthbert towards the door. He looked over his shoulder.

'Open it!' he shouted at Chanson.

Corbett gestured at his groom to obey. The door to the chamber swung open even as Archbishop Wallasby collapsed to the floor in an ever-widening pool of splashing blood. Aelfric hurried across and turned him over. The desperation on the Archdeacon's face and the jerking of his body showed he was past help. Corbett watched in horror. At first he thought Perditus was going to release Prior Cuthbert. He drew his arm away but then swiftly slashed with his knife. Corbett closed his eyes. Prior Cuthbert stood, a look of horror on his face, hands clutching his throat. Perditus sent him crashing forward and was out of the door in an instant, pounding down the stairs.

Ranulf ignored the chaos and commotion. He thrust Chanson aside and followed in pursuit. Perditus had already cleared the steps and was out through the door. Ranulf, hastily drawing his sword, chased after him. As he slipped and slithered on the ice, Ranulf was almost unaware of the monks he pushed aside: he had eyes only for the hurtling figure ahead of him, grey robe hitched up, running like the wind, past buildings, across courtyards, twisting and turning. Ranulf followed. At first he thought the assassin was heading for one of the postern gates or even the stables. He shortened the gap between them. Perditus had reached the cellar steps and hastened down. Ranulf followed, surprised that the door wasn't locked or bolted. He pushed it open and slipped into the darkness. The slap of sandals echoed back as Ranulf paused to regain his breath. He put down his sword, took out a tinder and lit one of the sconce torches. Once this was burning brightly, he grasped his sword and made his way gingerly down the passageway, hugging the wall, stretching the torch out in front of him. He passed the cavernous storerooms, wondering what Perditus intended. Behind him Corbett shouted his name.

'Go back!' Ranulf yelled.

Perditus was a skilled enemy, a trained soldier. Ranulf was fearful he'd taken a bow and arrow and was preparing an ambush. A pool of light glowed at the end of the corridor: Perditus was in the storeroom at the end where Abbot Stephen had found the mosaic. Ranulf watched the light carefully, expecting to see Perditus, armed with bow and arrow, appear in the doorway. Apart from a moving shadow, he could detect nothing. Closer and closer he crept. At the doorway he stopped and threw the torch in onto the floor. He slipped down the steps and paused in astonishment. Perditus, sword and dagger on the ground beside him, was kneeling, staring at the mosaic.

'It's beautiful, isn't it?' he whispered, tracing the outline with his finger. 'Abbot Stephen loved it, you know. He wanted to take it up and put it in the sanctuary. Don't you think it's beautiful, Ranulf?'

'Yes, yes, I do.'

'It shouldn't be kept here,' Perditus continued. 'These mumbling monks don't know true beauty when they see it.'

'You have killed Archdeacon Wallasby and Prior Cuthbert,' Ranulf declared.

'I am not bothered about them. They were marked for death anyway. It's a pity I couldn't have finished the whole tiresome business. I was never going to kill you though. Abbot Stephen would have liked you. I tried to warn Corbett. I just wanted you to go and leave these sinners to my justice.' He caressed the mosaic again. 'I have only two real regrets: I should have acted faster to ensure the deaths of all those damned monks. My second regret is that I never met my mother.' He smiled at Ranulf. 'But it's best if she didn't see me as a felon, hands and feet bound, eh? Tell me the truth, Ranulf-atte-Newgate: they'll hang me in London, won't they?'

'If you were considered mad,' Ranulf replied, 'the King might have mercy and immure you for the rest of your life . . .'

'Ah well.'

Ranulf knew all the street-fighting tricks: Perditus had gone slack, shoulders drooping. He stepped back. The assassin grabbed sword and dagger and sprang to his feet, slightly crouched. In the torchlight he looked composed, eyes serene, a dreamy, faraway expression on his face.

'Put up your weapons!' Ranulf ordered.

Perditus danced forward, sword and dagger flickering out. Ranulf parried. The cellar echoing with the clash of steel and the shuffle of feet. Ranulf watched carefully. Again Perditus's arm came snaking out in a feint, then a lunge with his dagger. Ranulf blocked and parried. He concentrated on nothing but this figure dancing in the torchlight, backwards and forwards. Perditus was no bully-boy from the alleyways but an accomplished man-at-arms. Time and again he came in, feinting, parrying. Each time Ranulf blocked. Perditus stood back, chest heaving, sword and dagger down. He pulled up his sword in a salute then brought it down, the tip aimed directly at Ranulf's face.

'This is the way it should be, shouldn't it, clerk? Warrior against warrior. Sword against sword.'

He came dancing across. Ranulf moved to parry the expected thrust but Perditus, as he lunged forward, suddenly brought sword and dagger up, exposing his body. Ranulf couldn't stop and thrust his sword deep into Perditus's chest. He withdrew it quickly. Perditus let his weapons fall with a clatter and fell to his knees. He clutched at the wound, the blood bubbling out. He stared up at Ranulf.

'I can taste death already. It's better this way'

He collapsed onto his face. His body shuddered for a while and lay still. Ranulf, crouching down, felt for the blood beat in his throat. He could detect nothing. The sound of running footsteps drew closer, and Corbett and Chanson appeared in the doorway.

'He's dead,' Ranulf got to his feet. 'He walked onto my sword. I think he intended that.'

'It's better than the scaffold,' Chanson remarked. 'Where did he get the sword and dagger from?'

'He probably had weapons hidden in all the caverns along the passageway,' Corbett remarked. He sat down on the steps and put his face in his hands.

'Cuthbert and Wallasby?' Ranulf asked.

'Oh, they are both dead,' Corbett took his hands away from his face. 'I made a mistake, Ranulf, I should have had Perditus bound. Yet, if I had, he might not have confessed.'

'In his eyes Wallasby and Cuthbert deserved to die,' Ranulf remarked. 'And God forgive me, Master, I believe that to a certain extent they brought their own deaths upon them. Do you really think Wallasby killed Taverner?'

'Yes I do,' Corbett got to his feet, 'though it would have been very difficult to prove. If Perditus had killed four times, why shouldn't he kill five? Our Archdeacon was intent on revenge. *Cacullus non facit monachum*: holy orders is no protection against murder. Wallasby would certainly have been disgraced and Prior Cuthbert a broken man. The Abbey of St Martin's has been turned into a battleground, a place of killing . . .'

He paused as he heard voices from the far end of the passageway.

'What will happen?' Ranulf asked.

'The abbey will have to be reconsecrated. The King and the Archbishop will demand a new Concilium be sent in to restore harmony and order.'

'And Perditus?'

'Bring his corpse. He can join the rest.'

The following morning Corbett stood beside Lady Margaret as she stared down at the waxen face of her son's corpse. Brother Aelfric had prepared the body for burial. Lady Margaret stood upright, no tears in her eyes. She caressed the young man's cheek and, leaning down, kissed him on the lips before pulling the coffin sheet up over his head.

'I would like to be alone, Sir Hugh.'

Corbett bowed. 'Madam, the clouds are breaking, there will be no more snow for a while. We must return to Norwich.'

'And my crime?' she asked. 'My sin?'

'I can speak for the King, Madam, and I say you have been punished enough. There must be an end to all this. All those who know the true story have taken an oath of silence.' He gestured at the sheeted corpse. 'What you do with him, where you have him buried, is a matter for you.'

'I feel nothing,' she whispered. 'The ground outside, Corbett, is frozen, and so is my heart. I suppose that's what happens,' she glanced back at the corpse, 'before the heart breaks. Such a high price!' she whispered. 'Such a high price, Sir Hugh! For one night of passion! A few golden hours and this!'

Corbett was about to reply. She held a hand up.

'And yet,' she continued, 'we could have stopped it

at any time. We hid our sin when we should have told the truth from the start.' She stretched out her hand. Corbett kissed the icy fingers. He glanced once more at the corpse, crossed himself and, picking up his cloak, left the death house, striding through the silent abbey grounds.

Ranulf and Chanson were waiting for him in the stable yard. The horses had been saddled, and the sumpter pony had their baggage lashed firmly on its back. Corbett put on his cloak and swung himself into the saddle. He looked over his shoulder once more as if memorising the gables, turrets, cornices and towers of the abbey.

'To Norwich, Master?'

'By nightfall, Ranulf, if God is good and the weather is clear.'

A lay brother swung open the gate and they cantered through. The Watcher by the Gates was standing by the trackway, staff in one hand, a large bundle strapped to his back. Corbett reined in.

'Where will you go to now?'

'As far from here as possible, Sir Hugh, at least for a while.' The Watcher brought up his shaggy cowl to hide his tangled hair. 'A job well done, eh clerk? The malefactor exposed, justice carried out.'

'I wouldn't call it well done,' Corbett retorted, leaning down from the saddle. 'All my life, sir,' Corbett held the Watcher's gaze, 'I've believed in logic and reason.'

'But hate is stronger.'

'No, sir, love is stronger: that was the root cause of all this. But it's like a two-edged sword. Love frustrated can yield a terrible harvest.' Corbett gathered his reins. 'And the reaping time always comes!'